DROP DEAD GORGEOUS

DROP DEAD GORGEOUS

Heather Graham

ONYX
Published by the Penguin Group
Penguin Putnam Inc., 375 Hudson Street,
New York, New York 10014, U.S.A.
Penguin Books Ltd, 27 Wrights Lane,
London W8 5TZ, England
Penguin Books Australia Ltd, Ringwood,
Victoria, Australia
Penguin Books Canada Ltd, 10 Alcorn Avenue,
Toronto, Ontario, Canada M4V 3B2
Penguin Books (N.Z.) Ltd, 182–190 Wairau Road,
Auckland 10, New Zealand

Penguin Books Ltd, Registered Offices:
Harmondsworth, Middlesex, England

First published by Onyx, an imprint of Dutton NAL,
a member of Penguin Putnam Inc.

ISBN 1-56865-821-4

 REGISTERED TRADEMARK—MARCA REGISTRADA

Printed in the United States of America

PUBLISHER'S NOTE
This is a work of fiction. Names, characters, places, and incidents either are the product of the author's imagination or are used fictitiously, and any resemblance to actual persons, living or dead, events, or locales is entirely coincidental.

To some folks in the Grove who always make life more pleasant for me—

The people at Planet Hollywood,
Cindy, Louie, Phillip, Annette, Leslie, Ryan, Amy, Jonny, Lucy, John, Heath, Aurora, Camel, Brian, Jacquie, Iliana, Jennifer, Kelly, Michaela, Adam, Edwin, and Steve—thanks for always being so nice.

The guys at Paolo Luigi (great Italian food!)

Colleen and everyone at Borders (great bookstore!)

And especially for Mrs. Mary Stanley and Mr. James Parrot, because teachers do make a difference!

DROP DEAD
GORGEOUS

Prologue

The guy had the kind of smile that just sent shivers racing down her spine.

Eleanor Metz hadn't seen too many men like him, and at nearly thirty-three, she felt she'd seen a fair quantity of men. She might have even said that she was a connoisseur of men. She'd married three of them. They came in all varieties, and some were nice, and some were jerks. Unfortunately, it seemed that most of the nice ones looked like Pillsbury Dough Boys, or beanpoles with BVD's, but that was okay. It took all kinds to make the world, right? She tried to be nice to nice guys.

But really good-looking guys were hard to come by. And since most guys in general were about as honest and dependable as the route of a tornado, it made sense to enjoy the company, body, and talents of a good-looking guy before he departed—since not even the Pillsbury Dough Boys or beanpoles could be counted on in a pinch.

She had glimpsed him just briefly.

The South Beach dance club was busy on a Friday night. She saw him through the crowd, and then he seemed to disappear into it. There were dancers everywhere; the music was played by a young disc jockey who kept the place rocking. Right now the English group *Republica* was blaring over the laughter and the pickup lines, and the room itself seemed to pulse with the beat. With all the movement, she simply couldn't figure just which way the guy had gone.

He had looked familiar—like a face from the distant past. Or maybe not so distant a past. It was disturbing, maddening. Who the hell was he?

Did she care? Hell, no. She just wanted to find him again.

It would be nice, of course, if she did know him. If they did share a *past,* if her mystery man was someone she had known, and with whom she could laugh over some bygone incident. Break the ice. If there was ice. She just had a feeling about this guy. . . .

But she couldn't see him anymore.

She sighed, having just refused a second go-round with the paunchy tourist with the heavy accent who was watching her now. She pretended to sit with her friends as if she were just exhausted and didn't want to dance again. Her tourist might be chubby, talk funny, and be the last guy in the world she'd ever want to sleep with, but she didn't want to hurt his feelings. He was one of the nice guys—but about as sexy as a mackerel.

"Slim pickings tonight," Abby Denhoff said. Abby was older, nearly forty, and often had a world-weary look about her. She'd been married twice, and agreed with the general premise that all men were primates. She was looking for an old guy—the older the better. Both of her husbands had left her for younger women. She now wanted a man so old that he was about to kick off any minute—he just had to have money. That way, when he left her—death being another way to depart—she'd be able to afford a lifestyle, at the least.

"Yeah, slim pickings," Eleanor said, not about to share her excitement over the strangely familiar, drop-dead-gorgeous guy she had just seen. Abby was looking for an old guy to marry, but obviously she wasn't going to find too many of them in this club. She still liked younger guys to play with.

Eleanor picked up her cocktail glass, toyed with her straw a minute, then anxiously finished her drink. Her third. She usually stopped at two; tonight she was feeling restless. She'd gone through one more husband than Abby, but she wasn't nearly as bitter, since she'd been the leaver instead of the leavee. She felt badly about the husbands she'd left, but she liked spice and variety in life, and she'd always been a sucker for a good-looking man.

The Chivas and soda she'd downed was strong because the bartender was a primate, and had tried to pick her up by making killer drinks. God, but did some of these orangutans think that any woman over twenty-five was an easy lay? Fool. Unfortunately for him, he had green teeth. He wasn't even a primate who could be enjoyed for sheer entertainment purposes.

"See anyone interesting at all?" Jenna Diamond asked, curling a strand of hair around her finger. She was twenty-eight with wide brown eyes, not as cynical as Abby. They all worked at a downtown

Miami bank, and being single and friends, they tended to do their clubbing together on Friday nights when the work week was done.

"No," Eleanor lied, "but maybe I'll go look around." She winked. "If I don't come back, don't worry about me!"

"I'm probably going home soon," Abby said, yawning. "And I won't be worried about anyone except for the men in my dreams. Both of you behave decently now—we're not hard up enough yet to mate with primates. See ya Monday."

"Monday," Eleanor murmured, moving on through the crowd, looking for the elusive, familiar stranger—Mr. Right.

She bumped into a tall, thin fellow who was kind of cute and she danced with him, thinking that he had promise, but then his toupee began to slip and he lost appeal. She smiled, thought of an excuse, and slipped away. She still couldn't find *the* guy, so she danced next with a short, friendly Latino who reminded her of a small version of Desi Arnaz. Then, hot, winded, and discouraged, she stepped out into the back alley of the club.

He was there, standing by his car. He grinned when he saw her. That killer-gorgeous kind of a smile that sent her heart racing. God, he was hot. And it wasn't that she would stoop to a one-night stand with a primate, and she wasn't easy or anything of the sort; it had just been so long since she'd even seen such a guy that she was . . .

Dying.

She could already feel him on the inside.

Okay, so tonight she'd be easy. Besides, maybe she knew him. There was that strange *something* that was familiar about him. . . .

"Coming with me?" he asked her. Cocky. Damned cocky. He had a right to be.

"Maybe," she told him, smiling as she walked toward his car. But as she neared him, she saw something in his face change. A warning bell went off inside her. Confusion stirred within while she thought madly and then . . .

Her eyes had fallen and she could see inside his car. See what he had in the front seat.

Oh, God. Her mother had warned her, her friends had warned her. Watch out. Your lifestyle is too loose. Playing around may be fun, but watch out, be careful. Some men are worse than primates. Some men are deranged.

And some are killers.

She dragged her eyes back to his, feeling a paralyzing, instinctive fear take hold of her. He was still smiling. She wanted to scream; her heart slammed against the wall of her chest.

She couldn't scream. It was as if she were living out a nightmare; her vocal cords were frozen. He was familiar, hell yes, he was familiar. She didn't just know him, she knew him *well*. And she suddenly knew a truth that had eluded her for years.

She knew truth . . .

And terror.

She turned and started to run. And it was then that the tire iron slammed against her skull. And she saw and felt no more.

Chapter 1

The ringing of the phone sounded like a five-alarm fire. Jerked cruelly from a sound—and admittedly, slightly drunken sleep—Sean Black reached over to pick up the receiver.

He encountered flesh as he fumbled for the telephone. The woman next to him made a grumbling noise and wiggled her rump. He stared at the blanket-covered feminine mound at his side, surprised that she was still with him and trying to remember more of the night gone by. He didn't think he'd had quite that much to drink in a very long time; it had been years since he'd actually been drunk.

Coming home had done it.

"Hello?" he said, staring at the sheet-covered curves of the woman. What had her name been? Maggie, Molly—something with an M. Pretty woman, thirtyish, sleek dark hair cut in a short, sophisticated style, good body, good face, great lips and tongue—and a talent for using them. She was a freelance writer who did travel articles for a number of papers and local interviews for an area literary magazine. Molly-Maggie—or whatever her name was—had been fun, the kind of woman who didn't play games, who liked sex, wanted sex, and was good at sex. Yeah . . . he liked her. He just hadn't remembered asking her to stay all night, but since she hadn't wanted dinner, he'd seen to it that they got a great dinner from room service, and hell, how many bottles of wine had they had? He should stick with Jack Daniel's or beer when he drank, he told himself, running his fingers through his hair. Wine in little crystal stemmed glasses was a killer. His head was pounding.

"Hello?" he repeated, his voice growing more terse.

"Hey, Sean, Ricky here. Hope I didn't wake you."

He winced, shrugging. He hadn't seen Ricky Garcia in about thirteen years until a few days ago. Ricky was trying to make up for lost time, so it seemed. But Sean refrained from telling his old friend that hell, yes, he'd wakened him. Ricky was with the Miami-Dade homicide unit. He was supposed to have grown up to become a lawyer, like his dad. Somehow he hadn't quite made it. Which might have made him a better person. Sean liked him better now than he had when Ricky had been a rich kid. But then, when he'd left town all those years ago, he hadn't much liked anyone here.

"It's all right," he said.

"Oh, hey, I did wake you. How did you like the club?"

"Fine."

"Have a nice night?"

"Sure."

"Meet anyone?"

Sean glanced over at his bed partner. "No," he lied.

"Hey, good, I'll pick you up in twenty minutes."

"What? Why?"

"We had a murder last night."

"You have half a dozen murders a week here, so it seems when you read the papers." Sean murmured dryly.

"Shootings, we've had a lot of trouble with shootings," Ricky admitted. "And stabbings," he added reluctantly. "Gangs, drugs, stuff like that in the crack neighborhoods. All right, throw in some domestic violence and stray bullets. That's still a low blow coming from a guy who chose to live in L.A. But this wasn't a gang killing or a guy who freaked out because his wife turned off the sports channel. It's different."

"Yeah?"

"Beautiful girl, dead after a hot night out at the very same club I sent you to."

Great, he thought. They'd probably be throwing the book at him any minute. He sat stiffly as a sensation of ice water swept through his veins.

No, maybe not. Not anymore. He was among the "rich kids" now.

God, but he could still remember what it had been like—the cops coming, dragging him out of the house by the hair, slamming him up against the car to slip the cuffs on him. His father crying, his brother protesting, the cops shoving Michael back as they took him away. He remembered telling his dad he was innocent, that he hadn't done anything, and his father had believed him, but it hadn't really mattered. His dad had started dying that same day. . . .

"She wasn't killed at the club, and she disappeared from it late Friday night, early Saturday morning. She wasn't found until the wee hours of this morning—2:23 A.M. Monday, that's what I've got on record—and so far the M.E. estimates she'd been dead at least twenty-four hours before she was found. She wasn't killed *last* night,'' Ricky said. ''Still, it seems like one of those 'looking for Mr. Goodbar' kind of things. I thought with what you write for a living . . . you did ask if you could drive along on anything important. Poor woman is my case, and I'm going in for the autopsy. Something about it is making me a little crazy at the moment, but I don't know what. Like I knew her or something. Like something is familiar and I should recognize it.''

Breathe, Sean told himself, loosen up.

''What was her name?'' he asked.

''Metz. Eleanor Metz.''

''Doesn't ring a bell with me.''

''I didn't get a good look at her face yet—she was pretty banged up, bloodied and bruised. And you know . . . decomposition sets in early down here. With the M.E., tech experts, and photographers all busy, I couldn't try to figure it out at the scene. She's at the morgue now, though, and the doc on this one is a friend of mine, and a big fan of yours. Or 'Michael Shayne's,' I should say. Whatever made you write under a pseudonym?'' Ricky asked.

Might it have been the fact that he had been acquitted of murder himself? he wondered dryly.

''I was teaching at the university when I first started writing,'' he told Ricky. ''And what I do is commercial fiction—sometimes the academic types don't like that.''

''Oh, yeah, sure. I guess. Still, if it had been me, I'd have had my real name all over everything. Anyway, just bring my friend Dr. Kate Gillespie an autographed book, and I can bring you in.''

Sean was quiet for a minute, fighting the ice, his jaw clenched, as time ticked by. Ironic. A cop was going to bring him to see an autopsy. It was a damned strange world. For a moment he thought that the last thing he wanted to do was attend the autopsy of a beautiful young woman in South Florida. The whole damned thing was ridiculously ironic.

He was about to refuse.

Then he didn't.

Hell, he didn't have another idea for a book at all at the moment, while he'd resigned from his position at the university five years ago when he'd realized his enthusiasm for fiction. He could probably have latched on to some kind of an interesting field trip, but he'd been feeling too restless.

And when he'd agreed to come here on the publicity tour, he'd called first to arrange to have the Coconut Grove stop be his last. Then he'd arranged to close up his Malibu Beach house to spend a few extra weeks. Then he'd determined he was going to spend at least a month here to work. He'd meant to come back for a time, long enough to dispel a few ghosts of the past. So he was here. To work.

If he was going to work, he might as well take advantage of the opportunity to attend the autopsy of a murder victim. He'd be a damned fool—or one hell of a poor writer—not to.

It was just that . . . Here. Of all places.

Miami did forgive a guy. Apparently, anybody could be forgiven. Still, it was bitter. Damned bitter.

"Sean?"

Maybe it was, at long last, simple justice. Maybe he'd always wanted to come back home as a hot shot just to have revenge. Tear a few things down to size; let a few people know that two could play games when there was so much in life that could be bought.

Then again, maybe he just wanted peace. He'd had his pride, he'd made his way—he'd become a success. But he'd never found peace with what had happened.

He looked over at Molly-Maggie. Lots of affairs, good fun. But there were times he felt as if he were copulating like a damned battery bunny and still coming out of it empty as all hell. Empty was better than pain, he reminded himself. No damned commitments for him. The Molly-Maggies of the world were just what he intended to keep in his life.

"Sean?"

He remembered Ricky on the other end of the line. Ricky had held out an olive branch. Of course, he'd held it out to a *New York Times* best-selling author with three movie deals in the works instead of to a poor kid from the wrong side of the street.

Cynical. Hell but he was cynical.

"Yeah," he told Ricky. "Thanks, I'll be ready."

He hung up the phone. Molly-Maggie had pulled the sheets from her face, and she stared up at him. "Leaving? Another interview?"

"Yeah, something like that." He shrugged ruefully. "Sorry we can't have breakfast. Or . . ."

Molly-Maggie was pretty. Good face, good body. Great lips. He felt himself hardening as he apologized. "Sorry we don't have more time," he said huskily.

She shook her head, pretty brown curls bouncing. "Honey, I don't need a lot of time." She grinned wickedly, and it sounded as if she purred just like a cat as she added, "And I do just fine with protein for breakfast!"

So saying, she threw the sheets over her head and rubbed her body down the length of him until she had him in her hands and mouth. His blood swiftly quickened . . . damn, but she was good. A matter of minutes and she was on top of him, moving like a jockey.

He had five minutes left to shower, and was downstairs waiting when Ricky came by in his unmarked patrol car. He swore softly at himself as he got into the car.

He'd still forgotten to ask if her name was Molly or Maggie.

Lori Kelly Corcoran pulled her Jeep Wagoneer into the driveway, studying the old house on Alhambra as she did so. Great old place, a real Merrick home, one of the houses built by the founder of the city for his own family. It had balconies, fireplaces, a curving staircase, two stories, and three bedrooms—all around a central courtyard.

What it didn't have was decent plumbing or electricity, but then, if it had possessed such simple marvels of contemporary living, she wouldn't have been able to afford the place. And she did love the house. She just hoped that Brendan would grow to love it, too. As it was, coming here might be a bit of an adjustment for a fourteen-year-old boy. He hadn't seen the house until now; she had been *inside* only one time herself. She had once thought that she was never coming back to the Miami area—not on any kind of a permanent basis. But that had been before Gramps had taken sick. He didn't intend to leave. His roots were here; her mother, father, and brother were here. She'd asked him to come to New York, but he couldn't leave the others he loved and who loved him as well, even if he had always had a soft spot in his heart for her.

You can't go home again—wasn't that what people said? But here she was, back again, despite all her resolve. And in a way it was wonderful. She had missed her old haunts. She loved the foliage, loved the old houses, Mediterranean and Deco, the bougainvillea that grew all over, crawling over houses and walls, the whole look and feel of the area. She liked heat, sunshine, her easy access to water, and even, at this stage of her life, her nearness to her folks and her brother. And, of course, to Gramps.

Naturally, she'd miss New York, though she was pleased with her new job, taking over for one of the first-grade teachers at a highly acclaimed experimental grade school. Mrs. Linitz was due to give birth in two weeks, so come a week from Thursday, Lori would be teaching twenty-seven little darlings on a daily basis. Leaving had given her another source of income and expression—she'd been do-ing designs part-time for the up-and-coming fashion duo of Yolanda Peters and Elizabeth Woodly—Yoelle Designs—and when they'd heard she was leaving, they'd asked her to create an entire line of elegantly casual resort wear for tropical and semitropical climates. Things looked good; she loved designing clothing, and she loved teaching, and here she was going to have the best of both worlds. She'd been authorized to arrange shows with some of the leading retailers in the area, and with Bal Harbour, Coconut Grove, and Palm Beach easily accessible, there would be plenty of opportunities to do so. She could be excited about the future.

Naturally, she was excited.

Uneasy too, she admitted. And bitter still. The past went away; life went on. But a sore spot had been left, like a bruise, and it never quite healed.

Get past it, get a life! she chided herself. She'd blamed an entire county for the events that had occurred long ago, and that was foolish. Still . . .

She wasn't a kid anymore. She was an adult woman, and she did have a life, and a super son. Her grandfather, who just happened to be one of the greatest people she had ever met, needed her. As a bonus, she'd made all her family happy as larks. She should have come back long ago with a simple fuck-you attitude toward anyone rude enough to plague her about the past. But that was ridiculous in itself—surely, everyone had forgotten the past. What had happened at the rock pit that day was just yellowed newspaper now, locked away in library files.

Except, of course, for Mandy Olin's family.

And the Blacks.

"Mom. Earth to Mom."

She turned. Brendan was staring at her with the patience and res-ignation of a maturing young man.

"Mom, we're here. That usually means it's time to get out of the car."

She smiled and nodded. "Yeah, sure. What do you think?" she asked, glancing over at the passenger seat where he sat, now staring back up at the house as she had been doing. He gazed at it gravely, and she felt a sense of maternal pride stirring. He was a great-looking kid. He'd inherited her light hazel eyes, but his hair was dark whereas hers was a reddish blond, and at fourteen he was already two inches taller than her own height of five foot nine. He liked sports, and was slim and lithe, coordinated, and decently good at his studies as well. Watching him, she felt a sense of wonder swell within her. Her trip to England all those years ago had begun out of trauma and a desperation to escape. Brendan made up for any trauma she might have suffered.

"Brendan," she said anxiously, "what do you think about the house?"

He shrugged. "It's—neat. Looks kind of like a castle. Except that it doesn't have any turrets—hey, it does kind of have a tower. Is that a tower?"

She smiled, nodding. "Yeah, it's a tower. There's a winding staircase in the back, and it goes all the way up to a little tower room in the rear of the house. I don't know what it was for—except that it gives you a great view of the area. I'd hoped you'd like the house. We're probably going to have a few problems with it, but . . ."

But, thanks to Jan finding the place for her, she'd found a house she could afford, in a neighborhood she liked, near her folks' house— but not too close—and near the hospital where Gramps received his treatments.

"Let's bring our things in. We'll work a few hours or until we feel like we're going crazy. Then we'll drive around and go into the Grove for dinner and a movie."

He grinned. "Are you going to show me all your old high school hangouts?" he asked her.

"Maybe," she murmured, lowering her eyes.

Like the old rock pit? she taunted herself. No. Definitely not.

"Well, then!" Brendan opened his door. "Mom, this is what you do to get out of the car—open door, step out. You look as if you're afraid of sinking into quicksand or something."

"Hey, they do have quicksand here, out in the Glades. Quicksand, alligators, moccasins, rattlers, coral snakes, scorpions—"

"All that in this house?" he teased. "Hey—cooler than I thought."

"The Everglades is one of the most unusual and beautiful natural environments in the country," she informed him loftily. "You wait until you see just how neat. We'll take a drive out next weekend."

He nodded, his eyes slightly averted, and she remembered that he had just left all his friends behind. The trip would be fun; he'd always been great about going places with her. But it was probably a sad thing for him to realize he might as well say yes to his mother, since he hadn't a plan in the world for the weeks to come.

He looked at her and grinned, hiding the fact that the move might have been in any way traumatic. "Next week, Mom. We've still got to get out of the Jeep now."

"Hardy, har!" she replied lightly.

But she stepped out of the car and Brendan followed suit. She guiltily realized that she'd been brooding on this move, worried about adjusting to home again herself when Brendan was still a kid. She did have friends here. He didn't. Hopefully, they'd fix that soon.

She was startled when she felt him beside her, an arm around her waist. He gave her a little squeeze. "It's going to be all right, Mom."

"Yeah. Thanks. You've been great about this," she said softly. "Well, come on, kid, let's get cracking, huh?"

But he'd already left her side and was busy pulling his in-line skates out of the back of the Jeep. "Well, come on, Mom, let's get cracking, huh?"

At somewhere around fifty-five years of age, Kate Gillespie was trim, slim, silver-haired, and smooth. She accepted Michael Shayne's latest thriller with thanks, but he discovered that it was his degree in forensic anthropology which had actually allowed him entrance to her autopsy.

She was professional to the core, commenting on his presence as well as Ricky's into the small recorder that was clipped to her white lab coat. She then walked around the gurney that held the dead woman and described the victim as a young woman in her late twenties to early thirties, five feet six, approximately one-hundred-and-twenty-five pounds. Cause of death appeared to be strangulation, contusion and trauma to the throat being obvious, the appearance of the bruising such that it must have occurred prior to death. Dr. Gillespie described the contusions and abrasions on the body, including the trauma to the head which had damaged the skull and facial bones. She took samples of blood, fluid, pubic hair, and scraped beneath the victim's fingernails. While she was so occupied, her assistant was busy taking mud samples from the face and then carefully cleaning away the remaining blood and dirt.

Midway through the gentle facial bathing, before Dr. Gillespie could slip her scalpel into the corpse, Ricky gasped out loud and Sean felt the blood drain from his face—it felt as if all oxygen were being ripped out of his lungs.

"What is it?" Gillespie asked sharply, staring at Ricky.

Ricky cleared his throat, looking at Sean. "I know her. Knew her. We—" He paused again, then gave himself a shake, still staring at Sean.

"We both knew her," he said.

Chapter 2

There was no way out of the fact that unpacking was a pain in the butt. By four o'clock Lori and Brendan were both grouchy and tired. She called it quits for the day, amazed to realize that most of their things were still coming by way of professional movers and UPS. She'd brought most of their clothing, Brendan's various pieces of sports equipment, and her portfolios and the majority of her fabric samples for the lines she was working on.

The house needed central air; now it was on units. Thankfully, since it seemed as if it was going to be a killer spring, the main unit was working really well.

Brendan showered, and she had just stepped out of the master bath herself when she heard voices downstairs. She walked carefully to her door in her towel—she and Brendan were taking her folks to breakfast in the morning, and she hadn't expected to see them until then. But just as she tiptoed to the stairway, Jan Hunt, standing below, looked up. "Hey!"

"Hey, yourself!" she said, with just a little bit of false cheer. She'd wanted to spend some time adjusting with just Brandon tonight, but then, Jan was a good friend. None of them had really kept in touch right away after their senior year. Lori had left for London almost immediately, and most of the others had carried through with their college plans. But when Lori had left London for school in New York City, Jan had written. She'd eloped. With Brad Jackson, of all people. She'd wanted Lori's forgiveness—which Lori, who'd barely remembered Brad by that time—readily gave.

The marriage hadn't lasted more than two years. Jan and Brad were still on-again, off-again lovers, and even when Jan was ready to kill

Brad, she mused philosophically that Brad had given her Tina, their daughter, and Lori could understand that reasoning. Especially when she'd met Tina. The girl was just thirteen, and stunning. Like both of her parents, she had huge blue eyes and, like her father, platinum-blond hair. She already had quite a little shape on her, and she had a very sweet way about her. From Jan, Lori knew. She didn't remember a whole lot about Brad, but 'kind' was one adjective she never would have cast in his direction.

"I wanted to introduce the kids!" Jan called up. She grinned and started up the stairs. "I've introduced them. Brought in your paper, too!" she added, lifting the *Miami Herald* high in her hands.

"I didn't even know I got the paper."

"It was on your lawn."

"Well, good, I guess. Give me just a second, Jan, I've got to get dressed."

"Oh, come on, our lockers were next to one another in the old showers!" Jan laughed immodestly, ignoring Lori's bid for privacy and barging on up the stairs. She hugged Lori, wet towel and all, and curled up on the bed—one of the few pieces of furniture she'd arranged to buy and have delivered for Lori—and waited, stretched out on an elbow.

"Damn, you look good for thirty-two!" Jan told her, shaking her head. "But then you're tall. Tall always makes people *look* skinny. Except that you are thin, too, anyway. Good shape. You always had a good shape. I'd kind of hoped you'd have gotten at least some cellulite by now."

Lori arched a brow and rummaged through the hastily arranged closet for a halter-top knit dress, glancing at Jan as she slipped it over her head and dropped the towel. "I've got cellulite, everyone does. And we're only thirty-two. We're not supposed to have decayed already, you know. Besides, aren't we supposed to be getting better, not older, or something like that? Look at what Jane Fonda did for women and the process of aging? Hmm?"

"But thirty *is* over the hill," Jan said with a sigh, idly spreading out the newspaper. "I'm wrinkling. It's like I've been folded, spindled, and mutilated already. Gray hairs are settling in! I've got crow's feet that slash through my zits—since I can't seem to quit breaking out."

Lori laughed, then frowned as it appeared that Jan seemed earnestly worried. Jan had never been overly concerned about her appearance before. She was a beautiful woman with brunette hair she now highlighted with a sophisticated streaking, sky blue eyes, and a buxom figure.

"Age is all relative, you know. My mom still thinks of Andrew and me as kids. And Jan, you look like a million bucks. Better than ever," Lori assured her.

"You think? You were always so decent to everyone, Lori. So nice. We could be so catty when we were kids, except that you didn't say bad things about anyone. Beauty and decency—I hated you before I liked you, you know. You were just so damned perfect, and you had the nerve to be nice at the same time! In all honesty, when we were kids, I had to be your friend—or else eat my heart out with jealousy."

Lori grimaced. "Jan, we were kids. Don't go making me sound like Mary Poppins—I'm not and I wasn't. But honest to God, I like my thirties better than my teens—"

"You can say that now because your teenager is a boy and mine is a girl. I just love my baby to death, but sometimes I look at her and see that she has the world before her, and I just feel all used up. That will teach me. If I ever bear a child again, it's going to be a man-child!" She sobered suddenly, her eyes growing very grave. "Hey, but have I got news for you! Speaking of males in general—"

She broke off, suddenly dead silent, her face pale. Lori realized she was staring down at the newspaper she had just brought into the house.

"What is it?"

"Do you remember Eleanor Metz?"

Lori shook her head.

"You must! You do, I know you do. How could any of us ever really forget."

"I don't remember the name Metz—"

"Wait, Metz was a married name! I know you remember *Eleanor*."

"Eleanor. No. Wait, you mean—Ellie?" Lori asked.

"Yes."

"Why, what's happened?"

Jan continued to stare at her, white as a sheet.

"Jan?"

"Eleanor is dead!"

"So you like to read?" Tina Jackson asked, twirling a strand of her long blond hair around a finger and studying her newfound friend, Brendan Corcoran.

Amazingly, this was coming out all right.

She'd been irritated to death with her mother for making her come here to meet some awkward, friendless, clueless guy from New York. Not that she was mean or anything. She really had a fair amount of homework, she was a cheerleader and they had a game tomorrow, and her mother had a tendency to think that she should be a one-woman welcome committee for the kids of anyone from out of town to whom she sold a house. And she had *really* wondered about Brendan Corcoran. Her mom had been friends with his mom from way back, his grandparents were here, his uncle was here, his *great*-grandfather was here—but he'd never been to Dade County before. Weird. And he'd been born in London. She'd expected him to sound like the guys from Oasis or the girl from Republica—or the old Beatles. He didn't have an accent, of any kind. He'd grown up in New York City, but he didn't even have a New York accent—only certain areas really acquired that accent, he'd explained to her. New York City was great, he'd told her. Busier than she could imagine, with people from everywhere in the world. It was her personal opinion that nowhere in the world was as great as South Florida. They could water-ski, go boating, diving, lie in the sun, swim, play—on almost any day of the year. But though she explained that to Brendan, she didn't argue about New York. Because she liked him. Really liked him. He was bright, fun, polite—and cute. Cute as could be. *Gorgeous.* Tall, dark, handsome, and cool. He had a great smile, a husky voice, and a lanky, laid-back way about him that sent her heart skittering wildly. He wasn't going to have any trouble fitting in anywhere. Wait till her friends saw him. She definitely wanted first dibs.

He was tired, having spent the day trying to make a home out of a new house, but he had been great anyway.

Though he had kind of kept going, refusing to give up the concept of turning the house into his own place—mostly fooling with setting up his CD player on a bookshelf—he had talked with her all along.

Now, at last, he took a break. They sat together on the antique sofa that had come with the place, drinking cans of soda.

His hazel eyes—great eyes, with little flecks of pure gold in them—focused on hers. "Love to read," he admitted. They'd gotten into the conversation because she'd brought a sci-fi book with her just in case the two of them didn't have anything to say to one another.

As if!

So far they hadn't stopped talking. He grinned. "See all those boxes that say 'Sports Stuff' over there?"

"Yeah?"

"Books," he admitted sheepishly.

"So you don't really play hockey?"

"Yeah," he said, laughing. "I play hockey. Or I did," he corrected with a shrug. "Who knows what I'll be doing now?"

"Go to my school and you can play anything you want," she said morosely. "It's a private school, and you know, there just aren't that many jocks for the coaches to choose from."

"I'm going to public school," he told her.

"Well," she said philosophically, "you're still in good shape. This is just your freshman year, and the teams don't begin to get serious until you're a little older, you know."

He grinned, shrugged, and shoved a long lock of his dark hair back from where it had fallen sleekly over one eye. "Who knows, we'll see." He lowered his voice, just in case the women upstairs could hear them. "Too bad I'm not going to your school."

She wrinkled her nose. "I'd rather be in the public school. But hey, it doesn't really matter. Lots of my friends go to Gables. We still hang out together on weekends and sometimes after school. We'll get to see each other, and I'll get to introduce you to lots of people. Like Friday night. A group of us are going to the movies in the Grove. Want to come?"

"Sure." He shrugged. "The Grove—I imagine my mom will let me."

Tina grinned. "Mine was a tough nut to crack at first. It's kind of a touristy area, but it was a hangout when our moms were kids. Dad thinks it's one big area of burned-out drug pushers."

"Is it?"

She laughed. "A few. But it's really okay. Mom used to come with me all the time, it was the only way she'd let me go. Now, as long as we're in a group of at least five kids, she lets me. Just long enough for a movie and a hamburger—there's a curfew down here, you know. She'll be extra glad if I'm with you—you're the tallest guy my own age I know. Mom always thinks that girls are in danger," she said, and made a face.

He laughed. "Let me clue you in—moms worry about sons too. My mother actually made a map of where I was and wasn't allowed to be in New York. Give her a few days. I'm sure I'll have one for down here, too." His stomach suddenly growled, and he went dead still, looking at her, blushing.

They both started to laugh together.

"Sorry," he mumbled. "Hey, where do you think we'll wind up for dinner? I guess it's pretty obvious—I'm starving."

"Do you like pasta?"

"Sure."

"Good. Because I think we're going to an Italian restaurant in Coconut Grove. You'll get to see the place, and see what I mean about it. Hey—do you read Michael Shayne?"

"Sure. He's one of my favorite writers."

"Well, guess what? He was here. Signing at a bookstore about two blocks away from the restaurant."

"He was *here*? I thought the guy didn't come out to meet his fans."

"I guess he's making a few appearances with this new book," Tina said. "Whatever—he was here!" She punched his arm lightly. "Score one for Miami!"

He didn't seem to notice the taunt. He was disturbed to realize he'd missed the signing. "He was here—but he's gone now?" Brendan asked, disappointed.

"Who knows where he is—but I didn't get to go, either. I was at a mandatory cheerleading session—you had to be there or be dead. But Michael Shayne left some signed copies at the bookstore, and I have a friend who works in the coffee shop there—he promised to see that a few got stashed away until I could get there. Like I was telling you, the Grove is cool anyway. We'll eat, we'll walk around—it will be great."

"Yeah." He was looking at her, smiling in a way that made her feel warm. "Maybe it will be cool." He squeezed her hand, got up, and headed for another box.

She looked at her hand, grinning. She was falling in love.

"Dead. *Dead*—how?" Lori asked.

"Murdered," Jan said, shaking her head as she stared at the paper. "She was at a South Beach club—the Stork—with friends, and then she left. Her car was left at the club, and her body was found dumped off Alligator Alley outside Fort Lauderdale. I guess someone tried to bury her, but she surfaced. That's all the information the police are releasing right now," Jan said.

"How sad, how horrible!" Lori said.

Jan shook her head again.

"Had you seen her lately?" Lori asked.

"Oh . . . a few times—over fifteen years," Jan said. "She married, divorced, married, divorced. She split from the last guy about a year ago—I'll bet the police are going to question him. He was kind of a character, I think. But then again, so was she."

"How so? I don't remember."

"Well, she was kind of like Mandy. She could be outrageous. She was always nice, but she was written up once for dancing naked in a fountain, and she was arrested once on a DUI. I think she was kind of living life in the fast lane, you know, looking for something she couldn't quite find. But," Jan added wryly, "aren't we all?"

"It's still terrible. I don't care how fast she was living—no one deserves to be murdered." Lori murmured. Suddenly, she remembered Eleanor clearly. *She'd come to the rock pit with Mandy, that last day when they'd all been together. She could remember how she'd looked in her bikini, laughing, running off with Mandy toward the water. Then, later, with the rest of them . . .*

When Mandy had been dragged up and Sean had been bent over her, desperately trying CPR, except that the cops had been convinced that . . .

"You're right," Jan said with a long sigh. "It's sad and terrible, and I sure hope they get the guy. I didn't mean that Eleanor deserved it or anything like that. It's just that a fast lifestyle can get you into trouble with guys you don't know, and these days it's kind of like anyone can be a homicidal maniac. Though, I admit, I used to like that club, but I guarantee you, I won't be there for a while!"

"You're going to stay home and be an angel?"

"For a while. Well, I'm going to stay home—or away from clubs and nights out on the town. Maybe I'll give Brad a call and see what he's up to for the next few weekends."

Despite the circumstances, Lori grinned. "Ah! Knowing what kind of monsters are out there makes the old husband look good, eh?" Lori arched a brow at Jan.

"Well, he's an ex-husband, remember. But a woman does have her needs, so maybe I will be nice to him for a while now," she murmured. "Scary stuff."

A shriek from downstairs caused them both to freeze and stare at one another. Lori pelted to the door and down the stairs, Jan at her heels. Her heart was hammering as she wondered what could have happened.

She jammed to a stop at the bottom of the stairs; Jan crashed into her.

Tina was sitting on the sofa while Brendan was going through a box of CDs, Tina shrieking with laughter. She looked at Lori and her mother with surprise, then apologized quickly. "Oh, I'm sorry, he was just telling me that he loves the Monkees! The Monkees, can you imagine?''

Lori sagged against the stairs.

Brendan looked up at his mother. She was relieved to see that he was happy, enjoying Tina. What wasn't to enjoy? The girl was as pretty as could be and nice as well.

"She's got no taste, Mom. Sorry, Mrs. Jackson."

"The Monkees?" Jan said, sniffing and staring at Lori in defense of her daughter. "And I go by my maiden name, Hunt, Brendan, except you can just call me Jan."

"Yes, ma'am," Brendan said politely. "Mom, I'm really starved," he added. "Are we possibly going to get something to eat sometime soon?"

"Of course," Lori said, looking at Jan. It seemed a little absurd now that Tina's shrieks of laughter had sent them into such a wild panic. They looked at one another somewhat sheepishly, in silent agreement that in front of the kids they would put the murder of an old acquaintance behind them. Even if it made both of them feel uneasy as hell.

"Yeah, dinner, my treat," Jan said, looking from Lori to Brendan, and back to Lori again. She forced a grin as she cheerfully added, "I did make a nice commission on this place!"

"Hey, fine, you can treat. Where are we going?" Lori asked.

"Coconut Grove. A great little Italian place, new since you've been here." Lori noticed that Tina elbowed Brendan—she had obviously known where they were going, and she wasn't displeased.

"Hey," Jan continued, "I'm treating, but I think we should take both cars. You and Brendan might want to hang around awhile, and I have to pick up a contract if the old geezer gets around to signing it. Things have changed, though, in the past fifteen years. Wait till you see how much!"

"All right. Let me just go up and grab my purse," Lori said absently.

Jan followed her upstairs. "Lori?"

"Yeah?"

"You're acting weird. Are you all right with this?"

Lori took her purse off the bed and headed back to the doorway, frowning. "I'm not acting weird."

"You looked white when I was talking about dinner."

"Oh . . . well, I guess I couldn't stop thinking about Eleanor."

"I know, but it's not like either of us was really still friends with her. You hadn't seen her in fifteen years, and I'd seen her maybe three or four times.''

"Still . . .''

"Lori, we just can't take everything to heart. You always hurt for everybody else all the time, but you should have learned by now, you just can't do that. Life's a bitch.''

"And then you die yourself?'' Lori queried, using the cliché dryly.

"Right. Bad things happen. Lots of kids we went to school with are dead. Petey Fitzhugh finally passed away from his hemophilia. Larry Gonzalez died at twenty-seven from cancer. That's the way it goes.''

"Ellie was murdered,'' Lori reminded her.

They stared at one another. Lori thought that maybe they were both about to say, "*So was Mandy!*''

But neither of them said the words. They hung there on the air between them, like a miasma. But then, way back when, the kids would never have thought that Mandy had been *murdered* that day; it was the cops who believed that she had been, the D.A.'s office who had come up with the charges.

"Mom!'' Brendan called.

It was a mournful sound. The kid was starving. Jan was right. She couldn't bleed for every evil thing that happened in the universe.

"He must be really hungry—we didn't go shopping yet. I've got milk, coffee, orange juice, and sodas, and that's it. Let's get going.''

"Right, let's get going,'' Jan agreed.

"Except—'' Lori murmured.

"Except?''

"Except, are we safe?'' she murmured softly.

Jan sighed. "Honey, where we're going is wall-to-wall tourists. Great. You don't want to move down here and get paranoid right away! I even let Tina hang around the Grove with her friends on weekends, as long as they stick to the main drag. Lots of cops on the streets all the time. Ellie was snatched from a South Beach club where she was probably trying to pick up guys.''

"I guess I'm just spooked,'' Lori said. But as they exited the house, she thought that a good alarm system was going to be her first investment.

Spooked. That was it. She'd lived in greater Miami, London, and New York. All big cities. Places you learned to be street-smart, places where murder did happen far too frequently. There wasn't anything astonishing about a murder in Miami.

Except that . . .

The victim had been an old friend of hers.

Old friend, yes, old friend, someone she hadn't seen in fifteen years. She had to let it go. . . .

She didn't think that she could, but then, getting out was good. Driving down familiar streets that weren't quite so familiar anymore took Lori's mind from what had happened to Ellie.

Things *had* changed. Coconut Grove had gotten busy—really busy, even on a Monday night.

The area had always been trendy; it remained so with artsy shops mixed in with larger, popular chain stores. She couldn't get over all the new construction in the area, the multitude of cars—and people. Tour buses were parked on Main Street in front of a Planet Hollywood. She might have been back in New York, there were so many languages being spoken.

The Italian restaurant Jan had chosen was small and apparently very good because it was full. Music played from another place across the street, car horns honked as people tried to get through the congested streets, and as they waited for their table, they had to speak up to be heard by one another. Once they were seated, Jan introduced Lori to everyone who worked in the restaurant who happened to pass them by. This turned out to be good, because Jan's beeper went off almost immediately and she disappeared to make a phone call, then returned and apologized, but prepared to leave them.

"Tina, I'll take you home," Jan said.

"Mom can take her," Brendan protested.

"If she doesn't mind," Tina said sweetly.

"But, Tina, you told me you had lots of homework and a million things to do after dinner tonight—"

"I think I'll be okay if I stay out a little later," Tina said, flushing slightly.

Lori quickly lowered her head, hiding her smile. Tina had been afraid that Brendan Corcoran might be a weird kid, or a dork, and naturally—at her mother's insistence—she had agreed to come and welcome him and be polite. Then she had discovered that he was cute and charming.

"I'll be happy to get her home, and we won't be late," Lori assured Jan. "Look at everything you've done for me."

"I sold you a house."

"And sat around for furniture to be delivered and cable installed and all kinds of hideously mundane things!" Lori reminded her.

"All right, then. Ciao, guys!" Jan said, and breezed on out.

The food was delicious, the service was superb, but by the time they had finished eating, Lori had acquired a pounding headache. Tina was telling Brendan about the various shops in the two malls and about some of the different places down Main Street and off into the side roads.

"Hey," she protested, "I know you two would probably like to walk around a bit, and I'm sorry, but honestly, I'm really exhausted."

"Can I just run into the big bookstore at the Mayfair?" Brendan asked, hazel eyes anxiously on hers. "Tina says that Michael Shayne was down here, and he left autographed copies of his latest at the store."

"We can come back—"

"They won't last," Brendan said, staring at her.

She sighed. She was vaguely familiar with the name. She loved to read when she had the time, though Michael Shayne was a little on the gruesome side for her. Still, she was glad that Brendan liked to read so much, and she always encouraged his interest in books. "All right. Go on down and—"

"There's a coffee bar in the bookstore. Maybe we could have ten minutes and you could meet us there?" Tina asked hopefully.

She smiled. It was a Monday night, a school night—for other kids, even if Brendan wasn't starting right away. There probably wouldn't be too many kids hanging around now, but she sensed that maybe Tina knew a few of her friends might be in the area seeing movies, shopping—or hanging out at the hamburger joint on Main Street. "You can have fifteen minutes, how's that? But really, Brendan—"

"Fifteen minutes. We'll be ready," Brendan promised.

The kids left. Lori discovered that Jan had paid the bill before taking off, so she thanked the staff and left. Threading her way through the surprisingly crowded streets, she headed toward the Mayfair and the bookstore. The mall was big, encompassing a hotel and dozens of shops with a courtyard between split sections of the edifice. The restaurant had been closer to Cocowalk, a second mall in the area. The night was nice, though, and walking along, she realized the scope of the place. Greater Miami, encompassing all the little municipalities, was big and densely populated. Somewhere around three million people. Constantly changing and growing. She hadn't seen a soul or a single thing she actually recognized. She'd come home, but home was different. She could relax.

Yeah, home was different. Eleanor had been murdered.

Suddenly, as she walked, the street and shop lights around her went out. She heard shouts, cars crashing into fender benders, alarms ringing.

An area blackout, don't panic! common sense told her. She heard a policeman cursing, and auxiliary lights began blinking on here and there.

Yet she suddenly felt a sense of alarm. *Brendan.* If anything happened to Brendan, she would die. She began to run.

In the shadows cast by a pale moon, she turned into the courtyard area of the mall, jogging swiftly up a few steps just in time to plow into another human being coming from the opposite direction. Their impact was such that she staggered back, nearly falling. Strong arms reached out for her in the gloom, steadying her. She didn't fall. Neither could she move.

Clouds moved over the moon. It was darker than ever.

It occurred to her that Coconut Grove could be a rough place. This guy was big, powerful. In the distance she could hear shouting. Nearby, there seemed to be nothing, and no one.

They were alone, surrounded by darkness. Fool! she charged herself. Don't panic!

A deep male voice startled her. "Hey, are you all right? Damn, lady, what's the rush, where's the fire?"

The man was both honestly concerned—and irritated. Rightly so, she decided. His grip on her was very firm and steadying. He hadn't accosted her; she had plowed into him. Maternal instinct had sent her running like a maniac.

"Oh, God, I'm sorry. My fault. I'm really sorry." He was still holding her. "Excuse me. My son—never mind, I'm sorry, if you'll just excuse me, I—"

She broke off, feeling herself break into a cold sweat. She knew him. Shock made her shake. She wondered why her reflexes had taken so long to warn her that she recognized his voice. It had changed. A little. Not much.

Naturally, the brief blackout chose that moment to come to an end. The lights in Coconut Grove suddenly came back on—brilliantly so.

Yes, it was him.

He had changed.

Of course he had changed. She hadn't seen him in nearly fifteen years.

A little. Not much. His shoulders had broadened; his physique had filled out. His dark hair was a little longer, and the character lines on his face were definitely etched in more deeply. He was tall, lithe, well muscled, ruggedly attractive. All the promise in the boy had been fulfilled in the man.

The darkness, the impact, had blinded her at first. And still, for some reason she didn't trust her eyes. He had gone away. Fifteen years ago. She hadn't known that he had come back. No one had warned her, no one had told her.

"Sean?" she said, sounding as if she were strangling over the name. She cleared her throat. "Sean?"

"Lori . . ."

He was taken every bit as much by surprise. His eyes were naked, startled. Alive with dark emotion.

Then they narrowed.

And his husky, masculine voice grew harsh.

"What the hell are you doing back here?"

Startled by the hostility in his voice, she stared at him mutely, aware that he honestly seemed more surprised to see her than even she was to see him. His eyes were so dark in the shadows that they appeared black rather than blue, ebony hued with anger. His hands were still gripping her shoulders, and his fingers were tense, biting into her flesh. "I asked you what the hell you were doing back here?"

"I—"

"Ah, hell! Visiting the family? *Now?*"

She realized later that she should have told him then and there to go to hell—her whereabouts were none of his concern. But she was still so disarmed simply to see him, and so taken aback by his animosity, that she snapped out a reply instead. "I'm not visiting. I've moved back."

"Moved back!" he exclaimed. The words were close to a roar. "Moved back—*now*? Oh, God—that's rich. That's just—that's just fucking perfect!"

He stared at her, realized he was holding her, and not gently. He released her abruptly. "Sorry," he said coolly, stepping back. She watched his striking features as he fought for control and gained it. His face was completely impassive as he stared at her then. "Sorry," he repeated.

He stepped around her, as if she were a total stranger he had just bumped into, and his long strides quickly took him away from her, down the street, and into the crowd.

Chapter 3

Sean. Oh, great. Just what she needed.

She was shaking! As if fifteen years hadn't gone by. As if she hadn't gotten herself a life.

Get a grip! she warned herself.

But she was still standing there. Just standing. And despite herself, she kept standing there, as a wave of memory that seemed as fresh as the night breeze swept over her.

She had met him way back in junior high. He'd walked into her life when she'd been just thirteen, and she hadn't forgotten him since. Thirteen. She'd been a year younger than Brendan when she'd met Sean, a tough age. She'd already been five-eight, slim—but maturing. She'd had breasts. Most of the boys in school then were gawky, pimple-faced, and squeaky-voiced. Trying to appear mature but not quite there. Her first day of eighth grade, a group of boys had been torturing her. Ricky Garcia and Ted Neeson had been the worst.

"Hey, new girl, want to come to a meeting of our four Fs club?"

"Four Fs—what's that?" she'd naively asked.

Ricky had looked at Ted. He'd moved closer to her. "Find 'em, feel 'em, fuck 'em, and forget 'em!" he'd told her, bursting into gales of laughter.

At the time his use of the four-letter word had stunned her. Her cheeks had gone crimson. She'd been absolutely humiliated.

"Come on, wanna play?" Ted had urged.

They were both pressing her closer and closer to the lockers, and she didn't want to be scared, unnerved by these creeps. Jan Hunt, in second period, had told her that Ricky and Ted were popular guys, in the right crowd. Now they were doing this to her, and if she freaked out, she'd be the laughingstock of the school for the rest of her life. She was trying to say something smart and strong, but no words could come to her lips. Then Sean arrived.

He was tall and lanky, dark hair parted at the side, a little shaggy, falling over one eye. He stepped right up to Ricky, caught hold of his shirt at the shoulder, and pulled him firmly away from Lori. "Give the girl a break, you asses. She's new here—she'll think we're all a bunch of delinquents."

"Ah, come on, Sean, we're just trying to see if she has a sense of humor."

"She's laughing on the inside. Now, leave her the hell alone. Get going, both of you."

And they did. They turned around like two chastised puppies and slunk away down the hall. "They're really not so bad. They're just jerks at times," Sean told her, smiling ruefully. And at that moment, that precise moment, she'd fallen in love. He had a little dimple in his chin. His eyes were a devastating deep blue.

His voice had already changed—no squeaking out of him.

"Thanks," she told him.

He walked her home.

And he'd made her laugh, and he'd been devastatingly good-looking to a thirteen-year-old girl, but beyond that, she had just *liked* him, his casual, natural ability to be warm, decent, friendly, funny . . . strong on the inside.

Her parents had hated him. Not *personally,* of course. But they'd said right away that he just wasn't the right kind of kid for her to be hanging around with. He was the wrong-side-of-the-tracks kind of a kid, even if there were no "tracks" dividing them. Her parents had simply rejected him as no good, even before the awful day at the rock pit.

Maybe, in a way, they'd all been destroyed that day. No matter what games they were playing at life now.

Life and death. Ellie was dead now as well.

But Sean was here. And after all these years she'd never really gotten him out of her heart. Her soul. No, her mind. God, no, her conscience. He'd always been there in the deep, dark corners where she knew she'd been wrong, a coward—where she hadn't tried hard enough, done enough, protested enough. . . .

Told the whole truth . . .

"Mom?"

Lori started, realizing at last that she'd been just standing on the sidewalk like a zombie. Frozen. Embarrassingly gaping. For how long?

Long enough. Brendan—the precious child whom she'd all but forgotten—was standing on the sidewalk in front of her, Tina at his side. The two had left the bookstore to come looking for her. She gave herself a mental shake.

"Are you all right, Mom? You look as if you've just seen a ghost or something," Brendan said.

She shook her head. She tried to smile. Her teeth felt brittle, her smile even more so. Ghost. Yeah, a ghost from the past. Haunting her.

"No, no . . ." she began and broke off. "Sorry, kids. The blackout scared me. Are you all right?"

"Of course," Tina assured her, smiling patiently.

"Good . . . good. Did you two get your books?"

"Mom, that blackout was no big deal, and the bookstore dealt with it just fine. They must have some kind of emergency system because it was only dark in the store for a half a second. Oh—and yeah!" Brendan said enthusiastically. "We both got books. Tina has a friend who was holding *signed* Michael Shaynes for us, first printing. Isn't it great, look!"

She looked, reminding herself that she was a parent, supposedly a good parent, and she needed to show interest in something that was so important to her son. She didn't really see the cover, or the title, but she nodded, still smiling stupidly, trying to share Brendan's pleasure with his acquisition. Then Brendan turned the book over, and she went into shock all over again. The author's picture was on the back of the book.

It was him. *Him.*

Michael Shayne was Sean Black. Or Sean Black was Michael Shayne. Jesus.

"Mom?" Brendan said worriedly.

"You're awfully white, Mrs. Corcoran," Tina murmured, and she glanced at Brendan. "Are you sick? I can beep my mom—"

"No, no, I'm fine," Lori said. "Fine!" she added cheerfully. "Let me get you two home. It's late. And, Tina, you've got a busy day coming up, huh? Cheerleading . . . school, all that stuff. Come on."

She turned and headed for the parking garage, aware that the kids were staring at one another, wondering about her mental health.

She was glad she didn't have far to go. Jan's house was in the Gables as well, so it was easy to drop Tina off. Lori continued to feel as if she'd been doused with a pail of numbing ice water as she watched her son walk Tina to her door. Tina went inside, waved, and then locked up.

Lori felt Brendan watching her as they drove. And once they got home, Brendan hovered around her, perplexed, convinced that something was wrong, no matter how she protested. She finally convinced him that she was just overly tired, and that he needed to get some sleep as well.

She knew her son. He wasn't convinced. He went to bed, but he went to bed worried.

Well, what had she expected? She'd nearly passed out cold when she'd seen the new book by Michael Shayne and realized that her son's favorite author was really Sean Black.

Lori walked into the coolness of the tiled kitchen. She stood still for a moment, then walked to the refrigerator. Milk, orange juice, soda. And thank God. A bottle of chablis—Jan's welcoming gift.

She got a water glass from a cabinet and filled it with the white wine, slammed the refrigerator door shut, and walked back to the living room. She pressed the cold glass to her forehead.

She should be glad. He'd been maligned, abused, and all but nailed to a cross. He deserved success.

But he was here. Who in God's name would have imagined he might ever come back here?

Who in God's name would have ever thought that he'd become a writer under the pseudonym of Michael Shayne? Or that the city of Miami would embrace him with such love and enthusiasm. But then, Miami had often been described as a whore of a city, falling in love with any entertainer, sports figure, or personality that happened to pass through.

Sean Black.

She hadn't seen him in nearly fifteen years. *Fifteen years!* What difference could any of this make to her now?

It made a difference because she'd never been able to forget. All of their lives had been changed forever.

She'd been seventeen that day. . . .

God help her; she could remember it just as clearly as if it had been yesterday.

She stood up, swallowing down her wine. She walked back into the kitchen, poured herself another glass, and swallowed it down like water. Wine would help her sleep, and she was going to sleep, and sleep well.

You won't think about him, she told herself. You won't, you won't, you won't. . . .

So determined, she started up the stairs. Then she remembered that Ellie had been murdered, and that some kind of a psycho was running around the city.

Lots of psychos were probably running around the city. It was a big place.

But she needed to forget Sean and be a responsible adult. Make sure that her new home was secure. She resolutely checked her doors and windows, went upstairs, changed into a tailored cotton nightgown, and lay down.

Poor Ellie.

Sean . . .

She could remember Ellie's face that day at the rock pit when Mandy . . .

When Mandy had died.

When Mandy had been murdered.

Now Ellie was dead, too. Murdered.

And Sean was back in town . . .

Jesus, no, dear God, what was she thinking?

No, Sean wasn't responsible.

Go to sleep! she raged silently to herself. *Forget it, don't think, don't dream.*

And for God's sake . . .

Don't remember.

Sean sat in his hotel room, staring blankly at the television. The news reporter was rehashing the information about Eleanor Metz.

Hell. Ellie was dead. Even though the pretty young reporter was far more dramatic than a newswoman should be, her description of the death Ellie had faced didn't begin to come up to the horror he'd realized seeing the body. He hadn't seen Ellie in fifteen years, but time had eroded painfully for him as he had stood there, seeing her as she lay naked, cold, brutalized. He shuddered, stared at the glass of scotch in his hands, and swallowed down two inches of the stuff. Then a fearful, creeping feeling came over him, and he remembered why he'd poured the drink in the first place. Memories. Ellie made him think of Mandy.

And Lori Kelly. Corcoran. She'd married; his brother had told him about it years back, but the husband had died long ago as well, and she'd been living in New York with her little boy. And he'd thought, good for her, God bless her! With so many assholes in the world, there had also been a few Lori Kellys. She'd been a cherished friend.

Except that for some reason after that day at the rock pit, his bitterness against her had been, in a way, greater than that he'd felt toward the others. The assholes were just assholes. Lori should have . . .

Should have what?

She'd testified at his trial. Soft-spoken, determined. She'd been loyal, trying to defend his character. But the lawyer from the D.A.'s office had grilled her as if she were on trial, and she hadn't been able to lie on the stand. She had admitted that Mandy had been acting wildly and that it would have been natural if he'd been in a jealous rage. When it had been over, her parents had all but jerked her away from any contact with him as if he were diseased—or as if they were afraid that he was a homicidal maniac and would make her pay for her words—and he hadn't spoken with her since.

So long ago now. So fucking long ago.

She didn't look any different. Tall, slim, still classically beautiful with her huge hazel eyes and the long reddish blond hair that still waved down her back. She had a way about her, a way of listening, or responding, or really hearing, of looking beyond the obvious, of seeing . . . even what he hadn't wanted seen. She'd always been his friend, since that first day. Even if she'd dated ye olde preppy boy-friend of yacht club status, while Sean had sown wild oats with Mandy. He found himself thinking of the cartoon character Jessica Rabbit. Mandy hadn't been bad; she'd just drawn herself that way. She'd wanted so much, and she'd been in such a hurry to get it—a Madonna ahead of her time. He'd cared about Mandy, but they never would have made it. And he hadn't been angry with her—things between them had died long before Mandy had lost her life that day.

Mandy had needed a ladder, a guy to crawl up. She wanted every-thing the world had to offer, and she didn't care who she teased or slept with to get it.

Lori had always been there, a friend. A ray of light, a streak of chemistry. Passion promising to happen. He'd never wanted to push anything, thinking there was something special there and the timing just wasn't right.

Bad, bad timing.

But then, Lori had been with him when he was in pain. She'd eased the worst night of his life, despite Brad, her folks, and anything else that might have stood in the way.

But she hadn't really stayed with him long enough, and she hadn't fought hard enough. He had left, but she could have found him, written, called. Instead she had fled as well, and they had gone their separate ways.

"To you, Lori Kelly!" he said softly, lifting his glass. So long ago. So many women in between. Yet he wondered suddenly if there had been so many simply because of Lori, and maybe Mandy as well, and a determination *not* to get involved in relationships that mattered.

He drank. Great. Miami was going to turn him into an alcoholic.

But things here were strange. No, life was so damned strange. Mandy had been dead a long, long time. Now Ellie was dead as well, and Lori had suddenly—literally—walked into him.

A chill assailed him, unlike anything he had ever known, and he finished the last of the scotch in his glass. Stupid, foolish. Bad things happened. Lots of bad things in a metropolis this size.

Don't go getting paranoid. There's nothing you can do, and there's no conspiracy, none whatsoever. Ellie was living a wild life, night-clubbing it, going out, looking for men. . . .

Right. And why wouldn't Lori be doing the same things now that she was back? There was no reason a widow shouldn't spend a few nights out, dancing, having a drink with friends, enjoying some music and dancing.

He swore impatiently, rose, fixed himself another scotch. What the hell was the matter with him? Ellie had been murdered, and nearly fifteen years ago Mandy had been murdered. Well, he had supposedly been the murderer, so where was the correlation?

He knew, of course, that he hadn't even been near Mandy until Andrew had pulled her from the water.

He shouldn't have come home. *You can never come home.* Everyone know the old adage.

Still, he found himself walking to the phone on the desk and dialing Ricky's home number.

"Hello?" Ricky answered.

"It's Sean. Lori Kelly's in town."

"Oh, yeah! I heard. Her brother Andrew said that she was coming back because her grandfather wasn't doing so well."

"Do you have a number for her?"

"No, but I can get it. Jan married Brad, you know. They're divorced, but still friends, and Jan kept up with Lori, found her a house. I'll get back with you."

"Great."

Sean set the receiver back in its cradle. The newscaster had finally moved on to other stories, recounted with similar dramatics. Over the weekend there had also been two shootings and a fatal car crash.

Tragedy was a fact of life. He heard horrible stories every day.

But he had known Ellie. Known her as a kid, seen her laugh, flirt, play, study—seen her hurt, confused, smiling and in pain. And when you knew someone, and then saw that someone dead and naked on a stainless steel gurney . . .

And Lori Kelly was back in town.

They were all together again. It seemed. The survivors.

Ricky Garcia held the receiver in his hands for a long time. Ellie was dead, and Lori Kelly was back in town, and Sean Black was here as well. What a homecoming.

He shook his head, aware again of the newswoman talking away on the television. Pretty woman, but melodramatic as all get out. What had happened to the simple facts?

He hesitated, then turned up the volume. Just what were they saying about the murder? The media had a penchant for screwing up law enforcement here. As if it wasn't a tough enough place already. Crack heads all over, pushers, dopers, gangs, mafia in half a dozen nationalities . . . and half the population whining all the time that the cops were bad as well. On the take. Bullshit. They didn't begin to know the meaning of bad.

He stared at the newswoman, so intense, going over and over the terror of what had happened, trying to make a name for herself.

Poor Ellie. All right, so she had been something of a prick tease. Still . . .

How strange. How damned strange. If Ellie were alive, they'd all be back now. All of them who had been there that day.

He remembered that Sean had asked him to get Lori Kelly's phone number. He dialed Brad Jackson.

Just what would they say on the news?

The killer watched the television, feeling a rush of pleasure that was almost as good as the chase. . . .

As the act itself.

The media. What fools! They spilled everything. Absolutely everything.

Now a half dozen psychos would confess to the crime, and the dumb cops wouldn't know the difference.

At last the newswoman went off the screen, and a white-haired man appeared. Some retired stiff from the FBI. He described the murder as a typical sex crime, and warned women that they should be very careful, think carefully, act carefully. When such a murder occurred, people tended to think that it had to be carried out by a monster, a devil with visible horns.

Sex crimes were usually carried out by men of the same race as their victims, men who were most often in their mid-twenties to late thirties. Younger than that, and they usually hadn't yet reached a level of such overt savagery. Older than that, and they'd usually tripped themselves up somehow.

I'll drink to that! he mused. Except he wouldn't do so.

The man on the television went on.

Such killers were often men women trusted on sight.

The average Joe.

Average!

He smiled tautly.

Average, hell!

He lifted his drink.

And drank to himself again, terribly pleased. They'd soon know that there wasn't anything average about him at all.

He heard a knocking at his door, his name was called, and he smiled. She was here. He did know how to play at *being the average Joe.*

But only a man way above average could begin to do it half so damned well.

Jan Hunt stood on Brad's doorstep, looking around as she waited. It was dark. Despite the lights out on the street, it was dark. In the residential area of Coconut Grove, it could be dark as a black hole at night. One of the prime attractions of the area was the tremendous amount of foliage around, and she usually loved it. Trees, vines, bushes, flowers—she'd lived around the general area all her life, didn't know the names of half of it, but loved it just the same. Except for tonight. Reading about Ellie had really disturbed her. Then, when she'd picked up the signed contract for the new condo for the old geezer, she'd seen nothing but the murder on the news. Unnerved, she'd called home, found that Tina was safely in with the doors locked and the alarm armed, and she'd headed for Brad's.

Dumb move. They had an agreement. They always called one another. She hadn't called him tonight. He might be with someone. And here she was, goose bumps rising on her flesh because she was afraid to be standing here, in the dark. There was a breeze, and every time it ruffled a leaf, she felt certain that a homicidal maniac was crawling around her, watching her, waiting to pounce, already beginning to hunger for a taste of blood. . . .

The door opened.

"Jan!"

"Hey!" she said nervously.

Brad was dressed—that was good, she reasoned. He hadn't just come popping out of bed. He was casual, in jeans and T-shirt, barefoot, blond hair neatly combed, looking good.

"Can I come in?" she asked.

"Yeah, sure." He backed away from the door, and she stepped in.

His place was nicely, simply decorated. It was a contemporary house, no more than fifteen years old, and he had some modern art on the walls, with most of his furniture being leather, chrome, and glass. The floors were cool tile, the kitchen was state-of-the-art—sporting far more utensils than Brad would ever use, but they were there if needed. His bedroom was huge, complete with a big bath that held a whirlpool encircled by glass walls that looked out over the lush foliage in back, enclosed by a redwood privacy fence. It was the perfect place for a prime-of-life, divorced, up-and-coming attorney. A great place to bring women.

Absurd, too, because she had sold it to him.

"I should have called—" she began.

"It's okay," he told her. He shrugged, and grinned. "I'm kind of glad to see you. There's no one important in my life right now . . . and I guess you heard about Ellie. I've been drinking since I heard about her."

Jan arched a brow. "Had you seen her lately?"

He shook his head. "No . . . I've run into her now and then over the past few years. She dated a guy from my office about five years ago. It's just that it's so . . . awful. When something like that happens, something so horrible, even to a casual acquaintance . . ."

"I know. It's scary. I couldn't help wondering what happened, how she met the guy, how she felt. . . ." She shivered fiercely.

"So you came to see me?"

"Yeah."

"Because you're scared."

"Maybe."

"Ah. You want some action, but you're afraid of the exciting new guys you might meet, so you're going for the humdrum but safe?"

Jan placed her hands on her hips. "Fuck you."

He grinned. "If that's what you want."

She started to get mad, then threw up her hands. She looked down unhappily before staring at him again. "I never said that you were humdrum, Brad. Just the opposite. I never knew where you were."

He looked at her and nodded after a moment, then smiled. "I'm glad to see you," he admitted. "But do you remember that you were mad at me last week?"

"You didn't want to help me pay for Tina's field trip, and that day they've got planned for her art class is nearly a hundred bucks!"

"I wasn't sure if I wanted my thirteen-year-old going on a week-end field trip!" he said. "Where is my thirteen-year-old?"

"Home, locked in tight. I should be home with her. I can't stay long—"

"Yes, ma'am, stud service on demand. Fast, too, if that's what you want."

She shed her clothing as she walked into the bedroom. It was dark, but she was familiar with the layout of the furniture. Brad didn't turn on a light. He was naked when he tackled her from behind, already aroused when they crashed down on the bed together.

She was glad of the darkness, confused by the rush of emotions that assailed her as they coupled. It was odd to discover that the awful news of a murder had made her need Brad, not just to talk to, but to be with in a sexual way. And it was somehow even more disturbing tonight to realize again that he was an exceptional lover. Tears stung her eyes as she climaxed, because she'd had such dreams once upon a time, when she'd been young, and things just hadn't worked out the way she had wanted. Sometimes she could pretend . . .

He started making love to her once again. He was needy, but not quite ready.

"Talk to me," he whispered.

And she knew what he wanted. His fantasy was two women. He liked to hear what she'd be doing to someone else while he was doing what he was doing to her. . . .

Sometimes she could play the game. Sometimes she couldn't.

She suddenly wished that she could see her watch. He was a good lover, and she was in the middle of this, but she was suddenly worried as well. She should be home. She couldn't be rude enough just to say so. She'd gotten what she'd come for . . . he hadn't quite. So she began to talk, saying what he wanted to hear.

And it was all right. His growing state of arousal turned her on more than she'd imagined possible, and they exploded together into a deliciously erotic climax. Moments later, lying at her side, he stroked her hair.

"Too bad you didn't agree to do it for me. Just once," he told her. "All kinds of awful things could have been avoided."

For a moment she felt a strange, cold fear inside.

"Like what?" she whispered.

"Our divorce."

He rolled around, and she felt him trying to study her features. "Of course, we can still do it."

"What?" she inquired, annoyed. "Brad, we are divorced. You do what you want to do. And you make big bucks. You could hire five women at a time if you wanted."

She vaguely saw the motion as he shook his head. "I want *you* and another woman."

"You're a pervert."

"No more so than any other red-blooded American male."

"You're cruel to me."

"I'm complimenting you! I want *you,* and another woman."

She shook her head, impatient as if she dealt with a child. Then she stroked his beautiful blond hair. "I've got to go."

"Think about it, Just me and you, and another gorgeous woman. Just once. My birthday is coming up."

She smacked him lightly in the jaw. "Pervert!"

"Hey, my old girlfriend is back in town as well. You and Lori Kelly. What a lineup."

"Lori Kelly apparently had the sense to know that you were a pervert when we were in high school. And don't do fantasies about my friends. It makes me uncomfortable."

"It's a great fantasy."

"Brad—"

"All right! I'll keep it in my head."

"Great. Now I'll feel awkward any time we're together."

"Hey, don't. 'Cause you know something?" he said softly.

"What?"

"I do love you, you know."

She smiled. He held her close. Just held her. It was nice. "I've got to go," she said unhappily.

"I'll give Tina a call, make sure she's okay. You can stay a little longer, then I'll follow you home. How's that?"

"Nice, Brad, thanks."

She watched as he dialed their daughter, talked to her, ascertained that everything was all right, and made her swear that she had the doors properly locked and the alarm on. He hung up, flicked on the television, told Jan he'd make them a couple of drinks, and padded out of the room.

She stared at the television. The late-night news was rehashing the earlier news. About Ellie.

"Turn it, please," she said as Brad came back into the room, handing her a Jack Black and Seven.

He quickly flicked to the Playboy channel. Jan groaned softly as a two-women, one-man sex scene popped onto the screen.

"So I'm a pervert, huh?"

"Yes," she said primly.

"Aw, come on, just watch," he said.

A few minutes later he was making love to her again. When it was over, he whispered, "We perverts need our fixes. Just once, Jan. For my birthday."

She turned away from him, pulling the sheets over her head. "You want me to go pick up some girl?"

"Sure. Or I can pick her up for you. Or take you places where a woman would come on to you."

"Pervert!" she said. "Think about it! What would you do if some girl came on to your daughter?"

He was quiet.

"Huh?"

"Kill her. Or him."

"You couldn't kill."

"Yes, actually, I think that I could."

Chapter 4

Brad Jackson lifted the receiver quickly as his bedside phone rang.

He usually let the machine get it.

But Jan had dozed off, and he had changed channels to watch the news again. Ellie. Poor damned Ellie.

"Hello?"

"Brad?"

"Yeah." He frowned. "Ricky?"

"Yeah, it's me."

"Anything new on Ellie?"

"No," Ricky said impatiently.

"You have any inside information?"

"Are you kidding? There was a leak somewhere in the department—you know there's actually a half dozen teams on this case—and someone spilled just about everything we know. That news lady seems to have more information than I do. If I learn anything that I can tell you—"

"I'm just kind of worried. I have a wife and daughter, you know."

"Ex-wife."

"Whatever, you know that I'm concerned about her."

"Yeah. Well, Jan is a sensible woman; she'll know to stay away from strangers."

"Yeah," Brad said dryly. He frowned. "You know, Ricky, it's late—"

"I'm sorry. I needed a favor. You know that Sean Black is in town?"

"Yeah, yeah, I know," Brad murmured. He couldn't help but know. Yeah, yeah, everyone had told him already—including Ricky.

The great Sean Black was back. Poor boy/school hero. Football genius. Famous writer. The guy who muscled up by just waking in the morning. He'd almost been convicted of murder—and now people were half killing themselves to get the guy's autograph.

"He wants to reach Lori Kelly. Or Corcoran, or whatever her name is now."

Brad felt a prickle of annoyance run down his spine. He wasn't really jealous of Sean Black, never had been. He'd had the advantages all his life; Sean had just been a hard-luck kid. But it had irritated him way back when that Lori had been such good friends with Sean—when he had supposedly been the hottest thing around and she'd been his privileged choice. That had been a long time ago. A lot was forgotten, but feelings, emotions, *annoyances* remained. He'd had a lot of knockdowns since then, but he liked his life now. Jan was a great ex-wife. Available—without the nagging. He really did love her, and his daughter was a beauty queen and a brain, the perfect child. He did what he wanted and never went without.

But he had to admit, he'd been really curious to see Lori Kelly again himself. All right, so it was unlikely he'd get Jan and Lori into bed at the same time. He'd still like to see Lori.

Seemed Sean Black wanted to beat him to the punch.

"Do you have Lori's number?" Ricky asked.

"Do I have her number . . . ?" he repeated, then smiled, shaking his head with amusement as he looked to his side, where Jan was beginning to stir beneath the sheets. He smacked a hand on her rump, covering the mouthpiece on the phone with his other hand. "Hey—what's Lori's number?"

Jan turned over, hair tangled, eyes heavy—and still suspicious. "Why?"

"I'm going to call her over."

She tried to hit him. He laughed, stopping her.

"Seriously, Ricky wants to know."

"Ricky?"

"Ricky Garcia wants the number. For Sean."

"Oh. For Sean!"

Jan sat up, hugging her knees to her chest. "I saw Lori tonight. I meant to tell her that Sean was in town . . . but then I saw the paper about poor Ellie and I blanked on that. Let's see, her number is four-four-four . . . four-four-four . . . damn! I forgot. But she's listed. Under L. Corcoran, on Almansa."

Brad conveyed that information to Ricky, told him to keep in touch, and hung up. Then he pretended to dial information and ask for the number, and then dial the number.

Jan sprang up. "What are you doing?"

He looked at her innocently. "Hey, I don't want to let Sean get in there first, and there might be danger out there on the streets. She's your friend, you should share. I'm calling Lori Kelly Corcoran to see if she wants in on my great stud service—"

Jan wrenched the phone out of his hands, her eyes wide, her features taut.

"Hey, now!" Brad teased.

"You leave Lori Kelly out of this."

"Jan!"

"You were nuts about her in high school."

"We were kids!"

"You said she was great."

"She was."

"You said you never touched her."

"One of us is lying," Brad said, eyes sparkling.

Jan made a point of slamming the phone receiver down, and he started laughing, pinning her to the bed. "All right. all right, so we won't ask Lori over. We'll let her take the chance of picking up a homicidal maniac."

"Sean always liked Lori; she can pick him up."

"And maybe Sean is a homicidal maniac."

"You're a pervert, so maybe you're a homicidal maniac, too."

He ignored that. "Okay, so we'll have to pick another woman. Just once. Then we could get married again."

She inhaled sharply, staring at him.

"I'd have it all out of my system," he said.

"Really? How could I ever be sure?"

"I'm getting older. Tired."

She stared at him skeptically.

"Honest."

She groaned.

He smiled. "Honestly honest. I wouldn't take vows again without meaning to be faithful. Think about it."

"Wait a minute. Are you trying to bribe me?" she said indignantly. "Marriage isn't something decided because of a bribe."

"Think about it," he insisted.

True to his word, Brad followed Jan home.

"Think about it!" he whispered one more time, nuzzling her earlobe on the front porch.

"I've thought!" she protested.

"Naw . . . I've sown the seeds. I know it."

"Good night, Brad."

She let herself in, reset the alarm, and checked on Tina, who was sleeping soundly.

In her own room she turned on the television, thinking she'd watch a movie until she fell asleep, and that would get her mind *off* Brad's absurd proposal. But the channel was on CNN, and the news came blaring out at her again.

She did forget about Brad.

A serious, attractive young blond woman was talking about the awful thing that had happened to Ellie.

And all she could think about was murder.

Chapter 5

At first Lori hadn't been able to sleep. All the wine in the world wouldn't have helped.

Then Lori dozed.

When she slept, she dreamed, reliving the past, knowing that she was reliving the past, unable to stop the frames of memory that played before her eyes.

She was seventeen that day at the rock pit. Her mother had told her that she was at the prime of life, with everything in the world going her way. She was young and literally a beauty queen, having just been elected to the title of Miss Orange Blossom for their end-of-the-year dance and parade.

And her heart was breaking.

Over Sean.

In the endless days to come, she knew that any small twist of behavior on anyone's part might have changed destiny, might have changed what happened, destroying so many young lives. But all she knew as the day began was that she was dying . . . over him.

Naturally, no one knew. She was Lori Kelly, and—partially because of Gramps and his wisdom!—she could pride herself on being kind and decent, but then, admittedly, she was a teenage girl, and she did have her ego and her pride. And though things might have been her own fault, she was crushed by what had happened between her and Sean.

Supposedly, she was in love with Brad Jackson. And they were the *perfect* couple. He was an honor student all the way, Key Club, quarterback, blue-eyed, blond-haired, could-trace-his-ancestors-back-to-the-*Mayflower* great. But beneath his polished veneer—just every once in a while—he wasn't quite so nice. Her folks never saw it. They saw his all-American parents, officers in the yacht club, civic duty to a T. And Brad was okay. She knew him well enough, liked him—but knew what not to like as well.

Sean dated Mandy Olin. She was his age, voluptuous, a little wild, mad about him—and the child of rich folks as well. They didn't approve of Sean. That might have been half the reason Mandy dated him. Except that he was great. Everybody liked Sean. He never backed down in a fight, but he never started one, either.

Lori had always been in love with Sean.

Secretly, of course. She had her pride, and as long as he was with Mandy, she'd never let him know. Even those few times when they'd met on some different level, she'd been flippant, keeping her true feelings quiet.

And now Sean was leaving. They were all going in different directions, of course, but since Sean would be taking summer courses at college, he'd be leaving soon. They were just kids—that's what Lori's mother told her all the time. Just kids. They shouldn't take things too seriously. Lori was too young to really be in love with anyone. After all, her whole life stretched in front of her. Naturally, if she continued a relationship with a nice boy like Brad, it would be good. Just so long as she stayed away from kids like Michael and Sean Black. Bad blood. Lori needed to go to college and create a promising future for herself. She came from well-educated people, and she had the chance to go for everything—a master's degree, a doctorate! They weren't poor folks, not from the wrong side of the tracks, and she didn't want to wind up pregnant, saddled with a child.

Normally, her mother was all right. A parent, but a decent sort of parent. Lori loved her mother. But in this instance her mother was blind. She didn't begin to realize that there was no chance of Lori running off with Brad or, heaven forbid, having a baby with Brad. Although she was beginning to feel a little nervous about what had happened with Sean.

Her parents still gave her a hard time about their friendship. He lived in a tough section of Coconut Grove. His father was some kind of a security guard, for God's sake. His mother was simply gone. He had a brother, Michael, one year older, who was constantly in trouble. He had another brother, Daniel, twenty already, in the service—no other choice, there'd been no future for the kid. They didn't want her to be prejudiced against kids less fortunate than she was. It was just that Sean, with no mother, a broken-down father, and a brother with a record, didn't have much chance; he and his kind were just bad news.

Except that he wasn't. Gramps understood. Sometimes Sean could swagger. He was on the football team, and he was good. He had an after-school job at a bookstore, and he still managed to keep a high B average. He was going to Florida State University on a scholarship—just a state school, but half the rich kids in the city went on to the same state schools, mainly because they could get in, and because they were known as party schools. Some of the state schools even had really great programs. But really smart rich kids went to Harvard or Yale, lazy or dumb rich kids went to state schools. Smart poor kids made it to state schools, and dumb poor kids wound up sleeping under bridges and drinking cheap booze out of brown paper bags. That was the way it went, according to her parents. Thankfully, Sean was a smart poor kid.

Not that it should have mattered. Sean thought he was her friend. No matter what emotions she was harboring all those years, he was in love—or lust, as the 4F club insisted—with Mandy. And Lori dated Brad.

Except for those few occasions when she and Sean met alone by chance, then there had been that one night . . .

Which was haunting her like crazy today.

They were all at the rock pit. The whole in crowd. They probably shouldn't have gone swimming there all the time, but they did. It had been dug out for construction, then abandoned, in the southwest section of the city—it was dangerous, but cool. It ranged from twenty to fifty feet deep, and old wrecked cars had been junked in it, pines grew all around it, and it was off the beaten track. The ground around it was all like a white powdery sand, and it was great to stretch out on and tan, and the pines all around it provided perfect shelter for picnics. The way the ground had been dug out, there were all kinds of dunes and little private, tree-shaded copses as well.

Sean hadn't been there when Lori had arrived with Susan Nichols and Jan Hunt. Neither had Brad. Last night had been grad night, and they'd all stayed out really late, and some of them were waking up slowly that morning.

Lori had a new bikini. It was cobalt-blue, and skimpy. Working carefully, she'd managed to get her pale skin to a fine tan, and she'd touched up her natural blond locks with a combination of vinegar and lemon—she could get away with that, her mother wouldn't allow her to use any store-bought bleaches. She looked good that day, and she knew it. Her mother had wistfully told her that youth was beauty in itself, and she hadn't even chastised her for the skimpy bikini. She'd just told her that she was beautiful. "Every kid's mother tells her that, Mom," Lori had protested. "No, honey, for real, you're beautiful. Inside and out." She should have felt great. Her folks had their hang-ups, but they were mostly all talk; they really weren't too bad, and they did love her. They might have warned her against the Blacks, but they were always decent to Sean when he was over with the gang. She had one summer left, then she was off to college herself. Her brother, Andrew, one year her senior, just back from college for the summer, had quit acting like a complete jerk this year. Rather than constantly threatening to tell on one another now, they kept each other's secrets.

Arriving at the rock pit, Susan, Jan, and Lori laid out their towels, popped open cans of soda, turned on the radio, and stretched out.

After a while Jan yawned and stretched. "I'm burning up. I'm going to hop in the water. Anyone coming?"

"I'll go," Susie said. "Lori?"

"Umm . . . not yet. I'm just beginning to feel the sun," Lori said. That wasn't true. She was hoping that Sean would show up, see her stretched out in her new bikini, decide that she was beautiful—inside and out—and profess his undying love and devotion.

"Okay, bake then. The guys should be along soon, huh?" Sue said. She was dating Lori's brother, Andrew. Ugh. There was no accounting for taste. But then again, Andrew was better than Ricky Garcia—who was still a creep in Lori's eyes—and Jan and he had been a hot item now for two years.

"Yeah, sure, the guys will be along soon," Lori said.

When the other two girls left her, more people began to arrive. Andrew showed up with their cousin, Josh, who was a senior as well, and Jeff Olin, Mandy's brother, Andrew's age. Her brother was a traitor, hanging around with Jeff, she determined. But, of course, she couldn't tell him so. She had to smile through her teeth, or else she'd give herself away. Her brother knew her too well.

Josh tickled her and called her kid. She was glad there was no one there to see. Josh could just act so damned superior—unless he was being nice to her because one of his college buddies had a crush on her.

Mandy arrived—without Sean. She came with a girlfriend, Ellie LeBlanc. They were both nearly naked, Ellie in a dark-patterned suit that complimented her light complexion and dark hair, and Mandy in an animal print that complimented everything about her. The two of them flirted with Andrew and Josh, then Ricky Garcia arrived, still hanging around with Ted Neeson, as he had been since junior high. Then Brad showed up with Michael Black. Brad came down on Susie's towel next to Lori, running his hand over Lori's bare midriff and kissing her lips. She tried hard not to make a face, or push his hand away. "What's the matter with you?" he asked her, pale blue eyes flashing angrily.

Just call it off with the jerk, she told herself.

But she felt guilty right away. Lots of the kids were sleeping together; she just didn't want to sleep with him. He was the most popular guy in his class, he was smart, he was good-looking—she just didn't want to. But if she could keep up the facade of being a steady *thing* together with just a few kisses and a little petting . . .

"It's just hot," she lied.

But staring at her, he shook his head angrily. "It's more than that. And you know what, Miss Orange Blossom? If you don't want to do it, there are other girls who will."

She stared at him, hoping that the others, still standing and talking, were unaware of the exchange.

"Look, I'm just not ready," she lied.

"I'm a grown-up guy," he told her. "With needs. It's not like we've just started dating. God knows, I love you. Everyone is convinced we'll get married."

"But not yet. What if—"

"First of all, we'll use protection. And if you get pregnant, we'll just get married early."

Her stomach tossed and turned.

"Brad, I'm just not ready."

"Well, fuck you, then!" he said, his voice a taut whisper.

"Brad, don't be mad—" she began, spurred by more than a twinge of guilt.

But he had stood, and already flirted with Mandy and Ellie along with the other guys. She closed her eyes, casting a crooked arm over them to shield them from the sun. "Hey, we're going on down to the pit, kid!" her brother called to her. She waved a hand in the air. She heard laughter as they all headed off toward the water.

Her arm was still over her eyes when she felt someone come down beside her again. And then a subtle scent of well-known aftershave just lightly teased her senses, and she sat up with a jerk. Sean was next to her. He wasn't laughing or smiling, and he wasn't about to tease her. "Lori," he said gravely.

"Sean." She was instantly nervous, so afraid of making a fool of herself, of letting her heart show—and being rebuffed. She inclined her head. "Mandy headed for the water."

Just at that moment Ted Neeson came loping back toward them. "Hey, Lori, you gotta come see this one! Mandy's got her top off, and the guys are playing keep-away with it. I—oh, Sean! Uh, hey, Sean! When did you get here? Sorry, buddy, I didn't mean—"

"It's all right," Sean said evenly, dark blue eyes level, lips ruefully curled. "Mandy's a big girl, a free agent. And her brother's in the water, isn't he?"

"Uh . . . yeah!"

"Then, I'm sure if she needs a rescue, he'll provide it."

"Yeah, sure," Ted said, and quickly went back the way he had come. He looked nervous as hell, as if he wished he hadn't been the one to bring such sordid tidings to Sean's attention.

"Mandy's a free agent?" Lori inquired. When pushed, Sean did have a bad temper. And he'd broken up with Mandy once before in their junior year when he'd been out of town with the football team and rumor had arisen about Mandy fooling around with Ricky. Mandy was a wicked flirt—but she always proclaimed herself madly in love with Sean—the only "real man" among the crowd. Rumor was that she'd been ready for a "real man" too, when Sean came along—she'd already fooled around with a number of older guys when they'd started dating, and she knew—in Jan's words—just how to satisfy a guy.

Sean lifted his hands and shrugged. He was shirtless, and though he was still lean, he was already well muscled due to his football playing and the fact that he picked up any odd jobs mowing lawns and moving furniture for people whenever he could. He worked shirtless in the hot sun, so he was handsomely tanned, and he wore jeans cutoffs in which to swim. He had a serious look about him today and she found herself thinking that neither money nor a fancy home had much to do with making up a person; Sean was handsome with an arresting, strongly sculpted face, penetrating eyes, and a great height and body. She wanted to slip her arms around him then and there. She flipped back her hair instead.

"I'm off to school in just a few days. I'm headed to Tallahassee, and Mandy will be in Denver by September." He shrugged, staring at Lori again. "Besides, she's always been something of a wild woman, huh?"

Lori arched a brow. "You're furious."

He shrugged. "Not really. She's—she's just kind of a . . ." He paused, hesitating, then shrugged. "She's just kind of a slut, and I can't change that. While . . . God, Lori. I'm sorry about the other night. Really sorry.''

Her face burned. She looked straight ahead. He wasn't going to tell her that she had changed his life, that he'd discovered he couldn't live without her. He was just sorry. He'd behaved badly.

She didn't speak.

He continued. "I was just so hurt . . .''

He had been hurt. Crushed. Five months ago, his brother Daniel had been reported MIA. He'd been assigned to a base in the Middle East, and had disappeared during a training mission. His status had been changed just the day before she'd come to see him. Daniel Black's death had been confirmed. His body had been found in the desert—he'd been shot in the back of the head. Sean, who never drank, had been drinking. When she'd arrived, he'd been crying. Sean, who never cried.

Mandy hadn't been with him. She'd had to go to some function at the Historical Society with her folks. Sean's father had been out with old military friends, and his brother Michael had been with his own girl. Lori hadn't been able to stay away. So they'd been alone. For hours and hours, and he'd talked, and talked, about how he'd loved Daniel, how Daniel had wanted to make a difference, how he'd told his brother that the service would pay for his education and help them all along. They'd get their father a fine new home eventually, pay him back for just loving them all and trying to do his best for them at all times. . . .

"I'm sorry,'' Sean said again, shaking his head. "So damned sorry. I'd never want to hurt you, Lori.''

She flipped her hair back again. "Don't be stupid, Sean. You can't hurt me. I mean . . . just as long as you never say anything. I wouldn't want Brad to know what happened—or my folks.''

He arched a brow, staring at her hard, and there was a disappointment in his eyes that caused a savage twisting of her insides.

"Lori, I think that we really need to talk. I have to say good-bye, and I want you to know—''

"Oh, God, please, I don't want to talk—''

"Lori—''

"I don't want to remember!'' She leapt to her feet. "I don't want to talk—and I don't want to be caught alone together. Go find your wild girlfriend. Say good-bye to *her*.'' Oh, God, she was going to burst into tears. He was sorry for her. Sorry. He pitied her. She was in love with him, and he pitied her. She couldn't bear it.

"Lori—''

"Damn you, don't be sorry! Mandy's going to Denver, you're going to Tallahassee, and I'm off to New York. All decided. Just leave me the hell alone!" she told him, and she jumped up and spun on her heels, almost running toward the water.

She plunged into it.

Everyone was involved in the keep-away game—even the other girls. Even Jeff—who seemed to be okay with his sister's constantly outrageous behavior.

But when Mandy saw Lori, her laughing humor suddenly seemed to fade. "All right, that's it, everybody's had a good time, and every one of you pricks has managed to cop a feel. Now, give me the damned thing!" she demanded, when her bikini top landed in Brad's hand. Her mountainous breasts bounced at surface level as she tied the top back on. "Assholes!" she accused the guys.

"Hey!" Andrew protested.

"What do you want from a cunt?" Ricky demanded.

"Ricky, come on, now," Jeff said uncomfortably.

"Fuck you all," Mandy told them.

"Ooh—sit on my face, baby!" Brad told her.

"Don't you wish, frat-boy!" Mandy taunted. "What's the matter, the prom queen won't let you get it up, honey?"

The group hooted and catcalled, with only Lori feeling sick and crimson.

Then they all fell silent, one by one, as Mandy, then Brad, and then the others saw Sean standing at the jump-off point. His blue eyes were nearly black. A blue vein beat a furious pulse at his throat.

"Sean . . ." Mandy breathed placatingly. She swam hard, crawling quickly from the water, approaching him. But when her hands fell on his shoulders, he turned away.

"Sean!" she cried, grabbing him again.

But he shook her off, and walked away.

Laughter was gone. They all emerged from the water. Brad stared at Lori, but she turned away from him, hurrying into the pines. She sat in the shadow of a group of trees, shaking.

She heard snatches of different arguments. Male voices, female voices. Then silence. She leaned back against a tree while the sun burned down around her and the morning ticked slowly by.

At last she emerged. Sean didn't love her; Brad was an asshole. She could live with that. She was nearly eighteen; nearly an adult. Time to move on.

Except that . . .

Fear rushed through her once again. *What if . . .*

Then she heard the screaming. "Oh, God, oh, God, oh, God, someone help!"

The first person she saw was Jan, who had been looking for her and was walking toward her on the path. Jan looked at her, lifting her shoulders. They stared at one another, then Lori leapt up.

They recognized that it was Ricky Garcia crying out. They both started running down the path that led to the water, and then around the rooted trail that skirted it. They could see Andrew, Jeff, Ted, and Ricky on the shore, with someone stretched between them. Then they could see Sean, racing like a madman toward the group of them, falling down beside them.

It was Mandy on the ground, and at first, as they came around the large rock pit, Lori thought that Sean was trying to kiss her and hold her. Then she realized that he was giving artificial respiration to her.

"Oh, Jeez!" she cried to Jan, grabbing her by the arm and starting to run hard.

They piled up against Brad and Ellie as they reached the far side of the water where the others hovered over Mandy. Mandy's lips were blue; her face was stark white against the background of her deep auburn hair. They heard sirens, an ambulance coming. Lori felt her brother by her side then, putting an arm around her. "Susan's called 911; help will be here any minute."

"What—what happened?" Lori said.

No one answered. All eyes were on Mandy and Sean.

Sean eased back for a moment, drawing in a deep breath, his face drawn, eyes glistening.

"Oh, God!" Ellie moaned. Ellie was Mandy's best friend. "Oh, God, oh, God . . ."

"No!" Jeff Olin shrieked, covering his face and slamming down to the ground on his knees.

"She's dead," Ricky said incredulously. "Jesus H. Christ, she'd dead."

"She can't be dead!" Brad cried. "She can't be—she's seventeen, she's a kid. Where the hell are the damned paramedics?"

Sean started up with CPR again. Then the sirens screeched closer, and in a matter of minutes, professionals in neatly pressed blue and white uniforms were pushing through the crowd of kids. A man knelt down by Sean. "I'll take it over from here, son."

Sean rose, and stood numbly. More of the paramedic crew arrived; a syringe was shot into Mandy's arm. Within minutes she'd been situated on a stretcher, and they were carrying her away.

The kids followed.

They were all there as she was loaded into the ambulance, Jeff barely coherent as he explained he was her brother and that he had to ride with her.

The ambulance pulled away.

The rest of them watched—Lori and her brother, Andrew, and their cousin, Josh. Michael and Sean Black. Ricky Garcia, Ted Neeson, Ellie LeBlanc, Brad Jackson, Susan Nichols, and Jan Hunt. All watching as the ambulance drove away.

"All right, who wants to tell me what happened?"

They all spun around. A tall, heavyset, white-haired man stood behind them. He'd come in an unmarked car right after the paramedics; until now they'd all been too stunned to pay him any attention.

He wasn't wearing a uniform, but he had "cop" written all over him.

Lori stared at him numbly.

"She—she was tangled up in some vine thing down there by one of the rusted-up old cars. I dragged her up, I called for help . . . Sean came running," Andrew said.

"All right. I'm going to take down all your names, and then you get in your cars and go home. I'm off to the hospital, but . . . I'm going to need statements from all of you," he said, walking past them.

"But . . . but she's going to be all right, isn't she?" Brad demanded.

The man stopped and turned around, staring at them. He shook his head. "You're all big kids, aren't you? Big, wild, independent kids, doing what the hell you want, thinking you're grown-ups. Well, then, you're big enough to know the truth. I've seen a lot of death, and I'm sorry to say your friend is already dead. That's bad. Real bad. But now, one of you might have made it happen. That's worse." He pointed at them, moving his stretched-out arm from right to left.

"Dead—*deeeaaad!*" Jan gasped, and she started to cry.

"Oh, God, Mandy's dead, and he's looking at us—" Susan stuttered.

"And next thing you know," Ricky wisecracked, "he's going to be telling us that none of us better dare leave town!" There were tears in Ricky's eyes, belying his tone.

"Yep, son, you're right," the cop told him.

"Dead! Oh, God, oh, God, oh, God!" Ellie kept moaning, and she sank to her knees, screaming hysterically. "Mandy is dead, Mandy is dead, Mandy is dead . . ."

Some of them didn't cry until later. Shock, said the therapist the Kellys hired to help their children through the trauma of the incident.

Shock . . .

How could they help it? Police divers found one of the vines from below, and proclaimed that there was a strong possibility that someone had purposely tied it around Mandy's ankle, and left her fighting desperately for her life beneath the water's surface. She had rubbed her ankle raw in her pathetic efforts to live.

By the time the cops were in the middle of their questioning, the kids all had lawyers, and none of them knew what they had said or done anymore—much less what they had felt.

In the upshot Sean was arrested. He had quarreled with Mandy, he was furious with her. She had humiliated him, she had threatened to ruin his life. He had been suspiciously near Mandy; he had motive, he had opportunity, and the strength to carry out the deed.

They refused to let him out on bond—partially because of his brother's record, and partially because he couldn't hire a hotshot lawyer like the others. He sat in jail until his trial, when a jury found him not guilty—due to a lack of any real physical evidence.

When they let him out, he was no longer a boy, or even a young adult; in a matter of months, he had become a hardened and cynical man. He packed his bags, and left town.

His father and brother mourned.

And Mandy's folks, and all her family, would grieve until their dying days.

But for the parents of the other kids who'd been at the rock pit that day, it was over.

Come to an inevitable end. And it was time to move on.

Sure, Sean had been one of the most popular kids in school, but what could you expect? He'd really been nothing but a no-good kid from a broken family, and in the end bad blood had told all.

So Sean paid . . .

But from the very beginning, Lori suspected that they were all keeping secrets about that day.

She knew damned well that she kept one herself.

Lori woke, flying up to a sitting position in bed as if she'd heard something, as if she'd been startled awake. Her room was in semi-darkness; a night-light burned in the hall. The house was quiet. Yet she had sworn that something . . .

It had just been the dream. She hadn't been able to escape the past, not by telling herself she wouldn't remember, not by seeking oblivion in sleep.

Fifteen years ago . . . it had all been nearly fifteen years ago, Lori reminded herself again. She was in a new home, back in the city where it had happened. Maybe it was natural to start off with a wretched night's sleep.

Lie back down! a rational voice in her head commanded. There's nothing wrong.

But she jumped again, hearing a pounding on her front door.

It was so late! Maybe it was Gramps. Her folks. She was at home again, something could be wrong with her mother, brother, father . . . Gramps.

She catapulted out of bed, raced out to the hall and down the stairs to the door. She frowned, dead still, as she realized that there was no peephole in the front door. She did have a screen door in front of the wooden one, and it was locked, but really, only a fool would open her door . . .

The pounding began again. She didn't want Brendan wakened unless something were really wrong, so as the pounding continued, she threw open the door, reminding herself even as she did so that she really had to be an idiot—a murder had just taken place in the city. But murderers didn't normally knock first.

Through the screen door, she saw him. Sean.

She froze once again. Just staring.

"Damn it, Lori, let me in."

Sean Black. The bastard had haunted her dreams—not to mention her life.

Now he was standing on her front porch.

Chapter 6

Lori wasn't sure why, but she responded to Sean's command and opened the screen door. Maybe it was the look in his eyes, and the fact that he'd probably stand out there banging until the police showed up if she didn't let him in.

He entered her house, closing and locking the door behind him, his eyes never leaving hers.

"What the hell brought you back here?" he demanded, his voice thick.

"What the hell brought *you* back?"

"Lori, I asked you what the hell brought you back!"

"And I asked the same thing."

"Well, I damned well asked first."

If he weren't so angry and tense, the situation might have been funny. And it was certainly strange that the years could wash away so quickly, and she could feel that she *knew* him when he was really such a stranger. But she did know him, the way she could gauge his anger by the tick in the vein at his throat, the tension in his face, the way he dragged his fingers through his hair. Certain things just didn't change about people; characteristics might fade with age, might be refined, but they were still there.

She shrugged, determined to be casual. "My grandfather is very ill, and though you might not remember, he and I were always very close."

His eyes remained locked upon her. She was annoyed to realize that a note of distress had touched her voice. However, he seemed to ease somewhat, leaning against the door then, though he crossed his arms over his chest while watching her.

"I remember," he said softly.

"So what are you doing back? Lording it over us all?" she demanded.

There was a look of anger—and amusement about him. "People are fickle, I've discovered. If they decide not to hang you, they put you on a pedestal. I was sent here by my publishing house. I thought I should stay on a while. I write crime. There's lots of it here."

She was quiet for a moment. *Hell, yes, lots of it! He had come back into town, and one of the most heinous murders since Jack the Ripper had taken place!*

She felt her mouth go dry, and she swallowed hard. Ellie had been Mandy's best friend. Now they were both dead. And what the hell was she thinking? She had loved him, really loved him—though adults had a way of saying that all juvenile feelings were crushes— and she knew damned well, deep in her heart, that Sean Black couldn't possibly murder anyone.

Yet his eyes narrowed as he watched her; he was reading her thoughts.

"Wonderful!" he said bitterly. "You think I came back into town, my murderous capability honed by fifteen years of maturity and growth, to butcher Ellie?" he inquired softly.

"No!" she protested. "No!" She shook her head vehemently. Why did it sound as if she was lying. No matter what she said or did right now, it just wasn't going to come out right.

"Why are you here, now, tonight?" she asked.

"Because it's scary, all this coincidence. It's damned scary."

It was; Jan had known it, she knew it.

Lori crossed her arms over her own chest. "It's a big city. What is the greater Miami population now? Over three million. It's not New York City, I grant you, but in this kind of population—"

"You have drugs and domestic violence. You have guys who shoot down gas station attendants for the fifty bucks in the cash register. You have gangs and juveniles shooting at one another. You have the guy who gets carried away on a date. The woman who freaks out and shoots her husband. But *this* . . . there's a bona fide psychotic killer out there, and he's out there somewhere close."

Chills suddenly shot up her spine. He continued to stare at her, as if she might somehow invite the murderer right over.

"So why are you here?" she demanded again.

"To tell you to go back to New York."

"You can't tell me to go back to New York. I can't go—I came here for a reason. You go back to—wherever it was you came from."

"I'm not in danger!"

"How do you know you're not in danger? How do you know you're not in the most danger? Hell, how do you know that Ricky won't turn around and arrest you—"

"Because I'm not so vulnerable anymore," he told her softly. "And you're missing the point here—a woman was brutally tortured and murdered."

"And it's horrible, but it's happened before, and people are tortured and killed in New York—"

"Not people we know."

She held her breath for a moment.

"Lori, get the hell out of here," he said simply, and with authority, as if he could make her do it.

"You get the hell out of here, Sean, out of my house, and out of here—"

"Mom?"

She broke off, feeling another cold sweat assail her as she realized that her voice had risen, and that she'd awakened Brendan.

He was coming down the stairs. Tall, lanky, wearing cotton boxers, determined to defend her from whatever trouble was at their door.

"Mom, is there a problem?" he began, and then he saw who was standing just inside their front door, and his entire expression changed. His face lit up like a candle. "Michael Shayne? Michael Shayne?" He glazed at his mother, hope in his eyes. "You two know each other?"

Lori couldn't quite find an answer. Sean responded.

He stepped past her, offering Brendan his hand. Brendan shook it.

"We went to school together, way back. My name's really Sean, Sean Black. Nice to meet you, Mr. Corcoran."

He had a way with kids, Lori thought. Her palms were damp.

"My name is Brendan," her son told him, still in awe.

"Call me Sean."

"My mom really knows you?" he repeated.

Sean smiled. His nice smile. Lori knew the smile; he was pleased, of course, yet not at all sure why he evoked such admiration, and he was uncomfortable still with too much adulation. He'd been like that at school when he'd made a great play on the football field, or had come up with an amazing essay in English class or argument in debate. She was tempted to touch him. Just reach out, stroke his face.

She gritted her teeth together and stood perfectly still.

"I've read everything. Everything you've ever written," Brendan told him.

"Hell, I hope not. Some of my early stuff was so bad I keep it in a desk drawer, and I've never let it out. I think about burning it now and then; but then again, I like to remember how things started, and how we can all learn and grow."

"I want to write," Brendan told him.

"Then, do it."

Brendan was still staring at him. "Wow. I just can't believe I'm getting to meet you. In person. But . . . wow. So you've really come home, huh? I thought you were just here on a book tour. Don't you live in California?"

"I do, but I'm here for a while. Research."

"That's great. If you need anything, maybe I could help you. Run errands, do the post office bit, whatever."

"Brendan, maybe he likes to work alone," Lori put in quickly. "And you've got a new school—"

"Yeah, brand-new school, not a lot of friends," Brendan murmured dryly.

"You will have lots of friends," Lori said, aware her voice was tightening, but unable to stop it. "And you've got to get back to bed now. Mr. Black was just leaving."

"Mom!" Brendan protested.

"I was just leaving."

"You just came—and you're leaving?" Brendan said.

Sean's cool blue gaze flickered over Lori. "I haven't seen your mother in a very long time. I was surprised to learn that she was back in town as well."

"Just back in town. I mean, this is really incredible. We just came in today."

"Today, umm, I guess you did just arrive. Anyway, I really was going. I just came to see that . . ." he broke off, hesitating, then shrugged. "It's a strange homecoming. I was just trying to see that your mom was safe."

"Safe?" Brendan said, and sounded confused.

Sean didn't miss a beat, realizing that she hadn't told her son that an old friend had been brutally murdered.

"New home and all. Needs an alarm."

"We'll be getting an alarm system installed. Right away," Lori assured them both.

Sean nodded, still staring at her. "Going back to New York might be better."

"You like New York, too?" Brendan said. "I loved the city. This move was kind of tough, except that . . . my great-grandfather is a great guy—''

''I know,'' Sean said softly.

''Oh, yeah, of course, you went to school with Mom. And Jan.''

''Jan, Brad, your Uncle Andrew, a lot of folks,'' Sean said.

''Yeah. We're really okay, you know. I mean, I've got to make new friends, but we've got family here.''

''Yeah, I know,'' Sean said. ''Well, good night then.''

He turned to the door, opening it, exiting. Brendan followed after him like a puppy. ''Can you come back. Like Friday night, for dinner, or something?''

Sean turned, amused, arching a brow at Lori. ''Son, your mother might have plans for Friday night.''

''No, she can't. I'm sure she can't. Mom, he can come, right? I mean, you tell me all the time to invite my friends over—well, all right, Sean is actually your friend, but that kind of makes it even, right?''

Lori felt as if she'd been frozen in place. No, it wasn't all right. The last person in the world she wanted to become buddy-buddy with her son was Sean Black.

But she couldn't seem to protest. With any luck Sean would refuse to come.

''Sean is a busy man these days,'' she managed to say. ''Very busy.''

''We'd sure love to have you,'' Brendan said passionately.

Sean looked right at Lori again, curious as to whether she'd buck her son and tell him he wasn't wanted.

''Sure,'' she said flatly. ''We'd just love to have you.''

''Well, then,'' he said very quietly, ''I'll definitely be here.''

He turned, and walked into the night without looking back.

Sean's phone rang at the crack of dawn. He'd been lying there awake and alone without a hangover. No drinking last night, and no women. The darkness had been peopled with haunting images of the past.

He wasn't surprised to find that it was Ricky at the other end, but he was startled when his old friend told him he was calling him on behalf of Dr. Kate Gillespie.

''Gillespie wants to consult with me?''

''She asked me if I could call you and bring you in this morning,'' Ricky said. ''Didn't exactly say why, but she called me just after five, which is early for me, too, I can tell you. The lady is a martinet.

She rips into her stiffs bright and early. You can say no, of course. You're a writer, I'm a cop. She makes us all jump through hoops, but you—''

''I owe a lot of coroners,'' Sean said briefly. And he liked Gillespie. He was curious as to why she would want to see him again.

''I'll be by in ten minutes,'' Ricky told him.

''I've got a rental; I can meet you—''

''Naw, I'll come by. You're the most interesting thing that's happened in my life in years.''

''Ricky, you're a homicide detective in the big city.''

''Yeah, sad, ain't it?''

Things grew more interesting at the morgue. After traveling lengths of corridors and halls to find Gillespie's theater of operation, Ricky stood by Sean, watching as Gillespie worked on an older man stretched out on a gurney. ''Looks as clean as a newborn babe,'' Ricky said. ''Not a scratch on him. This guy is a murder victim?''

''Killed with kindness. His wife made him one apple pie too many. Heart attack,'' Gillespie said briefly.

''Then—'' Ricky began.

''Heart attack—we think by a good, educated guess. According to the laws of the state, since the poor fellow was alone when he expired, we have to make sure. Now, Detective, thanks for bringing me our friend the author. When I'm done with him, I'll send him home, and you can quiz him later.''

Ricky glanced at Sean, both amusement and resentment apparent in his gaze. ''Okay, Doc, as you say. But I will quiz him later, you know. And we're old high school buddies. Guys talk, you know?'' Ricky waited a few seconds to see if he would be invited to stay anyway.

He wasn't. Sean didn't intend to help him. He was too curious to know what Gillespie was up to.

''All right, then . . .'' Ricky said, starting out.

''All right, then. See you soon,'' Gillespie said cheerfully.

Ricky finally left. Dr. Gillespie spoke into the mike, describing the deceased as a man of about seventy-five years of age, six feet in height, two hundred and thirty pounds. She described the outer signs of coronary on his body, the condition of his skin, etcetera, then prepared to make her initial cut. She hesitated—yet Sean was certain the hesitation was a ploy—and turned off the mike.

''An autopsy doesn't bother you, Mr. Black, does it?''

He stared into her eyes and shook his head. ''No, ma'am. I had to perform several to get my degree, and assisted at a number of them.''

"Yes . . . as a crime writer—or because of your major in forensic anthropology?"

"Both. And since you seem to know so much about me, why are you asking?"

She smiled, and he liked her more. A stern old broad with her salt and pepper hair, she could dig into the human body and mind so it seemed, with both thought and compassion.

"I do know a lot about you. I know of some of the people with whom you studied, and I've heard from them that you're the best. Pity that academics lost you to popular fiction."

"You can put a lot of academics into popular fiction. You can say a lot as long as you do it carefully and keep from being sued. So . . . why am I here? Not to watch you carve up a victim of a heart attack."

She shook her head, then sighed softly, glancing at the mike again to assure herself that she had turned it off. "I've been here a long time. I can't tell you what that means in a city like this. Battered babies, cruelly abused by those whose role in life is to protect them from danger and pain and the little hurts. The awful results of gang violence. The kids who got in the way on drive-by shootings. A husband burned to death by his wife. Plane crash victims. Automobile fatalities. The horrors go on and on."

Sean nodded, feeling a constriction in his throat, newly impressed by the compassion in this woman who worked with death—violent death—so closely.

"I understand," he said quietly.

"I performed the autopsy on Amanda Olin."

Sean felt himself tighten, top to bottom, as if he'd just been encased in shrink-wrap.

"Yes?" he said stiffly.

She studied him. "Well, in my educated opinion, Amanda Olin was murdered. It's possible to become entangled in vines, but the way the abrasions and bruises surrounded her one ankle . . . well, it was murder, even if it couldn't be proven beyond a doubt."

"I didn't murder Mandy," he said, his tone low, but his voice trembling with a deep fury and bitterness he would never resolve.

"I believe you," Gillespie said. "Don't go getting defensive on me."

"I was the one accused."

"But you weren't the only one there, were you?"

He exhaled. "No. And I'm damned sorry, but I can't agree with your call on that one, Dr. Gillespie. We were kids. All just kids."

"All right. Fine. You've got your opinion, I've got mine. I've seen kids do some pretty stupid vicious things, but no matter. We probably can't go back and prove a fifteen-year-old crime anyway.''

Sean lifted his hands, still feeling shaky, resentful. They said that you couldn't go home. He was a fool to have come here. Even the people he liked seemed compelled to thrust knives into him.

''So . . . what's this about?'' he demanded.

''I've got some bones I want you to look at.''

''What?'' he said incredulously.

''Bones. They're your specialty, right? Well, they were, before you became mister fame and fortune. Didn't you work in forensic anthropology?''

''Right, but—''

''I know some folks up at the University of Florida who thought you were pretty special.''

''Did you?'' he inquired quietly, somewhat amused at last. ''That's nice to hear, but—''

''I'd send them out—we send a lot of work like that to the folks at the Smithsonian, you know, or up to UF, but since you're right here . . . I thought you might want to look at them for me and give me a few preliminary thoughts.''

''Sure. Except that something tells me you're expert enough yourself.''

''I'd consider yours an outside expert opinion, which would make me happy. You know as well as I do that when we have almost nothing to go on, whatever we can learn is appreciated.''

Indeed, he knew. That was what had most aroused his curiosity and his compassion in school—bones talked the longest. In his first criminology course, he had heard a guest lecturer give an eloquent speech regarding the dead—in today's day and age, the dead could tell tales. Murderers were inventive; corpses could be dismembered, decomposed, soaked in acid, destroyed by the elements. But bone was strong, bone was man's superstructure. Bone could be destroyed, but even burned bone could tell tales. There was nothing in the world so cruel as murder, the theft of life, and there was nothing in the world so heinous as a murderer walking away scot-free from his crime. The dead cried out for justice. Bones could cry the loudest and the longest.

''Naturally, I have my own thoughts,'' Gillespie said.

''Want to tell me what you're thinking?''

''No—I want you to look over the bones first.''

He shrugged. He still liked Gillespie. So she'd knifed him a few times. Ricky would call her a broad with balls. And now his curiosity was truly piqued.

"Fine. Lead the way."

Gillespie smiled.

"Mom, Dad, Gramps!"

Lori greeted her folks with fierce hugs; she was more gentle with her grandfather, but he sensed her care and gave her a bear hug when she would have pulled away.

"Gramps—" she began softly.

"I'm not dead yet!" he told her firmly, his eyes, the hazel from which she had inherited her own, shining with a golden sparkle.

"Dad!" her mother said, appalled.

"Now, Gloria, I don't want my granddaughter treating me like glass. Affection is something I certainly have the strength to stomach, and since she left a happy home in New York City to be with me, I want a good old, bone-crunching hug!"

"Fine! I'll crunch all your bones!" Lori laughed.

"And I can crunch harder," Brendan said, doing so.

Her father, tall and lean, with thick snow-white hair and a handsomely aging face, was walking into the house, surveying the place. He looked at her with a smile.

"Great."

"Thanks, Dad."

"All kinds of problems, though," her mother said worriedly, "you should have bought new."

"Mom, I like the old."

She was braced, ready for an argument, but then her mother smiled and nodded and ruffled her hair. "You're right, it's got plenty of character, and you always did want to go your own way. You're doing it well, so I'm going to learn not to criticize."

Lori looked at her father with surprise. He shrugged. "Just goes to show, you can teach old dogs new tricks."

"James! Are you calling me an old dog?" her mother inquired in mock outrage.

"Never, my darling, never!" her father protested quickly, slipping his arms around his wife's waist and offering a look of baffled apology that sent Brendan into gales of laughter. Lori was bemused herself. She didn't remember her parents getting along quite so well when she was young, nor had she realized that they could be so affectionate to one another.

"Where's that breakfast you promised?" her father demanded quickly.

"Come in, come in, come in!" Brendan invited, and lead them all into the dining room.

Brendan was a great help, fetching plates, pouring juice, replenishing coffee. Lori was delighted that her bacon, eggs, toast, and waffles came out so well, and that her homecoming was going so well. She'd dreaded this; maybe they had dreaded it, too. And then, inevitably, the conversation veered to the past, where it could not help but intrude upon the present.

"Lori, did you hear that Sean Black was in town? He's become some famous author—" her mother began.

"Michael Shayne!" Brendan chimed in enthusiastically.

Lori frowned, but Brendan didn't notice.

"Gramma, he came over last night. I couldn't believe that Mom knew him—he's my favorite, I mean my absolute favorite!"

"Lori, should he be reading slasher books like that—" her mother began.

Lori was about to defend her son's reading habits, but she didn't need to. Brendan could take care of himself. "Gramma, he doesn't write slasher books. I learn so much reading his novels. They're all about DNA and science and police procedure and medicine and all kinds of stuff. And what's better than that, he writes about great people, and he makes you understand how people think and work and . . . well, you're just going to have to read one of his books to understand!"

"Well!" Gloria said. She looked at Lori, biting into her lower lip and asking softly, "So you've seen him—*already*?"

The inference was there, of course, that she'd seen Sean Black before she'd even seen her parents.

"Yeah," she said, sipping her coffee, then looking up to realize that not only her mother but her father and Gramps were staring at her hard. She tried to sound casual. "Small world, isn't it? Jan took us to supper in the Grove, and I ran right into him on my way to the bookshop to get the kids after we ate."

"Then he came here!" Brendan said with awe. "Can you believe that? Sean Black came here!"

There was dead silence. Lori waited for something awful to happen. Like the roof caving in to bury them all so that they could keep staring at one another while encased in white plaster.

"Well," her mother said.

"Sean? Came to your house?" her father said.

"Why?" Gramps asked.

"Well, he just stopped by to see if I was okay—" Lori hedged.

"Why?" Gramps repeated.

"Because their old friend was so horribly murdered, of course!" her mother said.

Lori almost spit coffee all over.

"Yeah, can you imagine, he comes back into town, and his old flame's best friend is butchered," her father said, shaking his head.

"Mom?" Brendan murmured.

"Dad," Lori protested.

"Oh, God, sorry, it's just that these things upset me so much," her father murmured. He was a retired stockbroker, one of the social elite, past commodore of the yacht club, and friend to many an attorney—yet passionate in his argument that criminals walked far too freely, criminal rights were far too often set above victim rights, and that most of the fellows making his friends rich should be "fried." He was an avid proponent of Florida's electric chair, known as "Old Sparky." There had been a major debate set in motion recently when a condemned man caught fire in the electric chair. Those against capital punishment had labeled the electric chair dangerous and inhumane. Lori's father had been quick to point out the fact that the chair was supposed to be damned dangerous, lethal actually, and that criminals should realize that there were dangerous consequences to crime.

"Mom, a friend of yours was killed?" Brendan asked, looking a little pale.

"Someone I went to school with, someone I hadn't seen in years," Lori said.

Brendan looked at his grandfather. "What was she to Sean Black?" he demanded.

Lori gritted her teeth together, wary of the answer.

"I'm really sorry, Brendan," her father said. "I shouldn't have spoken so freely with you here . . ." He paused, looking at Lori.

"We lost another friend when we were in school," Lori said, staring back at her parents. "The girl that Sean was dating at the time. She . . . drowned."

"I guess the cops wanted somebody to be responsible," her mother said. "They tried to accuse Sean of the crime. They let him go. Unfortunately, this second girl was one of her best friends at the time."

"Wow," Brendan said. "Poor Sean."

Lori frowned, watching her mother. She'd always been down on

Sean Black. Now, amazingly, it almost sounded as if she was defending him. Lori just wanted the matter put to rest for the moment.

"Things like this are always scary, and they warn us to be very careful," she said, rising. "Dad, more coffee? Gramps?"

"Sure. Hey, young lady, how are the designs going?"

"Great. Want to see some sketches?"

"Of course."

"Yes, yes, of course!" her mother said happily.

Lori had to drag her portfolio out of the pile of stuff still stacked upstairs, but she was glad to do so, and pleased when her family showed more than filial duty in their responses to her work. After, when she was putting things away, she found that her mother had followed her up to her room.

"It really is a cute place," Gloria told her, smiling awkwardly as Lori looked at her.

"Thanks, I like it."

"And we're close."

"Yep."

"Think you're going to like being close to us?"

"Well, of . . . of course."

Her mother was an attractive woman, slim, petite, much smaller than Lori herself. She wore her hair stylishly short, and her makeup was always perfect. At fifty-six she remained energetic, had gone for a laser peel once, and exercised with discipline. "Sweetheart, I'm happy you're home. I'm going to try not to be a pest . . . but it's hard to be a parent and not a pest. I'm going to respect your opinions, and I'm going to try really hard to respect your privacy. Of course," she hesitated, vexed, biting her lower lip. "Of course, with such a horrible murderer out there, it isn't going to be easy. And now with Sean back . . ."

"Mom, I'm sorry that you never liked Sean. But he's not a murderer."

Her mother looked startled. Then she smiled suddenly. "I'm sorry, that's not what I meant at all. I was wrong about Sean. Dead wrong. Oh, God, what a choice of words."

Lori hesitated, hands on her hips.

"Mom, what are you saying?"

Her mother shrugged. "Oh, dear, it's so hard these days . . . I mean, people just so seldom stay together, and young people just don't see the things that will matter later in life. When you're very young and in love, you don't worry about things like money, career, religion—love itself is so overwhelming. But then, being broke can

be downright ugly, and living in poverty can be demeaning and humiliating and miserable and . . . I admit, I was just so afraid of that
boy's family because I had friends who fell in love and had babies
with no-good men and went on welfare and wound up hating their
beer-guzzling husbands. One was even a wife beater. And Shelly—
that was my friend's name—couldn't leave the louse. She always
had a black eye, he was abusive to their kids . . . but she got into this
trap and couldn't leave him. I always knew that Brad would make a
good living, and so I guess I wanted you to be with him, and I was
horrible about Sean. Well, I was wrong about him. It's not where or
what a man comes from that's important, but what he is himself. I'm
sorry that we didn't fight harder for him. I'm sorry he wound up the
one accused, and that we were all so willing to crucify him. I'd like
to tell him so, if I ever get the chance.''

Lori was stunned. So stunned that she just stood there as her
mother shrugged and turned away. Gloria started down the stairs.

''Mom!''

Her mother waited.

Lori hurried to her, and hugged her fiercely. Gloria hugged her
back.

Soon after, her folks left.

And despite the fact that Sean was in town and a friend had just
been brutally murdered, it didn't seem so terrible to have come home.

''A young woman, an adult, early twenties, I'd say,'' Sean thoughtfully said aloud to Gillespie, who was watching him as he carefully
looked over the display of human bones, which didn't quite complete
the human body. She'd been approximately five feet six in life, and
at some point suffered a fracture to her right tibia. ''It's difficult to
diagnose cause of death, especially with the skull missing, but I can
tell you that the head was severed from the body—before or after
death, I don't know.'' He stepped back and looked at Gillespie without asking the obvious—where had the bones been found and under
what circumstances?

Gillespie wasn't giving such answers yet anyway—she was frowning. ''How can you tell the head was severed? Maybe the vertebrae
just fell away.''

He shook his head. Stepping forward with his surgically gloved
hands, he showed her a vertebra—and the marks that still, indisput-
ably, showed signs of a sharp instrument.

Gillespie nodded. ''How long dead?''

''When and where was she found?''

"Muck, Everglades, near Shark Valley."

"Sometimes such entombment helps preserve a body, but she must have decomposed before becoming buried in the mud. That makes it tough." He shook his head. "I'd say she's been dead three to ten years. I don't think I could give you a closer estimate."

Gillespie nodded, sighing. "She becomes another Jane Doe."

"Another?" he said, frowning.

Gillespie nodded.

"You know the statistics, so you can't be too surprised. Hell, work at the Orange County morgue for a few weeks, and you become immune to the corpses that pile up around you in the damned hallways . . . half of them victims of crimes we'll never solve. This is the third pile of bones we've uncovered in the past few years."

He watched her, well aware that although Gillespie was talking statistics, she thought that she was onto something.

"You've got a theory?" he asked, peeling off his gloves and standing back.

She nodded. "Yeah, I've got a theory. I've studied some in the behavioral sciences, criminal psychology—profiling. Most guys who get into the heavy-duty sick sex crimes don't just go out and kill and mutilate. Maybe they start by pulling the tales off lizards. Throwing rocks at dogs. Sometimes they become rapists, going a little further with every crime. Then, the ultimate thrill. Murder. A simple kill at first. Then torture before the kill. Maybe necrophilia. And killers can be smart, good-looking, and damned clever. I think we've had someone—God knows, maybe more than one—killing women down here for some time now. I mean, like years. Heaven knows, we've got our share of unsolved homicides! Getting a little bolder as time goes by, bolder, and bolder still." She shrugged and looked at him. "That's why serial offenders tend to be a certain age, isn't it? Too young, and they haven't gotten into doling out the heinous deaths that really cause media attention. Too old, and they've tripped themselves up somehow. You're the writer. Isn't that how it's supposed to work?"

"I deal in fiction," he hedged.

"Fiction—based on fact. You know your facts. I've read your books."

He shook his head. "Well, I can't have killed all these women over the years, Doc. I stayed out of Miami. I can prove it."

"Oh, don't go getting defensive on me, Mr. Black. Or is it Dr. Black."

He felt as if he were talking through a locked jaw. "I've got the degree, I just don't use the title."

She smiled. "I'm just giving you a story, you know. You are the author."

"Yes, but this story doesn't have an ending, does it?" he asked her.

"Hey, I'm just a hardworking civil servant," Gillespie said, lifting her hands innocently. "It's a big city. Not New York, not L.A.— worse, maybe. They say the heat's a killer. People come to South Florida from all over to commit their murders. What are a few dead girls over the years? No, there's not an ending. Not yet. But you are the author. Use your imagination."

He arched a brow at her.

She tapped her head. "Your imagination."

"You want to know what's going on," he said quietly. "Doc," he went on, shaking his head. "You're right. It's hot down here. People come from all over. Thousands of people disappear every year in the United States. Different criminals commit different crimes, and it's a damned crime in itself, but half of them never will be caught. The cops need to find out what's going on with these bones."

"Yeah, they do. But they're busy as hell, and they've got just about nothing to go on but the hunch of an old M.E."

He didn't really understand what she was getting at. What the hell could he do? Especially him. Some of the people he met set him on a pedestal—he made big bucks writing books. Half of them still condemned him as a killer who'd walked away from his crime.

He lifted his hands. "Hey, you're right, I'm an author, an out-of-towner. This isn't my story."

"Make it yours," she told him.

"Doc, I don't think that I can."

"And I thought you had balls."

He smiled, unoffended. "I damned well know you've got a pair," he told her. It was a compliment. She took it as such.

"Well, thanks for your time. I've got another patient waiting. Of course, he won't go anywhere . . . but neither will I if I don't get my work done. You can find your way out, right? See you around, Black."

She turned and left him.

Chapter 7

"Hey! Lori!"

Lori saw Andrew rising from a table inside the air-conditioned café.

Snowbirds might find it fun to eat outside.

Natives usually opted for the coolness inside a restaurant.

She had agreed to meet her brother on South Beach. Since he'd been working on wrapping up one of his projects, he hadn't been able to join the initial family breakfast at her house.

Brendan had gone over to Jan's, and Lori was alone as she came to greet her one and only sibling. Despite the fact that he had continued to date enthusiastically—and occasionally kept a girlfriend for a stretch as long six months—Andrew had never married. And he was damned good-looking, she thought. Charming when he chose to be. But he seemed to shy away from commitment, and at some point the women he dated usually wanted more than a casual sleeping arrangement. His bachelorhood was not a state of being that pleased either of their parents, but though he hadn't gone into any of the work fields that would have really passed muster with their white-collar tastes, her parents were still proud of his filmmaking. Andrew directed documentaries. He'd done shows on the endangered crocodiles of South Florida, and shows on the alligators—which had made an incredibly healthy comeback in the last few years. He'd done programs on the Everglades, on the state of Florida schools, and he'd traveled as well, doing some footage with sharks, dolphins, whales, and more. He was happy, loved his work, and since Lori understood what that meant, she also understood that he didn't need to make a fortune to be happy—though it seemed he did just fine. He drove a late-model Mercedes, his clothing was designer, and he never seemed to want for anything, though he could be very evasive about his affairs.

Lori had spent her adult life being fairly evasive herself, so she also understood her brother's desire for privacy.

"You're beautiful!" he told her, sweeping her into a hug as she reached his table.

"You're pretty handsome yourself," she told him, drawing away to study him. Not a gray hair in sight. The years had been good to Andrew. He'd gained character, not wrinkles. He had a healthy tan and was tall, muscled, and yet still lanky. He was their father all over again. Like her, he was light-haired, with eyes slightly more amber in color.

With the fights of childhood long gone by, she and her brother were friends. She liked Andrew, even though they hadn't been able to see each other more than once or twice a year since she'd left home.

"Wow!" he said, pulling out her chair, then sitting across from her, his eyes not leaving her face. "So the prodigal child has come home."

She smiled, sipping the ice tea he'd already ordered for her.

"I'm the prodigal child?"

"Sure, running off to England, marrying without a by-your-leave, procreating without parental blessing. Don't you remember how horrified the folks were when you not only married a foreigner right off the bat, but then did the unthinkable and reproduced immediately as well? How are the old dears, by the way?"

"Haven't you seen them recently?"

"Not in a couple of weeks. I've been working really hard."

"Oh, the folks are good, Gramps looks like hell. And actually, Mom and Dad were wonderfully well behaved. You wouldn't have believed it," she told him. She wrinkled her nose. "Oh, we're being awful, aren't we? Here we are talking about them. Judging them, while we condemn them for judging us."

He shrugged, then smiled ruefully. "Lori, siblings are supposed to talk about their parents and discuss why everyone is so dysfunctional."

"We're old enough to be understanding, aren't we?"

"Yeah. Okay, so they're all right. Maybe. They're improving with age, at any rate. Still ... isn't it terrible? I'm in my thirties, still worried about what my parents will think if they ..."

"If they what?"

"Oh, nothing, really. You know, just what the folks will think—
is this effort good enough, would they be proud, disappointed, all
that, you know."

"Well, you shouldn't worry. Dad was telling me about your latest—the one he calls the croc doc—and he seemed awfully proud.
So what are you up to now?"

"What?"

"What are you up to? What kind of a film are you making now?"

"Oh . . . now . . . well, I'm working on something for the PBS sta-
tions."

"Yeah? What?"

"Umm . . . oh, there's the waitress. Let's grab her. I'm starving."

Lori spun around and waved to their waitress. The pretty brunette
responded quickly. Her smile at Lori was sweet. Her smile at Andrew
was dazzling.

"Lori?" Andrew prodded.

"Uh . . . the spinach and pine nut salad." Lori said.

"It's great," the waitress assured her.

"I'm a meat boy myself. A carnivore all the way. The steak sand-
wich, with fries." Andrew said.

"How would you like that cooked?"

"Rare. The bloodier the better," Andrew said.

"If that's the way you like it . . ."

"That's the way I like it," Andrew said.

She offered him another smile, and left them.

"Teaching and sewing. How domestic. I never saw you that way,"
Andrew told her.

She shrugged. "I love kids. I guess I never knew it, growing up,
because you were older, and we were just busy being teenagers. And
I'm designing, not just sewing, but I'm really happy with my work,
and it's going well. So?"

"So . . . what?" he said.

"You never told me what you were working on now."

"Oh!"

"Well?"

"Yeah, I'm doing a documentary on South Florida wildlife. More
emphasis on the soft and cuddly, this time. You know, deer, otter,
squirrels, rabbits, and little foxes."

"Great. I'd love to see you filming one day."

"Sure. It's more tedious than glamorous, you know that."

"That's all right. I'd like to see you work."

"Great."

"When?"

"Um . . . I'm not sure yet. We'll set up a date. I'll have to find a time when I think I can impress you, okay?"

She wondered why he seemed so evasive, then realized that she was pressuring him. "Whenever you're ready. Just remember that after Mom, I'm probably your most ardent fan."

"I appreciate that," he said, then sobered suddenly. "You heard about Ellie?"

"How could I not?"

"It's all over the news, huh? Isn't that awful? And isn't it strange as hell, too? With Sean just back in town."

"Andrew, you can't possibly think—"

"I don't."

"Then—"

"It's just strange as hell, that's all. We're all here. Or kind of here."

"All?"

He grinned somewhat awkwardly. "All of us, the in crowd, the cool kids—the beautiful people. That's kind of what we thought of ourselves back then, wasn't it? But we're all together again. In spirit, anyway. I live here, you're back. Jan never left, Brad never left. Ted Neeson is a cop in Coral Gables. Ricky is a Metro homicide cop. Your old friend Susan Nichols owns a couple of coffee shops: one in the Gables, one in the Grove. Sean's brother, Michael, lives in the Keys, just a little more than an hour south of here. Our cousin Josh is practicing law—a nice divorce practice, I might add. Ellie was in Miami Lakes. Jeff Olin, Mandy's brother, is also down here—a corporate attorney. He's had some hot cases, fighting like a tiger and winning when others have stepped on the toes of his clients, I can tell you. He still lives in the Kendall area. I wonder what he thinks of all this."

"He was devastated when his sister was killed. Broken. I'm sure that Ellie's death will hurt him terribly."

"I imagine. But I guess we'll find out."

"Will we? When, why?"

"We'll all go to the funeral, won't we?"

"I . . . yeah, I guess. When is Ellie being buried?"

"Tomorrow. Ten o'clock service at St. Theresa's. You know what, I'll pick you up, okay?"

"Yeah, sure—" Lori began. Then she broke off, startled to hear her brother's name called. Loudly.

"Andrew! Andrew Kelly, why, hon, what a living pleasure!"

Startled by the saccharine drawl. Lori turned to see a bleached blonde come waddling toward them. The woman was anywhere from twenty-five to thirty-five years old and very voluptuous. Her hips were round, and her breasts were melons. They spilled over the edge of her low-cut tank top. Her face was pretty, but overly made up. Her smile was genuine.

Andrew looked at her totally aghast. His bronze face had gone pale. He looked like he would have hidden beneath the table if he could have done so.

Since he couldn't, he stood.

"Muffy," he said sickly.

Muffy? Lori thought. But she waited for an introduction. This busty blonde wasn't her brother's usual woman. Andrew dated them tall, sleek, and fashionable. He usually liked brunettes. But then again, in truth, Muffy was actually a brunette.

"Hi!" she said to Andrew. "What a surprise to see you here, hon. Oh!" she said, glancing at Lori. "I don't mean to interrupt—"

"It's all right," Lori said quickly. "Andrew, introduce us," she prodded softly.

"Oh, uh, Muffy, my sister, Lori. Uh . . . Lori, Muffy occasionally . . . uh . . . works for me."

"Occasionally! Why, I work for this handsome young charmer every single chance I get!" Muffy said, totally enthused. She pumped Lori's hand. "And to meet his sister . . . why, it's an honor. Just an honor!"

Lori smiled. She was dying of curiosity, and she couldn't help but like the woman who was so enthusiastic about her. "Thank you, Muffy. It's a pleasure to meet you, too," Lori told her.

"But we were just having lunch." Andrew said pointedly.

"Oh, well, oh, I am sorry—" Muffy began.

"You could joi—" Lori began.

"No! Uh, I haven't seen my sister in ages—we're catching up," Andrew said quickly.

Rudely, Lori thought.

But Muffy didn't seem to mind. Lori was sorry to think that maybe people were so frequently rude to Muffy that she didn't realize it, and didn't take offense.

"You two just catch up on old times. Truly, Lori, it's a pleasure to meet you! Don't get up now. Later, Andrew!" Beaming, Muffy moved on. She disappeared toward the rear door and the tables out back.

"Andrew, you were mean to that woman—"

"No, I wasn't.''

"You were.''

"I wasn't! Look, I'm not working right now, I'm seeing my sister, and I don't want to be bothered by employees!''

"Employees?''

"A coworker, whatever.''

"Just what does Muffy do for you?'' Lori asked.

"What is this, twenty questions?'' he demanded, annoyed.

"No, of course not, I just—''

"Damn it, Lori, I'm sorry, I just want to have lunch with you, and not be bothered by work, okay? Damn, you're making me feel as if I'm out with my mother. Can we please just drop it?''

"Andrew, what does Muffy do?''

"She prepares—things.''

"The set?''

"Yeah, sort of.''

"She works with props, cameras?''

"Yeah. Can we talk about something else?''

"I guess.'' Lori realized that she was annoyed, and hurt. Andrew didn't know everything about her life, but he knew more than anyone else. She couldn't begin to understand why this woman had upset him so much.

The waitress chose that timely moment to bring their food. She was good at her craft, politely making sure that they had everything without being overbearing.

By the time she left them, Andrew had calmed down and completely dismissed the episode.

"You know, old Sean got really famous. Top of the heap. Movies out of his stuff and all that.''

"Yep.''

"I'm glad for him. Sean was cool. He sure got a bum wrap.''

"Yeah, he took a lot of grief for an innocent guy.''

Andrew debated that carefully for a minute. "I guess. Though . . .''

"What?''

Andrew shrugged. "Well, if he did freak out and kill Mandy, she kind of had it coming, the way she all but waved a red flag beneath his nose.''

Lori felt her temper soar. "Andrew, there's a big difference between being angry with someone and murdering someone! You're being horrible!''

"Well, I don't mean to be. I'm just being logical.''

"Logical! You think a man has a right to kill a woman just because she—"

"She was acting like a total whore that day."

"It isn't legal to kill whores, Andrew. What's the matter with you?"

He sighed, staring at her ruefully. "I don't mean that. No, it isn't right for a guy to hurt a girl for acting like a cunt. I know that! That's the obvious. I just mean that guys have feelings, too. Maybe she humiliated him so badly that he freaked out—temporary insanity, that kind of thing. That's all I meant."

Lori shook her head, spearing her spinach angrily. "He didn't kill her."

"Okay! I didn't really think that he did. I mean, none of us thought that any one of us would ever do anything like that—it was just plain tragic. Mandy was trying to be a hotshot in the water, and she tangled herself in the vines. That's the way I saw it. If I ever had any evil thoughts, the damned cops caused them."

Lori exhaled. Well, that was true. The cops were the only ones suspicious that day.

"Things are different now, though, of course."

"What?"

"Well, Ellie Metz was no accident. She wasn't just murdered, she was butchered. Pass the ketchup, will you, sis?"

A security guard at the exit stopped Sean before he could leave the morgue.

"Mr. Black?"

"Yes?"

"Detective Garcia asked me to give you a message. He's having a late lunch with friends at Monty's—wants you to come. Says he promises it will be interesting."

"Thanks," Sean said.

He left the morgue, pausing just outside to stare up at the blazing sun. Hell. He'd told himself that it was possible to be here, and not live in the past. He'd barely been back, and he was becoming buddy-buddy with those who had—unwittingly, perhaps—half skewered him a lifetime ago.

But as he hailed a cab, he knew that he would be heading for the restaurant.

He'd liked Monty's as a kid; it hadn't changed much. There was an indoor restaurant, and an outdoor restaurant. Wood decking, palm trees, cats, a bay breeze. On the water, shaded, the tables were cool enough, and he discovered Ricky out at a table directly on the water with two other men. They'd obviously ordered some time ago, and were just finishing up. Ricky's friends were apparently on duty while Ricky was off. Ricky had a beer, the other two were drinking ice tea. Ricky was in cutoffs and a T-shirt, the others were in dockers and polo shirts.

"Hey, Sean!" Ricky called, rising.

His companions started to rise as well; Sean waved them back down, sitting himself.

"Bill Crowley, Alex Hanson," Ricky said. "Sean Black."

They all nodded.

"These guys are on my team," Ricky said.

"Team?"

"Task force. There's ten of us, hunting down clues on the Eleanor Metz murder," Crowley explained. He was fortyish, balding slightly, with a basset-hound look that seemed to state he'd been in homicide a long time. He smiled.

"Ten cops, one murder, a task force, that's interesting," Sean said.

"Well, the publicity on this one calls for immediate action," Hanson said. He was younger, late twenties, crew cut, the kind of physique that meant he spent several hours daily at a gym. "The mayor is convinced we're going to plunge the place into a rep so bad, we'll never crawl out if we don't get the guy fast."

"And Dr. Peterson—one of the force shrinks—thinks this guy probably started out abusing women, maybe turned to rape, and then murder," Bill Crowley said. "He thinks that—" Crowley broke off, then shrugged. "We weren't sworn to confidentiality, but we don't want this out, either. Anyway, the shrink on this one thinks the guy has killed before, and his victims were buried well enough to decompose so that the murders just weren't discovered." He looked at the others guiltily, as if he shouldn't have spoken.

"Sean isn't going to say anything. He's been at the morgue already. Gillespie is using him," Ricky said.

"Oh, yeah? I thought you were a writer?" Hanson said.

Sean started to answer, but Ricky was a step ahead of him, slamming him on the back. "My old buddy here is a lot of things. He's got a doctorate in forensic anthropology."

"Hey, great," Hanson said. He swallowed a long swig of his ice tea, then shrugged. "All right, what the hell is that?"

Sean grinned. "My specialty is bones. I started with a lot of field digs . . . ancient peoples, that kind of thing. Digging up ancient burial pits, we can learn about evolution and the way that people lived. That kind of thing. And we can also study more recent bones. Find out what happened to people.''

"Murder victims," Crowley said.

"Yeah. And sometimes, not. Bones can tell a lot of stories.''

"How do you know if someone was stabbed without flesh and blood?'' Hanson asked.

"Sometimes, you can't. Mortal wounds can be inflicted without striking bone. But murder victims usually fight, and murderers can seldom be so careful that they can make sure they don't strike bone. Scratches, abrasions . . . a lot can be seen on bone.''

Crowley sat back, looking at him. "So that's why your stuff sounds so good.''

"You read my books?''

Crowley nodded. "I had just figured you learned about cops and court from the time you were arrested here.''

"Ah," Sean said.

"That was a bad rap. They were just looking for something. Couldn't haul in any of those rich kids back then, though I think things are getting better now.''

"You were on the force then?''

"A rookie. It was a dumb call all the way around when they arrested you.''

"I wasn't there," Hanson said, "but I met Rutgers, and he was one asshole.''

Rutgers. The cop who had been the first plainclothesman at the rock pit. The cop who had insisted there had been a murder, long before the M.E.s had ever taken a look at Mandy's body.

"The D.A.'s office issued the warrants," Sean said evenly. Seemed like he could never get away from it. Miami. Big city. Lots of crime. But people didn't forget.

"On Rutgers' insistence; and they made a mistake. Obviously. They didn't have enough evidence, and that came out at the trial. They wasted the taxpayers' money, and they ripped up a lot of lives,'' Crowley said. Rising, he offered his hand to Sean. "Must have seemed like the whole city was out to lynch you, Mr. Black. There were a lot of us on your side all the time. Alex, we've got to head back in. Ricky, see you at the office. Mr. Black, nice to meet you.''

"Nice to meet you," Alex Hanson agreed, pumping Sean's hand. "Hey, I don't mean to impose, but—''

"If you'd like, I'll have Ricky bring you both some signed copies of my books," Sean said.

Bill Crowley beamed. "My wife will sure be impressed. Thanks.''

Ricky slammed Sean on the shoulder again with his palm in a good old boy gesture. "Man, you're all right, Sean. You always were, way back when. Hey, Brenda!" he said, calling to the waitress. "We need a couple of drafts over here. Thanks, Sean. This is really great of you. Crowley is a big fan."

"Yeah. No problem."

Dark eyes alight, Ricky was in a good mood, new murder or no. Yeah, they were buddies. Except that Ricky, like the rest of them, had basically turned his back on Sean when his folks had told him that he was just bad blood.

What the hell had he expected? They'd all been kids.

The drafts arrived. Ricky lifted his glass. "To Eleanor LeBlanc Metz. May the poor bitch rest in peace. Jesus," he said, setting his beer down and running his fingers through his hair. "Jesus, Sean, isn't it strange. I'm homicide, I do this for a living, and suddenly it's Ellie on that slab, and I'm feeling as sick as a kid and remembering . . ." He paused and looked at Sean. He lifted his beer again. "I was one royal shit back then. If you'd thumbed your nose at all of us, it would have been simple justice on your part."

Startled, Sean lifted his beer to Ricky. "We were all just kids," he said.

"Yeah," Ricky murmured, an awkward smile on his face as he accepted Sean's forgiveness. "Just kids. Want to go to the funeral with me tomorrow?"

Ellie's funeral.

"Sure."

Somehow, he knew that they'd all be there.

Lori ran into Muffy in the rest room.

She was powdering her nose, but saw Lori in the mirror as Lori came in. "Oh, hi! Nice to see you again, sorry, I really hope that I didn't disturb you. I guess I'm just overly friendly, too trusting and too much like a puppy in need of affection—that's what my dad always said, and of course, that I kind of talk on and on and don't stop. Oops, sorry, guess that's what I'm doing now."

Lori laughed, walked up to the mirror, and set her purse on the counter to pull out her brush. "It's great that you're friendly, Muffy. Don't let people tell you otherwise."

Muffy closed her compact, smiling. "You know, that's really nice of you to say. Andrew always made it sound like his kinfolk were all snobs. You're not like that at all."

"Thanks. Have you worked with Andrew long?"

"Oh, on and off. I don't work with him all the time, you know. Depends on who is directing what."

"I guess there's a lot going on down here."

"Oh, yeah, the market for this stuff is huge down here."

"You like working in film?"

"Well, I'd like to be in the films more than I am."

"Oh, well . . . you're in the business, surely you can get into the pictures more—"

"Oh, yeah, some, but I'm getting old. They like the young chicks to actually be in the pictures. As far as getting the dudes up for it, there's really nothing like an old broad like me with lots of experience."

"Excuse me?" Lori said, confused. Then she felt her cheeks flame, and she felt like an idiot.

Muffy hadn't noticed. She was patting her hair. "I know what I'm doing, and I'm good at my job. I make a lot of money at it. I can take a guy from zero to sixty in seconds flat. Saves the producers a bundle, because there's nothing like waiting around for the guys to get to it when they've already shot a w—" She broke off then, staring at Lori, and blushed furiously herself. "You know," she said awkwardly, "young guys, they get to it quick, and then they're like wet noodles. Young girls just don't know what I know that can . . . get a noodle going again, you know what I mean?"

"Yeah, sure. And I'm sure that you are great at what you do."

Muffy smiled broadly, "Well, I'll be seeing you. I hope. Take care, Lori."

"You take care, too, Muffy," Lori said.

She waited a few moments after the other woman had left.

Then she returned to her table.

Andrew had just ordered them coffee. She thanked him, and sipped her coffee.

"You know, Andrew, I don't mean to be a pest, but I'm still confused. Just what is it that Muffy gets ready for you on your sets?"

Andrew almost spit coffee. "Muffy, uh . . ."

"She gets things ready," Lori said, staring at him. "What things."

Andrew stared back at her. "Well, she, uh, she just prepares things . . ."

Lori leaned forward. "What things?"

Andrew was bloodred.

"Body parts?" Lori inquired sweetly.

"Oh, Jesus—" Andrew began, eyes lowered.

"Why the hell did you lie to me? Why do you pretend to be making nature films—"

"I *am* making nature films, and I do work for PBS—"

"Please don't tell me that Muffy does animals."

"Jeez, Lori—"

"Jeez, Andrew!"

"Who the hell are you to judge me?" he demanded angrily.

"I'm not judging you. I'm just your sister, and I don't understand why you lied to me, why you didn't trust me with the truth!"

He sat back, stared at her sulkily. "You don't always tell me the truth."

She hesitated. "I share a lot with you."

He sighed. "I am doing everything I said I was doing. I didn't lie. I'm just doing a little bit more, that's all. And you've got to know all the truth, well, Muffy is a fluffer. They call her Muffy Fluffy, and she's so good at what she does, she could probably raise the dead. She's actually a really nice person—"

"Yeah, she seems to be," Lori interrupted softly.

Andrew sighed, looking at her again. "Lori, the folks would just die if they knew."

"I know that, but I'm not the folks."

He nodded. "It's not something that I want to do, but I do want to make films, and I just wasn't surviving. I can do one porno flick and support myself for months, and help finance my other work."

"I'm not judging you, Andrew, honestly."

He shook his head angrily. "Okay, so I'm judging myself, and I'm disappointed in me."

"Andrew—"

"Let's get out of here. I didn't expect to see anyone I work with here—I do my adult stuff in other counties most of the time."

"Andrew, look, I'm really sorry. If I can help, let me know. I won't tell anyone—"

"Oh, some of our friends know," he said dryly. "Old Brad needed money once, and he 'acted' for me."

"What?" Lori said, startled.

"He said he needed the money. I think he had a good time. The girls all thought he was just drop dead gorgeous, and they fawned all over him."

"Did—did Jan know?"

"No, of course not! He'd die if his daughter ever found out! Lori, you wouldn't—"

"No, I wouldn't say anything!"

"And don't forget, our folks would have heart attacks on the spot—"

"Andrew, I won't say anything. Anything at all."

"I'm quitting as soon as I can."

"You're all grown-up, Andrew. That's a decision you have to make for yourself."

He'd been so anxious to leave. He suddenly settled back. He smiled at her. "You know what, little sister?"

"What?"

"It's sure good to have you home."

She smiled. "It's good to be home."

She wasn't sure if she meant it or not. But one thing was sure; home was just chock-full of surprises.

When they finally left, Andrew kissed her cheek before she slid into the driver's seat of her car. "I'll pick you up at nine-thirty tomorrow morning."

"Nine-thirty?" she asked.

"Ellie's funeral," he reminded her. "Bright and early."

"Ellie's funeral, bright and early."

"Hail, hail. I'll bet the gang will all be there," he said.

He closed her door, waved, and walked away.

Chapter 8

Ellie's coffin was brass with handsome crosses at the edges. When Lori and Andrew arrived, a soprano was singing a sad lament about God's will, and the priest was consoling her family in the front pew. Andrew urged his sister toward a rear pew. By rote, Lori slid to her knees at the pew and lowered her head. She tried to say the right words for Ellie, yet she couldn't really remember her friend, and in her mind, her prayers sounded hollow. When she thought about the horror of the murder, however, she was able to pray that Ellie had found peace. She then found herself raising her eyes, though her head remained bowed, and she watched as others began to pour into the church.

There were a number of women who were sobbing with a true emotion that tore at Lori's heart. She was startled when she felt a tap on her shoulder, and realized she had been studying the women so fiercely that she hadn't realized that her cousin, Josh, had come to sit next to her. She rose from her knees to the seat, offering Josh a warm hug. She sat back a little, looking at him. She hadn't seen him in several years, but he hadn't changed much. He was a striking man with reddish hair, green eyes, and a handsome tan. Her mother had told her that his folks were proud of him, but deeply dismayed. He had a great state-of-the-art bachelor condo, a red Prowler, and a yacht—but no steady girlfriend, and no prospects for fatherhood in the near future. He looked happy and healthy to Lori, however, and she was convinced that Josh was doing just fine. He certainly wasn't over the hill, and his only real problem was that he was an only child and his folks were really anxious on the grandchildren issue.

"Good to see you, kid," Josh told her.

"You, too," she whispered.

"You look great."

"Thanks. You're not bad yourself."

She stared forward again, and saw a man rising from the front pew to greet another man.

"Two of her exes," Josh whispered to her. He shrugged. "I worked on her last divorce."

Lori nodded, then asked Josh, "Do they think that any of the men in her life might—"

"Those guys were both out of state," Josh whispered.

"How do you know?"

"Ricky has headed up a lot of the investigations," Josh said simply.

"Ah."

"There's your old friend Susan Nichols," Andrew said, nudging Lori from the other side.

Lori had kept up with Jan, but she'd only heard about Susan through Jan now and then. She leaned forward. Susan was still very pretty, petite and well built, with long dark hair, dark eyes, and beautiful ivory skin. Right now, however, she looked rough. Like the other women who had come in earlier, Susan was suffering real, close, and personal grief, crying so that rivers of tears fell down her cheeks, no matter how she tried to staunch them.

"They hung out now and then," Josh offered, whispering in Lori's ear.

"Did they?"

"They were both divorced, no children, you know."

She nodded, then leaned forward frowning as she tried to place the man who followed in after Susan, tapping her on the shoulder, then holding her in a close, comforting embrace when she turned to him. The man was tall, brown-haired, with clean-cut, yet ruggedly handsome features; he wore an expensive Armani suit very well, being both well muscled and lean.

"Don't you recognize him?" Andrew asked her.

"Jeff Olin. Mandy's brother," Josh offered.

Jeff looked good, really good, tanned and healthy, and prosperous. Andrew had said that he was an attorney. Lori was glad for him; he had taken his sister's death hard, and the last time she had seen him, he had been stunned and numb, a lost little boy.

"And hail, hail, as I said . . ." Andrew added as someone else entered the church.

Lori turned. Ricky Garcia, Ted Neeson, and Sean and Michael

Black were entering together. Lori found herself smiling slightly. They looked like a team out of *Baywatch*, all dressed up for the church shot. Big guys, young, handsome, bodyguards out of the *Bold and the Beautiful.*

She remembered they were there for a funeral, one of their own. Ellie lay in that box, sewn back together the best the mortician could manage. There had been viewing hours the night before, but her coffin had never been open. Lori turned back to look toward the altar. A picture of Ellie in life, bright and laughing, sat atop the coffin. Somehow, it made it all the sadder.

The priest left the pew with Ellie's family and headed for the pulpet. He folded his hands together. "Let us pray," he invited the gathering, and they all rose.

Sometime during the service, she became aware that Ricky, Ted, Michael, and Sean sat in the pew behind them. Before mass, one of Ellie's coworkers gave the eulogy, and broke down in the middle. One of Ellie's exes rose and finished, saying that she was full of life, giving, warm, and generous, and that her friends would all miss her very much. He left it to the priest to tell the gathering that they must somehow try to understand God's will, and that there was an eternal justice—her murderer would surely be caught, and in truth, Ellie now rested in a better place than this earth.

The coffin was taken from the church. The congregation rose, and exited.

Lori was somberly leaving when she felt a touch on her shoulder. "Lori! Lori Kelly, oh, my God, it's so good to see you!"

She turned to find Susan Nichols staring at her, trying to smile despite her blotchy cheeks and tearstained eyes.

"Susan," Lori said.

Susan threw her arms around Lori's neck, still in a highly emotional state. Lori hugged her back tightly.

"Ladies, we should move on out, shouldn't we?" Josh suggested.

Her cousin's hand at her back, Lori started on out from the church.

"Are you going to the graveside?" Susan asked Lori.

"I—" Lori began.

"Yeah, sure, of course, Sue," Andrew answered for her.

"Good. We'll talk after," Susan said.

Ellie was buried at Woodlawn. The drive from the church to the graveyard wasn't long, but Josh decided to ride with Andrew and Lori, explaining as they rode that Susan was especially upset because she might have joined Ellie and her friends the evening she was killed, but backed out at the last minute because of a headache.

At Woodlawn Andrew led her toward the graveside. Somehow, their old crowd formed a group toward the right of the coffin and tent. They greeted one another discreetly, Andrew and Josh shaking hands with Michael and Sean, Susan kissing Sean, and Jeff Olin coming up to offer Lori a warm hug. Jan and Brad arrived together, and the handshakes and kisses went around again.

The graveyard service began; it was brief and bittersweet. One of Ellie's exes tossed the first handful of dirt into the grave, and then family members tossed flowers into the grave. The company had been invited to the home of one of Ellie's cousins; her folks having died in the last few years and her exes now living out of town.

Lori didn't know Ellie's cousins; at the graveside she offered her condolences, and went to the car to wait for Andrew. Jeff Olin found her there. He reached for her hands. His smile was warm and confident, though duly somber for the occasion.

"Lori. Lori Kelly. You look like a million bucks! What brings you home—not that it isn't wonderful that you're here."

"Thanks, Jeff. Gramps is really sick, that's why I'm home. You look great, of course. But I'm sorry to see you under these circumstances . . ."

"I know, this is really bad, isn't it?"

She nodded glumly. "Had you seen much of Ellie lately?"

He shook his head. "Not a lot. Now and then, in passing. I cared about her, though. She'd been Mandy's best friend. It's funny, though. Seems we all have some kind of bond from way back when, huh?"

"Yeah," she said softly, then hesitated. "How have you been, really, Jeff? What happened with Mandy was tough on everyone, but in a way, the rest of us were just bystanders, you were the one really hurt, you and—" She broke off, realizing that not just Jeff, Mandy's brother, but Sean, Mandy's accused killer, were both attending this funeral.

"Yes, I was hurt. Mandy was my sister. And yes, you're right, Sean was hurt, too, wasn't he?"

"You didn't think that he killed her, did you?" she asked, dismayed at the anxiety she heard in her voice.

Jeff smiled, shaking his head. Age had done wonders for him. He was really handsome, with a smooth, warm charm. "I *couldn't* think that, could I? If I did, I wouldn't have shook his hand, I'd be over there trying to strangle him now. I can't begin to tell you how bad it was at first, my mother crying night after night, my father praying constantly, trying to soothe my mother. I guess, in a way, it's good they're both gone.''

"Gone? They left the area?''

He shook his head. "Gone, passed away. They were in a car crash, just a few years after Mandy died.''

Lori clamped her hand over her mouth, stunned, then drew it away and managed to stutter out an apology. "Oh, God, Jeff, I'm so sorry. Your sister, and then your folks like that, together . . . I am sorry, I didn't know, my folks never told me . . . Andrew didn't . . .''

"They might not have known, Lori. I went away to school, and only came back summers. They died right after one of my school breaks, and if your family didn't read the name in the obits, they wouldn't have known. I wasn't really talking to any one back then.''

"It's really amazing that you're talking to us now.''

He smiled. "I need friends,'' he told her.

She offered her hand. "Well, I am your friend, you know.''

"Thanks, Lori. And you can call on me anytime you need me, too.''

"You're an attorney now, right?''

"Right. A good one. I defend rich crooks, but only the ones who go out and commit white-collar crimes. I admit to keeping them out of jail, but since our jails don't have room for the violent offenders, I can do my work well and feel entirely guilt free.''

"I thought you were a corporate attorney.''

He grinned dryly. "I am.''

"Ah!'' Lori murmured, looking past him to where her brother and cousin stood with Sean and Michael, Brad and Jan, Ricky Garcia, Ted Neeson—and Susan Nichols.

"Susan has taken this really hard,'' Jeff commented.

"Well, she and Ellie were still rather close, I take it.''

He nodded, then looked at her. "And she's scared. She's divorced and alone.''

"It's scary enough out there these days without something like this,'' Lori murmured.

He nodded. "I know, it is. It's really a shame that folks just don't seem able to stay together in our society. I hear you have a son.''

She smiled. "Yep.''

"Congratulations. A little late.''

Her smiled deepened. "Thanks, it's never too late.''

"But your husband . . . ?''

"He passed away.''

"Oh. Now it's my turn to be sorry.''

"Thanks. He was very sick, and we knew it was just a matter of time, and . . ."

"And?" he inquired.

"And I think we made the time we had together a whole lot easier for one another," Lori finished. "Anyway, Ian Corcoran has been gone a long time now, so you needn't be sorry. Brendan and I do very well, and it seems like coming home has actually been good."

"I'm glad to hear it." He sighed softly, glancing at the others. "Listen, I'm going to go and see if I can give Sue a ride home, ease her mind a bit, let her know she has friends around."

"That would be nice, Jeff."

"Hey, don't you go forgetting that you have friends around."

"I won't."

Jeff left her, walking over to join the group. She was glad to see him talking to Sean, as if nothing in the past had ever come between them. Sean was wearing dark glasses, but he grinned at something Jeff said. Maybe time did heal wounds. And maybe Jeff really thought that what was done to Sean was just as much a crime as his sister's death.

Someone in the group laughed, then she heard her brother say, "I don't know. Let me check with Lori."

Andrew strode toward her. "Lori, we all thought we'd slip over to the old Italian place on Coral Way and have coffee, food, alcohol, whatever. Have you got a little time? What's the story with Brendan?"

"Brendan's all right—he's got a number for the folks if he has any problems."

"You up to lunch?"

Was she? Sure.

It was strange. Damned strange. The last time he'd been together with this group it had been in the courthouse, Sean realized as they were brought to a table and took their seats.

He was at one end, Susan on one side, Ricky on the other. Lori was down at the other side. Somehow, Michael wound up next to her on the one side, Ted Neeson on the other. She seemed comfortable enough between them.

Sean remembered suddenly how he had met Lori the very first time, how she'd been this angelic waif, lost to the harassment of Ted and Ricky. He'd thought her the most fragile and delicate creature he'd ever seen. She'd hated both Ricky and Ted for years—then she'd decided they were just jerks. She'd told him that the night she'd stayed by his side when he'd learned that Daniel had been killed. The worst night of his life. Not even sitting in jail, listening to the cops tell him that the D.A.'s office meant to throw a murder one rap at him and he'd fry in the electric chair had been as bad as learning that Daniel had been killed. She'd been there for him then. Not so fragile. He'd discovered his angel had an inner core of steel.

Then again, none of them were kids now. The 4F Club was far behind them all. Ted and Ricky were both working cops, and they seemed to have their heads glued on right, something Lori couldn't help but notice.

Next to him, Susan inhaled on a shaky breath.

"All right?" he asked her.

She squeezed his hand, her fingers delicate on his. "Sean, I just can't believe it! Something so awful. I mean, I've seen stories like this on the news, in the papers, but for something like this to happen to Ellie . . . oh, God! I read an article that talked about her wild life-style, as if she was asking to get killed because she went to clubs. Can you imagine!"

He shook his head. "Susan, people know that stuff like that is a bunch of crap. Ellie was single, Ellie went out. She didn't owe any-body any explanations."

"She just wanted to be happy, Sean. She was looking for the right guy. And having a little fun. She wasn't doing drugs, she was honest, hardworking . . . oh, God, I'm so scared!"

"Don't be scared. If you're really worried, just lay low for a while—"

"It wasn't a *bad* club she was hanging out at. I've been there—"

"I went there, too. You're right. There was nothing wrong with the place. She just met the wrong guy there."

"God, Sean, it's really good to see you."

"Thanks, Sue."

"If you get the urge to move in with me, let me know, will you?"

He smiled. "You know what? It's a tempting offer, but you're a special friend, and I want to keep it that way."

"Don't want to sleep with me, huh?"

"You're as sexy as they come. But no. I've had lots of women, Sue, and not many friends. I value my friends."

"Think I should buy a gun? Or a Doberman?"

"I think you should keep your door locked and be smart."

She nodded. "You're right." The waitress went by, and Sue lifted her glass. "Excuse me, I'll have another Merlot, please." She smiled at Sean.

It was her third glass of wine.

"Sue, where's your car?"

"Don't worry, I took a cab to the funeral—my eyes were too red for me to drive. You can get me home."

"Ricky brought me. He, Ted, Michael, and I came together."

"Good. I can get driven home by two cops and two hunks."

"You got it."

Smiled. Looked into her wine, and started crying again. Sean set his hand on hers, and looked down the length of the table. Lori was listening to Michael, watching him. He wondered what his brother was saying.

Lori enjoyed lunch. She felt guilty, enjoying the occasion when they had just buried Ellie, but her brother and Ted were fun and pleasant, and they were both as interested as she in what Michael was telling them about his work.

After high school he'd followed Sean to California, where his brother had told him they were both going to pull up out of the muck, make lives for themselves, and take care of their father. They'd taken jobs in restaurants, and gotten into UCLA. Following Sean to a biology class one day, Michael had developed a crush on a marine biology major. The affair with Sara lasted only six months, but his love for the water became a lifelong thing. He was now working at a place called Anderson's Cay, just south of Islamorada. His main work was with dolphins, though he did a lot of work with manatees as well, since they were endangered. People killed them with boat propellers, or maimed them and left them to die under horrible circumstances.

He was earnest, passionate about his work. Lori found herself watching him, thinking that he was a lot like his brother, his eyes so intense, dark hair unruly and prone to fall over his forehead.

"Michael, man, it's great that you've done so well," Andrew told him. "Remember the rap sheet you had as a kid?"

"I was a punk," Michael said flatly. He shrugged and looked down the table. "But after Sean went to court over Mandy's death . . . well, the world got pretty serious. Turned me around."

"And Sean," Josh murmured.

Michael shook his head. "Sean never needed turning around. He was always on the straight and narrow. Life's funny, though. He might not have been such a popular commercial success as an author if things hadn't happened the way they did. I thought he'd go into law, after what happened—a way to get back at the system. But he went into forensics instead. Then he started with the writing . . . damn, it's good to have him here, though. Hope he stays awhile.''

"How long does he intend to stay?" Lori heard herself asking.

"I don't know. Probably long enough to do some research. I can't see him coming back for good, can you? To a place that all but crucified him?''

An hour later they paid the bill and rose. Outside in the parking lot, they hugged one another, saying good-bye, agreeing to get together again. Lori was alarmed to realize that she was trying to keep her distance from Sean.

"We need to have a party," Jan said.

Brad sighed softly. "Jan, we've just been to a funeral—''

"I know. And that's what happens when people get old and drift away. It's like families—people only get together for weddings and funerals, and funerals are sad and terrible and I don't want the next time we get together again to be another funeral.''

"You have a point there," Lori said, defending Jan.

"The ex-women in my life!" Brad said, and groaned.

"Very, very ex on my part," Lori reminded him. She inadvertently glanced at Sean and flushed when she realized he was studying her. She couldn't tell what he was thinking. He was wearing the Ray•Bans again. "I should get home. Check on Brendan," she said.

Andrew slipped a brotherly arm around her. "We'll get you right home, sis.''

"I think a party is a great idea, too," Jeff Olin said.

"Why not?" Andrew murmured. He glanced at Sean. "Would our visiting celebrity attend?''

Sean nodded behind the Ray Bans. "Yeah, sure.''

"We'd have our own cops on the scene," Ricky supplied.

"And attorneys—should we decide to sue one another," Andrew said.

"My house, Friday night," Jan said.

Lori glanced at Sean. It eased her out of a private dinner for him on Friday night.

He was watching her. He was thinking the same thing, but he didn't protest. He seemed amused.

"I'd love a party!" Susan said wistfully. "I'm so scared now, it's probably the only time I'll have any fun in the next year!''

"Then, it's settled. Jan's house, and you're all invited," Brad said.

"Wait a minute, if it's my house, I should be doing the inviting," Jan said.

"Not when I'm still making the payments," Brad told her.

"I love it when you talk alimony," Jan murmured sexily.

"Cute, isn't she? And they call women the weaker sex," Brad moaned.

He had his hand on his ex-wife's back and was propelling her toward his car. Lori had the feeling that they'd be together for the next hour or so, even if they did both have to get to work later.

They should just remarry, she thought. It was the nicest divorce she'd ever seen.

"Party, Friday night! Eight o'clock!" Jan called.

"Let's get going, shall we?" Andrew said.

Lori nodded, wondering if Sean was going to say good-bye.

But he was already gone, seated next to Ricky in his Mercury Cougar.

Tina Jackson wasn't supposed to be in the Grove alone. But she was there, after school, determined on her plan of action. Her friend, Bobby Sue, had copped out on the shopping mission, and with the excitement of a very special new guy in her life, Tina had to have some new clothes. She'd gotten a ride from a school friend's mom, and she figured if worse came to worse, she'd have to splurge on her spending money and take a taxi home. Her mom and dad both had the funeral that morning, so they'd probably hang out together for a while in the afternoon—nostalgia and all—and then, her mom had clients scheduled from four o'clock until seven. It was unlikely that she could get caught.

In a funky store just off Main Street, she found the perfect jeans, and the perfect top. The jeans hung stylishly low. The top hugged her growing breasts. Seeing herself in the mirror, she was excited by her image. She looked at least sixteen. Maybe seventeen, since she would be fourteen almost any day now. If she only had a pierced navel! Of course, that wasn't happening, but a delicate little ring would look just fantastic . . .

No body piercing, her mother had commanded. Maybe she'd break her down in another year or two.

At the moment she wasn't going to whine to herself over what she couldn't have. She liked the outfit so much she paid for it, and kept it on. She had friends working in some of the stores in the area— older brothers and sisters of schoolmates. She could try out the outfit. The clerk said she looked like a million bucks. She hoped it was true, and not just sales talk.

*   *   *

The killer cruised down the street, anxious for little more than a good dinner before heading home.

He was in no great hurry to kill again: he still felt remarkably sated from the last kill. And he was careful, he was fastidious. After all, he was not crazy, he was totally in possession of all his faculties; he could wait.

Then he saw her. Walking along the street, looking far older than her years. Tall, slim, budding, beautiful. Long blond hair down her back, belly bare. She was growing breasts, she was . . .

Ripe. Man, that was it, ripe for the picking. He gazed at the smooth length of her throat, and envisioned his fingers there. Smooth, oh, yeah, her flesh was so smooth. So young, so beautiful. He saw himself ripping off her clothing, saw the fear in her eyes as his hands went all over that perfect smooth young skin. He itched to touch her, ached . . .

And somewhere, in the back of his mind, he felt the rage growing, despite his determination that he was not a crazy, he was a smooth operator, invisible, because he was just so damned normal. But the rage was there. She was a tease. So young, so quick, she was a tease. Like her mother, like her mother's friends, like all women. She was just a cunt.

And her time would come.

Tina saw *him* and nearly passed out. Darn! She'd had it all figured out, and now . . .

"Hey, gorgeous!" he called to her. He sounded angry. Was he going to tell? Order her home? Her mom would ground her for a month.

She smiled and hurried over to his car. "Hi!"

"What are you up to down here all by your lonesome?"

"Shopping."

"All alone?"

"Yes, but don't tell Mom, please, please, don't tell her if you see her!"

He smiled. He knew it was a drop-dead gorgeous smile, and that she would be charmed. "It's our secret, sweetie. We'll never tell on one another."

"Never," she agreed.

"Want a ride?"

Tina hesitated. She should take the ride, get the hell home. Before she could get caught.

"Tina!"

She started and looked up. Bobby Sue was across the street, waving to her madly. Her friend had come to meet her after all, and that meant Bobby Sue's mom would be coming to pick them up in an hour or so.

"No, but thanks! See ya!"

She moved away from the car, waving.

The killer sat still, watching her. Behind him, horns began to beep. He started to drive away.

His smile faded, and he was not gorgeous anymore.

He caught a glimpse of his own eyes in the mirror. They were pure evil, he thought, terrifying.

That thought cheered him.

And he smiled once again.

Gorgeous . . .

He could take any woman he wanted.

And he would. And they'd never catch him.

Everyone trusted him; he was smart as a whip. They'd never get him.

That thought made him laugh. And he laughed. And laughed.

Chapter 9

That evening, Sean went back to the South Beach club with Ricky.

The bartender was a pretty woman of about thirty, a little world-weary, but still friendly, and unafraid of dealing with the police. She seemed glad that Ricky, point man on the homicide task force, had returned to ask questions again.

"You guys just can't give up on this one," she said, smoothing back a lock of medium brown hair. "I wish I could help you more. I remember the girl who was killed, I just can't remember seeing her with anyone special . . . except for the German fellow, and you said that he's in the clear?"

Ricky nodded. "He was with friends the rest of the night, in plain view at the News Café."

The woman, Shelley, smiled at Sean. "I remember you."

"Thanks."

"Well, you're the writer, right? A celebrity."

"Only in his own mind," Ricky teased.

Sean smiled. "He's jealous."

"Yeah, but I admit it," Ricky said.

"Shelley," Sean said, leaning forward, "Ellie's friends and co-workers apparently thought that she was especially nice—that she would dance with most guys who asked her, that she had a kind word for most people. Still, you don't need to be trying to remember a monster. If killers all had horns, we'd recognize them right away. Was there anybody you saw her especially interested in . . . someone she may have left with . . . ?"

Shelley shrugged. "We had several good-looking guys in here that evening—we used to be busy," she said glumly. "Honest to God,

I'd help you if I could. She was here, she left. Her friends left, all about the same time. If I can think of anything, anything at all, I will let you know. Can I get you another drink?'' she asked Ricky.

"No—he's driving,'' Sean answered for him. "Give him a soda. I'd love a beer.''

He smiled. She smiled back. Nice girl. Ricky frowned at him, laughed, and drank his soda.

Sean wanted to sleep, but he couldn't. Ricky left him off after midnight. He lay on his bed in his hotel room. Alone.

Around one he dozed.

At three he was back up.

He walked over to the desk where he'd set up his computer. He was a writer, he was supposed to be here writing. The city was full of stories. Sad, tragic, frightening, amusing. The stuff of life.

He stared at the blank screen in the darkness of his room.

Then his fingers started moving over the keys.

He wrote about Ellie. About how beautiful she had been in life. Beautiful in her enthusiasm and kindness. They said she'd kept from bitterness, an accomplishment in itself, when the years began to go by, when fine lines began to move into the face, when the heart had begun to fill with the dreams that remained just out of reach.

And then he wrote of her death. Of seeing her on the autopsy table, the last terror she felt in life still somehow there within her once lovely eyes ...

He hit the power key, deleting all hc had written.

He pressed his head between his palms, plagued by a sudden unease that seemed to make no sense.

He showered. Dressed, prowled his room.

At six, he called an old friend.

"Sean?'' Arnie Harris said, hearing his voice. Arnie was up, sipping his coffee. Sean could see him seated at the table on the porch of his hilltop retreat. Arnie had been retired for five years. He still woke promptly at five-thirty, and sat with his coffee by six, watching the day begin over his Virginia farmland.

"Yeah, how are you, Arnie?''

"Waiting for your call.''

Sean arched a brow, staring at the phone.

"Hear there's been some trouble down there.''

"How'd you know I was in Miami?''

"The dates of your tour were listed in *PW*. Maggie told me what you were up to. My wife is always careful to watch for your comings and goings. She considers you a personal victory.''

Sean laughed. He did give Maggie Harris credit for getting his writing career going. He had been with Arnie, describing a theorized death scenario after studying a cache of bones, and Maggie had suggested he turn his imagination toward paper. ''And fiction! Make it fiction. You don't want to get sued by anyone, and since you have been involved with so many real people . . . well, people who were once real . . .''

''So what's up?'' Arnie asked. ''Have the local police allowed you in on this sensational murder case? One corpse, and they're shouting serial killer.''

''Yes, some of the cops are old friends.''

Arnie snorted over the phone wires. ''Where were they way back when?''

''Arnie, I knew the girl.''

''Yes, I know,'' Arnie said after a moment.

''You do?'' Sean inquired.

''Well, I'm retired, not dead. And I still have access to information from all over the country. I pulled the files on Eleanor Metz, found out that she'd gone to school with you, and studied the old newspaper articles from there.''

''She was Mandy's best friend when Mandy died,'' Sean said.

''Interesting.''

''Mandy drowned. I was there when it happened. And I was at the autopsy for Eleanor Metz, Arnie. It was different. Ellie was butchered.''

''Completely different.''

''Yes.''

''But . . . you think that you're seeing a connection between something that happened nearly fifteen years ago and this murder?''

''I don't know. Am I just spooked being back here? Talk to me, Arnie. How can there be a connection? So many years have gone by. The M.O. is nothing at all alike. But something bothers me terribly here. You were with the first profilers, you studied psychos, you know what makes them tick, how they'll act. What's a killer like who shreds a woman the way this guy killed Ellie. She was knocked out, but not killed by the blow to her head. Her throat was severed. *After* she'd been beaten and stabbed. The body was found without clothing or identification. Half buried in the mud. She might never have been discovered except that you know what Florida's like heading from spring toward summer. Thunderstorms almost daily. Rain might have washed her up.''

''The killer sounds very organized,'' Arnie said. ''He was careful not to let her be identified too easily, and he was probably careful when he disposed of her body. I'd need to see more on the victim and study her habits, see the autopsy report itself, and find out what else the police know to give you a really educated opinion on this. But if you've got a victim who was totally savaged, this probably isn't the killer's first victim. Was the girl raped?''

''Yes.''

''He might have started out as a rapist, then moved on to rape and torture, and then to the ultimate thrill—the kill. He needs to be in control, needs to feel powerful. I would imagine, though, that he performed some pretty wicked deeds before this murder; he probably worked up to it over many years.''

''Right,'' Sean said. He'd listened to Arnie's lectures, heard his friend's advice to law enforcement officers desperately looking for any clue with which to help nab a killer.

''What you're really asking me,'' Arnie said, ''is whether someone might have drowned a girl fifteen years ago, and come back to slay another one of your friends. While you just happen to be in the city. You do sound spooked. And a more frightening thought is this—if there is such a connection, people might be thinking that it's you.''

Sean gritted his teeth together. ''I didn't kill Mandy, and I sure as hell didn't kill Ellie.''

''I know you didn't. I know you.''

Sean let out a sigh, disturbed to realize just how deeply the old wounds still cut. Why had he been the scapegoat way back then? *He'd been the outsider. The others had drawn together, leaving him on the outside looking in . . .*

''You there, Sean?''

''Yeah, I'm here,'' he said softly. ''Thanks, Arnie.''

''You don't need to thank a friend for being a friend, Sean,'' he said gruffly. ''Why don't you take a few days and come up and see us? Maybe get the hell out of there for a while. Might do you good.''

''Maybe I will, but not right now. I've got a few things here I've got to settle.''

''Anytime you need some help, call. I like retirement, mostly. But every once in a while, I feel about as useful as a potted plant. If the soup gets any thicker, bring me what you've got. Maybe I can help.''

''Thanks. I may take you up on that.''

Sean said good-bye and hung up. Still restless, he looked at the clock.

What the hell. It was creeping toward real morning. He just couldn't shake the uneasy feeling. He felt like a caged tiger.

Time, he thought, to move.

Lori had just poured her first cup of coffee when she heard the horn beeping. She ignored it, thinking someone was picking up a neighbor for work, but then she heard the pounding on her own door and hurried toward it. She checked her watch. Seven-thirty.

Sean was on her doorstep. She hated the way her heart seemed to leap at the simple sight of him; the way her palms felt clammy, and adrenaline seemed to race through her. This wasn't good, it wasn't healthy.

"Sean. Do you know how early it is?"

"Yes. Michael said he asked you down to the Keys yesterday, and you said yes."

She stared at him. She was holding a coffee cup, wearing a terry robe. Her hair was half up on her head; she had no makeup on.

He, in contrast, looked good. Cutoffs, T-shirt, sandals, dark Ray•Bans, baseball cap. He was freshly shaved; his hair remained slightly damp from a shower.

"The Keys? Now?"

"Yeah. Why waste the day? He said that you wanted to come down."

"I—I—" she stuttered, then waved her coffee cup in a circular motion. "I didn't say that I wanted to come at seven-thirty this morning! Michael told me about working with dolphins and manatees and I said I'd love to see the facility—he didn't say when—"

"Well, why not go before you have to start work?" he asked.

"Yes, but—"

"Today looks like a good day to me," he said. "Brendan home? Maybe if you're not up to it, he'd like to come along with me?"

She took a step back, somewhat outraged. But then, they had been best friends years ago, so there wasn't a thing in the world wrong with him suggesting he take her son for a drive. Not if she honestly believed in his innocence.

"Brendan's got to go to school soon, right?"

"Yes, I decided to give him a few days to adjust."

"So?"

"He's adjusting."

"Let him adjust in the Keys. He'll fall in love with Florida."

"We don't have to be in such a hurry—the world does still recognize weekends, doesn't it?''

Sean smiled. "Cop out. What's the matter with today? Make up for that Friday-night dinner you're getting out of.''

"I've had no warning, that's what's wrong. You just came barging in here—''

"Mom? Who's here?'' Brendan called. He came into the living room, shirtless, barefoot, wearing just his jeans. "Hey!'' he said with pleasure, seeing Sean. "Hey, great. Want some coffee, Mr. Black?''

Lori cast her son an evil glare. He didn't notice. Sean did, but he chose to ignore her. "I'd love coffee.''

He stepped past Lori, following Brendan into the kitchen. Lori swore, slammed the door, and fumed.

"I'm going to shower!'' she called to them.

"Dress in a bathing suit,'' Sean called after her.

"Why?'' Brendan asked, his eyes widening.

"I'm taking you two down to the Keys with me,'' Sean explained.

"Wow. Great. Cool!'' Brendan said happily.

"Lori?'' Sean's brow arched, but his tone remained polite.

She could protest, she knew. But it would just make her look bad in the eyes of her son. A drive down to the Keys would be nice for Brendan. It was a beautiful day. They did have to get going with life soon, and Michael's work had sounded fascinating.

"Sure, what the hell?'' she muttered.

Thirty minutes later she was in the front passenger seat of Sean's rental car, and they were heading south on the turnpike. Brendan had come up with the idea to call Jan and beg her to let Tina play hooky. To Lori's amazement, Jan had agreed. She was going to drive down later and meet them at a restaurant called Marker 88—fittingly, since it was at mile marker 88 along U.S. 1, the ribbon of road running from Miami to Key West.

It wasn't hard to keep conversation flowing on the way down— the kids never shut up. Tina was thrilled to be out of school, and Brendan was thrilled to have Tina with them. They talked about the latest movies, music—who was coming to what arena next—books, birds, plants, and crocodiles.

They stopped in Key Largo at a mom-and-pop place for breakfast; it was rustic, pleasant, and right on the water with a little spit of beach. While Sean paid the tab and the kids wandered back toward the car, Lori found herself doffing her shoes and strolling out toward the water. It was glorious. With a clear blue sky above her, the bay was at its most beautiful, true turquoise in color, the waves rolling in with a gentle, beguiling motion.

She closed her eyes, feeling the warmth of the sun as it touched her flesh. The sweet, deceptive coolness of the breeze swept over her. She loved the feeling. She had missed it. New York had water, and the world's most spectacular skyline. But this was home, this tropical balm, her flesh being kissed by a soft spray of salt, the radiant fingers of the sun, the caress of the breeze.

She opened her eyes, aware that Sean stood just slightly behind her, watching her. He'd stripped off his shirt, and was barefoot. He might not have been living in the intense heat of South Florida, but he'd spent some good time in the sun. His muscled shoulders and chest were deeply bronzed, glistening in the heat of the day. Hands on his hips, he surveyed her thoughtfully. She caught his eyes, flushed. "Great day, isn't it?" she said.

He nodded. "I've missed it."

"You've been away for years."

"Yeah," he agreed, then shrugged, looking across the water, eyes reflecting the blue of ocean and sky. "The Pacific is quite different, of course. So much time has gone by . . . so why did you hesitate when I asked you to come with me today?"

"You—you surprised me," Lori said.

"Really?" He walked toward her, and she was tempted to back away. But just a foot away from her, he stopped, not touching her, studying her eyes as he spoke. "I always cared for you. You knew that."

"You dated Mandy. I dated Brad—"

"Right. Until the day at the rock pit. It was over between Mandy and me before the tragedy. I think it was over between you and Brad as well."

"We would have gone on to different colleges—"

"You cared about me."

"Maybe I did. It was a long time ago."

"And your parents told you not to speak with me—I was a no-good kid from the wrong side of the tracks no matter whether I'd killed Mandy or not."

"That's very bitter," she said.

"Damned right. I get bitter now and then."

"Then, why come back to me?" she asked softly.

"Because, unless I'm missing something, you're a free agent. An adult free agent. As I am myself. There's no Brad, no Mandy. You've been widowed more than a decade."

"So you think we should date?" she asked.

He smiled suddenly. "Yeah, I think we should date. It's what people do, you know."

She was dismayed to find that she was shaking; her eyes slipped from his.

"Lori, I care about you. To be honest, I always cared about you, even when I hated caring about you. You're here, I'm here . . . I don't see anything in the way."

"Because you don't know where to look!" she murmured in a soft panic.

"What?"

"Sean, I just don't think that you really know me, that's all—"

"People never really change."

"Yes, they do."

"I don't agree. Not in the soul."

"You didn't really know me, Sean. I'm not so great a person. I've done some really horrible things—"

"Like what?"

She stared at him, thinking yes, now was the time to tell him just how horrible she had been.

But she didn't. She stared at him dumbly.

He smiled again, and she remembered the old Sean, the way he had been just gorgeous from the first time she had ever seen him, the way his slow, sexy smile had sent her heart catapulting . . .

"Why don't we avoid confessions for the moment," he said. "And if things do evolve . . . ?"

"From what to what?" she whispered. "Sean, I don't think it's such a good idea. Dating. I mean—"

He was suddenly behind her, arms slipped around her waist. He drew her back against him, and his words were husky and hot against her earlobe.

"Ah! I believe you are thinking about sex. Heat, sand, water, a few margaritas . . . a tall, dark stranger out of the past."

"Sean, the kids—"

"I didn't exactly mean here and now!" he teased softly.

She struggled against his arms, turning, finding herself face-to-face with him, and unable to avoid a smile. "Right! Not here and now, Sean—"

"Fine. When?"

Her smile faded. "You know, I actually did try to call you—"

"When?" he demanded, his amusement fading and his eyes guarded.

"Your father said that you left, and that you didn't want to hear from anyone. He said he'd tell you, but either you just didn't care, or he didn't bother to tell you. So you always talked about my parents being prejudiced, but he apparently decided against me—"

"No, he didn't."

"He must have because—"

"He died. He didn't tell me anything after I left, because he never had a chance. He died. I left and went to California, and sent for him and Michael. They were both eager to come west. They wanted to start over. Michael did. My father had a seizure on the plane, slipped into a coma, and died in California."

"Oh!" She stared at him, her mouth formed into a circle, wishing that the sand would swallow her up. She hadn't known; no one had told her. Maybe no one had known. Mr. Black, who had lived and worked hard, providing a simple life for his sons, had been a quiet, unassuming man. Death and scandal had rocked his family, and he had died. He hadn't made any headlines, and there had been no one left to whom Sean might send the news. His father had died as quietly, as sadly, as he had lived.

God, I'm sorry.

She wanted to say the words, but couldn't. They'd sound hollow anyway, even if she was sincere.

I would have loved your father; just as I always loved you. You never knew what an awful, painful, crush I had on you, you never knew, you never knew . . .

So much.

He released her, stepping away. He turned toward the parking lot.

Lori needn't have worried about Brendan and Tina watching them—the two were far too involved with one another, laughing as they drank sodas from cans.

"Sean!" she whispered.

But he didn't hear her. He was already walking away, and nearly at the car.

"Sean!" she repeated, coming after him.

This time he heard her. But so did the kids.

"What's up, Mom?" Brendan asked her.

"Um . . . nothing," she said, smiling. "Is Michael expecting us?"

Sean nodded slowly. "Yeah."

"I can't wait to see this place!" Brendan said, opening the rear door of the car.

"Will your brother really let us work with the animals?" Tina asked excitedly.

"Sure," Sean told her.

She flushed happily, getting into the car. Both rear passenger doors closed.

Lori looked at Sean over the top of the car. "How can Michael know we're all coming?" she asked.

He had his sunglasses on. His shrug offered little.

"Sean—"

He smiled, and her awkwardness eased a bit.

"I'm sorry about your father. Really."

"It was a long time ago now. No one can hurt him anymore. And I try to believe in heaven. If there is such a place, then he's with Daniel."

"Yeah."

"We should get going. The kids are going to wonder."

"Yeah. Sean . . ."

"Yes?"

No more confessions! he had said. *And how could she possibly talk about the past? Brendan and Tina were in the car.*

And yet, maybe, like it or not, this was the moment. The moment she had missed when it might have really mattered.

"Mom! Puh-lease! It's a hundred degrees in here!" Brendan called out.

Sean grimaced.

"Right!" Lori called back.

She slid into the car. Sean did likewise, revving the motor.

She glanced at him, then looked to the road.

The moment was gone.

The moment she should have taken.

She had missed it again.

Chapter 10

Michael was pleased to see them.

He'd been shy back in their school days, a strangely quiet bad boy getting into trouble and following around the wrong crowd. Sean, though a little younger, had been the outgoing one, standing up for his brother when he could make a stand, making his own way through life when he couldn't.

Apparently, working with animals had given Michael the complete turnaround he had needed. He was far more confident now; he hadn't gotten so much as a traffic fine since he found marine biology and animal psychology, according to Sean.

He met them at the gate where he worked, a private lab funded by a salvage concern with government contracts, people mainly interested in the use of dolphins for search-and-rescue techniques. But, as Michael explained to them while they walked around to the different pools, his company worked with all kinds of marine mammals and fish as well, since they were studying sharks and rays and their immunity to cancer. He introduced them to a few of the people in the main building, mostly dressed in swimsuits, shorts, and lab coats, some of them student assistants from various colleges, and some of them full-time animal behaviorists and researchers. Then he led them through the whitewashed halls to the outside, an area oceanside.

He brought them first to meet Rebecca, a pregnant manatee who'd been seriously wounded by a propeller in an upstate waterway. "No matter how you post these things, some people just don't care. They speed through zones where the animals live and breed, and this is what you get," he said unhappily. He was seated at the side of the natural pool, legs dangling into the water. Lori was instantly smitten;

the sea creature, big and bulky, nicknamed the sea cow, was, in truth, not a particularly pretty creature. But her eyes were large and dark and somehow soulful; her whiskered face had an appeal that only a mother should love, yet she somehow reminded Lori of a large, affectionate puppy dog. She came right to Michael, sliding her face onto his lap, looking as if she sighed in luxury while he scratched her head. Lori, at his side, reached out and scratched her, too.

"Can I touch her?" Brendan asked.

"Sure." Michael eased Rebecca's head from his lap and rose, allowing the kids room to sit.

"She's trusting," Sean commented as Rebecca happily slid up against Brendan, who laughed with pleasure.

"Too trusting. We'll never be able to release her. She'd be with people again, right smack in the middle of propeller zones. That's the main reason people have to be so careful with wild animals. Boaters down here, nice people, good people, thinking they're helping the dolphin and manatees out, feeding them. Especially with the dolphins, they sometimes give them bad fish, tainted food. Bacteria grows quickly. Worse than that, they make them trust people. And we're the worst creatures in the world to trust."

"Are we really that bad?" Lori asked.

Michael looked at her, appearing very much like Sean at that moment. "Yes. We're absolutely awful. Want to meet my girl?"

"You have a girlfriend down here?" Tina asked.

"Not exactly, but . . . come on. You'll see."

Michael led them to another lagoon pool, where they stood by a platform and a set of wooden steps leading down into the water. He explained that the seven pools in the compound—all connected with the ocean—although not natural, had been dug out decades before when Flagler's railroad—doomed to a later hurricane—was first being built to connect the Florida Keys. The railroad had washed away, but the work on it had become the basis for U.S. 1, connecting the chain of islands to the mainland to this day. Over the years the sea had encroached, allowing Michael's company to come in about forty years ago, dredge some of the pools deeper, and put in pumps to keep the seawater coming in and out on a daily basis.

"There she is, the love of my life, the only female I know who is totally trustworthy," Michael said, winking at Lori.

Lori gazed at Sean, who shrugged innocently. "He must have had a few bad dates recently, what can I say?"

She arched a brow at Michael, then looked out to where he pointed. At first she saw nothing. Michael made a swirling movement with his hand, and suddenly, a streak of blue arose from the pool in a jet and spray of motion. A dolphin rose high out of the water, turned, and dove back down.

"Marianne," Michael said softly.

"A porpoise!" Tina said, clapping her hands.

"An Atlantic bottlenose dolphin," Sean corrected her. "There's a difference between dolphins and porpoises."

Michael smiled. "My little brother is right. He apparently listens to me on occasion, so I'm flattered. There is a difference. They both actually belong to the whale family, but they're distinct species. Porpoises are much smaller, and they're fond of deeper, cooler water. You'll see these Atlantic bottlenose all up and down the coast, and in the Keys. You'll see them ocean side and bay side. You'll always recognize them because it does appear that they have a bottle for a nose. It isn't really a nose—it's a rostrum, an extension of the upper and lower jaws."

"Is she as affectionate as Rebecca?" Brendan asked.

"She's wonderful. And she's special. I'll show you. Lori, swim on out there and pretend to be dead."

"What?" Lori said incredulously.

"Michael—" Sean began to protest.

"No, seriously. Lori, you still swim like a fish, I'm sure, so there's really no danger."

Lori looked at Sean. "Your call," he told her.

"If you're afraid—" Michael began.

"No!" Lori protested. "I trust you. Both. I think. Even after that comment you made, Michael Black," she said.

"I'll go, Mom," Brendan offered hopefully.

"Let your mom go first," Michael said, smiling and watching Lori in a challenging way.

"Mrs. Corcoran, they have special programs for swimming with the dolphins just up at Theatre of the Sea," Tina said. "I've always wanted to go—"

"Everyone will get a chance," Michael said.

Lori pulled off the black cover-up she'd been wearing and slipped out of her sandals. She dropped both where she stood and headed straight into the water. "Now what?"

"Go float face down in the middle of the pool as if you were dead!"

Lori swam out, then did as Michael had instructed. She waited, holding her breath, wondering just how long she could do so. Once

she had been good in the water. Great. They'd all grown-up surrounded by water, and spent their lives playing in it.

Often at the rock pit.

Now, to herself, she could admit to being a little nervous. She
couldn't see anything around her; the water itself was clear and beautiful, totally temperate and comfortable, but there was a lot of seaweed in the pool, the salt stung, and she didn't have much vision.

She was about to rise—to breathe, first—then ask Michael just
what she was doing when she felt a rush of water around her. She
nearly gulped in water, startled, as the dolphin suddenly came upon
her.

The creature was huge. She hadn't appeared quite so large from
the shore. But she had to be at least nine feet, with eyes that were
strangely human as they met Lori's.

She gently butted Lori in the midsection and started swimming.
Her speed was incredible. Lori felt as if she flew through the water.
Split seconds later she was deposited on the steps leading into the
pool, where Sean and the kids were applauding.

"Isn't she magnificent?" Michael asked, speaking of Marianne as
if she were a favored child.

"Absolutely," Lori agreed, smoothing her wet hair from her face.

"May I try?" Tina begged.

"Sure, she loves people. Some dolphins don't—they're really just
like people. Some are social, some aren't. We train them through
positive reinforcement—"

"Food?" Brendan asked.

"Sometimes," Michael agreed. "But Marianne isn't even really
food oriented. She likes to be scratched on the back of her head, she
loves a belly rub—and applause! She's an incredible ham."

Lori sat on the steps while the kids took turns being rescued by
Marianne. Sean went in with the dolphin as well, and she watched
as he and Michael worked through a training routine with the animal.
But to her surprise, when Michael paused, explaining something to
Sean, Marianne swam over to where she sat on the steps. The dolphin
stared at her, angled on her side, one eye out of the water.

"Hey. What are you doing? You must think you're one big puppy
dog."

Michael came up on the steps beside her, dripping. "She likes
you."

"She doesn't know me."

"Dolphins are instinctive creatures. She instinctively likes you.
Smart girl," Michael said.

It was a quiet compliment, and Lori smiled. She looked down then, her smile fading.

If he only knew.

"Go swim with her."

"The kids are both in seventh heaven. I think I should—"

"They'll have all morning. Take a turn. Then I'll give you and Sean more of a tour of the place."

Lori shrugged, then eased back into the water. Michael had been right—Marianne liked her. The dolphin swam at her side, dove when she dove, surfaced when she surfaced. She reached out, and Marianne swam away, then came back. The second time the dolphin allowed her to slide her hand along her side. She found herself entranced. The creature was beautiful; powerful, gentle. Playful, and indeed, affectionate.

She left Lori for a few minutes, and Lori looked around the pool to realize that Marianne had decided to join Sean. He suddenly started laughing, calling out to his brother, "Michael, what's this! She's pushing me!"

"She wants you to move, obviously."

"What if I don't want to move?"

"What are you going to do, spank a dolphin?"

"What do you do?"

"I give her a time-out—like they do with grade-school kids. But why don't you see what she wants?"

Sean arched a brow, then stared at the dolphin, who lifted her head in front of his and let out a squeal.

"What?" Sean demanded, laughing.

She pressed her rostrum to his chest and began swimming. The next thing Lori knew, Sean was flying through the water, straight toward her.

He crashed into her, and they went down about a foot together. Sean instinctively reached out for her. They surfaced together, water streaming from their hair and faces. His hands were still on her rib cage as they tred the water. Big, powerful, she felt the length of his fingers over her ribs. His slow smile, along with the glittering reflection of the water in his eyes, was devastating. She was alarmed at the simple, sudden hunger for sex that seared through her just as hot as a stray ray of sun. *It was wrong, all wrong, there had just been too much emotion in the past.*

Even as those thoughts flew through her mind, she was startled by a large patch of seaweed drifting against her ankles. Seaweed, vines . . . the strength of his hands was immeasurable. And that was surely why the police had believed he'd gone into a fury and tied Mandy Olin down in the fresh water of the rock pit with a vine . . .

"See? Everyone is a matchmaker," Sean teased, his voice husky, sensual, bringing a leap of sweet fire into her veins once again and a sense of pure heat to the very center of her sex, unlike anything she had felt in years.

But Sean's smile faded—it was as if he read the suspicions of the past in her eyes.

He started to turn away.

"Sean!"

She reached out to stop him; he had already begun to move, and though she had intended to close her fingers around his arm, she caught him right below the belt line instead. He stopped, swinging back, pure surprise in his eyes.

She hadn't let go quite quickly enough to avoid feeling the instant growth of his erection. Her mouth went dry. He was staring at her with a brow arched high.

"I didn't mean—I'm sorry—" she stuttered. She felt absurd, younger, and more uncertain than she had been in high school, and it was just so foolish. "I think we should make love," she told him flippantly.

"Here?" he inquired politely, a glance indicating Michael and the kids.

"No," she said, shaking her head, laughing.

"Where? When?"

"Somewhere . . . sometime."

He inclined his head slightly. "You got it," he told her casually. "If you'll excuse me, I think I need to swim away from you right now."

Sean took a long time to come in. Lori and the kids were already dried off and dressed and ready to go into the research buildings to see the work going on with rays.

Sean made no further reference to sex with her, but it hung between them all day.

Andrew Kelly arrived first at the Irish pub in the Grove, where Brad Jackson had asked him to come join him for a late lunch.

Andrew ordered a beer and nursed it while he waited for Brad to arrive. His friend came in about ten minutes later, greeting the bartender and a few friends at the bar. He saw Andrew at the booth in the back and headed toward him.

"I'm glad you could come."

"No problem. What's up?" Andrew grinned. Brad had been extremely successful of late, so he was teasing when he said, "Need a job? A little extra cash? Tina asked for a Maserati already?"

"No, but that wouldn't matter. Her mother asked for the moon when we divorced."

"From what I hear, Jan does well enough with her real estate."

"She does. And I'm halfway kidding. The divorce was over a long time ago. We get along well."

"Still planning a party?"

"Jan's still planning a party."

"At the place that's half your house?"

Brad shrugged, threading his fingers through his still blond hair to smooth it back. Brad had always dressed immaculately—preparing for the business world long before he had become an attorney. In school even his jeans, Calvin Klein boxers, and T-shirts had been pressed.

"I don't think her idea was so bad. Do you?" Brad asked defensively.

Andrew shrugged. "No, it was a good idea. She invited my folks, you know."

"I think she invited everyone living."

"It's probably not quite that bad. And maybe she's right—I mean, family and friends drift apart. You get together for a funeral and wonder what happened to all the years."

"Ellie's funeral was tough, huh?"

Andrew nodded glumly, picking up his beer. "Yep."

"Susan was sure as hell upset."

"Yeah, I felt bad for poor Sue."

"Remember that last year . . . you were in college, but you and Sue still managed to be pretty hot and heavy back then," Brad said.

"Sue was a hot little ticket," Andrew agreed.

"What happened?" Brad asked.

Andrew shrugged. "Who knows? I think that after what happened to Mandy . . . I don't know."

Brad narrowed his eyes. "I do. We all closed ranks. It would have been bad enough if we'd just buried Mandy, but the cops pointed their fingers at Sean, and we all looked the other way."

Andrew studied his beer. "Yeah, maybe. And then we all figured we'd been assholes—even if we'd been encouraged to be assholes by our folks—so we kind of closed off against each other. Each family to itself, survival of the fittest!"

"There were a lot of casualities there. Mandy. Then the Olins dying in a crash. That Jeff is sane and walking and talking—and a well-respected attorney to boot—is amazing.''

"Sean and Michael came out of it okay,'' Andrew said.

"Sean Black could always fall into a pile of shit and come out smelling like a rose,'' Brad said.

Andrew arched a brow. "Sounds like there's still a rivalry going there.''

"There never was a rivalry. We came from different places, and we were going different ways. And you came out of it all okay, Jan and I are fine, your cousin Josh happily lives a life of pure decadence, and Sue did all right for herself. Ricky Garcia and Ted Neeson became cops—and though lawyers are considered sharks and cops are often considered pigs, both are respectable ways to make a living,'' Brad pointed out.

"So none of us is living under a bridge. You and Jan divorced, Lori rushed into marriage with a sick guy she couldn't have loved who kicked the bucket right away. Ellie was divorced, twice, I think, and Sue does well in business, but she's divorced. The rest of us happy decadent bachelors—that we appear to be—are incapable of maintaining any kind of a meaningful and long-term relationship.''

"Damn, I didn't know we were so miserable,'' Brad murmured.

"I didn't say we were miserable. Just screwed up.''

"We're from the generation that gave new meaning to the term dysfunctional,'' Brad said impatiently. "But maybe we are getting older and better. Instead of worrying so much about ourselves, we can start looking after each other as friends again. I know that Sue is glad we're here. She's really scared.''

"Why?'' Andrew asked.

"Why? What happened is awful—''

"Awful, but random. Ellie ran into a killer. For Sue to run into the same person . . .''

"Don't you find it just a little bit scary?'' Brad asked.

"Well, yes, of course, but . . .''

Brad leaned forward suddenly. "What if Sean Black did kill Mandy in a rage?''

Andrew felt uneasy, having had that same thought himself.

"What if?'' Brad repeated. "And he's always had a thing on Lori. I think she was really pining after him when we were dating . . . that was just great on my ego, I can tell you!''

"You want me to tell my sister she can't see Sean Black?'' Andrew inquired.

Brad sat back. "No, no, of course not . . . it's just . . . it's weird. That's all."

Weird. That it was, Andrew thought. He suddenly felt a strange impatience to be away from Brad. He looked at his watch. Nearly three.

"We need to order. I've got—things to do this afternoon. And hell, I almost forgot. What's up? You invited me to lunch," Andrew reminded him.

"Yeah, I know," Brad said. He was hedging, twirling his knife. Andrew found his behavior peculiar. Brad was never at a loss for words. In Lori's grade he and Sean had been the top guys, Brad the star quarterback, Sean the running back. They'd taken turns getting top honors in both sports and academics. Andrew had always been smooth, Sean a little rougher around the edges. In a debate, Andrew decided, he'd back Brad. Left in the wild with one person to help him survive, he'd opt for Sean. He liked Brad, and despite what Brad had just said, he thought that Lori still liked him, too, but then, he was sure that he knew things that Brad didn't. He'd been curious to see what the relationship might be when Lori came back, but she had chosen to cool things years ago—despite everything that happened— and she appeared not just content but pleased that Brad and Jan seemed to have the best—possibly hottest—divorce in history.

"I've got a really weird request for you," Brad said, blue eyes serious on Andrew's, then flicking away as if he feared he might be overheard.

"Shoot."

"Really weird."

"Shoot."

"I need a woman."

Andrew stared at him, then burst into laughter. "Brad, the last thing you need is a woman. Women practically throw themselves at you. What's not to like? If not rich, you're in damned good financial position. Young, great car—you have all your hair. I don't mean to sound immodest, but I can say that I don't do badly myself; however, I'm damned certain you can get your own dates."

"That's not what I mean."

Andrew thought quickly, frowning. "What, you need a cleaning woman or something?"

"No!" Brad sounded as if he were struggling.

He exhaled. "Look, I'm honestly thinking about remarrying Jan—"

"What?" Andrew demanded, baffled. He lifted his hands. "Well, great, more power to you, but don't you kind of have the best of both worlds right now? She's there whenever she wants you, but she can't always get her hands in your pockets anymore—"

"Andrew, she's not a particularly greedy woman—"

"That's not what you said when you divorced."

"We married way too young, and we were both full of ourselves—jealous, and nasty, and furious most of the time."

"Right. And it's not going to happen again?" Andrew asked skeptically.

"That's not the point here. Before I do anything . . ." He broke off. "Andrew, dammit, I want to hire someone."

"A prostitute?"

"Shh!"

"Seriously?" He looked at Brad. That was exactly what Brad had meant.

He lifted his hand. "Hey, ol' buddy, you've lived in these here parts as long as I have. You know where they are—"

"I don't want someone off the street, someone—"

"Real?" Andrew said dryly.

"I'm looking for a high-priced call girl."

Andrew drained his beer. It seemed to burn all the way down his gullet.

He made porno movies. It was a living. It was a way to do the films he really wanted to do.

Yeah, he made porno flicks, the down and dirty kind, he knew the language, the people, the game. Yet even in the midst of nude, slick, oiled "actors," he had never felt as suddenly soul-dirty as he did now.

Brad seemed to think that he was a pimp.

Brad, who'd become ridiculously reticent, considering some of the things they had discussed over the years, was now talking nonstop, explaining what he wanted.

Personally, he didn't think that Brad could really talk Jan into it. But then, what the hell, what did he really know about women?

And maybe he did know the right person for the job. Someone who could consider herself a sex therapist, a marriage counselor, rather than a whore. Someone who liked money, was clean as a whistle, and perfect for the job.

"I know it's weird, but it's just something like an itch I want to scratch, can you help me?" Brad asked.

An itch.

Yeah.

"Sure," Andrew said. "I think I've got just the right person."

"Clean—" Brad began.

"Oh, yeah. Lily-white."

Brad looked as pleased as a well-fed cat.

Andrew felt sick. If he didn't take any money, was he still a slimy pimp?

He could do it. Hell, he'd lived two lives for a very long time. The PBS nature series specialist.

And the XXX king.

Sure. What the hell. He'd done enough other things.

Chapter 11

Since the new bookstore had come in nearby, Susan had been keeping her shop on the Mile open late. She was lucky to employ four excellent managers, two for each store, but since Eric Trainor, her evening manager, was on vacation, she was closing up shop herself. She usually stayed open until ten, right about when the bookstore closed, but since Ellie's terrible death, she had started to close the doors at nine-thirty. If she closed too early, someone might complain, and the city or the merchants' association would be down her throat. But since she didn't have any customers in the shop at the moment . . .

She started switching off her machinery. She was meticulously clean, which was something that made her Coffee, Tea, and Me shops especially popular—not to mention the fact that she did make some of the best coffee-specialty drinks in the business, her own recipes. As she wiped down the counter, the phone rang.

"Coffee, Tea, and Me. Susan speaking, may I help you?"

"Sue."

"Yes?" She recognized the voice but couldn't place it.

"Hi. I'm just calling to check in on you."

Puzzled, she smiled to herself. *That's really nice, but who the hell are you?*

"It's Brad."

"Brad?"

"How quickly we forget. Brad Jackson."

"Oh, Brad, I'm sorry. Thanks for calling, I'm fine, you're being really sweet."

"You're coming to Jan's party tomorrow night, right?"

"You bet. My new college student is going to close for me."

"Close for you—are you alone in there?"

"Yes, but there's really a lot of traffic—foot traffic and cars on the road—thanks to the theater and the bookstore. There are people all around."

"Really?"

"Sure." She looked outside. She didn't see a single car, or a lone soul walking anywhere.

"Will the student be all right?"

"He'll be just fine. He's a linebacker at the University of Miami, working for me because his mother is a friend and he needs to make what money he can on a part-time basis."

"Well, good. But you be careful. And listen, bad things kind of make us all think, you know? If you need anything, feel free to give me a call."

"I will. Thanks."

"See you tomorrow night."

"You bet."

She hung up. As she did so, she decided the hell with the time. She was locking up.

But even as she headed toward the door to close it, she swore softly, seeing a man approaching it. The door opened and she smiled, exhaling on a sigh of relief.

"Andrew! Andrew Kelly."

"Hi, Sue. How's it going?"

She stared at him, shaking her head. "You'll never guess who was just on the phone."

"Who?"

"Brad."

"Jackson."

"The same."

Andrew flushed. "Checking up on you?"

"Yes." She stared at him a moment, then sighed. "You're doing the same, huh?"

"No, no, I just happened to be in the neighborhood."

"You liar."

"I do live near here—"

"And I'll bet you haven't actually been on the Mile in a good ten years."

He flushed. "Not true. I checked out the bookstore when it opened."

"Want a cup of coffee?"

"Yeah."

"Sure. What kind?"

"Um . . . I don't know. The coffee kind."

She laughed. "French roast, rich and hearty, it will keep you up all night."

He sat at the spotless counter. She poured him coffee. "Thanks, Sue."

"No, thank you. You are checking up on me, and I appreciate it."

He shrugged and smiled awkwardly. Sue wondered what had happened between them. They'd had a good thing going once upon a time. But after Mandy had died . . .

"You were the first love of my life, you know," he told her.

"I was your first sex," she corrected.

"No, Kitty Armstrong was my first, Sally Oakley was my second. I should have been pretty good by the time I got to you," he said, laughing.

"You were," she told him. "You were just fine. Maybe too good. I expected other guys to live up to you."

"Ah, Sue . . ."

"Hey, it's all right, don't get maudlin. I'm grateful to have friends right now. I—" She broke off, looking out the glass panes that separated the shop from the street. "Andrew, someone just walked by . . . kind of furtively."

He got up right away, sharp, attentive, and strode toward the door.

"Andrew, wait! Don't go off half-cocked like that! People have guns these days—"

But her words went unheeded. He flung the door open.

"My God!" she heard him exclaim.

The day should have been great. Brendan and Tina had enjoyed every aspect of Michael's tour, and Brendan had assured Michael that he was going to major in marine biology. Tina became convinced that she was destined to be either a vet or an animal behaviorist.

At five, they had met Jan at Marker 88. The food was delicious, all of them opting for fresh fish prepared in different ways, and sharing an array of appetizers that were excellent. Lori didn't have to do much to keep the conversation going because the kids spent the entire dinner telling Jan about their day, making Michael repeat his thorough explanations of various aspects of sea life. Jan was as comfortable and natural as could be with both Sean and Michael, and Lori found herself thinking that Jan was their real friend—she believed in Sean and accepted Michael.

And she had never betrayed Sean in any way.

The only one who noticed that Lori was quiet was Sean, and he didn't say anything. He just watched her with enigmatic eyes, and she had no idea what he was thinking.

While the adults indulged in after-dinner coffees, the kids went out to watch the sunset from the dock. Jan talked about her party with enthusiasm, then remarked that she was still worried about Susan, who had seemed so upset.

"I guess we're all going to be staying out of the clubs for a while now," she said.

Sean shrugged. "I imagine that women will be safe enough if they stay together—in a crowd of at least three."

"How can you be certain about that?" Lori demanded. "What if someone has a gun? You can control half a dozen people with a gun!"

He shook his head. "This killer doesn't use a gun. He uses the element of surprise and then . . ."

"Then what?" Jan demanded.

"A knife," Sean said quietly.

"How do you know?" Jan asked dismayed. "I mean, how can you know just exactly—"

"Because I was at the autopsy," Sean said briefly.

"Oh," Jan said, her mouth forming a circle.

Lori studied him. "Why?" she asked him. "Because of Ricky, because of your books?"

He shrugged. "Well, that, and—"

"My little brother turned out to be a true student of science," Michael said. "He has a doctorate in forensic anthropology. Seems some of your M.E.'s in Dade County like to read, and happen to know some of the people Sean has worked with in the past."

Lori watched Sean, wondering just what kind of work he'd done in the past. So much time had gone by. She thought that she knew a lot about him, his past, and what made him tick. But she had missed the years when the young adult had matured into a man, and so she didn't really know him at all.

And yet she knew that she liked him still. And that she was more attracted to him than she had ever been before.

"I didn't know we had an expert in murder in our midst!" Jan said.

"Not an expert," Sean said. He shrugged. "But being accused of the deed does make you interested in the subject of proving guilt and innocence. Think we should head back? Hey, Mike, thanks, it was a really great day."

Lori echoed the thank-you.

"Shucks," Michael said, "come more often!"

Outside, Michael said good-bye to the kids, who happily fawned all over him and gave him more thanks. He finally managed to get into his Jeep and head south.

Lori was dismayed when the kids both opted to ride with Jan so that she wouldn't have to make the drive alone. She didn't want to be with Sean alone. It was very strange to feel such a physical excitement alongside an awkward emotional fear. Not that dating was ever easy . . .

But Sean didn't press any issues. He drove in silence, his eyes on the road. She found herself staring at her hands, then instigating a conversation.

"Sean?"

"Yes?"

"Thanks. Really, thanks. This was great for Brendan. I thought it would be so difficult, moving him here, but Tina has helped to make it easy, and today sure made the area look great."

"Michael was the one with the magic touch."

"Yes, but thanks for . . ."

"Making you come down for the day."

"Yes. It's been strange to come home."

"Damned strange. I arrived, Ellie was murdered—and you were here."

"It's all coincidence."

"Mmm."

"It has to be coincidence. I mean, you published a book and came on tour. I came home because of Gramps. And Ellie was murdered because she happened to be in the wrong place at the wrong time, and the police will get the guy," Lori said determinedly.

"We can hope."

"You don't sound sure," Lori said.

He shrugged, hesitating. "Statistics aren't always in favor of killers being caught."

"But . . . this guy is crazy. Surely. He'll have to trip himself up somehow."

He studied the road. "Lori, you've got to be careful. Really careful."

"I'm always careful."

"More careful than ever. You don't have an alarm system."

"I will."

"Let me loan you the money."

"What makes you think I need the money?" she demanded irritably. "I have a teaching post waiting, and I'm paid very well for my designs, thank you—"

"And it's an expensive world."

"My folks are well-off, you know," she reminded him coolly.

"How could I ever forget?" he asked her quietly.

"That again. You've got a chip on your shoulder as big as a boulder—"

"Well, you did drop a few rocks on me."

"I did. *I* did, all by myself?"

He was silent, staring straight ahead. Then he suddenly seemed to explode, his voice modulated but harsh, his knuckles white on the steering wheel. "A chip on my shoulder? No, I really shouldn't have a chip, and you know what? Usually I don't. But let's see, how did I get into all this? First, because I was thrown in jail. I had a kid for a public defender, fresh out of school, who was smart, who tried but who was intimidated by the tough, experienced district attorneys set to try the case. Then, let's see—some time in the Dade County jail, with every cutthroat, deviant, and sick cold-blooded murderer out there. There were the pictures they threw at me daily. Mandy's ankle, Mandy's face, Mandy's eyes, on the autopsy table. While all the rich, respectable kids sat home in a protected silence, all bonded together, nice as could be."

"Ahh, so at last I can tell what regard you have for me," Lori breathed.

He lifted one of his hands off the wheel. "I'm supposed to be sorry for being angry when I was the only one accused out of that many people?"

"Well, you were dating her!"

"I was done dating her."

"Conveniently."

"You of all people know that's the truth!"

"But—"

"But what?" he demanded harshly.

"But it's over! And I can't go back, and I sure as hell can't change things. So if you're going to resent everyone, you should just leave. You're the great Sean Black. You've beaten all the odds, you made something out of yourself, you met adversity head-on, and you climbed out of the gutter and up a damned mountain. Just who the hell do you think you are to be so stinking self-righteous—"

"I am *not* self-righteous!" he broke in furiously.

"The hell you're not!"

They were suddenly both silent. Lori found that she was shaking, and she didn't know if it was with anger or guilt. What the hell was she doing? Making matters far worse than they ever needed to be?

"You're going seventy, and the speed here is forty-five miles an hour," she murmured.

"I'm going sixty and the speed limit is fifty."

"Oh, good, let's argue about this, too."

"Lori, I'm sorry, you can't begin to understand—"

"Because you won't give anyone else credit for understanding, and you can't begin to understand yourself what others were going through," she interrupted.

"Well, forgive me. Try a few autopsies and a couple of nights in the Dade County jail," he murmured.

"And you should try—" she began and broke off.

"Try what?"

"Nothing."

"Lori—"

"Nothing. You're right, no one's experiences compare with yours."

"Damn you, that's not what I'm saying."

"It's exactly what you're saying."

He fell silent. She heard him gritting his teeth; his knuckles remained whitely wound around the steering wheel. He drove fast but competently—not too far over the speed limit.

They reached the turnpike and rode the distance from Florida City to Lori's house in dead silence. When he drove into her yard, she was startled to see a Metro-Dade police cruiser sitting in her front yard.

"Oh, my God, there's been an accident. Something has happened, Jan had an accident with the kids—" Lori blurted in a panic.

Sean shook his head, setting his hand on hers to calm her. She nearly jumped a mile high at the touch.

"No," he said softly. "It's just Ricky. He's come for me."

"Why? Why would Ricky be looking for you—and at my house?"

"I'm not sure," Sean said, and stepped out of the car.

Sue sighed softly; she'd been about to scream. Andrew Kelly was laughing.

"It's Jeff."

"Jeff?"

"Jeff Olin."

Sue smiled. It was great to have friends. Jeff had come right from work, it appeared. He walked in wearing a three-piece suit, loosening his tie, his smile handsome and rueful. "Hey, Sue."

"I know. You just had a sudden, uncontrollable urge for coffee, right?"

Jeff grinned at Andrew. "I guess Ellie's funeral was a shake-up for all of us. You were in such bad shape, Sue. Not physically—I mean, you look like a million bucks, but . . ."

"Thanks, that's nice, Jeff."

"You do look great," Andrew assured her.

"And you're just two of the most glorious hunks I've ever seen, and better than that, you're being the world's best friends."

"One of us can give you a ride home."

"Thanks. I've got my car. If one of you wants to follow me home, that would be great. I'm probably just being a big scaredy cat, right? Ellie disappeared from a club, so this monster probably crawls around bars and nightspots rather than coffeehouses, don't you think?"

"Right," Jeff agreed. "And you know what? I hear that you do make incredible gourmet coffee."

"Want some?"

"Of course."

"What's Andrew drinking?"

"French roast. Have the same?"

"Hell, no, I'll have something different," Jeff told her.

She smiled. "Friends are good," she told them, and poured Jeff a cup of Colombian gold.

Sean saw that Ricky wasn't alone. They really might have been back in high school—Ted Neeson, tall and lanky now and usually a little quiet in Ricky's presence, was with him. Ted was in his City of Coral Gables uniform. Ricky was in jeans and a T-shirt.

"Hi, Lori, Sean!" Ricky called, striding toward the rental Olds.

"Is anything wrong?" Lori asked anxiously.

"No, nothing," Ricky told her.

"Then how, what—"

"We were just looking for Sean."

"How'd you know I'd be here?" Sean asked. Lori still looked distressed, hazel eyes wide and glittering, face pale. Even worried, he thought, inwardly growling at his libido—Lori was looking great. She'd maintained what he considered a perfect female figure—she managed to be tall and slim and curved all at the same time. It had been a hell of a long time since he'd touched her, and he'd been drunk at the time, but it was odd how he remembered the way she felt, the full firmness of her breasts in his hands, the hollows at her hipbones . . .

Hell! This was definitely not a time to remember how her fingers had brushed him with such inadvertent intimacy.

"What's up, Ricky, Ted?" Sean asked. "How'd you know I'd be here?"

"Jan told Brad she was meeting you down in the Keys for dinner," Ricky said. "Sorry, Lori, I didn't mean to scare you. I was about to drop Ted off, and decided to ride by and see if I could catch you."

"There hasn't been another murder?" Lori asked anxiously.

Ricky looked at her, a strange expression in his eyes, then he shook his head. "There's always a murder somewhere, unfortunately. But no, not here, not that I'm aware of." Ricky turned to Sean. "Gillespie asked me to see if you'd come back in," he said. "That's all."

"Gillespie?" Lori murmured, confused.

"The medical examiner," Sean explained, not looking at her. "Is it any kind of an emergency?" he asked Ricky.

"She's not down at the morgue waiting for you now, no," Ricky said. "But she would like to see you in the morning."

"Sure."

"Why?" Lori demanded.

"She has old bones she wants to play sleuth with, that's all," Sean said. "How's it going in Coral Gables, Ted?" he asked, determinedly changing the direction of the conversation.

"Good, thanks. We're still mostly after traffic offenders, a few kids wandering the streets. A few more home invasions in the last few years—some violent deaths in the last decade, but knock on wood, not many," Ted said cheerfully. "I'm glad you bought this old place, Lori," he told her. "Nice neighborhood, good for you and for your boy."

"Thanks, Ted. It's great so far."

"It needs an alarm," Sean said.

"Well, you're in the right place as far as I'm concerned," Ted told her. "I happen to know all the guys on the force, and we'll keep an eye out for you."

"Thanks, that's good to know," Lori said.

"Speaking of which . . . we were about to take a ride to Sue's shop, make sure she closes up okay," Ricky said. "Want to come for the ride? She makes great coffee?"

"I have to wait for Brendan," Lori said. "He's in Jan's car."

As she spoke, Jan pulled into the drive. Like Lori, she instantly frowned at the sight of the police cruiser, jumping out of her car with a worried "What's wrong?"

"Nothing, social visit!" Ricky called to her. "Don't go getting your panties in a snarl, Jan."

She flashed Ricky a glance that assured him that although he might be on the Metro Dade homicide squad, he had not come so far from the 4F days. "Everything's all right?"

"Everything's all right," Lori said.

"We're about to go to Sue's for coffee. Want to come?" Ted invited.

"Sue's—coffee now?" Jan said, frowning.

"I think that the guys are being nice he-men, and that we should applaud them," Lori told her, smiling.

Jan shrugged. "It's a little late, but . . ."

Brendan and Tina were standing just behind Jan. Brendan stepped forward. "Mom, would you mind if Tina and I just vegged out and watched a little television until you all came back?"

Sean was somewhat startled to see that Lori glanced his way, almost as if she were asking his opinion. Not to lose the moment, he quickly spoke up. "Lock yourselves safely in," he advised.

"Don't open the door to anyone," Lori added sternly.

"Of course not, Mom." His glance at Tina stated that grown-ups were overly paranoid but it was best to humor them.

"Want to all go in the cruiser?" Ricky asked.

"I think I'll take my own car. Jan, Lori—want to drive with me?"

"Sure," Lori said.

Again, to his surprise, she slid into the front seat. Next to him. Jan slid in beside her.

Her arm brushed his. Little tendrils of her hair brushed his flesh. He was glad that the denim jeans he had changed to were of a heavy material. He locked his jaw, looked ahead, and revved the car into motion.

Sue, looking out the window as she chatted with Jeff and Andrew, suddenly started to laugh.

"What is it?" Andrew asked.

Sue smiled at him. "Your cousin Josh is coming from one direction, and your sister is coming from the other direction with Sean and Jan, and our neighborhood cops—Ricky and Ted—are coming in right behind them."

"You're kidding," Andrew said, rising.

"I guess I'd better put on more coffee."

"Hey, Sue," Lori said, opening the door. She flashed a smile at her brother and Jeff while the others piled in behind her. "Hey, Andrew. And Josh!" She ruffled her brother's hair and kissed her cousin on the cheek. Sue smiled, remembering just how wildly she'd been in love with Andrew Kelly back in high school, and how she, Jan, and Lori had talked endlessly about their hopes and dreams and fantasies. The Kellys were still remarkable. Lori had always been a beauty with her blond hair and tawny eyes; likewise, Andrew was as solidly sexy as an adult as he had been as a football hero. Josh Kelly, a bit leaner, still had a subtle grace and appeal. He had been captain of the debate team, Sue remembered. One hell of a talker. He was probably one damned good lawyer. Ellie had told her that she knew a number of girls Josh had dated, and that he'd talked his way into bed with every one of them.

"Hiya, Susie," Josh said, grinning. "Coffee smells great!"

"This sudden craving for coffee is just amazing!" Sue said. "But thank you, all of you, very much."

Sean looked at Andrew and Josh, shrugged, smiled. "Great minds think alike, or something like that."

"And, just think. It's safe as all hell—the cops are already here," Ricky put in.

"Safe? That's not the way I hear it—regarding you, Ricky Garcia!" Jan teased.

"He started those rumors himself," Ted told her.

"Well, we are all here," Jan said. She grinned at Sue. "I'm supposed to be having the party, you know," she teased.

"And don't you dare renege on it. I can't wait. And I'm sure you're going to have much better food, since I'm out of everything but day-old bagels and croissants," Sue said.

"Pizza!" Another voice suddenly announced from the door.

"Brad!" Jan said, startled.

"In the flesh," he agreed.

"What are you doing here?" Jan demanded.

"I called Lori's house to find out why you all weren't back yet, and Brendan told me you had come here. Seriously. I worked hard today and I'm famished. Let's order a pizza."

"Fine, I'll call down the street. They're open until midnight," Sue said happily. She picked up the phone and dialed, while the group lined up at her counter began to call out suggested toppings.

"No anchovies!" Josh insisted.

"We have to have anchovies," Ted complained.

"Anything but onions," Jan said.

"Oh, man, gotta have onions," Ricky protested.

"How about one plain cheese, one with meat, and one with onions and anchovies?" Lori suggested.

"If I can repeat all that!" Sue agreed, laughing.

When the pizzas arrived, the group ate, talked, laughed. In the middle of biting into a piece deliciously loaded, Sue looked up and exclaimed, "I don't believe it!"

"What?" Sean inquired, his eyes narrowed. Sue smiled at him. For all of his success, good looks, and usual confidence, Sean could still be very tense. Well, could she blame him? There was a time when the D.A.'s office had been threatening the electric chair.

"Your brother is here."

"My brother?" Sean said, astounded.

Michael Black stepped into the coffee shop, grinning sheepishly. "I thought the party was tomorrow night!"

"It is!" Jan assured him.

"What are you doing here?" Sean demanded.

Hands on hips, he told Jan, "I'm not supposed to spill the beans, but your daughter left her little knapsack in the changing room. There were prescription glasses in it along with her assignment notebook, and I was afraid that she might get in some trouble at school."

"Oh, Michael! You drove all the way up here for that! I'm so sorry!" Jan protested.

"It's okay, don't worry. I do the drive often enough—what the hell, it's only an hour and a half," Michael teased.

"She's always leaving things," Brad said, shaking his head. "When they're not attached to her, she just leaves them. Thanks, Mike, that was really nice."

"Honest to God, no bother. And, please, don't say anything. When the kids told me that you all were here, I told them I'd think of a story that wouldn't get Tina into trouble. I remember being that age."

"She should be grounded," Brad said.

"Can't ground her. You'll turn Michael into a rat if you do," Sean advised.

"But an hour and a half drive!" Jan protested.

"It's okay, honest, as long as there's pizza left," Michael said happily.

"Tons!" Sue assured him. "And what's your choice of coffee drink? The hot stuff, or an icy mocha, a mochaccino, a latte on ice—"

"Damn, I'm going to have to drive up more often," Michael said, taking a seat at the counter.

"Can I have another of these mochaccino things?" Ted asked.

"Sure."

"I'll help you," Lori said.

"I guess I'll set feminine rights back about twenty years and get up and do the woman-pours-the-coffee thing, too," Jan said with a yawn, rising.

"Oh, yeah, madam domesticity!" Brad groaned.

"Stuff it," Jan protested.

"Oh, baby!" he said huskily.

Jan sighed with impatience.

Sue smiled, happy. All her friends were there. It was like high school—they were all grown-up, but that didn't mean they were all mature! she thought affectionately. It was great. She'd been so scared. She'd felt so alone. And now, now . . . well, now she felt unbelievably warm and safe!

Asses.

They were all such asses!

The killer watched Sue flush, flip back her hair, gush all over. Little bird, foolish little bird. She was just like the others, didn't care what came out of her mouth, didn't care what she did, what she said. She'd sleep with a damned orangutan now just to feel that someone was watching over her.

Safe!

She thought she was safe.

In the bosom of her friends . . .

Well, she would see. And that was half the thrill of it, of course, seeing their faces when they realized they weren't safe at all.

Chapter 12

It had been a long, full day.

After Sean had dropped her off and Jan had left with Tina, Lori had started out to take a long, luxurious shower, washing her hair, letting the hot water steam over her. But then, strangely enough, she had begun to feel uneasy in the shower—certain that someone was lurking just outside the bathroom door.

Logically, she convinced herself that it couldn't be, but her mood was ruined, she was entirely spooked, and so she rinsed her hair and body quickly, turned off the deliciously steamy cascade of water, wrapped in her terry robe, and stepped out of the shower. She didn't dry her hair at first; she was too anxious to get to Brendan's room.

Brendan was sound asleep. It had been a great day for him. Sun, sea, and dozens of animals. Long, long hours. He was happily exhausted. She closed his door softly, leaving him sleeping.

She brushed and dried her hair, but the blow-dryer seemed to be making too much noise. She turned it off—listening.

She wasn't sure what she was listening for.

"Stop this!" she told herself. In the mirror her eyes looked too big. Frightened.

She sighed. Okay, so she did need an alarm. She couldn't borrow money from Sean. She could borrow money from her folks. Better yet, if she was going to be this panicky, she could just move in with her folks.

Well, maybe not. She loved them, but . . .

There was Gramps, of course. She was due to take him to the clinic in the morning, she reminded herself. She needed to get some sleep, to be wide awake and alert. She wanted to talk to his doctor, and with doctors these days she needed to be fast.

"I need to go to bed," she told her reflection.

But she was wide awake.

"There is nothing, no one, in the house," she told herself.

But just then she heard a thumping noise.

Coming from downstairs.

Coming from *inside* the house.

Two miles away, Sue Nichols remained awake as well. It had been great to have everyone at her shop. Just like homecoming. She hadn't been nervous in the least.

But now, in her pretty little ranch house where she was usually so happy . . .

She was nervous.

She was alone.

Late-night television failed to entertain her. She sat with Miss Priss—her white Persian cat—on her lap. If only she could curl up with the total ease of her feline—and sleep. She'd made decaf everything that night, but she might as well have consumed a ton of caffeine. No-doze pills, or some kind of uppers. She was just frightened, she told herself.

She nearly jumped a mile high—practically throwing an irate and squealing Miss Priss to the ceiling—when she heard a soft tapping on the door.

Standing by the sofa, she thought quickly. Should she dial 911? And what? Tell the emergency operator that someone was knocking on her door?

She looked around her living room. Her glass doors were locked; the brocade drapes were in place. No one could peek in at her. She kept her house as immaculate as her shops, and just as organized. All of her windows locked. Her doors had several bolts. She was safe.

But the tapping came again.

She walked to the door. If she ignored the tapping, whoever it was might just go away.

"Sue?"

She breathed a sigh of relief, recognizing the voice. She opened the door, smiling.

He had come.

How nice. Her heart began to flutter, responding to the expression in his eyes.

"Hey!"

He looked at her sheepishly. "Hey. Sorry, I know it's late, but . . . well, I just wanted to check in."

"I'm okay."

"I don't mean to be keeping you awake."

"I was wide awake. I don't know why."

"Then good. We can be awake together."

The way that he looked at her . . . God, he was so damned good-looking. And yet, oh Lord, what a fool she'd make of herself if she jumped him!

"I'm glad you're here," she told him.

He smiled. Then suddenly, he reached out for her, drew her to him. He was smiling still as his face lowered to hers, questioning her with his eyes, with the curve of his lips.

She laughed nervously. It seemed like forever since she'd been with a man. Actually, it had been only about six months ago, but that had been bad, a one-night stand with a clod who had pumped for all of two seconds like a broken jack, then snored until she freaked out, shook him awake, and sent him out of her house forever.

And now . . .

She had this opportunity. This fabulous opportunity to have good sex with a fabulous guy without a two-foot beer belly or a penchant for farting.

Sad but true. As she had gotten older, her requirements had slipped. The guy didn't usually have to be much—just clean and reasonably presentable, and capable of going a few hours without creating body emissions. And now tonight . . . she felt very young, innocent. She felt like laughing.

"You horny, too?" he asked wistfully.

"Oh, you betcha!" she said. She threw her arms around him. They kissed and kissed. She touched him all over, relishing the feel of firm muscle and smooth, toned flesh. She thought she was going to die as he played with her breasts, slipped his hand between her legs. . . .

"Oh, man, oh, baby . . . you're wetter than a slip-'n'-slide," he murmured huskily. "Where's the bedroom?"

Dazed, she pointed.

It was something out of a dream. He swept her up into his arms and carried her. Laid her down, stripped off her clothes, then manipulated her on the bed into a position he liked. He sighed, telling her how much she was turning him on. Then he paused, and she heard him ripping open a foil packet.

"It's—it's all right," she offered, suddenly feeling shy. "I'm—protected."

He lay down beside her, smoothing back her hair. "No, baby, I always use my own form of protection, for both of us, you know?"

She nodded, deliciously floating. She didn't gave a damn how he did it, as long as he did. . . .

The killer was amused. Man, she'd do anything. Anything at all. How long had it been since she'd had any? A while, that was for sure.

But it was amusing. There were some functions a woman definitely performed better alive than dead. Still, what a damned cunt. Like the others. She'd probably strip naked and bend over for him in the middle of the street if he asked.

At one point his fingers curled around her throat.

It would be easy. So easy . . .

Just press down and watch her eyes.

Maybe, maybe . . .

Wait? Or kill her now. Wait?

Or kill her now?

Lori slowly moved downstairs, one of Brendan's hockey sticks raised as a weapon as she tiptoed, praying the old steps and floorboards wouldn't creak.

She regretted at that moment that the house was shaped around a courtyard. She could possibly move in a circle—or square—for hours, one step behind an intruder all the while.

Or perhaps she'd run into the intruder immediately, and he would kill her before she could take more than a few steps.

Paranoid! she accused herself. She had just heard a noise . . . in an empty house. Not empty, Brendan was here. But he was upstairs. Sleeping like the dead. Oh, God, what if he—no, no! She had to run back up, check to make sure that he was breathing.

She had no choice. She eased her way quickly back up the stairs to Brendan's room. She bent over her son as he slept, set her hand on his chest.

Yes, he was breathing. Softly, deeply, his chest rising and falling. She felt like an idiot, but she was still afraid. She *had* heard a thump.

Once again Lori tiptoed down the stairs. She started into the living room, dining room, kitchen, family, office. She hesitated there, seeing that her sketchbook had fallen off the easel. That must have been the source of the noise.

But why had it fallen?

She stood dead still in the darkened office while the seconds and

then minutes ticked by. She still couldn't shake the feeling that someone was in—or had been in—the house. At long last she reached for
the telephone, called Sean's hotel, and asked for his room. To her
dismay, his phone rang and rang, and then a voice-message service
picked up. "Sean!" she whispered. Then, "Never mind, sorry!" she
added, and hung up.

What to do?

Stand in the office all night, afraid to move?

No, she was going upstairs. To sleep. There was no one here, and
that was that.

She walked upstairs, went into Brendan's room, and assured herself that her son was fine. She sat by his bed, in the darkness, afraid
to leave him, not willing to wake him and possibly make a complete
idiot of herself in front of her one and only precious child.

Long minutes passed. She began to relax a bit, leaning her head
back. Her eyes closed. She began to drift.

Then she heard it again. A thumping downstairs, or was it outside?

She bolted from the floor, racing toward Brendan's door, forced
herself to pause, to breathe. She stood very still in his doorway,
listening, trying to force her heart to stop beating so loudly that she
couldn't possibly hear.

She heard it again, softly. Thump, thump.

Then, just when she was about to lose control and scream, she
heard another sound. A tapping. Soft but insistent on her front door.

She flew down the stairs. The tapping continued. She heard her
name.

"Lori? Lori, it's me. Sean."

She lunged at the door, twisted the bolts, and threw it open. Hair
barely settled, eyes wide, she stared at him.

"Sean!" she whispered.

"Lori!" he whispered back.

"What—what—what are you doing here?" she demanded.

"You called," he reminded her pointedly.

"Yes." She nodded. "But you weren't there."

"I got your message and came right over."

"Right." She said, staring at him. Then she reached out, grabbing
his shoulder. "Get in here!"

"Yes, ma'am!"

"Please."

"I'm in."

He was in. She had him standing in the foyer.

"What's the matter?" He still was whispering.

"A bumping."

"What?"

"I keep hearing a bumping."

"Well, let's have a look."

"I'll get the hockey stick."

"The hockey stick?"

"We need a weapon," she insisted.

"Lori, how long have you heard this thumping sound?"

"The first time was a while ago. My sketch pad had fallen in the office—"

"Show me."

"The hockey stick—"

"I don't think that there's any one in here."

"How do you know?"

"Listen, go back upstairs, okay? Wait in Brendan's room."

"Sean—"

"Lori—"

"I've seen too many slasher movies. If I leave you—"

"You'll be with your son. Want to leave him alone?"

She wanted to kick him, but he was right. She turned around and headed for the stairs, racing silently up them on her bare feet. She hurried into Brendan's room, checked him, and came back to his door. She stood just outside it, barely daring to breathe.

Soon, she saw the lights coming on downstairs. She moved to the wrought iron railing, looking over it to the foyer.

"Sean?"

He came below her, smiling up at her from the foyer. "You've got a visitor."

"What?"

"A little kitten. Brendan must have put him in a box, but he wasn't inclined to stay."

"*A kitten?* I've nearly had heart failure over a kitten?"

"Come down. See for yourself."

She hurried down the stairs. Half hidden behind some still un-opened crates in the office area was a cardboard box. Air holes had been punched into it, and a saucer filled with milk had been set in it, along with an old T-shirt. The kitten, however, a little striped gray, was in Sean's arms, squealing away.

"A kitten!" Lori said, shaking her head with disgust. "I'm going to tear his hair out! Why didn't he tell me?"

"Maybe he meant to. He was probably just wiped out."

"He was half asleep when he got back tonight, but still, I can't believe he just picked up a stray and forgot to tell me!"

"Lori, don't be too mad at him. There're a lot worse trouble boys can get into at that age. Thirteen is tough."

"Fourteen," she said distractedly.

"Fourteen?"

"He just turned fourteen," she said.

"He's a great kid."

She nodded. "I don't mind a kitten. It's just that—I'm already so jumpy."

"You need an alarm."

"All right, all right, I admit, I need an alarm. I'll get one."

"I told you—"

"I'm fine financially," she lied. She smoothed back her hair. "Um . . . thanks for coming over."

"Don't mention it," he told her. His voice was deep, husky. The lazy sound of it seemed to brush along the length of her spine. Leaning against the door that separated the office from the kitchen, he studied her with an amused half smile as he stroked the kitten. He wore worn jeans that hugged his figure nicely and a tailored denim shirt with the sleeves rolled up and the front buttons down, exposing his throat and a V of his chest. There was something so naturally masculine and sensual about the way he stood there that Lori felt an alarming wave of heat radiate through her limbs.

Desperate to get a grip, she nonchalantly stepped forward. "Here, let me put this little invader back in his box," she said, scooping the kitten from his arms and nestling it in with the soft T-shirt. "You might have ruined my exclusive designs, do you realize?"

She straightened, turning to look at Sean. "I guess—" she began.

Her terry robe, tied only with a terry belt, chose that moment to untie. Sean remained against the door frame, casual, his gaze flickering slowly over the length of her before meeting hers once again. For long seconds he didn't move. His eyes darkened. Somehow she missed the obvious. She retied the robe.

His eyes remained locked with hers, and still neither of them moved.

He waited.

Then, apparently, he'd waited long enough.

He left the doorway and came to her. Lifting her chin with his thumb and forefinger, he kissed her lips. Very lightly at first. And still she felt the explosive heat in his touch, in his body, so close to hers. She wanted to step quickly back in panic, and she wanted to leap on him, feel his length with her nakedness. But as his lips rose above hers she whispered, "We—can't do this. We can't do this. We can't . . . honestly, we just can't."

He didn't seem to be paying attention. His hands slid into the opening of the robe. He had long hands, with long, tapering fingers. Powerful hands, bronzed from the sun, they were dark against her breasts as they cradled and stroked her flesh. His palms were rough against her nipples, creating a shower of sparks that became a stream of liquid heat, cascading down to settle as a searing ache between her thighs. His lips touched hers again, found her throat, followed an erotic trail along the valley between her breasts. He came down upon a knee before her, hands on her hips, lips and tongue moving lower. Her hands fell on the top of his head, fingers digging into the richness of his dark hair. "We can't . . . do this . . ." she repeated.

This . . . so different, yet the same. Some instinct remained within her that wanted him in the same way she had all those years ago. Wanted to touch him, feel his flesh sliding along her own, luxuriate in the heat of his body pressed against the warmth of her own. It was all the same, yet she'd been so inept then, not even really knowing what she'd wanted until she got it. And now, of course, she knew, but this was too fast, and she was so afraid of the lies of the past and . . .

"Oh . . ."

His hand stroked the flesh of her inner thigh, higher, lower, higher, lower, until his fingers and tongue were intimately between her. Her fingers had a death grip on his hair; her limbs and body were trembling. She couldn't stand, her protests were inarticulate. He had taken her from zero to sixty in split seconds, and she raced at a dizzying speed toward a sweet oblivion. He was entirely focused on her, his touch exquisitely experienced. She thought she was going to die on her feet, explode into a thousand pieces of glass and shatter to the floor.

She was dismayed by the force of the climax that ripped through her, choking back a scream that had formed in her throat. He stood, catching her in his arms when she might well have fallen, finding her lips in a heartbreakingly slow, tender kiss that tasted of all the years she had been alone and hungered for exactly this.

Her arms were around him. She clung to him.

Then to her amazement, he disentangled himself from her arms and turned away, walking through the kitchen toward the front of the house.

A cool wave of humiliation and anger washed over her. She wrenched her robe into place, passed him in the den, and walked through to the front door, opening it.

"Thanks. Thanks so much for coming over. I'm delighted to be such a source of amusement. Please, don't come again."

He stood still. He was smiling. "Actually, I'm not the one who—"

"Get out."

"Lori," he said patiently, "we're downstairs. You were right. You have a son, I was way out of line."

She exhaled on a long breath. He came over to her at last, closing the door. He touched her face lightly with the knuckle of his forefinger. "And then, I admit to being afraid."

"Afraid?" she breathed.

"I wanted to be with you from the time I saw you standing in that school hallway, your little nose up in the air as you tried to determine how you were going to deal with Ricky Garcia's aggression. I knew I was never good enough for the Kellys—"

"Don't say that, Sean," she murmured uncomfortably, her eyes falling. She moved her face so that his hand fell away, and she spoke with her eyes still averted from his. "I—I love my folks—"

"You should love them. And appreciate the fact that you have them. But they were down on me."

"They're not, really."

"They were. Maybe they're not now. I hope it doesn't matter now. I hope that you feel enough of what I feel to want to give this a chance, and that we're both old enough and mature enough to stand on our own feet, make our own decisions. I thought I should stay. On the couch. You were really unhinged when I got here. That's another thing. I really did take advantage of the situation . . . I'm sorry."

She didn't say anything. He was silent as well, so she looked at him again at last.

"Lori, now you're supposed to say that you wanted me to take advantage of the situation."

She smiled. "I . . ."

"Never mind. Want to get me some pillows and sheets? Or do you want me to go? I'd really feel better if you'd let me stay. I don't want you to be afraid—"

"I was afraid. And I do need to get some sleep. I've got a session with my grandfather in the morning. I'll fix up the couch," she said without hesitation. "Thanks."

She hurried up the stairs to the hallway linen closet, found extra bedding, and hurried back down. She started to make up the sofa, but he stopped her. "I can do it."

"Okay." She left the bedding and backed toward the door leading to the foyer and the stairs. "Thanks again for staying."

"Sure. Is that all?"

Lori frowned. "I don't know what you mean."

He absently smoothed back dark hair that had fallen over an eye. "You're supposed to say, you were terrific."

Blood rushed to her cheeks. She watched him for several seconds, then shrugged. "Thanks," she said huskily. "You were terrific."

Then she turned and sped up the stairs.

Lori Kelly's new house, Lori in it.

Sean in it.

Interesting. And what a way to go. Let Sean get his rocks off . . . leave his fingerprints everywhere, his semen, maybe even cut himself shaving . . .

Let it happen. And when Sean left, he could slip into Lori's house. . . .

Easy. The old place had no alarm.

There was the boy.

Just a boy, easily subdued, and if he could do the mother, why not the son?

Why not? He could make her watch, or make the boy watch what he did with her, one way or the other. . . .

He frowned, realizing suddenly that he needed more and more for the real thrill. At first it had been just seeing the terror he could instill. Then he had needed the real kill, and then to feel the blood against his flesh, warm, hot, in a rush. . . .

He liked the careful planning as well, he realized. Fooling the police, his friends—fooling everyone. Fooling his victims until the last possible minutes . . . then watching. The alarm, the fear, the disbelief, the despair . . .

But this . . .

This might well be the ultimate. Lori, his toy, until he tired of her. Killed her.

Then seeing Sean Black squirm . . .

And this time he would surely fry in Old Sparky. Maybe his head would even catch fire in the electric chair, as had been known to happen. He sat there and laughed suddenly. Death-penalty opponents had called the state's electric chair "dangerous." Well, what the hell was the damned thing supposed to be? If it all happened fast enough, there could be the rich, famous Sean Black, a.k.a. Michael Shayne, burning in the electric chair, protesting his innocence while his brains fried. . . .

It was just fucking perfect.

Chapter 13

Sean hadn't fallen asleep. He'd stripped down to his briefs and jeans, and lay on the couch, studying the ceiling. Life suddenly seemed damned good. Not that the years past hadn't been all right; he had managed to do well enough. He'd liked anthropology, and he liked writing, liked the people with whom he worked, the travel that was part of it all.

Things were just better now. Maybe he'd been running for a very long time, and discovered that he could never really run fast enough or far enough to escape the past. And maybe he'd been searching for something he had almost had once and needed to find again. What the hell. It was good to be home. Here. And lie on a couch somewhat frustrated, but still feeling the taste of the woman who had always fascinated him.

He heard a rustling sound, tensed, then smiled.

The kitten.

"Hey, thanks, cat," he murmured aloud. And Brendan—he owed the boy for bringing in the stray and forgetting to tell his mother.

He frowned, suddenly certain that he had heard a noise from outside. He rose in the darkness and moved to the window. Nothing. It was a pretty street, lots of foliage, bougainvillea from pastel shades to deep purple crawling over cement fences, brickwork, and the houses themselves. Sea grape tree, royal poincianas, and old oaks lined the walkways. Lots of trees.

Lots of places to hide, illuminated only now and then when moonlight broke through the clouds.

He stood for a long time by the window but saw nothing. Cars were mostly parked in driveways or garages; only an occasional vehicle sat on the embankment that flanked the sidewalks. Coral Gables strictly enforced its codes, and there wasn't a truck to be seen.

At last he turned away from the window and returned to the couch. As he did so, he saw headlights. He went back to the window and looked out. Ted Neeson going by, he thought. A City of Coral Gables police car was out front, pausing just briefly.

It moved on.

Sean headed away from the window, but even as he turned, he heard the stairs creak. He froze where he stood for a moment, waiting, listening. How could someone have gotten inside? But if they had . . .

He pushed away from the wall, hurrying on bare feet for the stairs. A body was stealthily creeping along. He rushed forward, instinctively turning to the old mode of his football days.

He set his arms around the body, and as they fell, he realized that he had tackled Lori.

On top of her on the stairs in the darkness, he demanded, "What are you doing?"

"What are you doing?" she demanded furiously in return.

"Trying to protect you! Why the hell were you creeping around?"

She hesitated, inhaling, looking up at him. Her eyes were pure tiger's eyes, glittering a true gold. Her delicate features were firmly set. Her lips, taut, suddenly became wide and generous, and she smiled ruefully.

"I was trying to sleep with you," she told him.

"Here, now?"

"Well, not on the stairs. I mean, I do have a sleeping child, and I'm not into the danger-of-exposure thing. I—I do have a bedroom."

He arched a brow slowly. "Door does lock, I take it?"

"Tight as a drum," she whispered.

"Think you can handle it?" he asked.

"Handle—it?" she inquired.

"I wouldn't want you getting too loud."

"I'll take my chances."

He'd lingered, he'd put on some bravado—he suddenly rose faster than the damned Energizer bunny. He reached down; she thought that he was helping her up, but he did more, sweeping her into his arms. She was tall, she was shapely, she felt light as a feather to him then.

He found her bedroom, right at the top of the stairs. She'd probably been pondering whether she really wanted to come to him or not for some time; she was still wearing nothing more than the terry robe, and he had it off her before he set her down. Idiot. He was going to be so damned good. As he looked at her now, pale, filtered moonlight bathing her body in a silver glow, sensory memory kicked in. He tasted her again, felt her, without so much as touching her. He felt a frightening rush sweep through him, and he was suddenly afraid that he'd ejaculate like a raw kid before he could perform, period. But Lori wasn't waiting. She rose from the bed, slipping her arms around his body. Her lips and tongue caressed the muscles of his abdomen, and he felt his flesh begin to ripple in response. A groan escaped him, and he threaded his fingers into the soft length of her hair. She undid his buckle, started on each button of his button-fly jeans. He felt he could pop the damn buttons. She hooked her thumbs into his waistband, but he caught her hands, stripped off his jeans, and fell atop her, bearing her back down to the bed. Good, he'd promised to be good, so he was going to have be good, and do it fast. He caught her knees, dragged them apart, and thrust into her, groaning as he buried his face against her neck, willing himself to pause and luxuriate in the moment.

Her fingertips snaked down his back, over his buttocks.

He found her lips, kissed her wetly, hot, openmouthed, while his hips ground into hers and spiraled into motion. Slow, dammit, slower, slower, he pleaded with his body, and he tried, determined to arouse, glad to arouse, groaning with each new thrust that seemed like a caress of pure silk around his cock. Then something white-hot burst inside him, and he was moving like a jackhammer, sweating bullets, taut as a fiddle string. He came with a violent climax that seemed to tear right through his guts, so full, so complete, so sexually good that the bulk of his weight nearly collapsed upon her, he was so sated and dazed. But he caught himself, falling to her side, realizing it had been remarkably like that first time when he had suddenly realized that he wanted her desperately and that she was there and willing. It had helped set aside any moral dilemmas he might have faced, considering that he'd been drinking his dad's whiskey and he'd been three sheets to the wind at the time.

Well, hell, so much for being so wonderful that she wouldn't be able to keep quiet . . .

Yet next to him, she suddenly sighed, something almost like a sob, and her slick body moved next to his, closer, her fingers fluttering over his chest. Her hair, damp, beautiful skeins of it, brushed against his flesh; her face buried against him. He exhaled, smiling, relieved, grateful to the power above that she'd been every bit as desperate, as hungry for him, and she hadn't even realized how they had sped through the act like a pair of teenagers.

They lay together, still for a long while. Then he touched her, stroking the length of her spine, simply because the dip in her back was beautiful and he was compelled to touch her.

Then he was tempted to kiss the little hollow at the small of her back.

Then she was turning in his arms.

Touching him. Kissing him. Just a little hesitant at first. But their lips melded, locked, their tongues dueled in a frenzy, and his hands were on her, all over her, and she was breathing heavily, in arousing little pants. Her heart was thrumming like butterfly wings. Her fingers encircled his sex, stroked, played. He felt her hair feathering around him, and then she was down on him. This time he managed to enjoy the pure torture of wanting while he kissed, teased, licked, stroked, her in return until they were both desperate, both awkward and graceful in their need to be together again. The first time was incredible; the second time was even better, more involved, more intimate. They were soaked, entwined. . . .

And he thought that it was the closest he had ever been with anyone, physically and more. The night was almost gone, but it didn't matter. It might have been the best night he'd ever had.

Dead still, he watched the house. He knew the area. His car was down the street—not too far, in case he needed it quickly—and he was well hidden behind one of the big banyan trees on the embankment in front of her house.

He shifted, stiff, growing irritated.

Sean Black was still inside.

Then he realized—Sean Black wasn't leaving.

He swore to himself, his temper soaring. "Do it, do it, do it, do it anyway!" a voice inside him cried out. The sound of his own voice startled him, and he realized in a panic that he was out of control, that he had actually spoken aloud. . . .

Do it. Just do Sean, too . . .

Dumb move, he told himself. Disorganized. Disorganized assholes were the ones who were caught all the time. He had to be smart; he wasn't crazy.

He managed to lower his voice, to swear to himself. Then he nearly jumped, feeling something brush his legs. He looked down. A cat. A dumb black cat. He stared at the creature, reached for it. He gripped it tightly. The animal started to mewl in protest. "Kitty, kitty," he

*said softly, stroking the animal. He glared at it with hatred even as
it began a soft purring sound. "Dumb animal!" he repeated, his tone
placating, his teeth gritted together. He gently stroked it once again.*

Then, with a single motion, he broke its neck.

*He tossed it toward the trash pile between Lori's driveway and
her neighbor's.*

*He needed the element of surprise to do them both. If he could get
in while they were sleeping . . .*

He looked up at the sky. Lots of clouds.

He waited.

*The moon was covered, and despite the streetlights it was very
dark. He'd see how tight the house was. He wasn't a fool. He
wouldn't try the front. It was a courtyard house.*

There would be other doors.

Time slipped away. Comfortable time. She remained next to him,
warm, supple, even as their bodies cooled, and she reached for the
covers.

"Lori," he whispered, slipping an arm around her and pulling her
even closer.

"What?"

"I think I love you."

She stiffened suddenly. She didn't pull away, but something had
changed. "Don't say that, Sean, not now, in the heat of the moment,
in—"

"Lori, the heat of the moment is *before* intercourse, not after."

"No, no, I mean, you don't really know me. We've barely seen
each other again—"

"You always meant something to me."

"You can't *know* that now, and you don't know what I'm like
now. You don't know if I've changed over the years. You don't—"

He shifted, pinning her, staring into her eyes. She swallowed hard,
staring back.

"Then, give me a chance to get to know you."

Her eyes were wide, glistening. He wondered for a moment if she
was afraid of him, and he felt the old tension seeping back into him.
But then she moistened her lips, and he thought that she looked *guilty,*
not afraid.

She smiled suddenly. "It seems I am giving you a chance to get
to know me again. I don't usually invite men up to my bedroom and
lie around naked with them."

He nodded somberly. "Glad to hear it."

She pushed him to the side, coming up on an elbow. "What about you?"

"I never invite men up to my room and lie around naked with them."

She smiled again. "Women?"

"Too many," he admitted.

"Do you tell them all you think you're in love with them?"

"I've never said it to another soul."

Her smile deepened. "Really?" she said softly.

"Really."

"Cool."

He cupped her face, anxious to feel her lips again, when he heard something.

What, he wasn't sure.

A scratching . . . a sound. But not from within the house. From outside . . . ?

"What is it?" Lori asked.

"I don't know."

He stood abruptly, walking to the window. He cracked the drapes, looked out. There was enough foliage to hide an army out there. But it was nearly dawn, and the black shadows had begun to turn gray.

"You have any lights out back?" he asked her.

"A big floodlight by the back door—it's near the kitten's box. If it's working."

He arched a brow at her, grabbed his jeans, and pulled them on. Lori stood, slipping into her robe.

"You should just stay here—" he began.

"Hell, no," she told him.

"Brendan is up here."

"The noise came from the back door," she said firmly.

Her eyes met his. She had heard it, too.

"Stay behind me."

She did. He moved out of her room, silent on his bare feet. She was just as quiet, coming behind him. They moved down the stairs and started around to the back.

Headlights suddenly flooded through the curtained windows in the den. Sean moved to the window and opened the drapes slightly, looking out.

"Ted's out there," he told Lori.

She nodded, glanced at her watch. "It's after six. Want to ask him in for coffee?"

"Sure." The night was over. He had no idea what time Brendan awakened, but he had no intention of taking any chances. He walked to the couch, reaching for his shirt. "I'll go out and see if Ted wants to come in."

Lori nodded. "Keep him outside for a minute. I'll get dressed." Lori turned toward the stairs, and Sean unlocked the front door, letting himself out.

Morning had come. Down the street he could see a garbage truck starting out on its rounds. Dogs barked; a neighbor in hair rollers was out getting her newspaper. The lady eyed him and waved.

Ted stepped from his patrol car.

"You work all night?" Sean asked him.

"Yeah, I pulled a shift for a friend," Ted replied. He looked tired. Rough and rugged, but tired, like a sheriff out of a western. He shrugged. "And I thought I'd keep an eye on our girls."

"Our girls?"

He flushed. "I kept driving by here—saw your car, so I wasn't too concerned. I also drove past Jan's and Susan's."

"Lori had a scare. Brendan picked up a kitten and forgot to tell her, so she thought someone was in the house. I figured I'd sleep on the couch."

"A couch, a hotel room . . . Me, I could never travel the way you do. I make a good cop. I like my hometown, like the people, like staying put."

"Sometimes seems strange that you and Ricky are cops."

Ted grinned. "Shouldn't. We always thought we were macho men, remember? This just kind of continues the pattern."

"Want to come in? Lori's making coffee."

"I don't mean to intrude. I was just watching out for her."

"You won't be intruding. In fact, I think someone might have been trying to break in when you showed up."

"Here?" Ted asked with surprise.

"I heard noises in back."

"Lots of cats and raccoons in the area. Even an occasional fox, though the way things have built up, there's not much habitat left. Actually, Lori's got one of the great remaining overgrown back lawns, planted decades ago. You probably did hear a fox or 'coon."

"Probably. Want to have a look around with me?"

"Sure. Why not? That's my job."

Ted followed him. Sean walked around back but didn't see anything unusual. He walked up to Lori's back door and studied the knob. It was old and scratched through the years. It was impossible to tell if there were new scratches or not. Had someone been trying to get in, or had they both simply been a bit too tightly wound?

"I don't see anything out of the ordinary," Ted said.

"Neither do I. Let's have some coffee."

They walked around to the front of the house. Determined to give Lori plenty of time, Sean rang the bell. After a moment she answered it wearing a dress, stockings, and heeled sandals, her blond hair damp but twisted back neatly in a knot at her nape. She smelled pleasantly of soap, shampoo, and a touch of perfume. Not a trace left of last night's activities. She was fast, damned fast.

"Hi, Ted, thanks so much for watching the house! That's really great of you."

"Well, I'm not just a cop, you know. I'm a Gables cop."

"I know." She smiled. "And you're still going above and beyond."

"Well, thanks, ma'am," he drawled teasingly as he followed her into the kitchen. "Seriously, there are things that time can't change." He accepted coffee from her, lifting his cup. "We were friends, and seeing you both again, it all just feels the same."

"Thanks," Lori murmured. She glanced at Sean. "And thanks for coming around."

"Sure," he said. She clearly wasn't ready to announce to the world that they were sleeping together. "I guess I'll get going, then," he told her.

She glanced at her watch. "I've got to pick up my grandfather by eight."

"If I can do anything, let me know," he said.

Her eyes lowered. "I wish there was something someone could do," she said, "but I do appreciate the support."

As he started to turn, they heard the front door opening.

All three of them stared at one another in surprise.

"Hey, Lori!"

It was her brother, Andrew. He walked into the den. "What's this, Grand Central at the crack of dawn?" he asked.

Sean shook his head. "Some watch dogs we are, huh?" he asked Ted. "Leaving Lori's door wide open for anyone to walk through."

"Oh, well," Andrew said. He flashed his sister a smile. "I just wanted to see if you wanted me to go with you to take Gramps. I have to film this afternoon, but—"

"No, thanks, I'll be fine. Mom and Dad offered to go, too, Andrew. I want some time alone with him."

"Sure thing. But since everyone else is having coffee, mind if I join you?"

"Sure."

She went to get her brother a mug, and Sean sat down to slip on his shoes and socks.

"Just how were you checking up on my sister?" Andrew asked Sean, hazel eyes narrowed suspiciously.

Sean didn't have a chance to answer. Brendan chose that moment to come flying down the stairs. It was obvious he'd just awakened, but he had dressed in cutoffs and a worn Rolling Stones T-shirt from their Voodoo Lounge tour. "Hey, Sean! Oh—hi, Uncle Andrew. And Mr. Neeson . . . hi."

He'd been filled with exuberance, seeing only Sean at first. But realizing that the den was filled, he became puzzled. "What's going on? Is Mom all right?"

"She's fine," Ted said quickly.

Sean grinned. "Your kitten gave her one hell of a scare in the middle of the night."

"The kitten . . . oh! Lucky!" Brendan said. "Oh, wow, it was just wandering around outside, crying. I think it was starving, so I brought it in and gave it milk."

"The kitten's name is *Lucky*?" Sean asked.

"That's what I called it," Brendan said. "Is Mom mad?"

Sean shook his head. "She was just scared, so she called me."

"I wonder why she didn't call me or the folks," Andrew murmured, staring at Sean.

He shrugged, determined not to take the bait. "She probably didn't want to wake your folks, and she might not have been sure that you'd be up. We'd been out all day, and I might have talked about the way I write really late at night."

"Yeah, maybe," Andrew said.

"So you stayed here," Brendan said, pleased. By here, he was indicating the couch. Close enough.

"Yeah."

"That was nice of you."

"Yeah, I'm sure it was real nice of him," Andrew remarked.

"What was nice?" Lori asked, returning with Andrew's coffee.

"Sean, coming over in the middle of the night."

"The kitten's name is Lucky," Sean said politely, looking at her.

"Lucky? Really?" She arched a brow, a subtle smile communicating just with him. "Brendan, you've got to tell me about your new pets from now on."

"I will, Mom, I'm sorry. Can we keep it?"

"I guess. We'll take it to the vet, though. I don't want any more little kittens, and we'll have to check it for worms and the like."

"Well, I've got to get going," Sean said. "See you all tonight at Jan's."

"Will I be there?" Brendan asked his mother.

"She's invited everyone, all ages," Lori told him.

"Hey, great," Brendan said.

"You won't be bored?" Andrew teased him, ruffling his hair.

"No . . . Jan's daughter is about my age," he reminded Andrew. "We're friends."

"The next generation is friends, too. That's nice," Ted said.

"Yeah, friends," Andrew said, studying Lori strangely. Sean gritted his teeth. Friends, hell yes. Andrew was supposedly his friend. But now he'd gone defensive over Sean being in his sister's house. Maybe things really hadn't changed at all.

"Sean, thanks," Lori said, walking with him to the door and then out.

He was glad that she had chosen to come out with him, except that Ted followed along, saying that he had to get back to work. Andrew came as well, followed by Brendan.

"Nice day, maybe no rain," Ted commented.

"Just so long as it doesn't rain tonight," Andrew said. "Jan will be heartbroken if anything ruins her party."

"Oh, Mom!" Brendan suddenly cried out. He rushed forward, toward the trash pile. Narrowing his eyes against the sunlight now beginning to fill the day, Sean saw what Brendan had seen.

A dead cat, tossed into the pile, just like trash.

"Damn, too bad the boy found it!" Ted muttered. "People speed through here, kill the damned things all the time."

"Oh, Mom!" Brendan repeated, holding the poor dead creature.

Lori hurried to him. "Brendan, honey, you can't pick it up, it might have had something—"

"It doesn't look sick, it was healthy! It was hit! Some idiot driver hit it and killed it and just threw it away!" Brendan said furiously. "Why do people do things like this?" he demanded, looking at Sean.

He could see that Lori was about to snatch the animal away from Brendan, aware of her son's hurt, but also mindful that dead animals did carry disease.

"Let me take it, Brendan," Sean said, going to the boy. "I'll drop by the vet's office on Bird Road, have it checked." And cremated, he didn't say aloud.

Brendan swallowed hard and nodded. Lori glanced at him grate-fully, her lower lip between her teeth. She set an arm around her son's shoulders. Sean thought at first that Brendan would shake off his mother's touch, but he didn't. He stood stiff and angry, but aware that what had happened was not his mother's fault. "People should be shot!" he said heatedly. He was getting older; he didn't like show-ing emotion, Sean saw. But Brendan was still young enough to feel that awful sense of loss, pain, and injustice when an innocent animal was hurt or killed through the carelessness of people.

Sean wished suddenly that he could go back to that time himself.

"It's terrible, Brendan," Andrew told his nephew. "But some peo-ple are just monsters."

He stood by Ted as he spoke, and looked at Sean.

Sean decided to ignore him. Andrew was Lori's brother, Brendan's uncle.

Sean's *friend.*

Oh, yeah. Right.

He set the cat in his car, slid into the driver's seat, and started the engine. Lifting a hand in farewell, he started out of Lori's driveway.

He came to a stoplight and glanced over at the dead cat. He frowned, studying the angle of the animal. He reached over, stroking a hand over it.

Brendan was right.

It had been a healthy cat. Nice coat, good body form and muscle tone.

He felt around the cat's midriff, the limbs.

And he realized that there was no way the cat had been hit by a car.

Its neck was broken.

Other than that, there wasn't a scratch on it.

Chapter 14

"Want to stop for lunch—or a soda?" Lori asked. She gazed anxiously at Gramps in the mirror.

His head was leaned back, his eyes closed. He'd lost some hair, but he'd had so much to start with that it still seemed he had a rich head full of snow-white locks. His face today was very gaunt and pale.

He looked dead.

She felt an awful emotion welling in her breast. He was good, he was wonderful, always thoughtful, slow. He'd always listened, all her life, carefully, before he judged any situation or any human being. She'd always loved him, from the time she'd been a very little girl and he'd bought her candy for being good until she'd been an adolescent and he'd surprised her with expensive art supplies for an exceptionally good report card. His talent, however, hadn't been in expensive gifts, but rather in knowing what was important to different people—a yellow canary once for Josh, the little lab mix puppy her mother still adored—even a ball python once for Andrew. He'd never been a politician. He'd never had ambitions to change the world. He'd just been great. He'd made money with his architecture, a lot of it. He'd created beautiful places. And he'd just gone through life being so decent. And now, this . . .

She felt furious. And totally impotent.

"Gramps?" she said softly, thinking that maybe he was sleeping. There was a slight sob in her voice.

She took her eyes off the road, glanced at him again. His eyes were open, and he was watching her.

"Lori, please, don't hurt so badly. Don't hurt for me, okay?"

"Oh, Gramps . . ." Tears she didn't mean to shed flooded her eyes.

"Yes, I want a soda. Hell, no, I want a drink. The Irish bar is just up ahead. I'm not a Kelly for nothing."

"Gramps, you're not supposed—"

"Sweetheart, am I still a functioning adult?"

"Yes, of course."

"I want a whiskey. I don't indulge often; right now I want a whiskey."

She pulled into the parking lot of the Irish bar. An institution, it had been there forever. Miami was a great place. The business next door was Hispanic. The Cubans and other Central Americans and South Americans in the area learned how to eat bangers and mash, bacon and cabbage. In turn, some of the signs in the restaurant were in English, Gaelic, and Spanish, with even a little Portuguese thrown in now and then for the Brazilians.

Inside, Gramps called out to the bartender, an old friend, a gaunt young man of about ninety.

"Hey, Mickey, a whiskey for me. And my girl will have a . . ." He paused, looking at Lori. "You're driving, but I think you can have one. One what?"

She hesitated. "A Guinness, Mickey. A big one."

"Oh, aye! Whiskey and Guinness coming right up," Mickey called.

"Well, that means about ten minutes," Gramps muttered, winking at Lori. He lowered his head. "Old Mickey looks dead, too, doesn't he?"

"Gramps!" she exclaimed, horrified.

"Ah, lass, that's what you were thinking in the car, wasn't it? You thought I was sleeping, but I wasn't. I saw you look my way, saw your eyes. And it breaks my heart to hurt you so."

"You're not hurting me."

"Death is hurting you, Lori. But, me love, I've had a damned good life. The truth of it is now, your brother, Josh, your folks, our more distant kin . . . everyone is there, everyone cares, everyone is trying to keep me from knowing. I'm not dead yet, but I am dying, and girl, it's all right with me. I've made all my peace with my Maker. I just want it to be all right with you."

Mickey wasn't that slow. He handed their drinks over. Lori quickly lowered her head over her Guinness.

" 'Tis good ta see you back, Lori Kelly," old Mickey told her, warmth in his voice. "This old man here has done nothin' but brag about ya all these years, and that's a fact. I tell the truth, Lori girl."

Lori nodded, wishing she could thank him but suddenly unable to speak. "She's crying in her beer," Gramps explained. "She can't stand that I'm dying."

"Aye, and what a wake we'll have!" Mickey said. "And that's a promise, by God!"

Mickey moved away.

"Gramps, I wish that you wouldn't—"

"Lori, if you must feel bad, hurt for your friend Eleanor. Now, there's a tragedy. If you love me, talk with me honestly—don't ever pretend that I'm a doddering old fool who can't make up his own mind about his treatments."

"But . . . I don't want you to die!" she told him softly.

"It's never easy to leave those you love, so it's not like I'm in a great hurry," he told her, lifting her chin, smiling broadly.

She managed to smile in return.

"No talking about me behind my back," he warned her.

"None," she promised.

"You may have to help me with your mother."

"Mom's a card."

"Aye, now, that she is. But she's been a fine daughter-in-law to me, she's loved me like she was my own child, and she's come a long way as well." He nodded, lifted his glass, and said. "To your mother!"

Lori smiled and picked up her beer. "To Mom. Stubborn as all hell, but a lady at all times."

He grinned, then sobered. "She's worried, you know. Says it's a shame that you came back right when your old friend was murdered. I mean, if you'd stayed in New York, it would still have been horrible, but you'd have been distant from it."

"She doesn't need to be worried."

He shrugged. "Well, she changed a lot, you know. After Mandy Olin drowned—and Sean Black went to trial." He picked up his whiskey again. "And you flew away—to England. Not a damned thing she could do or say to stop you, and the next thing we hear, you're married, and there's a picture of you with your husband in the mail, and he's a sad sack of a thing. Talk about a human walking around looking dead before he'd drawn his last breath!"

"Gramps—"

"It's all right, Lori girl. I just want you to understand that your mother has changed. You see, she thinks that she forced you to marry that Englishman, and that you had a disastrous marriage and became a widow and stayed a widow because of her. And so her judgments on people softened a hell of a lot."

Lori slipped her hand over her beer glass. The Guinness was room temperature, and for a minute it seemed to be making her dizzy.

"I'm okay now, and I'm happy."

"And how is Sean Black?" he asked.

She turned to him, eyes narrowed. "He's fine, he's good."

"Well, now, I hope so. This can't be easy for him, either. Frankly, the fellow ought to fly back to California and stay there, what with another girl in your circle being dead. But then, I don't suppose he will. Not with you back in town as well."

"Gramps, he stayed to work, not because of me."

"Do you really believe that? Well, we'll see. I'll be glad to talk with the fellow tonight. I always liked that boy."

She couldn't help but smile. "He's a good friend."

"More than a friend?"

"I don't know. There's a lot of past between us."

"Maybe you should talk about that past," Gramps suggested.

Startled, she looked at him. He always knew too much. She wondered just what he did know.

He smiled at her, not expecting an answer. Once more he lifted his glass to her. "I won't be going quite yet, lass, so don't go mourning me until I tell you it's time to mourn. I'll be around awhile, making sure you're safe before I go."

"Thanks."

She clicked her glass to his, and downed the Guinness.

"Well?"

Sean liked Gillespie, really liked her, but she seemed to have a habit of being dramatic.

They were at the morgue, and in a small room she had thrown open a plastic bag containing a pile of bones. Burned bones.

"Well?" she repeated.

He looked at her. "Burned bones," he told her.

"But you can still tell things from them, right? When you study them, you can tell me something about the person in life?"

He nodded. "I can. I can tell you what you probably already know."

"Indulge me," she said. "Bones shrink when they're burned, right?"

"Right. But taking that into perspective, I can still tell you if this was a man or a woman and give you an approximate age. And since the skull seems to be in pretty good shape, I'll bet you a forensic artist can give you something of a picture of the face."

"I'll leave you with them," she said sweetly.

She did, closing the door.

She had left him gloves, instruments, chemicals, materials, anything she thought he might need.

He was hesitant at first, but then he pulled on a pair of gloves and began carefully arranging the human skeleton. Time slipped away as a body came into being from the bones. He still found the work fascinating. He'd started off with one of the world's greatest professors, a man who routinely gave them tests, simple at first, with large pieces of bone. Was it human or not? The bone pieces got smaller and smaller. They did work in the field—bones purposely left in a building scheduled for demolition, and then the students went in to find the pieces after destruction and fire. To this day, Sean remained amazed by what bones, the most permanent feature of the human body, could tell. Bone in itself couldn't offer something so unique as DNA, but with new technology, even burned teeth could be tested to discover what kind of trace elements remained to prove what kind of dental work had been done. He didn't have that kind of capability here, but the fragments could be sent to the Smithsonian. Proof positive couldn't be offered for identification that way, but dental records could be compared for compatible results.

Gillespie hadn't given him any particulars, but he assumed that she thought the body had been burned to keep the police from identifying the victim.

This girl *had* been a victim.

The pelvic bone was in relatively good shape, enough to tell him immediately that the bones had belonged to a young woman. Despite the fact that the bones had been burned—before the body had decomposed, as the residue of burning body fat proved—they could still be read. The epiphysis had joined completely with the thigh bone, showing that she had finished growing, yet it was a recent union, making her a young adult. The skull, in relatively good shape despite the fragmented teeth, also proved her age through the tiny fissures still visible. Mid-twenties. He was sure that Gillespie had been able to read these obvious signs, and he grew more curious as to why she had brought him in.

While going through the vertebrae, he found marks suggesting that she'd been killed with a sharp object, such as a long knife or scalpel. He also found nicks on the ribs, suggesting that she had been repeatedly stabbed. What damage had been done to tissue he couldn't say, but the bones themselves told a very sad story. He was studying one of the vertebrae when Gillespie returned.

He looked at her. "I can't prove anything, of course, and this is pure theory, but I imagine you've got the same theory. She was killed by the same person who killed your other victim—and perhaps killed Eleanor Metz as well."

Gillespie opened a file she'd been holding and slipped on a pair of reading glasses. "Sariah Applebee, female, twenty-five years of age, five foot six, one hundred and twenty-five pounds . . . let's see, what's pertinent . . . she wore a size seven shoe. Could these bones have fit such a woman?"

"Yes, but they might fit descriptions of other women as well. You can send the bones and the teeth—"

"Yes, but I still won't have proof positive. I don't think that I can go much further than we've gone toward a total identification—unless we get the killer to confess."

"A study of the teeth fragments could agree or not agree with Sariah Applebee's dental records."

"They could. And if you suggest it, I will send the teeth to the lab. But for now . . . will you talk with someone for me?"

He frowned, shrugging. "Who?"

She smiled. "My husband. You'll understand in a minute."

He followed Gillespie down the institutional morgue hallway to her office. There was an older gentleman seated behind her desk. He was about sixty, with sharp blue eyes and steel gray hair. He smiled at Sean and Gillespie.

"My ex-husband, Lieutenant Trent, homicide. Joseph, this is Mr. Sean Black."

Joseph Trent rose, reaching out to shake Sean's hand. "Nice to meet you," Sean said, and looked at Dr. Gillespie, frowning. "I kept my own name when I was married," she explained. "I'd gone through medical school with it, and then, of course, Joe and I were divorced . . . he couldn't live with my corpses."

"She couldn't live with *my* corpses," Joseph Trent corrected.

"One would think you'd both be happy as larks, sharing corpses," Sean suggested politely.

They both smiled, then Trent explained. "My dear angst-ridden ex-wife has been convinced for some time before this last murder that we had a serial killer on our hands, but it's been difficult to get any real federal help when we've nothing but some old bones to go by and no real fear in the community."

"Well, I think you've got some real fear going since the Metz killing," Sean said.

They glanced at one another. "I admit," Trent said, "I was scoffing at Kate's suggestion that I didn't know my business, but I understand you've worked with some real experts, that you studied with some of the finest professors, and have consulted the FBI in certain cases. At first, you see, I told Kate that she had too great a fondness for fiction. She was trying to create a mystery when we were quite busy enough in homicide already. So, you see, she dragged you in on this to prove that her opinions were right. Can you prove her right?"

"I can't prove her opinion, but I do agree with it."

"Now, Joseph," Kate Gillespie said patiently, "you know as well as I do that for a killer to have gone so far over the edge, he must have started somewhere."

"Usually," Josegh said firmly. He looked at Sean. "There was the case of that young female marine who was abducted while she was out jogging and horribly murdered and mutilated. Her killer turned out to be a married man, and to the best that anyone has managed to discover, he didn't even beat his wife."

"Few killers beat their wives—they kill other women," Kate said with a sigh. "Please remind my husband—who has been through all kinds of behavioral classes!—that violence can be far more addictive than drugs or alcohol, and that the capacity for it can grow within the human psyche at a terrifying rate."

"He doesn't need to remind me, dear," Joseph Trent said. He sighed. "I believe what you're telling me, that—that among our other murders, and we do have other murders—we've had a specific sexual serial killer down here for several years now. A careful, organized killer."

"But I think he's growing less careful, more unhinged," Kate said. "Don't you think, Sean? Eleanor Metz's body was found before it had decomposed."

He hesitated, then agreed. "The fact that her body was so poorly hidden might be indicative of a carelessness . . . because he is either growing too confident in himself—or because he was afraid of being caught in the act. But I would say, yes, as his confidence continues to grow, he'll be more careless. And he'll probably grow to need bigger thrills."

"More killings, each more violent and *angry*," Gillespie said.

Joseph Trent rose. "Well, dear, we are on it. Honestly. But I still have to be careful; we don't want a panic." He started out the door, then paused, setting a hand on Sean's shoulder. "Actually, I'd like to keep our discussion quiet. From everyone. Including your friend, my associate Detective Garcia."

Sean frowned. "Ricky brought me in here."

"Of course. But just tell him Kate is interested in helping you with research." He glanced at his ex-wife. "He'll buy that."

With a smile, he left them.

Gillespie smiled broadly at him and took a bottle of brandy from a desk drawer. She didn't have glasses. She took a swig and handed it to him.

Politely, he took a swallow as well.

"There is someone evil out there," she said firmly. "Thanks!"

He nodded. "Thank you."

"For making you study more bones when you've got rich and famous as a writer?"

He grinned. "I still like old bones. But no—thanks for believing in me enough to want my opinion."

She drank from the bottle again and handed it back.

"Still, you're a lot richer. The brandy is on me. If I do prove my point and the cops get this guy, the champagne is on you. And it had best be good."

"So we're partners, huh?"

Gillespie arched a brow. "What does that mean?"

"I need a favor from you."

"All right."

"Come with me."

"Are you taking me somewhere dark and dangerous and scary?"

"Dr. Gillespie, you are the M.E. at the morgue—just what do you consider spooky?"

She shrugged. "Dark, spider-webbed mansions in gothic novels, I suppose. But where are you taking me?"

"Just to my car, and just for a moment."

Intrigued, she came with him. He opened the passenger-side door, and she wrinkled her nose—the cat was already getting rank. He hadn't realized he'd be at the morgue so long.

"You're not driving around with a corpse, are you?"

"Cat corpse."

"Oh?"

"I need a cause of death," he told her.

She frowned, watching him. "I imagine you think you have your cause of death already."

"Indulge me," he told her.

She grinned, slipped on a thin pair of gloves from her pocket, and reached into the bag for the cat. She looked at him. "Neck snapped."

"Could a car have done it?"

"No, a person did it." She frowned, watching him. "I'm sorry to say it, but lots of people get angry and kill animals, especially stray cats. It's terrible and they should all be arrested, but . . . where did you find this cat?"

"In a friend's trash pile."

"Probably has some nasty neighbors."

"Maybe."

"You think there's more?"

"I think that maybe . . . I don't know. Maybe I'm suffering from paranoia. . . ."

"Maybe," Gillespie said shrewdly, "you feel that you should keep a close eye on your friend?"

"Yeah, maybe."

"I'll get rid of the cat for you," Gillespie volunteered.

Chapter 15

Jan's party was a tremendous success from the minute it started.

Lori came early, having promised Jan that she would help setting up the food. Brad, too, arrived before the other guests and instructed the kids in setting up banquet tables on the patio while Lori and Jan made dips, cut veggies, and arranged pepperoni, salami, and trays of cheese.

Lori's parents and Gramps arrived with the Jacksons and Hunts, all still friends involved with one another through their country club. Jan's mom had made lasagna, Lori's mother contributed a shepherd's pie, and Brad's mom, the daughter of a pastry chef, had brought fabulous desserts. Within a matter of minutes there was a fair amount of confusion in the kitchen and beyond. More of Tina's friends from school came, Jeff Olin arrived, then Michael Black, then Andrew and Josh, Ricky, Ted, Sue, and finally, late, after their party had gotten going with kids racing in and out of the pool, squealing everywhere, Sean arrived.

He obviously hadn't been prepared for Brendan and Tina spreading the word that *the* Michael Shayne would be there, but as he entered the patio and was nearly knocked over by the throng of teenagers, he quickly rebounded and handled the situation with humor and courtesy.

Lori watched him, torn. She could see the teenage girls forming instant crushes on him while they chatted. He smiled back, polite, talked, handed out photographs.

"I think I'm going to save him," Jan said, watching. Their old group was sitting together at one of the plastic-covered banquet tables. The grown-ups had gravitated together, and the kids were all excitedly arranged around Sean.

"Why save him?" Brad demanded. "Let him bask in the adoration."

"He can deal with it," Michael said, a soft note of pride in his voice.

"He always was a hunk," Sue said. "When you think back to what we did to him—" She broke off, looking around, uneasy, because a number of the older parents who had jerked their children away from Sean after the scandal were present here tonight. Sue's dad had died, and her mother had Alzheimer's, but Ricky's parents were there as well as Ted's mother and the Jacksons, Hunts, and Kellys. And she was sitting across the table from Jeff Kelly and next to Michael Black.

"We didn't do anything to him," Jeff said. He reached out and set a hand on top of Sue's. "And it's all right. I never thought that Sean had anything to do with it. He and Mandy had their problems, but they solved them like normal people." He grinned. "They yelled a lot."

"It's still strange to realize that Mandy is really gone, much less Eleanor," Michael said.

"I still miss her," Jeff said. He lifted his bottle of Miller Lite. "Jan, thanks. This was a hell of an idea."

"I still think we should save Sean," Jan said.

"He doesn't look like he needs saving to me," Ricky commented. "Who is that cute little thing with the sexy curves? That girl can't be thirteen, is she, Jan?"

"You'd better not be talking about my daughter," Brad growled.

"Don't be ridiculous. I know your daughter."

"That's Jennie Larson, and no, she's my neighbor's daughter, ahead of Tina in school. She's sixteen," Jan told him.

"She thinks she's twenty," Sue said.

"Sour grapes?" Josh teased.

"No, she just knows that she's attractive, and she's experimenting," Lori said, smiling.

"Ah . . . so you were out to torment older men in your younger days as well!" Ricky accused her.

She shook her head, laughing. "No, I thought that thirty-somethings were decaying when I was that young. I was out to torment kids my own age."

"Honesty!" Jeff applauded.

"Well, I'll tell you. That little cutie is one hot ticket," Ted commented.

"Well, didn't we all think we were something back then?" Andrew asked.

Josh laughed. "We were. We were the 'Bold and the Beautiful' of our high school."

Sean was managing to extract himself from the throng of kids. A couple of the girls raced by the table with Tina. "Oh! Isn't he just gorgeous!" one of them said.

"Drop dead gorgeous!" the other agreed.

"Oh, God," Sue said softly. She looked around at them all, her eyes wide. "Ellie used to call guys that. When she met someone she really liked . . ."

Big tears started to form in her eyes.

"Sue!" Jan wailed.

"I'm sorry, I can't help it."

"Look at those girls over there! All talking away, spilling everything! Females will just talk, talk, talk!" Michael said, trying to distract Sue.

It worked. Sue looked. She turned back, grinning. "Well, at least when we age, we wrinkle, but we do learn a little discretion."

"Discretion has its place," Josh Kelly said sagely. Then he grinned at Sean as he finally joined the group. "Hail the conquering hero! Want a beer, you *hunk* you?"

Sean laughed, joining them at the table, accepting the beer. "It still throws me."

"You're surprised that people get all excited that you've written a book?"

He shook his head, grinned, swigged the beer. "No, no one got excited when I had just written a book. I wound up in *People* because of a movie deal. Millions of people see a movie, and I assure you, it's seldom that millions of people read a book, any book. I worked for a long time, wrote for a long time. Nobody noticed—then I had an offer for the big screen. The movie deals did it. Now people think that I actually have something to do with the movies."

"What a pity. Women throwing themselves all over you!" Jeff moaned, clapping him on the back.

"It can be," Sean informed him. "You haven't seen some of the women. They can be downright terrifying."

"Oh, hardy-har!" Jan told him. "But you know what? Come to think of it, I don't have an autographed book. I need one. How will

I ever prove that you're a friend when I'm throwing around names to sell real estate if I don't even have an autograph?''

"Well, Jan, I think I can manage an autograph for you," he teased back. "I mean, if you really think it will sell more real estate . . .''

"Hey, excuse me," Lori said, rising quickly. "It looks as if my folks are leaving.''

"How late is it? My neighbors are coming for their kids.''

"Elevenish," Jeff supplied. "Hey, maybe we should all get out of your hair—''

"Don't even think it! Let's let the old folks and the young ones go home, and then we can talk, just us, the old crowd. Don't one of you move!''

"I have to move, have to say good-bye to the folks, and Gramps,'' Andrew said, joining Lori.

"Let's all say good-bye and all sit back down," Ricky suggested.

They did. It was a long leave-taking, everyone kissing and hugging everyone else.

Lori's mother offered Sean a rueful smile. Lori watched tensely, glad to see that Sean kissed her cheek and answered something she was saying, smiling.

She hugged Gramps tightly. "I'll be talking to you!'' he told her firmly.

She pulled back. He sounded angry. He was never angry with her. "I watch, you know. I watch—and I know!''

But he wasn't going to say more then. He was upset, but he loved her, and he hugged her again before saying good-bye to his grandsons. Puzzled, she watched him, but his stern expression gave nothing away. She grew more worried, wondering if the cancer treatments weren't affecting his mind.

Brendan, worn-out, decided to go home with his grandparents for the night, delighting Lori's mother and father. She promised to pick him up early, but he told her to sleep late—he planned to do so himself.

Lori waved until they were gone. Tina kissed her and her parents good night, smiling to the others.

When the front door finally closed, Jan sighed. "Down to just us! Wow, I'm worn-out! Brad, would you get me one of those wine cooler things?''

"Yep. Anyone else? Call out your orders, now or never.''

Ricky and Josh opted to help Brad with drinks, and in a matter of minutes they were all grouped around the patio together, Jan stretched out with Brad on a lounge chair, Sue on the ground at their feet,

Ricky, in shorts, with his feet in the pool, Michael flat on the patio, Josh, Jeff, and Sean on chairs, Josh and Andrew seated Indian fashion between the loungers, Lori near her brother.

"To Jan, to a great party," Brad said, lifting his beer. "And hell, to us—survivors!"

Lori didn't think that Brad had meant that too literally, but Sue suddenly let out a soft sob.

"Ah, Sue . . . sorry," Brad mumbled.

"It's just we're here, all together, while Ellie . . . while poor Ellie . . ."

"Sue, it's all right. We all miss her," Jeff said.

"And Mandy, too," she whispered.

Lori involuntarily looked at Sean, painfully aware that all of them did the same. Sean rose and came over to Sue. "Sue, I didn't kill Mandy."

"I know you didn't," she whispered miserably. "It's just that . . . we were all so bad to you!"

"It's all right, Sue. Honest. A lot of time has gone by. I'm okay."

She smiled, then inhaled on a shaky sob again. "If Ellie hadn't been killed, maybe none of us would be here. I know that you all hadn't really seen much of her. She was really so sweet, just looking for something right, you know?"

"We know, Sue. And it's true, I hadn't seen Ellie in a very long time, so I can't feel what you're feeling. I can't really mourn her the way that you're doing, the rest of us. . . . I think that in a way, we mourn the girl we knew. We mourn a terrible loss of innocence, but then again, we all lost our innocence so long ago that I'm not sure that's exactly right, either. We do hurt, though, Sue. But if I remember Ellie, she'd be glad that she brought the rest of us together."

She finally smiled. She touched his cheek. "You came out all right, bad boy from the wrong side of the tracks."

"Well, excuse me!" Michael protested. "He gets his name in lights, while I just plod away trying to save humanity, and he gets all the accolades!"

"Ah, Michael, it's all right. None of the rest of us is rich and *famous* in any way. You've got to be careful of sounding jealous," Jeff warned.

"He's not jealous. That's just the Miller Lite talking," Sean teased. "You came out all right, big brother."

"We all came out pretty much all right, I think," Sue said. "Well, okay, let's see, Brad is a wealthy attorney, which we all expected."

"Ditto here, if I may say so immodestly," Jeff volunteered.

"Jeff, we expected no less," Josh Kelly said with mock severity.

"Jan, whom we didn't really expect to be anything but a pretty fluff ball on the PTA, is in the Million Dollar Club for real estate brokers," Brad said. He ended his sentence with something of a yelp as Jan slammed an elbow into his rib cage.

"Fluff ball, indeed!" she exclaimed indignantly. Then she shrugged. "And Sue's our entrepreneur. Lori teaches and takes the fashion world by storm. Ricky—"

"Ricky we always expected to be a cop, a macho man with a billy club bravado!" Brad said.

"Yuk, yuk!" Ricky said.

"Homicide. That's pretty serious stuff. Ted, as a non-homicide cop, what do you do when you see a body?" Jeff asked.

"When I see a body?" Ted repeated. "Hmm. Now, what should I do, or what would I do?"

"Both," Sue said.

"Well, protocol says that I ascertain if the body is a dead body, and radio in medical assistance or a homicide unit or both while I rope off the crime scene with yellow tape, see that no evidence is disturbed, et cetera, et cetera. I call in backup to assist me with crowd control, and I stand ready to report to homicide exactly what I found, saw, and so forth. Then I turn it all over to them, with two tons of messy paperwork, and wish to God I hadn't been first on the scene. I probably have to show up in court, and it's really nasty. So . . . in truth, if I found a body, I'd probably run like hell in the other direction and let the next guy on duty deal with it."

"Ted! You wouldn't!" Lori said.

He shrugged. "I probably wouldn't. But bodies are Ricky's bag. I like working with the community."

"Oh, yeah. Stopping the rich girls in their red Jaguars and blue Porches!" Ricky accused.

"You both seem happy enough with your work, and that's what's important," Jeff said.

"Are you happy, Jeff?" Sue asked.

He shrugged, stretching his shoulders. "Yeah, I am. Strange, I'm what I expected to be, and happy at it. I'm good at what I do."

"I'm lucky, too. I love my work," Michael said. "I don't need the fame—of course, a little fortune would be fine. Who knows, maybe I'll make a communications break-through one day and take the scientific world by storm."

"There we go—fame without the fortune," Brad said dryly. "I

like my work, too. I'm good at it as well. I just love a good verbal fight.''

"I'll agree with that," Jan offered.

Brad grinned. "You'd better, or I'll fight you."

Lori smiled. "I could probably use more time on my design work, but I love teaching."

Brad made a strange noise.

"Really!" Lori laughed. "I love kids, especially at age six."

"I guess six is a good age," Brad said. "It's before kids talk back too badly, want a car, and tell their parents where they should go."

"It's a great age. Their minds are wide-open, and they're eager to learn, affectionate, and fun. I really, truly enjoy what I do."

"You'll never get rich teaching."

"I'm not sure I need to be *rich,*" Lori said. "And I do love designing clothing—"

"You need to get rich enough to buy an alarm system," Andrew suddenly said.

Lori hesitated, seeing how Sean's eyes darted to Andrew and then fell on her.

"I'm getting an alarm," she said defensively.

"You need to do it tomorrow," Sean said.

"Yeah, tell her," Andrew said. "I told her I'd help her out if she needed the money."

"Any of us would help her out," Sean said firmly.

"The family can manage," Andrew said.

"*I* can manage!" Lori exclaimed, realizing that everyone was staring at her.

"Lori, I had a client with one of the best security companies around," Jeff Olin told her quietly. "He'll give you great terms."

"Thanks, Jeff, but—"

"Hey, anybody want another drink?" Jan asked, trying to change the sticky subject.

"Yeah, let's drink to the fact that we're all just thrilled to pieces with our jobs!" Michael said.

"Oh, yeah, so fucking happy," Andrew muttered.

There was a sudden silence, and he looked up as if he hadn't really expected anyone to hear him. He shrugged. "I always did want to make films. I didn't become the lawyer I was expected to be. But I'd be happy if only . . ."

"Ah, come on, Andrew!" Brad said impatiently. "You're not doing anything illegal or all that terrible."

"Yeah," Sue said dryly. "Brad should know—since he was in one of the films."

Jeff Olin suddenly cleared his throat. "Brad wasn't the only one." He found everyone staring at him, and he quickly added, "Hey, I needed the money for school, and it paid really well. Brad worked for Andrew, I worked for Andrew, Josh worked for Andrew—"

"Hey, *wait* a minute! Let me volunteer that information myself!" Josh protested, blushing.

"You guys all did . . . am I getting this right? . . . porno flicks?" Sue inquired, stunned.

"Adult films, if you don't mind," Andrew said.

"Hold on here!" Ricky protested. "You let all these guys do porno flicks—sorry, adult films—and you never called me and offered me a shot at it?" he demanded, feigning outrage.

"*I've* never ignored a live body," Ted put in.

Andrew leaned his head back, groaning. "I'm trying to be the next Fellini, Antonioni, Polanski . . . and this is what I get."

"Dreams change. We never quite get a real grip on them," Sean said quietly. "But if you want to make a certain kind of film, Andrew, you will. Just don't lose sight of the ultimate goal."

Andrew flashed him a sudden smile. "I probably could get by with a cheaper car," he mused. "A few less expensive dates . . . maybe get some investors and finance something I really want to try . . ."

"Do it," Lori told her brother passionately. "Do it, don't just talk, and don't just dream. Do it."

He shrugged

"Wait a minute!" Ricky protested. "Don't talk him out of doing porno films when I'm just about to get a starring role."

"Oh, you guys are still disgusting!" Jan declared. "Now you're old and disgusting instead of young and disgusting."

Sue started to giggle. "I think that we should just all be grateful that we're still in decent enough shape to be in porno flicks!"

"Is that an offer to work for me, too?" Andrew asked her.

Still smiling, she shook her head. "No, I'm the coffee entrepreneur, remember. A 'Mrs. Olsen' for our decade."

"I think you'd look damned good in one of my movies, Sue!" Andrew said.

"Here, here!" Ted agreed. "And, Lori, whew, we've got to get you into something hot and steamy—"

"Hey! That's sick. Lori is my sister!" Andrew protested.

"I can't be in that one," Josh teased. "Ugh. We'd have to be too careful of inbreeding. I mean, look at the royal family."

Lori rolled her eyes. "Sue's right—I feel as if I'm back in the halls at school and you guys of the 4F Club are all at it again."

"Yeah," Ricky said, "but Sean is back to put us all in our places again, so everything's all right, huh, Sean?"

"She was new to the school back then, and you were torturing her," Sean reminded him.

Ricky grinned. "The good old 4F Club. It was fun back then. We didn't have the least idea of what we were talking about."

"As if we do now half the time!" Ted said with a sad shake of his head.

"Don't be silly!" Sue told him. "We're all gorgeous, and, Ted, you can have whatever you want in life. Just go out and ask for it."

Jan suddenly yawned.

Sean was the first to stand. He looked at Lori, reached for her hand, helped her up. "Jan, this was great. Really great. Thanks."

"We have to do it again," Brad said.

"We should plan something once a month. Report on career achievements—and even failures!" Andrew said.

"Sounds good," Michael agreed. "It's fun coming together for a real reason."

"Lori can host the party next month in her new place," Andrew volunteered for her, setting an arm around her shoulder.

"Andrew!" Jan said.

"My place. Four weeks from tonight," Lori agreed. She hugged Jan and then Sue, and started to wave to the others.

"Excuse me, didn't you just forget your brother and your cousin?" Josh asked.

She grinned, hugged them both, and headed out the door. She heard Sean saying his good-byes, then heard him following her. She slipped behind her steering wheel, and saw him back by his car, saying good night to his brother. She started her engine, then discovered that he was at her window.

"Brendan went home with your folks?"

She nodded.

"Want to fool around?"

She nodded.

His dark blue gaze was devastating, his smile magnetic.

"With me, I mean."

"I'm going to hit you in a minute."

His smile flashed again.

"I'm right behind you."

She started her car, eased slowly onto the street. He was on her tail all the way.

She barely opened the door to her house before he was with her, urging her through, slamming the door behind them, fumbling for the bolts without looking at them, his eyes on hers.

Then the door was locked, and he was reaching for her. She cried out, throwing herself into his arms, leaping up at him and locking her legs around his hips.

He groaned, kissing her, fingers tangling in her hair. He raised his lips from hers at last. "I don't think I can walk up the stairs this way."

She laughed, starting to unwind herself from him.

"No, no, wait! Don't . . . don't move, let me try. It feels too good to stop . . ."

He didn't quite make it. They stumbled on the third step. Laughing, he eased them down together. She couldn't keep her hands off him, had to feel his flesh. She had his shirt out of his jeans, then her hands were in his waistband. Her fingers curled around him, freed him. He inhaled sharply, ripped at the snap of her jeans and tugged them off her where she lay on the step. His mouth fused with hers again.

Soon his body was joined with hers as well.

They were entirely unaware that a killer drove by in the night, thoughtfully studying the house . . .

But it didn't matter that they were oblivious.

The killer had other business that night.

Although Sue had been in bed for over an hour, she was awake and immediately heard the soft tapping at her door.

Her heart took flight.

He'd come to her.

It was a miracle, this feeling. It was special, unique, so wonderful . . . something she wasn't willing to share with anyone yet, because she'd been around, because it felt so real and so right, and yet she *knew* that you just couldn't count on things so easily. It might have just been sex, because the sex of course had been so good, even if at the end there . . . but no matter, she could deal with that kind of a situation.

What mattered was she was certain that he had come back.

She ran downstairs, prepared tonight. She had been out to the lingerie shop, purchased the sexiest black nightie with a matching robe.

She'd kept her makeup on—no, that wasn't exactly true, she'd added to it, enhancing it. She was a little tipsy, too—she'd had a few too many wine coolers at Jan's, but that was all right, too. It just seemed to add greater sensation and boldness to every move she made. She couldn't wait to touch him. . . .

If it was him. It might not be, she chided herself.

Who else, at this time of night?

She raced to the door and looked through the peephole.

She leaned against the door, her heart thundering.

It was him.

She fumbled with the locks, she was in such a hurry to open them, but then got something of a grip on herself and opened the door slowly. She could have played coy, but she decided not to.

"Hi."

"Can I come in."

"Of course."

He smiled. God, he was great. She almost came in her new thong pantics just looking at his smile. Who'd have imagined that *he* would want her after all these years?

"Wasn't it a great party? But then, of course, you'd expect no less of Jan. Nice, so nice to be together . . ."

He set a finger on her lips and stopped her speaking. He kissed her then, and she felt as if she were melting.

"Want to come up to the bedroom?"

"I like it right here. You know what I want."

She did know. And she was willing to comply.

He was more urgent tonight, rougher. And still, he was so charming and exciting . . . she was willing.

Even when what he asked hurt her.

"We need something more to drink," he told her, later.

Another drink would be good now, she thought. She didn't feel quite as excited, as filled with wonder, as she had before. Something was wrong; something was simply not quite right. She didn't understand, and she was wiling to laugh and joke and tease as they shared a bottle of her best champagne. She realized vaguely, leaning against the couch with him, that he didn't touch anything, or hadn't touched anything—other than her—until she'd come out with the champagne. And that they were drinking straight from the bottle.

He nuzzled her throat, his whisper a little drunken. "Let's go away."

"What?" she asked, surprised.

"Let's go away."

She giggled. "Great idea. Except that I've got a business to run."

"People work for you. Trust them."

"Go . . . ?"

"To the islands. Pina coladas, sun, sea, surf, we can just play on the beach all day, play in the sand . . ."

"Umm . . ."

"Let's be reckless. Daring. Let's do it."

What the hell? She had been careful in life, respectable, responsible. Where had it gotten her?

Here. Alone. With a cat.

"Are you serious?"

He smiled. "Dead serious," he told her gravely.

Why not? Run away to the islands for pure decadent pleasure. It sounded so exciting. So wickedly wonderful.

"All right . . . I have to pack."

He shook his head. "Just your purse, jeans, bathing suit, and toothbrush. We'll be naked most of the time. What we need, we'll buy."

Suddenly so thrilled she could barely stand it, Sue jumped up and raced upstairs. She packed, checked her makeup, washed up, wished fleetingly that there were just a few uncomfortable things that he wouldn't ask her to do. But now he was asking her to run away. . . .

Could she be falling in love?

She hurried back downstairs. "I'm ready."

"Great. Let's go."

It was the middle of the night. There wasn't a soul or another car in sight.

He'd parked down several streets.

She looked at him, puzzled.

"Didn't want your neighbors to talk," he told her.

"Oh." He quietly opened the passenger's door for her, quietly closed it. He came around to drive.

"Oh, dear God!"

"What?"

"I forgot the cat."

"He'll be all right."

"I just need to leave him extra water."

"Give me the key. I'll take care of the cat," he told her.

She handed him the key, smiling.

Trustingly.

He walked back to the house, slipping on gloves from his pocket before turning the key in the lock.

He stepped inside, flicked on the light.

He headed for the kitchen. He set down an extra bowl of water,

*found cat food in a pantry, and dumped some into a bowl. He didn't
need to bother, but he'd suddenly felt compelled to double-check the
house for any sign that he'd been there. For any careless mistakes.*
"Here, kitty, kitty!" he called softly.
A minute later the dumb puffball came padding into the kitchen.
"Yeah, baby, here kitty, kitty, pussy, pussy, pussy!"
The cat came close; he snatched it up.
Smiled. Stroked it . . .
*Gritted his teeth and snapped its neck. He dropped the cat. Pussy
fell dead to the floor. He knew it was stupid. A really serious mistake.
But he couldn't help himself. He felt out of control, yet . . . invincible.
Sue would be horrified, in another deluge of tears . . .*
But then, that didn't matter a hell of lot.
Sue wasn't coming home.

Lori awoke, amazed by the feeling of happiness that assailed her
just to discover that he lay beside her in the light of day, his flesh
bronze against her light blue sheets. She propped herself on an elbow,
studying him, the sheen of muscle that seemed to ripple nicely as his
lungs rose and fell with each breath, the smoothness of his skin, the
dark hair that covered his broad chest. . . .

He'd been thinner way back when. Always taut and muscled—
he'd been a natural athlete. But at eighteen he'd been a leaner version
of himself, always with his large, espressive hands, always with those
eyes that could say so much one moment and hide everything the
next.

She closed her eyes, leaning back, thinking of the time before the
nightmare with Mandy when he had faced a different demon, the
death of his brother. Sean had always loved his family; he'd gotten
into a fight once in school because a kid had called his father a loser.
He wouldn't instigate anything on his own, but attack his dad or his
brothers, and he was a tiger. And Daniel, who had been the oldest,
quiet, assured, determined, had gone off to serve his country, and
like a good soldier, he had fought, gone missing. . . .

And then his body was found.

When Lori had heard about it, she'd had to go and see Sean, try
to tell him that she understood how devastated he must feel. She
couldn't really understand, of course. She'd never lost anyone, not
Andrew, not her folks, not Gramps. But she imagined then that it
must be like losing an arm or a leg; it must be unbearable, the pain,
thinking that he loved Daniel so much, and he'd never, ever see

Daniel again, and Daniel had been so young, so beautiful, his whole future before him.

And Sean had taken it hard. She'd arrived at his house to find him drunk. She'd seen Ricky drunk and Ted drunk, even her brother Andrew and cousin Josh. Jeff and Mandy Olin were both prone to drink too much when they could get away with it, and Brad was always trying to get her to drink so that he could get her to let him do what he wanted in the backseat of his car or out at the beach. She always knew what he was up to—she just wasn't playing the game.

They were seniors and either first- or second-year college students, and though they were seldom dumb enough to drink or drive, they'd all tried liquor at one time or another—some of them more than others. Michael drank at parties, Sue had a beer now and then, and Jan liked to impress them all by ordering martinis she couldn't begin to finish just to prove that she could go out and drink without being carded.

Sean seldom touched alcohol. He was just too busy with school and sports and jobs. But he'd been touching it that night. Plenty of it.

He'd told her to go away at first, that he was in no mood for friends. But she'd insisted she stay, and suddenly he became very quiet. "Lori . . . Lori Kelly. You're an angel, you know. Always an angel. The rest of us . . . well, you're something special, you know? Hair just like a damned angel and eyes . . . eyes. Well . . . I'm not good company tonight, Lori Kelly."

"Sean, I know how much you loved him."

"Do you? I can't believe it. Daniel was good, the best, so Daniel is dead. So many assholes out there, and they're alive and walking around, and Daniel is dead. Fine, come on in, Lori Kelly."

So she came in, and sat with him on the sofa in his living room while he dragged out photos and showed her Daniel through the ages. Daniel, their father, Michael, himself. One picture—when the kids were all babies—had a woman in it. She was very pretty. Tall, slender, pretty.

"Your mother?"

He shrugged. "I guess. She didn't stick around. But it's okay; we didn't need her. Dad kept us together. Daniel taught us to make beds, get supper, wash ourselves, tend to our clothing . . . oh, God, Daniel . . ."

He sobbed. She put an arm around him. He put an arm around her. She wasn't sure just exactly when, but they started kissing. Petting. And the kiss deepened, and her skirt inched its way up her hips and he was touching her in a way that she never let Brad touch her, but she didn't want to stop him.

She'd been drinking with him, small sips of whiskey because she couldn't really stand the stuff. It was enough to make things a little hazy, but in reality she knew what she was doing. She realized, even as he fumbled about in his pain, that she was in love with him. Call it an unrequited crush, whatever, she felt for Sean something that she had never felt for anyone else. And so it was all right. He was young, drunk, and awkward, yet she was still aching for something when he kissed her, touched her, rubbed her. . . .

She knew what was happening, she wanted it, and it still hurt like hell and was humiliating—not at all what she had expected. He hadn't expected her to be innocent. He surely assumed that she'd fooled around with Brad—Brad had probably told the other boys that sure, they did it all the time—and so Sean seemed angry at first, swearing that he'd never have done anything if he'd only known. Embarrassed, expecting that it should have been so much more, Lori set out to seduce him into doing it again. . . .

And so she got more. Then he was upset about Daniel, and about her, and she lay with him, whispering that it was all right, that everything was going to be all right. He kept apologizing.

Until he passed out. And she stood then, hurried to his bathroom, straightened herself and her clothing the best she could, and fled home. All night she burned, wondering just how awful it would have been if Michael had come home, or worse, if his father had found them. . . .

And still, she didn't really feel any shame about what she had done. She loved him. Really loved him. And it was good to feel that she might have helped him through his misery. She didn't feel pain. She hadn't exactly discovered ecstasy, but she had discovered that she wanted to explore Mr. Sean Black—and what had happened between them—in a far more thorough way. Except that . . .

She was still supposedly Brad's steady, and Sean and Mandy were still supposed to be the hottest thing going.

Until the rock pit . . . Life changed forever after that awful day.

She inhaled and exhaled on a long sigh, then realized that although he hadn't moved, he was awake, studying her in return.

"Like what you see?" he teased.

"I always have. You are drop dead gorgeous, you know."

He inclined his head, smiling. "So are you."

"Thanks. Even in the morning?"

"Especially in the morning."

"Is that only because I'm so willing for sex?"

He laughed, shrugged thoughtfully. "It helps."

"Hey, you—"

She attempted to smack him with a pillow.

He caught hold of the pillow, stealing it away. Then he tossed off the sheets, rolled over her, twined his fingers with hers, pinning them to the bed. He kissed her, murmuring against her lips, "You're the most beautiful woman I've met in all my life, and I'm really afraid to say it, Lori Kelly . . ."

"God, you are good!" she whispered.

"You ain't seen nothing yet."

"Show me."

He did.

Chapter 16

Jan woke up to discover that she was alone, though the side of the bed where Brad had been sleeping remained rumpled. She knew that he had risen long ago, probably because he didn't want their daughter to realize that they were actually sleeping together in her home. Dumb. Tina was no fool, and kids were so aware these days. She thought she'd heard Brad go out and come back in; maybe he'd been thinking things over himself.

She hugged her pillow for a minute, musing about the party, the night gone by—and Brad. Could she ever trust him again?

He was bartering with her to remarry. That was wrong to begin with. He loved women in general, always had. She couldn't help but feel a little twinge of jealousy, seeing the way that he still watched Lori. Well, despite the things he told her now, she knew—having been Lori's best friend back in high school—that he hadn't managed to get into Lori's pants. Lori was probably the only woman who had ever said no to him. Maybe that would always bother Brad.

Would she always be upset that he had a crush on Lori? Had it actually been easier when Lori was living in New York, before their old crowd had gotten all buddy-buddy again, mourning Ellie's death?

She wasn't sure what she felt. One thing was certain, Brad wasn't a highly paid attorney for nothing. He could argue a point right into the ground. He didn't give up. He was still set on her playing along with his threesome fantasy.

What was she going to do? Sometimes, the way he talked, she had to admit—only to herself!—that she was intrigued. Sometimes she found it completely repugnant.

"Mom?" Tina knocked on the door hesitantly. Jan saw that the door was ajar, and she huddled more deeply beneath the sheets. Tina knew that she didn't normally sleep in the nude.

"Hey, baby."

Tina, blue eyes huge, face flushed and pretty, stared in at her. "Mom, Dad's here, in the kitchen! He's got coffee on for you—and Mom, get this, he's making pancakes and bacon."

"Bacon, good," Jan said. Two tons of fat and cholesterol, and she wouldn't be able to resist. A million calories. What was he trying to do? Fatten her up so that she couldn't possibly appeal to other men, and she'd be forced to give in to his fantasy, or not have any sex at all.

All right, so one breakfast of bacon and pancakes wasn't going to kill her.

"Mom, did he stay here last night?" Tina asked anxiously.

"I—I guess he must have slept on the couch after the party. You know Dad, he's good about not driving if he's been drinking."

"Yeah, I guess," Tina said. But she still hesitated in the hallway just outside the door. "Mom, that is so cool. Both you and Dad here as if we were a *normal* family."

Smiling, Tina turned and left. Jan jumped quickly out of bed and into the shower. Dressed, she came downstairs in time to discover that her ex had prepared the perfect meal, that he was joking with Tina, cute as could be in cutoffs and a T-shirt, blond hair disarrayed, blue eyes lazy.

"Hey, sleepy head."

"Hey. This looks fabulous."

"Tina helped."

"Did you, baby?" Jan asked.

Tina nodded happily.

"How's your schedule?" Brad asked her.

"Schedule?"

"Work. I made some plans for the weekend."

"Oh, really?"

"A trip down to the Keys. I called Sean's hotel and found out that Michael had stayed in Sean's room since it was late for him to drive back so far. And Sean was at Lori's place."

"What?" Tina asked.

Brad looked at his daughter. "He's sleeping on the sofa there, baby. Scary things going on here, you know?"

"Oh."

The look Brad gave Jan assured her that in Brad's opinion, Sean wasn't sleeping on any couch.

"Anyway, I gave them a call, and we thought it might be fun to drive to Key West together, stop at Michael's place, see what's got Tina all riled up, and then spend the night at some four-star place, live it up!''

"Oh, Mom, cool. Please, can we go?" Tina demanded.

"I did have a few appointments—"

"Mom! You have an assistant!" Tina said indignantly.

"Yes, but, baby, I sell my own properties," Jan murmured. But Brad was staring at her.

Challengingly. He was amused. Tina was on top of the world. Her mother, father—Brendan Corcoran and Sean Black, alias Michael Shayne—all in one weekend wrapped up pretty with a bow.

"Mom!" Tina wailed.

She shrugged. "I'll call Lisa."

"I'll call her for you. I'll do it right, I'll tell her something family came up—oh, thanks, Mom!"

Tina ran off to the den to make the call. Jan stared at Brad.

"You're getting her hopes up."

"I'm trying to get your hopes up."

She sipped her coffee. "Strange, I never thought that you were all that fond of Sean."

"That's bullshit. We were football heroes together. I never could have been such a celebrity if he hadn't been there to catch all my passes."

"I know you, though. You were jealous of him."

Brad shrugged. "What could you expect? Lori was mine, but I could see the way she looked at him all the time. And I knew, no matter how hot and heavy he was with Mandy, she was just a substitute for Lori."

"Brad, how can you know that? That was all so long ago."

"Yeah, right, my point. I like Sean. He's always been interesting."

"Yeah, right. When he was a suspected murderer, we all spurned him. Now he's rich and famous. If he moves back down here, he'll make a great client."

"Maybe."

She sipped more coffee.

"Or are we going for Lori Kelly?"

"Lori Corcoran," he reminded her. He stared at her. "Sure. Lori is a friend. Her kid is great. Level. Good head on his shoulders. He won't be in with any of the drug crowd, and you know damned well that some of Tina's friends are already smoking—dope and cigarettes. They've gotten their hands on liquor—hell, you know that we did, too."

"Just so long as we're not going for Lori."

"Jan, she's supposedly your best friend."

"I want to keep it that way."

"Fine."

"Just so long as you've completely squashed that stupid fantasy—"

He came and stood beside her, stroking her hair, looking into her eyes. "Lori is out of the fantasy. But I've found the perfect person to fulfill it."

"Oh, please . . ."

"But, Jan, she's perfect. You'll see her once and never again. She's a professional, clean as the snow, careful, expensive, good."

"Oh, God, Brad—"

"Think about it."

"You know this can't be right if you're bribing me—"

"I'm not bribing you. I'm trying to get my last great streak of wildness out and gone before I settle down again. What do you say? Once, I swear it. I'll sign away my life in promises, honest."

"Maybe," Jan murmured as Tina came bounding back into the kitchen.

Lori didn't get a chance to talk to Gramps alone, but he was still disturbed, she realized, when she and Sean picked up Brendan from her parents' house.

He was very polite to Sean, as he had always been. Her folks were nice as well. When Lori tried to ask him what was up, he told her sternly that he'd talk to her alone when she had the chance. She told him she'd pick him up on Monday morning.

She had been surprised that Sean had agreed to the weekend with the Jacksons, and she was surprised at herself for letting others know that she and Sean Black were spending intimate time together.

But they were both adults, they had both agreed, and it seemed just fine.

They could travel easily enough all together. Although Brad usually rode around in his sports car, he also owned a huge Suburban, and the six of them would fit easily enough in it, though Michael, who had remained in Coconut Grove until they were ready to drive down, offered to put Sean and Lori in his car for the first half of the ride.

It was a pleasant drive, a great day, with everything casual. Michael's marine facility was quiet since it was a Saturday and not a tourist destination, but Marianne seemed pleased to have the company, and once again she preferred to swim with Lori, as if she had made a bosom buddy for life. Brad was dismayed that the dolphin didn't seem to like him, but he kept a sense of humor about the situation, maybe because Tina was so delighted to be with the dolphin again.

"Some women just prefer the company of women," Brad said, shrugging, looking at Jan, who looked away.

They left Michael about five in the afternoon. It wasn't bad in the Suburban, Brad driving, Tina between him and Sean, Brendan in the back on the left, Lori in the middle, Jan on the right. They reached Key West just when the sun was setting, one of the most spectacular views imaginable—gold, crimson, magenta, mauve . . . beautiful, especially from the balcony of the huge southwesterly facing suite Sean had taken to make sure that he didn't jeopardize whatever Lori chose to tell Brendan about their relationship.

They walked on the hotel's private beach, played in the surf and sand while the sun fell, then changed for dinner, a rustic place on the water known best to the locals where the blackened fish and conch chowder were some of the finest to be had. Later, with the kids at a movie, they strolled the streets of Old Town, discussed Hemingway and his years spent in Key West and had what Lori considered a wonderful and refreshingly normal night.

She was still plagued by thoughts of her grandfather's strange behavior, and she was afraid she knew what he was going to say to her. But she pushed it all back into a corner of her mind. It wasn't time to deal with it yet. She wanted this simple time of pleasure and enjoyment with Sean, her son, and her friends.

Idly walking along, she found that Jan had come up beside her while the guys were behind them, discussing the triumphs and potential of the Panthers, the Marlins, and the Miami Dolphins. Jan linked arms with her. "Isn't this *fun*? I haven't enjoyed myself like that in years. I mean, it's almost like we're normal couples, real couples . . ."

"You and Brad are a real couple."

"Strange, isn't it? Me and Brad, you and Sean."

Lori shrugged. "Why?"

"Well, in school it was you and Brad. Mr. and Miss. Perfection, you know."

"We were never perfect. We didn't belong together. Our parents just thought we did. Other people thought we did."

"You really feel that way?"

Lori looked at her friend. "Cross my heart and hope to die. Honest, Jan, you've known me forever! I don't think things ever ended dramatically between Brad and me because there simply wasn't really anything there. And then, of course, after Mandy's death . . ."

"Everybody just went away," Jan said with a sigh. She chewed her lip. "Well, I believe you, but I don't think my ex-husband was so certain you shouldn't have been together. He still thinks you're incredible, you know."

"Jan, it really seems that he loves you. You two were just as cute as could be on that lounge chair last night."

Jan sniffed. "I think he was being a little proprietary because of the ratio."

"The ratio?"

"Women—there were three. You, me, and Sue. Men—there were a bunch. Michael, Jeff Olin, your cousin Josh, Ricky, Ted, Andrew, and Sean. And the one thing that's true here is, they are a beautiful crowd. Brad is probably the most classically good-looking—a *Baywatch* beachboy if I've seen one. Of course, he knows it. Sean is probably the sexiest, tall, those dark good looks and killer blue eyes . . . but, hell, I'd take Andrew in a flash—even if he is your brother. Sue always thought he was the most gorgeous thing in the world—and Ricky is a knockout with his Latin eyes. Jeff Olin is just about perfect, built like an Adonis, sexy as all hell when he flashes those pearly white teeth! Brad had good reason to stick close to me last night!" Jan said, grinning. "In fact, I think Susie is after one of our good friends."

"My brother again?" Lori said, surprised. Andrew seemed to be in the doldrums a bit, too concerned with his future to be seriously concerned with any one woman.

"I don't know, I have no idea. She was just talking to me while helping set out plates, saying it was great that we're all together, that some friendships become closer than others and it's so wonderful now because she's so scared."

"Interesting. It will be fun to find out just whom she's close with!" Lori said, pleased. Sue was a good person, always a good friend, quiet, honest, kind. She'd absolutely adored Andrew back in school— she might be just what he needed. But then again, maybe it wasn't Andrew Sue was seeing at all. She'd have to ask her brother—when he wasn't haunting her about an alarm system. "Think you and Brad will remarry?" she asked Jan. "You two just look so right for one another. I almost feel as if I'm out with Ma and Pa Kettle—in the nicest way, of course."

"Yeah, Ma and Pa Kettle. That's a laugh," Jan said.

Lori frowned. "Why, what's wrong?"

Jan sighed, glanced at Lori. "If I tell you, you've got to swear, I mean swear, not to say a word to anyone. Ever."

Lori smiled. "Jan, we are out of high school. But I swear, I swear."

"Brad has this fantasy . . ." Jan murmured, looking back to see that the men were out of earshot. "Oh, Lori, what should I do? Brad wants to remarry, but only after he's sown the very last of his wild oats."

"Meaning?"

"He wants to live out one of his fantasies."

"Oh?"

"He wants a threesome."

"A threesome?"

"Oh, don't sound so naive!"

"Sorry."

"Lori, I'm thinking about doing it."

"He wants a ménage à trois with you in it."

Jan nodded. "Please don't look at me that way! I'm not terrible."

"I didn't say you were!"

"It's supposedly a big fantasy for him, having two women."

"It could be."

"I'm not a horrible person."

"Jan, of course not, and quit defending yourself to me. I'm not judging anyone. Trust me, I wouldn't dream of judging anyone. The important thing here is you, can you do this, can you live with it, and if so, is it for the right reasons?"

"Oh, Lori, what should I do?" Jan wailed.

"You've got to do what you think is right," Lori told her, then sighed. "Oh, Jan, honestly, I wish I could give you real advice. It's a decision you've got to make for yourself."

"You won't quit being my friend?"

"Of course not!"

"You don't think it's too sick or perverted?"

Lori laughed. "Jan, it's what you think that matters."

"But you will still be my friend."

"Always."

"Lori?"

"What?"

"Do you think that Brad loves me, really loves me?"

Lori hesitated. Brad teased, he still teased. He had a powerful personality and liked women. But she had been pleasantly surprised to see how tender he could be with Jan, and how domestically intimate the two had been at Jan's house. There did seem to be a special bond between the two of them.

"Okay, Jan, pure honesty. I think Brad could be a jerk back in high school—but then, we were young, we were all idiots. I was surprised when you married him, not so surprised when you divorced him. But he seems to have come a long way—and yes, I think he does love you, and Tina, very much."

The smile on Jan's face was frightening. Maybe what Lori hadn't realized was just how much Jan loved Brad.

Jan gave her a hug.

"I'm so glad that you're home."

Sean, Lori discovered, was shrewd.

Rich, she decided, could also be a good thing.

The suite he had taken had a huge parlor area, one bedroom to the left of it and two bedrooms to the right. They looked like three separate hotel rooms, and they could be.

But the two rooms on the left of the parlor area were connecting, she discovered. She had been surprised when Sean gave her a casual nod good night, waved to Brendan, and disappeared into his own room. She bid Brendan good night herself and closed her own door.

A few minutes later, she heard a knock and noticed the door between the two rooms. He poked his head in, grinned, then entered, wearing a black velour robe. He walked over to her door, assured himself it was locked, and came over to stand before her.

He lifted her chin, kissed her. "Any problems?"

She shook her head, opening his robe, burying her face against the crisp hair on his chest. She breathed him in. He even smelled sexy. She moved her lips lightly against his chest, feathered her fingertips along his sides, then sank slowly down against him, eager to touch, taste, drive him into a frenzy, and make love.

She nuzzled his lower abdomen.

"Shall I . . . ?"

"Do it . . . oh, God."

A guttural groan emitted from deep within his chest. His fingers were hard as they threaded in her hair. He pulled her up by the arms, found her mouth, kissed her with wet passion, and lost the robe. Her knit dress never quite made it from her body, being shoved up to her waist while her panties were ripped away.

Later, he made love to her slowly, teasing and arousing her with such an intimate and instinctive precision that she found herself climaxing just from his subtle, liquid touch, then rising to meet him again when his body joined with hers. As she lay against him, half asleep, he murmured, "Where did you learn to do that?"

"I see a lot of movies," she teased.

"What kind of movies? Andrew's?"

She punched him in the shoulder, laughing softly. "No, I didn't even know what Brother was up until recently. No, it's just that . . . Sean, do a lot of men have a fantasy about sleeping with two women at once?"

He was silent for a minute, then asked her, "Why? Did you want to bring a friend?"

"No!" she exclaimed. "Oh, never mind, I was just curious. Is it really such a common fantasy?"

He shrugged after a moment. "Maybe."

"Do you have that fantasy?"

"Are you volunteering to fulfill it?"

"No!" she said, laughing again.

"Then, what is this?"

"I just wondered—"

"You."

"What?"

He rolled toward her, and in the shadowy moonlight that filtered into the room, she felt his eyes. "You. I lived a lot of fantasies. I did whatever the hell I wanted for years, nothing very kinky, I don't think, but I knew a lot of people, many of them pretty interesting and freethinking. In all that time, when I lay awake at night, alone—I wondered what it would be like just to have a real chance to be with you. Good enough?"

She smiled, trembling inside and out. She touched his cheek and tried to be nonchalant.

"God, you are good," she said lightly, but she bit into her lower lip and added, "Sean . . . ? I love you."

He arched a brow. "Can you really say that so quickly?"

"It's not so quickly. I've thought about it myself for around fifteen years."

He wrapped his arms around her and pulled her close, and she was really afraid because it was just too good.

Sean awoke first, restless, despite the fact that she lay beside him, lovely, content, warm, everything he might have wanted.

It was very early, but he showered and dressed, slipped into the suite's little kitchenette, made coffee, and took it out to the balcony.

He sat, watching as the sun slowly rose against the eastern horizon. *Would she have loved him if he hadn't been as successful?* Yes, probably, she had come to see him when he lived in a clean little shack in the wrong neighborhood—and she had comforted him when he was in pain.

Fifteen years . . . in just a month or so, it would be a full fifteen years.

And amazingly, he could still remember it. He could remember being hauled away to jail, and he could remember the jail. The doper with the slash across his eye who had spotted him as a possible victim, then decided that he was a little too big for an attempted rape. The two car thieves who had offered to tackle him for the doper, and the tough-guy gang member who had decided to help him out when he had taken on the three and sustained a black eye and a broken rib.

He could remember the assistant D.A., pounding him, showing him the awful pictures over and over again. Mandy dead. Mandy decaying. He had done it, he had done it in a rage. She'd just been such a prick tease. . . .

No, he hadn't done it, and he'd never be coerced to say he had.

Then there had been his own court-appointed lawyer, the fresh kid who had been willing to fight but was so inexperienced! He remembered the night that he had lied to his dad, assuring him he'd be okay, then listening to his attorney telling him that if he didn't plead to the lesser charge of manslaughter, the D.A. meant to get him on murder one and send him to the chair.

He could have died. A jury could have convicted him, and if so, he might have run out of appeals right about now and be heading for Old Sparky.

He sipped his coffee, realizing that he was in a cold sweat. He looked around. It was a great suite.

He wished he could have brought his father some place like this.

"To you, Dad," he said quietly, raising his cup. "Thanks, wish you were here!"

Could he really live in Dade County again? he wondered.

Maybe. There had been people who had hated him. Who had condemned him.

But there had been people on his side, and maybe even people who had loved him as well. He had run away from the bad, and God, yes, he could credit himself with creating a damned good life out of it all. But maybe he had run away from the good as well.

"Hey, early bird."

Lori was up. Wrapped in a long, slinky silk robe, hair mussed and wild, she smiled ruefully as she stepped out on the balcony with a cup of coffee and stared at the horizon. "Do you always manage on so little sleep?"

"I tend to be restless in the middle of the night."

"Dreams?" she asked quietly. "Nightmares?"

"Memories." He reached out a hand. She took it, sitting on his lap when he drew her to him. "Watch the coffee."

"I would wear scalding coffee for you any time."

She smiled. She was dazzling. As beautiful as ever. He felt shaky suddenly, as if she couldn't really be there now, available for him. Like so many good things in life, she might suddenly slip out of his grasp.

He didn't want to betray too strong an emotion, so he arched a brow at her.

"So who is getting into a ménage à trois?"

"What?"

"Who?" he asked again, grinning.

She smoothed back her hair. "I can't tell you that! Someone was talking to me in confidence."

"Brad wants Jan to do it, huh?"

Her sharp intake of breath assured him that he had nailed it on the first try.

"I can't tell you."

"You just did."

"Oh, God, don't say anything."

"Brad and I hardly share intimate secrets," he told her.

"But you are friends. You act like friends—"

"We're friends. On the surface, always. Maybe a little deeper than that. Sometimes, we needed each other, like on the football field, in certain classes . . . but he was always a little suspicious of me, and I was always damned careful of him."

"Why would he have been suspicious?"

She was staring it him with her hazel eyes wide and troubled.

He smiled. "You," he told her.

"Hey, Mom, Sean!" Brendan called, wandering out on the balcony. "Can we get something to eat?"

Lori tried to hop up; Sean didn't let her. She looked at him, alarmed, then settled back in his lap. She realized that she would just make herself look guilty if she jumped up.

"Sure. Let's call the Jacksons and get them down for breakfast. In fact, Brendan, will you do that? I've got to get dressed."

She rose slowly and started for her bedroom. Sean smiled,

shrugged to Brendan, and told him he could find a room-service menu on the desk in the parlor.

The Jacksons had been awake and soon joined Sean, Lori, and Brendan on the balcony for room-service breakfast. As morning deepened and the sun continued to rise over the water, the scenery was almost as beautiful as it had been at sunset.

Breakfast was delicious, and they ate it lazily, discussing what they could do with the day while remembering that tomorrow was a school day—Brendan's first—and people did have to work in the morning.

"Parasailing," Tina pleaded.

"I'll think about it," Brad said.

"No, I don't want her up in the air. What if something breaks or falls or—" Jan protested.

"Fishing," Brendan suggested.

"Snorkeling, diving, water skiing," Lori added.

"We'll rent a boat. A little fishing, a little snorkeling, a littie waterskiing," Brad said.

Lori watched him smile at his ex-wife. She thought that he did love Jan. She hoped that he wasn't just using her, raising her hopes. She thought about what Sean had told her, and she lowered her head, feeling a rush of fear. Every minute she was with him, she wanted him more. The relationship subtly changed each time they were together. At first it might have been mostly sexual. What the hell, she was an adult. She was allowed a relationship now and then, and he was attractive as hell and had pursued her. She liked him, wanted him, even if it wasn't forever. . . .

But she had loved him once before, and she was growing emotionally entangled at a terrifying rate.

She thought they were just beginning to share a feeling of commitment, a comfort in being together. Yes, sex was great. That was important. One of those things you didn't allow yourself to realize just how much you missed while you were missing it until you had it again.

But her feeling for him was much more. Waking beside him, talking with him with their heads still on their pillows, watching his slow smile as he listened to her, or like this morning, waking and feeling warmth where he had been, and knowing that she would see him again soon.

Scary. Damned scary.

Maybe she should pull back. Now. Create a distance between them so that they could start over again with . . .

With the truth.

"Lori, what did you have in mind?" Sean asked.

She shook her head. "Anything. I'm open. Except—"

"What?" Brad asked.

"I was thinking about going to church."

"Church!" Brendan exclaimed in dismay, then quickly tried to cover. "You always said that God didn't consider us terrible sinners for missing church now and then. You—"

"It's because of Ellie," Jan interrupted, staring at Lori.

"But, Mom, do we have to go—"

"Well, she wants to go," Sean said quietly.

"There goes half the day," Brad muttered.

"We'll pray for good weather for the afternoon," Jan said philosophically.

They went to church, returned to the hotel, and rented a little ski boat. Tina knew what she was doing; on his fifth try, Brendan made it to his feet and actually waterskied.

After they'd all taken a turn, they spent some time fishing, but threw back the few bone fish they caught. They weren't good eating, but they put up a hell of a fight, and Lori found herself ready to engage in fierce battle with the one fish that bit her line. At the very end Sean helped her, but she took her fish off the hook to throw back into the water.

Jan relented and allowed Tina to go parasailing with Brendan and Sean and Brad while she and Lori gathered up their things so that they could make their afternoon checkout time from the suite. She was just going through the rooms to make sure they hadn't forgotten anything when she suddenly heard Jan squeal out her name.

"Lori!"

"What?"

She rushed out to the parlor, where Jan, the consummate businesswoman, had been checking her messages.

Jan held the receiver tightly in her hand as she stared at Lori, absolutely ashen.

"Sue . . ."

"Sue what?"

"She's disappeared. One of the kids working for her called my house half a dozen times, worried because she didn't come to work. Oh, God, Lori, what's happening?"

Chapter 17

"She's just not home," Brad said firmly as they sat around a table having dinner at a seaside restaurant. The kids were off looking at the large aquarium in the center of the restaurant, so he could speak freely. "You can't go getting all panicky just because Sue's not home."

"Brad, she didn't show up for work. She didn't call in. Sue is reliable, dependable!"

Sean calmly folded his arms and leaned on the table to meet Jan's eyes. "Ted has gone ahead and started calling more of her coworkers and friends. He intends to take a look in her house—despite the fact that she's certainly not been missing for forty-eight hours. We just saw her Friday night! Late Friday night. And, Jan, didn't you say that she was hinting that she was seeing someone?"

"Yes," Jan agreed.

"Look, if she doesn't show up soon, then we can panic," Brad said.

"Don't even think about not sleeping at my house!" Jan warned Brad.

"I'll stay, don't worry." Brad glanced at Sean. His blue eyes were impassive. "I assume you'll be with Lori?"

"Brad," Lori protested. "I'm all right, I—"

"I'll be with Lori."

She could have argued the point, but she didn't. She didn't want to be alone.

"Let's start home, can we?" Jan said. "I'm anxious."

"Yeah, let's go," Brad said.

*　　*　　*

No matter where Andrew went lately, he seemed to be running into Muffy Fluffy.

He'd called her himself yesterday to make arrangements for Brad, but Sunday evening he'd agreed to meet Jeff and Josh for drinks at Fat Tuesdays in the Grove, and he *wasn't* looking forward to any business conversations beforehand. But he arrived first, ordered a beer, and was sitting at one of the tables looking down at Main Street when he heard a cheerful "Hi!"

He swung around, certain she couldn't be there.

But she was.

"What a pleasant surprise, Andrew."

"Muffy."

"Can I join you?"

"Well, I'm waiting for friends."

"I'll leave when they come."

"I don't mean to be rude . . ."

"It's all right. I understand."

"What are you doing down in this neck of the woods?"

"Oh, my boyfriend lives down here."

"Boyfriend?"

She shrugged. "Sure. You know, business is business. I also have a social life."

"I'm glad to hear it," he said, smiling. Interesting woman. She really was pretty, and very voluptuous. Brad was going to be pleased, even if Andrew still felt uncomfortable as hell.

Muffy smiled suddenly. "You're looking ill, Andrew. Don't. I appreciate you telling me about your friend. Sounds like maybe he does need just one final kick . . . and then he'll settle down. I'll make the wife comfortable, I promise. This is the kind of thing I really like, getting to feel as if I'm helping someone." She was dead serious, entirely sincere.

Andrew swallowed his beer and nodded. "Thanks."

Muffy grinned suddenly. "Does she know that you know? That you found me?"

Andrew shook his head. "No. Don't mention it, huh?"

"Not on your life. Are you kind of getting out of the business yourself, Andrew?"

She didn't mean it that way, but he felt more like a pimp than ever. He smiled at her, leaning forward. "Yeah, Muffy. I'm going to try to take a few chances and make some of the films I really want to make. Just as soon as we wrap up *Debbie and the Devils,* I'm going to turn my talents toward something I want to do more."

"You'll be a great loss to the industry," Muffy told him sincerely.

"Yeah, sure."

"You're one of the good ones, Andrew. Handsome, smart, honest. We'll miss you, but I'm happy for you, happy you'll be doing what you want."

"Thanks, Muff."

She winked at him. "I'll let you know how things go with your friend."

"Do that."

She grinned and stood, and he suddenly felt a deeper affection for her. "You're a good kid, Muffy."

"Thanks. You, too, Andrew."

With a cheerful swish of derriere she left his table. He was still watching her depart when he heard Jeff's voice, "Now, that's a . . . handful of woman, Andrew."

"Whoa, cousin!" Josh chimed in, grinning and climbing over a chair backward to lean on its back and face Andrew. "There's a wicked figure for you."

"Your latest?" Jeff asked him.

"No, just a friend," Andrew said.

"Or employee?" Jeff asked.

"She's been known to work a stage or two," Andrew said.

"Ahh . . ." Josh teased, then he smiled. "Muffy Fluffy."

"You know her?" Andrew asked.

"Hey, don't you remember? She was working for you way back in the days when we needed money and you needed cheap labor, and we still looked pretty good in the buff," Josh said.

"Yeah, I remember."

"Actually, I don't *want* to remember," Josh groaned. "You on for golf Tuesday afternoon?" Josh asked him.

"Tuesday afternoon . . ." Andrew mused, swallowing his beer. "Yeah, I can manage a round. About three-thirty, four?"

"That will be good. We'll get Brad, and have a foursome," Jeff said.

"Then we can run over with him to Jan's after, and jump in the pool and Jacuzzi," Josh added. "Oh, Lord!" he said, raising his voice. "The riffraff are here!" He was joking, and lifted a hand to slap Ricky's as he and Ted appeared, both off duty, in jeans and knit shirts.

"Speaking of riffraff," Ted said, shaking his head as he, too, pulled up a chair.

"How'd you know we'd be here?" Andrew asked.

"Didn't. We just stumbled on you," Ricky told him. "Who was the blonde, Andrew?"

Andrew groaned. "Old friend."

"Good friend," Jeff Olin teased. "Damned good friend."

"Do I want to meet her?" Ricky asked.

"Every man wants to meet Muffy," Josh said. "But she's gone now, so what are you are two doing out on the streets?"

"I came for booze, lots of it," Ted said.

"Oh, yeah? What's up?" Jeff asked, hiking a brow.

"Sue is missing," Ted said, suddenly serious.

"Missing!" Josh exclaimed.

Ted shrugged. "Her employees are all shook up because she hasn't come into work yesterday or today. You know we need forty-eight hours for a regulation missing-persons report, but since it's Sue . . ." He shrugged. "One of her neighbors keeps a key so we went in. It looks like Sue just decided to take off. According to the neighbor, the big handbag she uses most of the time is gone, and so is her little overnight bag. So it looks as if she planned it."

"So?" Andrew inquired carefully.

"Well, her car is in the driveway."

"That's not so weird," Jeff said. "She must have gone off with a friend."

"Yeah, well, that's possible."

"Then . . ." Andrew prodded. "What is it?"

"Her cat was there. Dead on the kitchen floor."

"Maybe she forgot to feed it," Josh suggested. "Or leave it water. Animals dehydrate so easily—"

"And sometimes they bite those poisonous frogs—" Jeff said.

"Toads," Andrew remarked distractedly. "I still don't understand why you look so worried, Ted. It's not like Sue, but maybe she did just take off on a lark. Maybe she got sick of being responsible—the small-business owner. If her purse and overnight bag are gone . . ."

"Yeah, it should look like she went off on her own free will. But Andrew, the cat didn't just die," Ricky said.

"No?"

"It's neck was broken," Ted explained.

Andrew felt a shiver go right down his spine.

He cruised the streets.

He liked to do it, just driving around at first, by Lori's house, then . . .

By the Kelly house.

The good old Kellys.

He could see inside. It was night, but the drapes hadn't yet been closed to the living room of the fine old Spanish mansion. Good old Mom Kelly was a great housekeeper, always had been, in line with the last generation's Donna Reed or June Cleaver. Pretty woman, she never aged. Her hair was always just so. She had kept a slim figure. He saw her now, walking away from the television, taking a seat on the couch. Talking with someone in another chair. Old Gramps?

He smiled. Who knew?

He warned himself that he had to be very careful. He was an organized killer. There were things that even stupid police felt they knew. Like the fact that killers liked to return to the scene of the crime.

Well, he was going to cruise by Sue's house anyway. Not that it was actually the scene *of any crime.*

It was actually damned funny. Sue's stuff gone with Sue, and a dead cat in the house.

They just didn't know what to think.

But they would. And soon.

Smiling to himself, he drove by Sue's house.

And then Lori's.

Sean was still there. But he wouldn't be forever. He'd be so surprised. So damned surprised. If he ever knew, of course. Now that would be a challenge. Lori dead, Sean about to fry for it, and him as free as a bird. To start over somewhere else. Everyone would understand, of course, when he chose to leave the area . . .

Sean woke up feeling like a million bucks. He shouldn't have felt so good. He should have had creaks all over. Instead he felt like a teenager again, starting off on the sofa, slipping up to Lori's room, waking himself with an internal alarm around four to slip back down to the sofa. He wondered if Brendan knew exactly what was going on, but the boy seemed to like him, and he liked Brendan—Lori had done a great job with the kid—and the subterfuge was definitely worth it.

He'd gotten in a few hours of sleep on the sofa, from around four to six, but was still the first one up. He rose, made his way into Lori's kitchen, and put the coffee on. In his jeans, barefoot, bare-chested, he stepped out on the lawn and picked up Lori's paper. The main headline was about the shake-up in the stock market, which had occurred on Friday.

Flipping the paper over, though, he frowned to see his name in big black print.

"*Acclaimed Author Sean Black Returns to the Scene of the Crime—And Another Woman Dies.*"

He felt instantly sick. A shot of hot adrenaline ripped through him, and he gritted his teeth as if he were powerless, turning into some monster through the force of his anger.

He quickly scanned the article. It hashed everything that happened when Mandy died—the situation at the rock pit, his arrest, his incarceration, his trial—and the fact that no one else had ever been charged with the crime. The article went on to state that another member of the group that had been at the rock pit that day had recently died under terrible circumstances—and now a third member of that same group was apparently missing. And he was back in town after a very long absence. Coincidence?

"Sean?"

He swung around, startled to see that Lori had come outside. He hadn't heard her.

"What's the matter?"

"Here."

He handed it to her. She glanced down, and went pale. "Let's not show it to Brendan."

"Why. He's not going to hear about it?" Sean demanded, hands on his hips.

"Look, I know you're upset—"

"Yeah, I'm upset!" he said, dragging his fingers through his hair. "And you shouldn't be a part of this—"

"Sean. I was at the rock pit, remember?"

"You were at the rock pit, yeah. But in a way, this doesn't concern you, and I don't want you dragged into it. Lori, I've got to find out whoever the hell is doing this, what happened to Ellie—"

"The police will find out—"

"Oh, yeah, right."

"They're qualified—"

"And I'm more qualified than you might imagine. Jesus, I'm beginning to think that someone close to us is doing this. It's just too . . . First Ellie, now Sue—"

"Everyone keeps saying that Sue just went away for the weekend."

"Maybe. But I've got to find out—"

He heard the phone ringing. Disgusted, irritated with himself for letting the article upset him so much, he shook his head impatiently. "Will you answer the phone, please."

"It can wait—"

"Answer the damned phone. Please."

She went into the house, but was back out a second later. "It's Jeff Olin."

"What did he want?"

"He wants to speak with you."

Sean stared at her, then went into the house. He picked up the phone in the den, watching Lori as she followed him in. "Yeah, Jeff, it's Sean."

Jeff's voice came to him, crisp, distinct, and outraged. "Sean, I've seen the paper—"

"I imagine most of the city has seen it."

"That reporter—that what's her name—Kathy Clines—is way out of line. Those of us who were there, who know you, know the truth. She's close to libel on this. I'll be happy to represent you to sue the ass off the reporter and the paper."

Sean felt some of the tension ease away. "It's all right, Jeff. I don't think I can actually sue on what's written, and frankly, I don't want to sue anyone, I just want to be left the hell alone."

Jeff was quiet a minute. "Want to have lunch tomorrow? Some high-profile place?"

"Jeff, you don't have to do this. I admit the article threw me at first, but I can deal with it." He hesitated. "I've dealt with much worse."

"We're going golfing tomorrow afternoon, Biltmore course, then to Jan's place after. Join us?"

He started to say no, then shrugged, watching Lori. "Yeah, what the hell? Thanks Jeff."

"Maybe Lori can meet us at Jan's."

He hesitated. Amazing how quickly everyone seemed to know just how deeply he and Lori were becoming involved. He should cut some distance from her with this going on. "Jeff, that will be up to her," he said.

He set the receiver down, looking at Lori. Her eyes were wide and troubled. "God, Sean, I'm so sorry."

He looked at her a long moment and felt the anger and tension draining from his body. He walked over to her, slipped his arms around her and drew her tight.

"You do know that I didn't do it?"

"With all my heart."

"God, I don't know, I'm afraid to leave you, afraid to be with you. I haven't known how to trust anyone in all these years, so many backs were turned to me, I thought that you'd betrayed me just like everyone else, and now, this isn't just a knife in my side, it's touching your life."

"You know, I've never liked the movie reviews in that paper. And some of the editorials quite simply suck. I'm not going to be bothered by something being said by a novice reporter trying to make a name for herself."

He pulled back, looking at her. "What about Brendan?"

"I'm going to tell Brendan what happened back then."

The phone was ringing again. Lori turned from him, and he went to pick it up. "Hello?" He covered the mouthpiece. "Michael," he told her.

"Is he upset?"

"Worried about me."

Sean quickly assured his brother, told him good-bye, and answered the call waiting.

Brad was on the line, offering to help him sue the paper as well.

He thanked Brad, and hung up. Sitting, he shook his head. "Lori, I'd like to go and talk to your son myself."

She stared at him a moment, about to protest. Then she shrugged. "Yes. I guess that would be right."

"It's his first day of school. People might be talking about this."

She nodded. "I'll get dressed. I have to get Brendan to school, then pick up my grandfather."

"You'll be with your family?" he asked her.

"Yes."

"Good. I've got to take care of some things. Call my publicist, some other people. You be careful."

He could tell by the way her hazel eyes met his—stubbornly— that she didn't feel she was in any danger.

"Lori, please be careful."

"I will be."

"I intend to solve this, not you."

"What could I do?" she asked innocently. Then she turned quickly, and left him.

He went upstairs, and tapped on Brendan's door.

"Maybe we should wait on this now," Jan told Brad.

"*What?*" Brad demanded.

"Well, this is going to be a rough day for Sean—"

"And what the hell can we do about it? I think he should sue the bloody paper. Jan, something is always going to happen in life. I've got the hotel reservation. I've—"

He broke off. Jan was in the bathroom in a black dress and little pillbox type hat with a veil.

"What in hell are you doing?" he demanded.

She flashed him a nervous glance. "I don't want anyone to recognize me, I don't want to be conspicuous—"

"Honey, trust me, you are conspicuous in that hat. You look like my grandmother."

"What? You mean that isn't one of your fantasies?"

"No, it's not," he said sourly. "People will notice you, and remember you, in that outfit. Put on a pantsuit or something."

"I've got a blond wig."

He groaned. "Fine. Wear your wig. But not the hat. It looks like we're going to a funeral."

"We may be going to a funeral again soon," Jan informed him. "No one's heard from Sue yet, and Ted seems to be uneasy about something."

"I spoke with him on the phone last night," Brad said, feeling a little uneasy himself about the dead cat.

"And?" Jan said.

"He said that her purse is gone, her bag is gone, what else can he say? It looks as if she went away on a romantic tryst of some kind. There were a bunch of receipts from that sweet-smelling lingerie shop you all like so much on her dresser. Sounds as if she was planning something."

"But not to tell anyone . . ."

"Jan, if you're really trying to get out of this—"

"No, I'm not. I said that I'd do it and I will."

Lori showered and dressed. When she came out of her room, she could still hear Sean and Brendan talking behind the closed door to Brendan's room.

She hesitated, then tapped on Brendan's door. "Come in," Sean told her, and she entered the room. Brendan was up, dressed for school. The newspaper lay on the bed between them.

"Sorry to interrupt, but we need to go soon."

"I'm ready," Brendan said. He stood, and Sean did the same. Brendan picked up his backpack, then offered Sean his hand. "It wouldn't have mattered what I heard, Sean. I haven't known you that long, but I know that you didn't kill that girl."

"Thank you," Sean told him solemnly.

Brendan grinned suddenly. "And you're still welcome to date my mother."

"Well, thanks again."

Lori smiled, her eyes meeting Sean's.

"You're no monster," Brendan told Sean.

Sean frowned at that. "I'm glad that you believe that, Brendan, but one of the scariest things in life is that monsters don't always come with horns and tails and vampire teeth. There are monsters out there that are hard to recognize."

"I know that. But monsters are hideous inside, and lots of the time, no matter what's on the outside of people, if you look hard enough, you can see the monster inside."

"You've got good vision," Sean told him quietly.

Lori smiled, proud of her son. "I'll see you later," she told Sean.

"I'll be out of here soon. I'll lock up."

Brendan hurried down the stairs ahead of her, was out the door and into the car quickly. She followed him, and eased out into the street. Things were still quiet, the traffic still light at this hour.

"You really all right with all this?" she asked him.

He was looking straight ahead, hazel eyes level on the road. His hair was getting longish, and she felt a sudden sinking in the pit of her stomach as he brushed it back. The gesture was amazingly familiar.

"Yeah, I'm fine, Mom. I was just thinking . . . I feel so bad for you all. You weren't much older than I am now when you had to face something so awful as the death of your friend—and then he was blamed for it!"

Lori didn't know exactly what Sean had told Brendan, but she was sure he had downplayed his experiences in the jail. "Bad things happen in life," she murmured.

"Makes you wonder why we go through it, huh, Mom?"

She looked at him, perplexed. Then she smiled. "Because good things happen, too." They were nearing the school. "Wow! Big place," Lori said, worried. "It's grown since I lived here."

"Things have changed since the dark ages, Mom," he teased. "Don't worry about me. I come from the Big Apple. Nothing's too big for me."

"Oh, yeah?"

"Yeah." He kissed her cheek. "I'll just jump out. Don't park or anything—there, right there, that's where everyone is getting out."

The school was on LeJeune, a major thoroughfare, but school-zone signs were posted everywhere, and it was true that all the cars ahead of her were dropping off in the same spot. She came to a stop and let Brendan off, and was proud again to see her son's natural, easy-going confidence. If he was afraid, he wasn't going to show it.

She didn't return home, but drove on to her parents' house, dreading what awaited her. As she expected, her mother opened the door with a worried look. "Lori, dear—"

"I know, Mom, I've see the newspaper. So has Sean."

"Well, I'm really trying hard not to make judgments—"

"Then, don't allow a newspaper reporter to make them for you, Mom!" Lori said with anger.

"Sweetheart, I'm just thinking of Brendan."

"Brendan is fine."

Her father had come into the living room. He didn't embrace her and kiss her; he kept his distance. "Lori, what if—just what if!— Suppose he did kill your friend Mandy in high school. He's back in town, and suddenly Ellie Metz is dead, and now Sue Nichols is missing. What if you and Jan are next, have you thought about that?"

She hadn't. She drew her breath in sharply, and stuttered out an answer, "Sue is just missing, Dad."

"Yeah, but Ted was by here the other night, and he's very concerned. She was supposed to be in this weekend to pay her mother's bill at the nursing home, and she didn't show. Sue is a devoted daughter, so Ted tells me. She never misses a visit with her mother, and she sure as hell never forgets to pay her bill!"

Lori put her hands on her hips, feeling ill. "Maybe something has happened to Sue, but—"

"Oh, sweetheart!" her mother interrupted miserably. "I don't *want* it to be Sean, either. I like him, honestly like him."

"We're just so damned scared for you, Lori," her father said. "What if Sean is innocent, and it's his brother—"

"If Sean is innocent, why should it be *his* brother who is guilty?" Lori demanded.

"Michael Black used to get into a lot trouble," her mother said.

"Kids do get into trouble."

"But you're seeing so much of Sean and Michael."

"Yes, I am. And don't be worried about me. I'm okay. I promised Gramps some time out. Is he ready?"

"Should be," her mother said. "I'll just—" she began, but broke off because the phone was ringing. "I'll just get that, and check on Gramps."

She answered the phone on the desk, and looked at Lori. "For you," she whispered. "Sean."

She arched a brow, and went to the phone. "Sean?"

"Yeah. Can you stay with your folks tonight?"

She frowned. "I'm sure I could. But why?"

"An old friend of mine is in Palm Beach. I'm going to go see him this afternoon, and I may run late."

"Why don't I come with you?"

She heard his hesitation. "Lori, I told you—"

"You want me safe, don't you? I'll be safe with you."

"Let me think about it. Call me at the hotel after you've gone out with your grandfather. But promise me, if we miss one another by any chance, you'll stay with your parents."

"Sure."

Jan had never been so nervous in her whole life.

Nor had she had ever been in such a hotel before. Heart-shaped whirlpool, heart-shaped bed, brass posts everywhere, pink sheets, heart-shaped champagne tray, heart-shaped chocolates.

"I can't imagine why they didn't manage a heart-shaped champagne bottle," she murmured to Brad.

He dropped the little case bearing their toiletries and wandered over to where she stood by the Jacuzzi. He kissed her nape. "This is the best gift I've had in my entire life."

"It's a one and only."

"I know. That's all I want."

Jan hoped that was true.

"Why don't we get into the Jacuzzi?"

"Sure."

Sure. She felt about as sexy as a watermelon; this was so awkward, and she still didn't really know how it was going to work. did they just introduce themselves to this woman: Hi, I'm Brad's ex-wife, the mother of his child, and then, oh, yes, how do you do, I'm the prostitute he's hired for the day, should we get right to it, or what?

There was a soft knocking on the door, and Brad grinned, then went to answer it.

Jan experienced a terrible moment of panic. Of course, she could still back out. She could back out until the very end.

She turned around. The woman was in the room, a bosomy blonde who certainly looked the part, and yet . . .

"Hi. I'm Muffy. Oh, a hot tub! Great, isn't this place just too much? Champagne, definitely the right way to start. May I have a glass?''

Brad was already fumbling with the bottle.

Muffy didn't get the first glass. Jan did. In fact, Muffy didn't get a glass of the first bottle at all because Jan just drank straight from it and wouldn't let it go.

She drank the whole thing.

Gramps was quiet as they drove. "Where are we going?" Lori asked him. "I think it's a little too early for even you to head for a bar.''

He arched a brow to her. "It's never too early for really old, sick Irish Catholics to head for the bar, but no, I don't want a drink, a breakfast place will be just fine.''

They opted for Denny's. The early crowd was gone, the place was slow. The waitress gave them coffee and took their order.

"Okay, Gramps, what is it?" Lori asked as soon as the waitress had gone.

He wagged a finger at her. "I may be old, and I may be sick, but I'm damned sure not blind as yet!''

"All right, I don't remember suggesting that you are.''

"Other people aren't blind, either.''

"Gramps, what are you getting at?''

"Brendan.''

She felt as if she had been doused by a bucket of cold water. She inhaled, "Gramps, I don't—''

"Right. You don't go taking me for a fool! His eyes are all Kelly, right enough, but you see him and Sean Black up close in the same room and . . .'' He lifted his hands, shrugging.

She sipped her coffee, feeling trapped, desperate, and really afraid.

"When are you going to tell him?''

She stared at her grandfather, about to hedge or lie again. "I don't know. I was ready to just blurt it out when I first saw him again, but . . . but I don't know. I missed the right moment. And now . . . well, now he's just trusting me, and I'm really worried about what's going on. I'm scared for Sue, really scared, and I'm scared for Sean just the same. He needs to trust someone right now, and if he discovers that I kept a secret like that . . . well, I didn't mean to, Gramps, I really didn't mean to, I tried to reach him before I fled to England, but his dad was never able to give him the message, and then it was as if he had just disappeared, all his family had disappeared, and I was alone, and I assumed he hated me, and . . . and I met Ian Corcoran, and he was my solution.''

She sat back, biting her lower lip, suddenly glad that she'd confessed the truth to someone other than the friend and husband she had inadvertently met, sobbing her eyes out in a coffeehouse her first night in London. A folk group had been playing; Ian had been the singer/songwriter, and he'd been good. He'd seen her sitting there, seen her wiping her tears. And she'd talked, telling him that everything was so horrible she wanted to die, and he'd told her that no, she didn't, he was dying, and it wasn't easy, but neither was living—life itself was precious, to be cherished. There'd been a quiet strength about him, and after a week of friendship, she'd been glad of his solution.

"I'll marry you."

"That's not fair to you. I couldn't—"

"It's hardly fair to you. Because I am dying, and you'll be with me, and it won't be pretty."

It wasn't pretty; and by the time he died, she had loved him with all her heart, despite the fact that their marriage had never been anything other than platonic.

"Lori," Gramps told her then, "I'm not telling you that you did anything wrong—hell, you were young, it was one hell of a bad situation! But I think you need to tell Sean Black that Brendan is his son. I can't believe he hasn't figured it out yet himself."

"We were only together once, Gramps."

"I told you, honey, I'm not judging you."

She nodded. "I'm going to tell him. But I am trying to pick the right time."

"I hope you get a 'right time' soon," he told her. "Where is that waitress? I could use more coffee."

"She's not as good as old Mickey at the pub, eh, Gramps?" Lori said. "Too bad we didn't go there."

"Why's that?"

"I could have used the drink today," she said dryly.

He grinned. "You're going to be all right, girl," he told her.

She smiled, but felt an inward shiver. Was she?

Chapter 18

It wasn't half so bad as Jan had imagined.

Of course, the champagne helped, but it didn't matter.

She drank a lot, and she was really lethargic by the time she somehow wound up in the ridiculous heart-shaped bed.

Muffy suggested a blindfold, and delicate little scarves that tied her wrists to the brass bedposts. She didn't really care at that point.

Then it began . . .

And it was just a blur of sensations and images. Brad's voice, his whisper, so excited. His kiss . . . it seemed really good to kiss him . . . then she realized, dimly, that if he was kissing her lips, then the lips moving so seductively over her other, extremely intimate places, had to be . . .

Didn't matter, didn't matter, had to be the champagne.

And yet . . .

Oh, God.

It wasn't bad, it wasn't horrible, it was . . .

Exciting.

Arnie Harris had come down to Palm Beach on Saturday morning.

"You didn't need to come down here for me, Arnie," Sean told him. "Anytime I need help, I call you, you know that.

"We're not writing a book here, Sean. I'm not giving you hypothetical advice for a character. This is your life. Besides, I didn't come for you, I came for Maggie. She just loves this old hotel."

He and Maggie were staying at the Breakers, a majestic establishment built during the twenties, and still lording it over the houses in the area where presidents, princes, and the simply filthy rich had their winter homes.

A fine strip of beach flanked the back of the hotel, and Sean walked it along with Arnie. They were both barefoot, pant legs rolled up, relaxed in their movements. But Arnie's mind was far from idle, and Sean knew that his friend had come down just to be near him because of the Eleanor Metz thing.

And now Sue was missing.

"Maybe you're not so paranoid," Arnie said after a moment. "But if you're not, it's a terrifying thought."

"What is?"

Arnie paused, squinting beneath the sun. "Say your old girlfriend Mandy was murdered. It might have been a spur-of-the-moment thing—hell, it must have been a spur of the moment thing. The girl in the water, the vine handy. So it wasn't a premeditated murder, just a murder of convenience." Arnie grimaced. "Murder . . . one, two, three, not planned, but easy. Young deviants don't usually plan to throw rocks at dogs, drown kittens, rip the wings off butterflies. The creatures are just there, and . . ."

"So he was losing it, Mandy was in the water, a vine was in the water . . . so he kills Mandy, but then waits?" Sean said. "And then *this many* years comes back for Ellie—and then Sue?"

Arnie shook his head slowly. "He wasn't waiting. Your Doctor Gillespie has been trying to convince the local police that there's a serial killer in your midst. You looked at those bones yourself; you know what you're doing. You don't need me to tell you any of this, you just want some reassurances on what you're thinking. The killer is good, really good. You want a profile? He lives alone, or is able to be alone, because he plans things out. He plans the occasions of his murders, and just where he'll find his victims. He knows how to dispose of the bodies so that they're *usually* almost totally decomposed before they're found. No fingerprinting to be done—the last victim, your friend, however, was found. Maybe he wanted that to happen. Maybe he knew you were back in town and wanted people associating you with the murder. She was raped. Any blood, semen, anything?" Arnie asked.

"Nothing was found, not a drop of blood, nothing. She didn't have a speck of flesh beneath her nails."

"He knows how he can be caught," Arnie said. "I imagine he has a deep-seated hatred for women, but he hides it with charisma. There's something very personal about his feelings—he goes into overkill. Someone this organized probably appears to be a respectably functioning member of the community.''

"But he's supposed to make a mistake somewhere along the line, right?" Sean inquired with a touch of bitterness.

Arnie looked at him. "I'm sorry to say that some of these killers have apparently walked away from their crimes. The Seattle murders have never been solved, there are high-profile cases in California . . . look how long Bundy got away with murder, how many states he traveled, how many *years* he killed before he was brought to justice."

"We're talking about my life here, Arnie. I have to find this killer, or spend my life with people looking at me, pointing . . . thinking I'm guilty."

"You know the truth."

"Yes, but how do you inflict that kind of life on anyone else, Arnie?"

Arnie shrugged. "If a killer won't trip himself up, you can try to give him a little nudge."

"I don't know who the killer is."

"But you do have a theory that goes back to Mandy's death . . . one of your old friends, your good old boys, is a killer. Start talking to them. Find out who has alibis for when. Find out who had a thing on Mandy Olin and—"

"And?"

"On you. But be careful. If you push too hard . . ."

"What?"

Arnie smiled grimly. "Obviously. He'll push back. You want him to make a mistake. Just don't let that mistake be you."

Sean hadn't waited for her. Lori found a note at her house; he'd gone to Palm Beach, he didn't know when he'd be back, she should stay with her parents.

She walked up the stairs to the small tower at the back of the house and surveyed her surroundings. She loved the lush foliage, the pretty old houses, some of them renovated, some of them ladies of fading grandeur. She was glad to have come home. Gramps was right, she'd lived a lie too long, and she wanted a life with Sean. He seemed to think that someone they knew might be involved in the murders. The same someone who had killed Mandy.

She stood. She probably would spend the night at her folks house, but she could go later. She went to her desk for paper and a pen, sat down, and started writing out a list. Who had been there that day? Ricky Garcia, Ted Larson. Brad. Sean. Her cousin, Josh, her brother,

Andrew, and Sean's brother, Michael. Ricky and Ted had become cops. Did that exonerate them? No. There were cases of bad cops. Josh, Jeff, and Brad, were attorneys. Did that make them killers? Sharks, according to some, but killers? Then there was Andrew. Her brother. Making porno movies, resenting every minute of it.

No, her brother wasn't a killer. She scratched out his name. She refused to accept such a concept.

No! Don't. *If you're making a list, you have to make a list!* she chastised herself. She wrote down his name again.

That left Michael. Sean's brother. Working with marine mammals and fish, trying to cure cancer. Gentle, decent. Couldn't be.

But their mother had left them. He might well resent other women. And Mandy Olin had been running around on his brother, acting cruelly, hurting Sean, embarrassing them all. And what had happened with Mandy had nearly destroyed his family, it had killed his father.

All the same things could be said of Sean.

And Brad, bless him, wanted his ex-wife to engage in a ménage à trois!

She laid her forehead down on the desk. There was Jeff Olin. An attorney, one of those ruthless sharks.

Jeff. Mandy's brother. And Ellie had been her best friend.

Ricky dealt with homicide every day. He'd know how to get away with murder. Ted had been inside Sue's house. Ted had been the one to tell them that her purse and bag were gone . . .

She groaned softly. There had to be a way to prove Sean innocent without indicting her other friends.

She sat up again. Okay, so she didn't want to put her own brother's name on a list. Why not start by eliminating him? She picked up the phone and dialed Andrew's number. An answering service picked up. When Lori said it was a personal call, the woman said that she'd have Andrew call back. Frustrated, Lori stared at the phone. She called again and put on a soft Southern accent. "Hi, honey, I'm trying to reach Mr. Kelly about today's shoot? I seem to have lost the address."

"They're filming on the Beach."

Bingo. South Beach.

"Do you have that exact address?"

The woman gave it to her. Lori started out of the house. She saw a car driving up and frowned, then realized that it was Jeff Olin. He swung into her drive, blocking her. What the hell, she could start with Jeff.

"Hey, Lori. Heading out?"

"Errands. I'm supposed to start teaching Thursday. But I have a few minutes. Want some coffee, a soda, lunch? What brings you by?"

"Coffee would be great. Actually, I came by to see Sean. Is he here?"

"No, but he might be back any minute. I really can't say." She wasn't sure why she lied; she just didn't trust anybody at the moment.

"Is Sean okay?" Jeff asked as they walked inside and through to the kitchen.

"Yeah, he's all right."

"He has to be upset. You don't have to bother with coffee, Lori. I thought it might be made."

"No, it's fine. It only takes a second."

She measured out coffee, smiling at him. "So how is the law these days?"

"The law is a beautiful thing."

"Because it protects the innocent?"

"Because it makes me a lot of money," he said, grinning. "Did your son go to school today?"

"Yes." It suddenly occurred to Lori that if she really thought there was a murderer among her friends it probably wasn't such a smart idea to quiz one of them in her house alone. "I think he'll be home about now, too."

"No, the school kids won't be out for several hours," Jeff said, looking at his watch. "I wonder how long I can wait for Sean."

"Well, the coffee is ready," Lori told him. "Drink it, and we'll see if he comes."

"Join me?"

"Of course." She poured herself a cup and sat with him.

"How is he, really?"

"Sean?"

"Yeah."

"Angry, I think."

"More upset than he's willing to say."

"Well, it is an awful accusation."

"I seriously think he should sue the reporter and the newspaper. Sheer speculation. They could damage him personally and professionally. He shouldn't let some little hot snot, trying to make a name for herself, get away with something like this."

"I'm sure he's glad that you feel that way."

"I've always liked Sean. My folks didn't care for him—they

thought that he corrupted Mandy. They didn't understand the strong will of a teenage girl.''

"I hope the reporter doesn't know that.''

"No one knew—except your parents, Brad's parents . . . the others. And they closed ranks tighter than the military when other people started questioning them. I've been thinking about making some kind of a statement, about the fact that I know Sean would never have killed my sister. I'm trying to decide whether I'd be going to far, or if it would be helpful. The reporter can still dig up the trial transcripts if she wants to, and some of the things we all said were pretty damaging, just because they did have a row that day and hadn't been getting along.''

"Sean will appreciate the fact that you're so supportive,'' Lori said.

He smiled at her. "In lots of ways, he's a lucky guy.'' He reached out for her suddenly, and she felt a moment's panic. *She was an idiot, letting Jeff in here when she was all alone, and now he was going to reach out and strangle her, drag her out, take her somewhere, kill . . .*

He brushed back a lock of her hair, smiling again. "He's lucky to have you behind him,'' Jeff said. He stood. "I've got to go. Tell Sean to call me if he thinks I can do anything. We'll see you all tomorrow, anyway.''

"Oh?''

"Golf.''

"I don't golf.''

"No, but we thought we'd meet at Jan's after for a dip in the pool and Jacuzzi—and a call to a pizza place that delivers. You'll come, won't you?''

"Yes,'' she said, following him to the front door. As she opened it, feeling like a fool and hoping he didn't see the sheer panic in her face, Ted was just driving onto the embankment in front of her house.

"What's up?'' he asked, getting out. He was in uniform, on duty.

"Just came by to see Sean. But he's not here,'' Jeff said.

"You all right, Lori?'' Ted asked. "Sean . . . ?''

"He's fine, thanks. And, of course, I'm all right.''

Was she? Even Ted was making her nervous. *A man in uniform, a cop, could make a vulnerable woman do almost anything, trustingly.*

"Ted, any news on Sue?'' Lori asked anxiously.

He shook his head. "Strange. I followed her home from lunch after the funeral, and checked up on her after the party. She didn't say a thing about going anywhere. But she packed her toothbrush, so she must have planned on being away.''

"It is strange," Lori said.

"Scary," Ted agreed.

She thought that Ted and Jeff might even be suspicious of one another, because neither of them moved. She finally excused herself. "Well, I've got some errands. Thanks, guys, for being friends.''

"Sure thing, Lori.''

They were leaning against the rear of Jeff's car, both watching her, as she drove away.

Jan was practically passed out when Muffy left. She lay on the heart-shaped bed, her head spinning, wanting only to sleep.

She felt Brad near her, whispering in her ear. "Jan, I love you. I know how hard this was for you . . . thanks.''

She mumbled something.

"Jan . . .''

He turned her over. She slit her eyes open, saw the diamond he held glittering, even in the subdued light.

"Marry me?'' He said. He suddenly seemed somewhat tense. "You know, I really need you now in my life. I need your support, I need to say you're with me . . . at all times.''

Her head really hurt. She did love him, and she wanted to marry him.

But not now.

She rolled back over. "It would serve you right if I ran off with another woman,'' she told him.

He might have kept talking; she'd never know. The champagne was just too much.

She passed out.

At last Jan was home.

The killer knew, because he watched her. He'd known about her whole day ahead of time; they said that women talked, but men were just as bad.

She showered. Forever and ever it seemed, just letting the water rush over her. She was totally unaware that he stood within the redwood enclosure that encircled the glassed-in hot tub and shower area of her bathroom. She was usually safe from prying eyes because of that privacy fence and the profusion of hybiscus bushes that surrounded the fence.

But he knew her house. Knew that the pool and patio area were hidden by heavy foliage as well. Hell, he even knew her damned neighborhood. The old bat next door was watching Oprah. *The couple in back both worked. The house on the other side was empty; snowbirds owned it, and they were back up north.*

Can't wash it away, Jan, can't wash away what you've done! *he thought, amused.*

But it was nothing. Nothing at all compared to what she was going to do.

Soon, Jan.

With me.

It won't matter if your willing.

It won't even matter if you're alive or dead.

Lori reached the address the woman had given her. It was one of the old hotels, and she discovered at the desk that MFOT Productions had rented a rear suite. She made a mental note to ask her brother what "MFOT" stood for, then walked around the hotel and saw the camera crews first. She followed a deli caterer into the back of a large suite facing the ocean, then saw her brother in a chair, and a pair of long-limbed young women cuddled up together on the bed.

"Did Muffy get in yet? We need to get to the stud shots soon."

"Muffy's in back, she's clocked in!" someone called back.

Andrew was swearing softly to himself, then he called out a direction, "Come on, ladies, you're looking bored as hell! This is a seduction for you, Tanya, and a discovery for you, Betty. Look like you're into it."

"Yeah, yeah, I'm into it!" Betty said, bored.

"You're paid to be into it!" Andrew snapped, gritting his teeth and pressing his temples between his fingers. He looked up, and saw his sister.

"Jesus!" he cried, jumping up. "Take five!" he shouted to his crew, grabbing Lori by the elbow and propelling her out of the suite and down the walk toward the beach.

"Andrew—" she protested.

"What the hell are you doing here?" he asked with dismay.

"Calm down, I know what you do—"

"And you know I pee, too, but I don't want you watching me!"

She smiled. "Andrew, I've seen porno flicks. And it seems that half our friends have starred in the damned things."

"Only Brad, Jeff, and Josh," he mumbled.

"Andrew, what's MFOT?"

He stared at her dully. "Money for Other Things," he muttered. She smiled. "Lori, come on. What the hell are you doing here?"

"I just came to see if you wanted lunch," she lied. He looked innocent as hell. Her brother couldn't have killed anyone.

He hadn't looked half so innocent when he had been yelling at Tanya and Betty. Did he hate women, somewhere down deep? Or just these so-called actresses?

"Lunch?" he inquired, puzzled. She realized he was looking past her, to the door to the suite. She swung around, stunned to see that Sean was standing there.

Talking with Muffy Fluffy.

Lori's heart slammed against her chest.

"Sean called before to ask me to lunch," Andrew said. "He said that you were busy."

"I—was," Lori said quickly, staring at Sean. He hadn't seen her yet, he was smiling, laughing at something Muffy was saying. He was wearing his Ray•Bans, his dark hair was slightly damp, he was in dark dockers and a casual but well-cut jacket and looked as if he could easily be the star of the show.

"You haven't started using Sean in these things, have you?" she whispered.

"Oh, yeah, world-class author with a death-defying desire to do adult films," Andrew said. "No, I think the newspaper thing was getting to him, and he honestly just wanted to have lunch with a friend."

Honestly. Right. She realized that Sean was doing his own investigation, and that *he* was starting with *her* brother.

He looked up from Muffy Fluffy and saw her. Despite his glasses, she saw the flicker of quickly controlled tension in his features.

"Lori!" Muffy said happily.

"Hi, Muffy. Hello, Sean."

"Lori. What are you doing here?"

"Just came to see my big brother."

"You were supposed to be out with your grandfather," Sean said.

"I was. I thought you were staying in Palm Beach?"

"I was. I decided to come back early."

"Oh."

"Well," Andrew said, apparently unaware of any tension whatsoever, "we can all go to lunch."

"Sure," Sean said after a moment.

"Umm," Lori hedged.

"I'd love to—" Muffy began.

"But," Andrew quickly interrupted, "they'll need you here; I'm going to have the assistant director finish up those close-up shots while I'm gone."

"Oh, sure," Muffy said, ever cheerful. "See you all later, then."

"Where to?" Andrew asked.

"Anywhere."

"Down the street there's a great little fish house. Great fried shrimp," Andrew asked.

"Great," Sean agreed.

Before they reached the restaurant, someone called out their names. They turned around to see that Ricky Garcia was following them.

"Ricky?" Andrew said. "I may not be winning the Nobel Prize, but I am within my legal rights."

"Funny. I just heard that you were here, Sean, seeing Andrew."

"How'd you hear that?" Sean asked.

"Talked to Brad."

"How did Brad know?"

"Don't know," Ricky said.

"Maybe he called here and talked to someone in production," Andrew offered.

"Why were you looking for me?" Sean asked. "I'm not under arrest yet, am I?" he asked dryly.

Ricky shook his head. "She's a jerky kid reporter, Sean. No one will take any of it seriously."

"Some people will. Doesn't matter. What's up?"

"I'm down here to meet Brad and Jeff Olin for lunch," Ricky said. "Why don't we all go together? One of you can treat. Cops don't get paid well."

Just at that moment, Brad and Jeff pulled up in front of the hotel.

Sean, Ricky, and Lori spun around, and shouted a greeting as the two came toward them along the street. They looked the part of attorneys, sharply dressed, neat haircuts, clean-cut features, handsome, serious faces.

"What the hell is going on?" Sean asked as they walked up. "How'd you know I was here?" he asked Brad.

"Little bird," Brad said, and grinned. "I'd called for Andrew, a production assistant told me that *the* Sean Black was waiting to talk to him."

"Ah."

"So, you looking for work again?" Andrew teased.

"Naw, just came to see you and give someone something I forgot to take care of properly," Brad said.

"Well, are we having lunch or not?" Ricky demanded impatiently. They went into the restaurant.

Once they had ordered, Sean became insistent. "Ricky, what's up?"

"I ran into Ted right after he left your house this morning, Lori."

Sean looked at her sharply. "Ted was at your house this morning?"

"Worried about you," she told him. She grinned across the table at Jeff. "Another friend was by—Jeff. He thinks you should really sue the reporter."

"Lori, did Ted tell you about . . . the cat?" Ricky asked.

"The cat?" Sean snapped so sharply that they all stared at him.

"Yeah, seems that what has him so upset about Sue is her cat. Her stuff really was gone, place was closed up as if she was going away and all that—but her cat was dead."

"Did it dehydrate?" Lori asked.

Ricky shook his head, watching them all. "It's neck was broken." They all stared at him.

"She broke her own cat's neck?" Andrew said incredulously.

"I doubt it," Ricky said impatiently. "If she went away with the guy, he's some kind of a real loser."

"Ah, Sue doesn't deserve such a jerk," Andrew said angrily.

"Jerk? He may be a killer," Sean said.

"Yeah. I just thought you guys should know."

"Ted had told me," Jeff said quietly.

"I don't want Jan to know," Andrew said. "She's spooked enough."

"Maybe she needs to know," Sean said.

"Maybe. Because it is getting a little scary here," Ricky said. "All right—real scary. Wierd, bizarre."

"Only for women, it seems," Lori said quietly.

"Lori, don't you even think about being alone anywhere!" Andrew warned her.

"I won't, Andrew, I'm careful—"

"Jeff knows good alarm people; he told you he did."

"I'll have an alarm put in—"

"Tomorrow. Before you go back to work at the school," Sean told her.

"I'll see to it, Lori," Jeff said.

"Tomorrow," she said. She would borrow the money from Gramps, and keep them all quiet.

"You need to keep an eye out, too, Andrew. This is a strange business you're in," Ricky told him.

"But I think I really am getting out of it soon. I've an appointment next week with some highly respected Hollywood types interested in a screenplay I submitted."

"Andrew! How wonderful!" Lori said.

"What is it?"

Andrew winced. "A movie about a serial killer in Miami."

Despite the topic, Lori made a point of being very supportive—he was her brother, her blood. It was all right for her to quiz him. She wasn't sure what she felt about Sean doing the same—except that he should have gotten her permission.

When she left the men, she didn't realize at first that Sean had gotten right into his own car to follow her, but he did so, bursting into the house right behind her after she had unlocked the door.

"What the hell did you think you were doing?" he demanded furiously.

"I told you, seeing my brother—"

"Bull!"

"Well, then, what the hell were you doing?"

"Questioning him."

"*My* brother. How dare you? How dare you?" she screamed, alarmed at the way her voice rose. She sounded like a shrew. But she was angry.

And scared.

"Oh, gee, now, why would I question the porn king of Miami?"

"Don't you dare call him that!"

"Don't you start being such an idiot!"

"He's my brother! He'd never hurt me—"

"How do you know that?"

"I trust him—I—"

"How can you?"

"I trust you!"

He stood with his whole body tense, blue eyes dark as cobalt, knuckles white, teeth audibly grinding. She knew that she must look the same. They were like two combatants, poised to go to war.

"Don't! Don't do it, Lori, don't start hanging around anywhere questioning people, not even your brother."

"And don't you dare go after my own family!"

"Why? Haven't you wondered if it wasn't *my* brother?"

"Haven't you?" she demanded.

Again, he was very still. "You know, if you were a guy, I'd be swinging right now."

"You are a guy, and I should slug you for being so suspicious of Andrew."

His jaw tightened, and he took a step forward. Adrenaline raced through her body at an ungodly speed. She wanted to fly at him . . .

He paused.

"Want to make love?"

"No!" she exclaimed incredulously. Then she realized that yes, she did, very much.

"Yes . . . maybe."

He swept her into his arms, tension and anger vented in sheer physical passion as he kissed her, fumbling with her clothing. She was half naked, kissing him back hungrily, when he murmured, "Want to go upstairs?"

"I don't care. There, here, the floor . . ."

He glanced at his watch, groaning. "Have we got time before Brendan gets out . . . ?"

"Not much."

"Then, the floor will be just fine."

Muffy didn't finish work at the shoot until late.

She left the hotel after dark, walking along the street. South Beach was usually busy, a great place. All kinds of people came here: punk kids, rich Arabs. Women walked by in veils—and in thong bikinis, almost nothing at all! And the guys . . . beach bums, the gay community, bodybuilders, some dopers . . . everyone. It was the most fantastic place in the world to be.

Tonight, it was kind of dark. Storm clouds on the horizon. People seemed to be staying in. The streets were nearly deserted when she heard the whistle.

She looked up and saw the van coming toward her, pulling to a stop at the curve. Funny, she didn't know anybody who had a van.

But then she saw the driver, recognized him, and brightened.

"Why, hi!" she said.

"Hi, Muffy," he returned, leaning far over to open the passenger side door. He smiled at her, and his smile was devastating. "You busy? Or just off work? Can I buy you a drink?"

"You want to buy me a drink?" she said. "Sure. Sure, why not?" And she climbed in.

*   *   *

Late that night Sean lay beside Lori, and she knew he was about to get up and go back downstairs to the sofa. Yet he was staring at the ceiling, tense, wide awake.

"Sean?"

He turned to her. "I'm really worried. I'm afraid for you, for me, for us . . . God, you've got to be careful. Let me call an alarm company."

"All right. I'll ask my grandfather—"

"Damn it, please, will you let me do this thing? If you love me, can you trust me enough to do something for you?"

She hesitated just slightly. "All right."

He pulled her still damp body into his arms, kissing her shoulder tenderly.

"Sean . . . is there something else?"

"Sue's cat's neck was broken."

"I know. Ricky said so."

"Remember that dead cat in your trash pile?"

She felt prickles of fear assail her.

"Yes?"

"Well, it wasn't hit by a car. Its neck was broken, too."

Chapter 19

"Damn!" Jeff swore, missing his shot. "Boy, am I over par!"

"Thank God we're not playing for money," Andrew said.

Jeff made a face. "I am playing for money. I bet Brad fifty bucks that I could beat you if no one else."

Andrew started to laugh. "Looks like you're going to have to pay up, though it doesn't seem Brad's faring so well himself back there!"

Sean, too, glanced back. Brad's swings were wild; his game was really off. They had divided up since they wound up with eight playing. Ted, Jeff, Andrew, and he had teed off first, followed by Brad, Ricky, Brendan, and Michael, who had come up that morning for a meeting with the Seaquarium about taking in a wounded dolphin discovered off Miami Beach that weekend.

Brendan was a surprisingly good golfer for his age; the older men had offered to give him a handicap, but Brendan was quietly beating the pants off most of them. The kid was a natural athelete.

"He's got a swing just like yours, Sean," Jeff commented. "Kid's good. Really good. Kind of like you, Sean, remember? Football, baseball, whatever, you aced it. The kid even golfs like you do."

"He swings like I do?" Sean said skeptically.

"Yeah, he does," Andrew agreed, walking forward to eye his shot, and then prepare for it. "He is good, even if I might be just a little bit biased regarding my blood relation. He's a natural—with everything he touches. All Lori needs to do is buy him good clubs, a guitar, a football, and a computer—and he'll make it rich somewhere along the line."

Andrew putted—the ball obediently fell into the hole, causing Jeff to groan.

"Nice shot, Uncle Andrew!" Brendan called cheerfully from behind them, adjusting his baseball cap on his head.

"Thank you, thank you very much!" Andrew said, and collecting his ball, he kissed it, and stepped aside for the others to finish. "I am personally ready for the Jacuzzi, if you all don't mind picking up the pace here. . . ."

Sean took his shot, surprised that his ball went where he wanted it to go when he felt so strangely disjointed. Even the comments about Brendan nagged at him. But his was the low score, and it amazed him that it was possible to keep functioning with such apparent normalcy when he wanted to shake his "old friends" one by one and demand to know who had killed Mandy, and just what the hell was going on now.

But as he looked around, he gritted his teeth, realizing that he was getting nowhere.

He was golfing normally, and his friends looked just as normal as could be. Of course, there was something simmering beneath the surface. Ellie Metz had been horribly murdered. Sue was still missing—and a dead cat had been found in her house. And a dead cat had been found at Lori's, and reporters were taking potshots at him.

One of them was a killer—or was he entirely out of line and a stranger was doing these heinous things and the world was full of coincidence?

Could it be Ricky, swearing violently now that he had missed his shot? Ted, the clean-cut Gables guy? Could either them of function quite so well as cops? Michael—was it possible to be so talented with animals, and hate people? Brad—he admitted to some of his fantasies, but did he have darker desires? Andrew dealt in the down and dirty daily. Jeff, Mandy's *brother*? Josh—Lori's cousin . . .

Where did he begin ruling out people? If he watched long enough, would the killer make a mistake? Do something that gave him away, gave a single clue?

"Maybe you should go back to California, Sean," Brad said, looking at the scores when they had all played through.

"Don't worry; I have my bad days."

"You're not going back to California soon, are you?" Brendan asked him anxiously. "No matter what that lady says in the paper," he added.

There was an awkward moment when Sean felt the others looking at him. He stared at them, then at Brendan. "No. I'm not leaving. I'm not running. Ricky's a great cop, and the guys he works with are going to catch whoever killed Ellie."

Brendan looked pleased. Andrew turned, starting for his car.

"You riding with me, Brendan?"

"Nah, my stuff is in Sean's car, Uncle Andrew," Brendan called back to him.

They all shouldered their golf bags, and started for the cars. Sean glanced over at Brendan. There was something about the kid's face, the way he walked, moved.

Andrew's words seemed to echo to him. *He's got a swing just like yours.*

He suddenly felt as if he'd been hit in the chest. He couldn't breathe; his face felt flushed, his heart was hammering. Jesus.

What a blind ass he'd been.

Lori was in the pool when the men arrived hot and sweaty from their golf game.

Visions of dead cats, and dead women, had swum before her eyes all day. The simple acts of walking and talking seemed strained.

The idea had been to order pizzas so that Jan wouldn't be put to any trouble, but she and Lori had prepared salads and dips, and there were bowls of chips and other snacks around. From the pool Lori heard Jan tell the guys she'd waited for them to arrive before phoning for the pizzas so that they'd be hot.

"Put in that call, honey," Brad told her. "We're all starving— since we rushed right here without so much as a breeze through at the nineteenth hole!"

A few minutes later Sean appeared, having changed to swim trunks. He dived in, swimming to her.

"Anything?" she asked him.

"I won," he said. She thought that he was studying her strangely, that he seemed tense.

Naturally. Dead cats, dead women, public accusations.

"Congratulations. Anything else?" she asked anxiously.

"Your son came in second."

"My son is a good player. Sean—"

He shook his head, eyes grave, reflecting the light from the pool. "Your son is definitely an excellent player. A real natural—"

Lori cut him off impatiently. "Thanks. But did you learn anything new about our old friends?"

"I learned nothing. Anything up with Jan?"

"I haven't been here that long, really. The phone kept ringing, and we were busy with salads and tables and the like. We haven't gotten to talk much," she told him.

"Neither have we—you and I, that is—or so it seems," he said pointedly.

Something about his manner gave her a chill, but Brad made a sudden dive bomb into the pool, distracting them both, and soon the others were piling in, too. Jan cried out, "Chicken! Let's have a chicken championship!"

"Oh, I don't know . . ." Lori murmured uneasily, but whatever she had seen in Sean was masked now as he came toward her.

"Come on," he told her, "let's play. We can beat them. You're tough. You know a good fight, and a good bluff."

She found herself on Sean's shoulders, playing a wicked game of chicken against Brad and Jan. She couldn't stop thinking that something wasn't quite right. What had happened during the game of golf to make Sean so cool toward her? But she found herself involved in the game, in the pursuit of winning. She even quit imagining dead cats and was laughing, still atop Sean's shoulders and struggling with Jan when the doorbell rang.

"Pizza!" Brad announced. "Off, woman! I'm starving!" he cried.

"We won!" Jan stated.

"The hell you won!" Lori protested.

"It's a draw!" Brad declared.

Sean allowed Lori to slip into the water. He didn't drop her; he just let her slip off. He had played the game hard, yet it suddenly seemed as if he was ridding himself of an unwanted touch.

She surfaced, smoothing back her hair. He was staring at her as if she was an enemy and they had suddenly discovered themselves to be at war. What could have happened?

She was suddenly afraid that she knew.

"I'll go get the kids," she said, swimming toward the steps.

Andrew, already out of the pool and mostly dried off, said, "It's all right. I'll get them. Are they playing Nintendo in Tina's room, Jan?"

"Yep!" Jan called.

Lori put on a terry cover-up, aware that Sean was watching her, though he kept his distance. She ignored him, slowly realizing that she was waiting for the world to cave in around her, trying to behave normally all the while. She went out to the picnic tables to help Jan open up pizza boxes. Andrew suddenly came striding out of the house, looking anxious. He beckoned to her, wanting to speak with her in private. She walked over to join him in a corner of the patio.

"Do you know what I found?" he whispered tensely.

"What?" she asked in sudden panic. What had he found? The kids, gone. Tina—injured?

"Your son and Tina—*kissing.*"

"Kissing," she repeated. "Here? In Tina's house, in her room?" She exhaled. "I'll talk to Brendan immediately. I can't believe that in Jan's house . . ."

"In Jan's house? Lori, that's . . . it?"

"Andrew, it's really not that terrible. Brendan is fourteen, she's thirteen, and that's the age when kids start experimenting like this. Don't look so horrified—"

"What do you mean, it's not that terrible?" Andrew demanded, hands on his hips, staring at her incredulously. "They were *kissing,* dammit!"

Confused by the depth of his concern, Lori just stared at him in return, frowning. "Andrew, don't worry, I intend to talk with him—"

"What—have you been living in a fantasy so long you've forgotten the truth? Tina is Brad's daughter! *Brad's.* Lori, remember genetics! Brendan—"

"Brendan what?" she mouthed carefully.

"Oh, come on, who else were you seeing? Brendan surely never belonged to Ian Corcoran!" Andrew said with exasperation. "Ian died of AIDS, and he had the disease before he ever met you."

Her jaw dropped as she stared at him. It had never occurred to her that her brother had assumed that her son belonged to Brad. "Andrew," she said slowly, enunciating her words, "pay attention to me. Brendan is not Brad's child."

His eyes widened. "He's not?"

"Andrew—" she began again, and she broke off, sickly aware that Sean was watching them from the other side of the pool, where he had appeared to be in casual conversation with Jeff.

Had he heard them? Impossible. Could he read lips? Or had her original fear that evening been well founded? Had he been slowly realizing the truth, and had he—sometime during the day—found himself being hit right in the face with it?

She felt her cheeks flame. She was hot, uncomfortable, and afraid.

"Hey," Andrew said awkwardly. "I'm sorry. I guess I was wrong. I always thought—I mean, you were dating Brad, and you had Brendan pretty soon after you left—"

"Andrew, please, can we talk about this later?"

He stiffened suddenly. He was staring across the pool, and Sean was staring back at the two of them.

"Lori, Andrew, what kind of pizza did you want?" Jan called from the picnic tables, looking over at her.

"Uh—doesn't matter. Plain, pepperoni, whatever," she murmured.

"Oh, God. It's him. Sean. And you never told him," Andrew said.

"That's right. But somehow, I think he knows now."

"Lori, I'm sorry."

She nodded, stared at her brother with eloquent eyes, then turned around quickly and headed for the pizza table.

She took a slice and bit into it, not tasting it at all.

People talked to her. She answered; she babbled. She didn't hear a word said in reply. She watched Sean eat, laugh with Ted, trade some kind of story with Jeff.

Minutes seemed to stretch into eternity. He *knew*. And he was just biding his time. Waiting.

Finally, he'd waited long enough.

She was aware when he headed her way.

She felt him come for her before she saw him. He reached her side, and took her by the arm. His grip was firm, his voice was calm. "Great evening, Jan. But I think we need to go now, Lori, don't you?" he asked her quietly. She felt her heart sinking. Felt the heated emotion that shot through his body to his fingers, where he held her. "Jan," he said, so casual still, "Is it all right if Brendan stays here for a while this evening?"

"Sure. Of course!" Jan said warmly.

"Brendan's welcome to stay the night—" Brad offered.

"I'll take care of Brendan," Andrew cut in, forcing a cheerful note to his voice. Apparently, he had come to Lori first, so neither Jan nor Brad was aware that the kids had been necking in their daughter's room. Andrew had no intention of letting things go too far between the kids.

"Thanks, Andrew. Jan, Brad, this was great," Lori said.

A minute later she was in Sean's car. He drove too fast, not speaking. She didn't speak, either, unable to talk about the truth that now lay between them, and certainly unable to suggest that the weather that night was almost balmy.

He jerked the vehicle into her driveway.

She got out of the car, strode to the house, fighting to remain calm and in control. It was hard to maintain her composure when the first explosive word out of his mouth once they were inside seemed to knife right into her heart.

"Trust?"

"Look, Sean—"

"How could you keep something like this from me? Damn you, Lori. What a fool I was! I should have guessed the moment I saw Brendan. But then, none of our crowd guessed the truth, did they. How ironic. I didn't catch everything your brother was saying to you, but apparently Andrew has gone all these years assuming that my son was Brad's? Ian Corcoran died of AIDS. You never had a sexual relationship with him, much less a child. So you had my son, Lori. A child, a human being! How could you keep something like that from him, from *me*?"

She backed away from him in the foyer. "Sean—"

"Brendan is *mine*; you lived a lie for nearly fifteen years!" he said, incredulous. He was losing control. She wasn't sure she'd ever seen him lose control. His voice was rising, his fingers tore absently through his hair, and she'd never seen his features so tense.

There were a dozen things she could have said, but she couldn't seem to find any words, and when she did, she stuttered defensively. "I—I—never—"

"You never *what*? You married a man with AIDS, for Christ's sake. You never knew you were pregnant from our night together? You assumed Brendan to be a divine surprise? All these years your family, and others, assumed him to be *Brad's*? Jesus, Lori, what were you, judge and jury, condemning me even when I was acquitted?"

"My family assumed him to be Ian's. Andrew's the only one who knows he died of AIDS—my folks thought it was cancer. I was really married to Ian Corcoran. He was a real, live, flesh-and-blood human being, and I did love him, and he did die a terrible death—but he cared for me. I wasn't trying to be judge and jury, don't be absurd. You don't understand how hard it was—"

"No? Then, what was your reasoning? No need to say anything, *ever*? Not to *Brendan*. Don't tell him, don't let him know that his father was tainted by a murder rap?"

"Sean, it wasn't like that at all—"

"Then, what was it like?" he demanded, eyes suddenly ink dark, arms crossed over his chest, stance firm and jaw clenched. He looked like a spring about to let loose, something lethal about to uncoil. "I'm waiting . . . I'll listen."

She didn't know if she was suddenly deeply afraid, more afraid than she'd ever been in her life, or simply so angry she couldn't bear it. She wasn't going to let him explode. She was going to do so first.

"Oh, will you?" she demanded. She strode the distance that separated them and slammed her open palms against his chest, trying to push him back toward the door. "You can just wait until hell freezes over if you want, I don't owe you any explanations! You—"

He backed up a step, but then caught her hands. "You do owe me one hell of an explanation. A jury let me go, but you chose to judge me—"

"Wait a minute!" she lashed back. "Where do you think your rights come in on this? You got out of jail, and you were gone. Gone! Simply gone."

"And what would you have done if I'd stayed? One thing I'll never forget is leaving the courtroom once the case was dismissed. Every one of you, my so-called friends, my good old buddies, turned away along with their folks as I was walking by!"

"But don't you see? If I'd wanted to reach you, I couldn't have done so—"

His fingers suddenly clenched so tightly around her wrists that she broke off, startled.

"My God," he said slowly, swallowing tightly. "He's really mine. All these years, I've had a son. I should have seen it before, but I didn't. Not until today. Then your brother compared Brendan to me this afternoon. And at first it was just like a hint of something, then it slowly began to sink in. I wouldn't have imagined that I'd ever owe such gratitude to your brother."

He said the last bitterly, and Lori found her temper rising again. "Sean, Andrew had nothing to do with any of this. I didn't even confide in him at the time. Don't start on my brother—"

"Oh, God, I'm not, I wouldn't. I haven't begun to finish with you."

Finish with her! She was suddenly furious with him . . . and sick inside. Did he have a right to be this angry?

"Finish with me? You don't need to finish with me, because I'll tell you right now—this is over. You were gone, and I was alone for nearly fifteen years, having him alone, raising him alone. You were involved *one* night! One night! I dealt with measles, shots, fevers, cholic—and you suddenly walk back into my life. No, oh, no, I am not going to feel any guilt over this!"

His grip around her wrists reflexively tightened. She almost cried out, but gritted hard on her teeth instead. He didn't even notice. "You were never going to tell me?" he asked.

"I didn't say that."

"When, then?"

"When the right time came."

"And when was that going to be? When he graduated from high

school, college? When he became a father himself and his kids were my *grand*kids?''

She wrenched her wrists free from his grasp, wishing that she could beat on him again, do something to change the awful distance that now gaped between them. They'd fought yesterday, and anger had led to passion. She wished she could throw herself against him, slam her fists against him . . . then feel his warmth. Have him tell her that it was going to be okay. Make love to her.

But it wasn't going to happen, not this time.

''Things haven't been that great around here lately, hadn't you noticed? Our friends being murdered is a little more important than an ancient secret.''

''Actually,'' he said, stepping back, folding his arms over his chest once again as if he locked them there to keep from doing her bodily harm. ''I thought that they were pretty great between you and me. It's not as if we didn't have any private time together.''

''Look, you've got to realize that you still weren't around when—''

''I was never given the choice.''

''I didn't have a chance to give you any choices. And quite frankly, I didn't feel that I had any choices myself. I went away, I was alone in a foreign country, I met a kind and generous man who would help me. Sean, I still don't owe you anything—''

''No, you don't owe me anything. But maybe you do owe Brendan. Maybe he has the right to choose if he wants me for a father or not.''

She stared at him, stricken. If only she could step forward, touch him, make things all right.

But she couldn't.

He turned around, and walked out on her.

Andrew called her a while later, and asked if it was okay for Brendan to come home. Lori told him it was fine.

Jan called soon after. Lori knew that Jan had sensed something was wrong, but not even Jan knew exactly what. It was obvious that Jan was dying to grill her, but that she wasn't going to do so with Brad listening.

''Let's get together tomorrow sometime, just the two of us,'' Jan said. ''Okay?''

''Yeah, sure.''

''Lori?'' Jan whispered suddenly. ''He's gone. Brad just left the room. Lori, is Brendan *Sean's*? Is that what's going on? I mean, I have to admit, if he is, I'm rather glad—I was always afraid that your child was Brad's. Brad told me, after everyone left, that seeing them together, he thought that Brendan was a lot like Sean. Is it true?''

Lori winced. ''Yes.''

Jan was silent for a moment, then she blurted, ''How—when you were my best friend—how could you have lied to me—''

''I didn't actually lie to you, I didn't lie to anyone. Certainly not to Ian. You never asked me if I'd been with Sean,'' Lori said wearily.

''Where is he now?''

''Gone.''

''Where?''

''I don't know.''

Jan was quiet. ''He'll be back, don't worry.''

''I'm sure he will,'' she murmured dryly. He would be back; certainly. To discuss Brendan. Her head was killing her. She had to hang up. ''Jan, I'll see you tomorrow, okay?''

''All right. And you will tell me all about it.''

Lori hung up. Soon after Andrew came over with Brendan. Her brother wanted to talk. She pleaded exhaustion. Andrew was awkward, but seemed to understand.

Brendan didn't particularly want to talk, either. He was just as anxious to slink away from her after telling her that his uncle had already yelled at him and Tina.

''What did he say?'' Lori asked carefully.

''He said, 'It's not that you can't share an innocent kiss now and then, it's just that, Brendan! In her room . . . that's like a betrayal of trust with her folks, you know?' '' Brendan paused. He didn't look at Lori, but stared at a little gadget he held in his hands. He sighed impatiently. ''Then he gave me the whole sex speech again, as if I didn't know anything about reproduction.''

Lori tried not to smile. ''Maybe he thought you needed to remember,'' she said. Then added, ''What Andrew said wasn't so bad . . . You're lucky Brad didn't tan your hide for taking advantage of his daughter.''

He looked up at her. ''Mom, she wanted to kiss me.''

''Like your uncle said, what you two were doing was a betrayal of trust.''

''I care about her very much, and we weren't doing anything wrong. Why is it that adults can get away with any outrageous behavior and it's all right?''

Lori opened her mouth and hesitated. ''Sometimes they get away with it, and sometimes they don't. I'm glad you like Tina, and her folks like you, too. Just cool it a little, huh?''

"Sure," he told her.

"What's that?'' she asked him.

"This?'' he said, surprised. He opened his palm. "Isn't it neat? It's a little pocketknife with a can opener, and a bottle opener.''

"Where'd you get it?'' Lori asked. It was a great little device, small, cleverly designed, and very useful-looking.

"Sean gave it to me. I couldn't get that new box of golf balls opened because it was taped, so Sean used this thing, and then gave it to me. It's all right, isn't it?''

"Uh . . . yeah, of course.''

"Can I go to my room?''

"Yes.''

He disappeared quickly. She went upstairs herself, wishing she could lie down, and instantly fall asleep.

Naturally, she didn't.

She lay awake, thinking that a dead cat had been found in her trash pile, a dead cat had been found at Sue's house. And Sean knew that Brendan was his child, and hated her for keeping it a secret.

Did it matter? Could it matter? There was a murderer walking among them, and it seemed he was coming closer and closer. Staying safe right now had to take precedence over the issue of Brendan's paternity.

She was tossing and turning in bed when she heard the doorbell ringing. She started to rise, then realized that Brendan had answered it, and it was Sean. She tiptoed to the landing just outside her bedroom.

"I'll get Mom,'' Brendan told Sean.

"No, don't. Don't wake her. I just wanted to stay on the sofa, keep an eye on the place.''

"No faith in me, huh?''

"I have a lot of faith in you, champ. But three people are better than one any day.''

It was apparently the right answer. Biting her lip, Lori hesitated. If Sean wanted to find her, he knew where she was. She went back to bed and lay there awake, thinking that she'd throw pride to the wind and go to him if it would do any good. But it wouldn't.

She worried that Sean might say something to Brendan, but apparently he had no intention of springing any surprises on his newly discovered son.

Nor did it seem he wanted to find her. She lay awake for a very long time. He did not come up. When she woke in the morning, he was already gone. Light had come again, the danger of darkness dispelled, and he had left her alone.

Sean had good reason to be up and out early.

He'd been called to the morgue.

"The media is already demanding to know what we've got," Gillespie said, looking at Sean and Ricky over the sheeted corpse on the autopsy table. "But this time, I do have something to give you. Something I intend to keep from the media as long as I can."

"What do you have?" Ricky asked, trying not to look at the sheet. "I know you'll give me the full report, but—"

"She was found in the swamp. But there was dirt under her fingernails. Not swamp dirt. More like a rocky sand. She was killed somewhere else, and then dumped in the swamp. Are you ready? We've cleaned up the mud."

Ricky and Sean glanced at one another.

Gillespie pulled back the plastic sheeting.

"Did you know her?" she asked. "Is it Sue?"

Sean felt Ricky's eyes on him.

"I knew her," he said quietly.

"Is it Sue?" Gillespie asked.

He shook his head. "I knew her, but no, this isn't Sue Nichols."

"Then, who the hell is it?" Gillespie demanded.

Chapter 20

At nine o'clock, just after she returned from taking Brendan to school, Lori received a call from Jeff Olin. "Hi, Lori. Listen, the guys from the security company will be over at about ten, if that's all right."

"The security company—"

"To put in your alarm system. Your brother, your cousin Josh, and Sean are all in on this, so don't go giving me any arguments. You'll make me look really bad."

"Jeff, but—"

"The guy who owns the alarm company owes me, so we're getting a great deal. And you'll be safe, Lori. Everyone thinks you need an alarm. Andrew, Josh, Sean, Brad, Jan, your folks—everyone."

"Didn't Sue have an alarm system?" she asked.

"I think so."

"Sue is gone."

"Right, but it appears she's off on a romantic vacation."

"She wouldn't just leave."

"How can you say that? How well do any of us really know each other anymore?"

"Sue's cat was dead, Jeff."

"I know."

"She didn't strangle her own cat."

He sighed. "There's still hope for Sue," he told her.

He didn't believe it, not for a minute. He was just trying to reassure her.

"All right, fine, thanks. I appreciate your help, and your concern," Lori said.

"Hey, what are friends for? The company is called SafeHome, and it will be two guys in a blue van."

"Thanks."

She worked on her design sketches, attaching bits of fabric to mix and match as she did so. Right before ten, she heard a car pulling into her drive. Assuming it was the alarm people, she went to the front. She was surprised to see that Michael Black had driven up in a white van with a big dolphin painted on the side.

"Company vehicle!" he called to her cheerfully.

"Cute," she told him.

He walked to the door, smiling, blue eyes a lot like Sean's, dark hair a little longer now, wild from the wind since he had apparently been driving with the window down. "My brother here?"

She shook her head.

"Do you know where I can find him?"

"No, Michael, I'm sorry, he didn't tell me where he was going."

"Hmm. Do you imagine he'll be back any time soon?"

"I don't have any idea."

"Do you care if I wait around a while?"

"No, of course not. Come in."

Even as she stepped back, allowing Michael to enter her house, she felt a sense of unease.

Sean himself thought that someone from their past was involved in all this. Naturally, he wouldn't want it to be his own brother. Just as she wouldn't want it to be hers. Or her cousin Josh, or . . .

Or any of them.

"Want something to drink?" she asked him.

"Sure."

She poured him a glass of iced tea. He sat at the kitchen table with her, smiling. He was as cute as could be, with a mischievous glint in his eyes.

"So . . . there was an argument last night?"

"An argument?"

Michael shrugged. "Oddly enough, I do know my brother. Something strange was going on at Jan's and thinking back—and being the observant chap that I am—I put two and two together. I think that maybe, yesterday, a lot of people put two and two together."

She sighed deeply. "Michael—"

"Sorry. None of my business. Maybe it is. He's a great kid. Lori, is he my nephew?"

"Michael, I—"

"Sorry, really. Honestly. I guess that isn't open to discussion yet.

But I hope we are related. I really like your son." He glanced at his watch. "Where the hell is that brother of mine? I've a meeting again with Seaquarium people . . ." He looked at her. "Want to come for a ride?"

"What?"

He wiggled his eyebrows suggestively. "Come for a ride with me. In my van."

"Where?"

"The Seaquarium. We'll open the windows, feel the breeze. It's a nice day. Maybe you'll relax."

"I am relaxed," she lied. She felt ridiculously tense, afraid. She didn't want to be in a van with Michael, she realized.

Alone.

To her relief, she heard another vehicle in the road. "Sorry! I can't. The alarm people are here."

"You're having an alarm put in?" he asked her sharply.

"Yes."

"Jeff Olin's friends are doing it?"

"Yes, why?"

He shrugged. "I don't know. I don't particularly trust Jeff."

"Why on earth not?"

Michael wrinkled his nose. "He's an attorney."

She laughed. "So is Brad!"

"Did I ever say I trusted Brad?"

"What about my cousin, Josh? You couldn't find a nicer guy."

"Really? You should ask a few of the women he's dated about that." Michael stood. "I guess I'm just not fond of attorneys—knew too many when I was young. Prosecutors, mostly, I've got to admit."

"Jeff does good work, defending the innocent—"

"And not so innocent, I imagine. Anyway, kid, tell Sean I was by. And watch out for any alarm Jeff Olin's friends install."

"I think he's done very well—Michael, what's up with you?"

"Sorry. I like dophins; lawyers are sharks! Just my opinion. And if you've got a houseful of other men, I'm leaving." He grinned. "Watch out, now," he warned.

"I'll watch out," she promised, humoring him. At the door she waved good-bye, wondering how long he would have stayed if the men from the alarm company hadn't arrived, and why she had felt so terribly uneasy in his presence.

As the two men started working, she realized the irony of the situation—she was letting two strange men into her house so that strange people couldn't break into her house. Michael had warned her to watch out, right when she had been thinking that she needed to watch out for Michael. She decided that absence was the better part of valor, gave her treasures up to thieves if that's what they proved to be, and drove to the fabric store for more samples while they worked in her house.

She came home to find Ted, Jeff, and Andrew standing around, watching the workmens' progress.

"Lori, you're not supposed to let strangers in your house and leave them there," Jeff told her.

"I thought I was being smart by leaving, so that I wouldn't be alone with strangers."

"You wouldn't have been alone with them; I was coming over to be here with you," Andrew chastised her.

She realized she wanted to smack her brother. He meant well, she supposed, but he was irritating her to death at the moment. He had added to the uncomfortable situation with Brendan, and now he was behaving as if nothing had happened.

"It's okay, Lori," Ted told her. "I've checked everything out; the van is empty—they haven't taken any of your household treasures!— and these guys are licensed and bonded."

"They can show you how to work the alarm," Jeff volunteered.

"Great," Lori said.

The two men installing the system were young, polite, and efficient. But when she had to give them a number code to punch in to set the alarm, she realized that Jeff, Ted, and Andrew were all right behind her shoulder.

One technician seemed to understand her dilemma, and he took her aside to speak privately. "No one should know your code, and certainly not Dave and me here. Just remember the number you pick. Once you punch it in, it's recorded at the office."

By noon she had her alarm system. Jeff left to return to work, Ted returned to his patrol car, and she was alone with Andrew.

In the foyer he closed the door slowly, then turned to stare at her. "Lori, look, you're my sister, my friend, we've kept secrets from one another, but I know that you're angry right now . . . and I'm sorry. I can't imagine how Sean could have heard me . . . I was upset, because I didn't know the truth. I thought my nephew was about to get heavily involved with his half sister or something. I knew that you had just married Ian Corcoran to give your baby a father, and since you hadn't shared the fact that you'd had an affair with Sean Black with me—"

"It wasn't an affair."

"Then, what the hell was it? Never mind, I don't want to know. At the moment Sean and I just don't get along anyway. If he did something . . . wrong with you—"

"He didn't force me into anything, Andrew. It was just one occasion, rather accidental, and not an affair, that's all."

"So he really, truly, is Brendan's father."

"Yes."

"If I caused you a lot of trouble—"

"Andrew, you didn't cause anything. Sean knew before you started carrying on. And he was bound to find out anyway."

"Why hadn't you told him?"

She arched a brow. Then shrugged. "At the time, I couldn't. He was gone. And now . . . now, I guess I just hadn't gotten to it."

"Did you tell Brendan?"

"Not yet."

"Are you going to?"

"Eventually, yes." She lowered her head and bit into her lower lip. If she didn't, Sean would. Eventually. For now, Sean seemed determined to hold his peace. If he had lost faith in her, he had not done so with Brendan.

"I'm sorry, kid, really."

She nodded. "You didn't do anything, Andrew. Really. I'm a big girl—with an alarm system now. I can manage my life. So, out. I've got some work to do before I pick up Brendan."

Obligingly, he left, telling her to turn on the alarm as soon as he was gone. She did. She returned to her work, becoming so involved that she didn't even turn the stereo on. At three she went to pick up Brendan. She stopped at an art supply store to buy Brendan some of the things he told her he needed for a drafting class, and then they drove to the Grove, where she was to meet Jan.

"Think Tina and I can still walk around alone together?" Brendan asked her defensively.

"In the right areas," she assured him gravely, trying not to smile. Ah, young love. She remembered it well.

Far better than she wanted to.

It was nearly five when they got to the bookstore and Brendan asked Jan politely if it was all right if he and Tina took off alone together. Jan said of course, if they stayed smart and on the main streets. "And behave!" Jan chastised them.

"Oh, Mom!" Tina protested.

Brendan didn't utter a word.

When they had gone, Jan took Lori's arm. "I need a drink. And surely, you must, too. Just no champagne."

"All right. But you love champagne?"

"Well . . . I really overindulged. It was the only way I could do it."

"Do it?" Lori said, puzzled. Then she gasped. She'd been so wound up in with her own fears and personal traumas, she'd forgotten about her friend's dilemma. "Jan! You—you went through with Brad's fantasy?"

"I told you, I need a drink," Jan said firmly. "If you want me to talk, I need a drink."

Lori couldn't help but smile. "You didn't say a thing to me yesterday!"

"I didn't have a chance."

"Of course I want you to talk. I'm dying of curiosity. Let's go over to the place on the first floor at Mayfair."

"Fine. I'll talk—and you can tell me about Brendan's daddy."

"I don't have much to tell. And how you and Brad knew that anything was going on—"

"Easy. You should have seen your face!" Jan said, winking. "Come on."

A few minutes later they were seated in the restaurant at the bar, sipping pina coladas. "Well?" Lori asked.

Jan went crimson. "You first."

"Quick easy story. He was mad."

"Naturally. You had his child, and neglected to tell him."

"It wasn't that simple."

"Of course not. But I don't want to know about last night. Tell me how on earth you managed to have his child when no one—I mean no one!—ever had the slightest inkling that you two were ever anything but friends. Want to hear something funny? Brad's ticked— all these years later—that you cheated on him. But then again, he was glad to hear it was Sean when he realized that many of us thought that Brendan might be his."

Lori shook her head. "People shouldn't think."

"They have no choice when other people don't tell them the truth," she remonstrated softly.

Lori sighed. "Jan! I was seventeen years old."

"You were always hung up on Sean."

"Maybe. I went to see him when he was down after his brother Daniel died. One thing led to another. That was it."

"That was it? Something that charged and emotional must have been traumatic. You never told me."

"I never told anyone."

"You were a teenage girl! You were supposed to spill everything to your best friend, me."

Lori shook her head, sipped her drink. "At first, I didn't know. And I had my pride. I mean, I think I did have a terrible crush on him, but I couldn't admit it, because as far as I knew, he and Mandy were hot and heavy."

"You didn't even say anything to me!"

"Well, I just did. Now."

"Almost fifteen years later—and only because you were finally caught!"

"All right, enough about me. I—"

"No, no, not yet. More about Sean. Was he really that angry? He covered it well at our house—you gave away much more than he did."

Lori frowned. "Yes, he's really angry. He told me what he thought, and left. And I haven't spoken with him since."

"I can't believe that. He's so protective of you!"

Lori shrugged. "He slept at the house."

"Ahh!"

"Downstairs."

"Oh."

"It's all right."

"It will be. You'll get it together, you know."

"Maybe. Now, Jan, your turn. You tell me about yesterday."

Jan flushed. "It was fine," she said, adding, "I drank a bottle of champagne in about five minutes flat."

"Really?"

Jan set her left hand on the table. A dazzling diamond twinkled from her ring finger.

"You're remarrying him!" Lori gasped.

"Well, I told him I wasn't sure yet. Oh, Lori, it was so strange, I thought I'd die. I refused to be bribed, and Brad said it wasn't bribery, just a last fantasy to be fulfilled before . . ." Her voice trailed away. "I—" she began again, then broke off. Lori saw that she was staring at the news that had come on the television situated on a ledge at the back of the bar.

"Oh, God, look!"

Lori looked. The young anchor was speaking in a dramatically grave voice, saying that another body had been discovered, apparently the victim of the same killer who had murdered Eleanor Metz.

"Not Sue—!" Jan breathed.

A picture flashed on the screen.

Not Sue.

Jan and Lori gasped in unison.

"Muffy!" Jan and Lori cried simultaneously.

The two women stared at one another. "You knew Muffy?" Jan demanded.

"Yes," Lori said. "She, er, worked for Andrew now and then. How did you know her?"

"She, she—" Jan stuttered, her face crimson.

"Oh, no!" Lori gasped. "Muffy Fluffy was . . . your third person?"

"Oh, my God! Just yesterday . . . and now . . . oh, my God, she's dead."

"All I can tell you is that there's something your mother isn't telling you," Tina said to Brendan. "I could hear my parents talking about it last night. Then my mom talked to yours on the phone and got all whispery. And your uncle! Did you see his face when he caught us in my room? He looked as if he were completely wacko!"

"He lost it," Brendan said, staring at a pair of boots in the window of a shoe store. "That's all."

"We're old enough to date."

"Yeah, but we were fooling around in your room at your house."

"There's more. Your mother and Sean Black went away mad—I know, cause the little big-mouth next door saw it all and told me. Brendan, your mother did something really wrong—"

"She did not!" he snapped angrily, but he was afraid, and he didn't want Tina to see it. Something was going on. He could feel it, and he was confused—because his mother should have been telling him about it.

"I don't think your father was your father at all," Tina announced.

"What do you know about my father? He was a talented musician; everybody liked him!"

"Don't go getting ballistic on me!" Tina said.

"Well, you've all but called my mother a whore and me a bastard!"

"Brendan, face facts—"

"I'm going into the sub shop for a Coke," he said. Spinning around, he left her.

"Did you want me to join you?" Tina called.

"Suit yourself!" he said angrily, assuming she would follow.

Watching him go, Tina bit into her lower lip. She hadn't meant to get mad, and she hadn't meant to make him mad. She had rather thought the whole thing exciting—apparently, Brendan didn't agree.

She stood on the street, feeling hurt, and very much alone.

She turned around. A van was moving along the street. She frowned, not recognizing it, yet the driver was slowing down as if he meant to talk to her.

Then the van suddenly sped up, passing her by.

She felt very uneasy, and she didn't know why.

Lovely, he thought. The girl was lovely. Fresh, innocent, pretty as a picture. Ripe. So deliciously ripe. He was tempted. Her eyes were so blue, her hair so light a gold. She'd be so good to touch. And she'd be so stunned and so terrified . . .

The compulsion was great.

Yet he had a different taste for death today.

Still, watching her, he could almost smell her, feel her soft young flesh, ah, yes, the taste . . .

Women!

They were enough to drive a guy nuts!

He was half crazy about Tina, and now she was giving him all this talk about his mother. He didn't want to hear it.

Even if he did know that it was probably true.

He strode angrily and quickly along the street, then stopped and looked back.

He didn't see Tina. She hadn't followed him.

He frowned, seeing that a van was slowing. He couldn't see the driver as yet, but he sensed a familiarity. The van pulled to the sidewalk right by him, and the driver called to him.

"Brendan! Brendan Corcoran, thank God! Come here! It's Tina . . ."

Hell, yes, he knew the driver, the man looking at him now with such concern. Brendan rushed forward anxiously. "Tina? What's wrong, what happened?" he demanded.

"Get in with her, hurry!"

He threw open the side door, worried sick. Had she tried to come after him, had she been hit by a car, hurt some way, what the hell . . .

"What is it, please, what's happened, what's wrong?" Brendan demanded, looking in.

The driver gripped him by the shoulders with powerful hands; pulled him in. No rear seats, Brendan saw quickly.

And no Tina.

"What's going on? If you've done anything to Tina, if you hurt her, I'll kill you!" Brendan said sharply, afraid, and determined not to be, and suddenly knowing . . .

"Hey, little man, tough guy, big talk from a kid. Tina's just fine right now. Her time hasn't come yet. It will. Trust me, it will. Can't wait to taste that young honey, but for now, son, well, boy, welcome to my party."

Like hell! He knew how to fight, and so help him, he would fight. Fight and fight . . .

But a wet towel was suddenly slapped over his face. He struggled to move it, trying hard to fight, to lash out. Make noise, if he could only scream . . .

But even as he inhaled, he knew there would be no sound. He breathed something sticky and sweet . . .

He struggled no more.

The fight was over.

Chapter 21

"I've got to go to the ladies' room," Jan said, staring at the television. She was pure green.

"Are you all right?" Lori said, not sure that she was all right herself.

"I think . . . I don't know . . ."

"I'll come with you—"

"No . . . no . . . I'll be right back," Jan said, offering her a weak smile. "Lori, Muffy's *dead*."

"I know. I saw. Listen, let me help you—"

"No, no. I'll be back."

Lori nodded, stared at the television, and thought about Muffy. Muffy Fluffy. So nice, so sweet, strangely innocent despite the way she had chosen to make a living.

Lori listened to the news, trying to register the facts. Muffy, too, had been discovered in swampland, out on Alligator Alley.

"Ma'am, can I get you another?"

Lori looked down. She'd inhaled her drink. She shook her head. "Water, if I could, please?"

He brought her water. The anchor continued speaking, telling more details about the ghastly murder.

Andrew had known Muffy well, worked with Muffy, was rude to her. Oh, God, Andrew . . .

Brad.

Brad had used her to fulfill his fantasy. Had that fantasy been much, much more than Jan had ever imagined?

"No," she whispered anxiously aloud.

"Excuse me?" the bartender said.

She shook her head.

It seemed that he was back immediately. "Sorry, is your friend coming back?"

"What?"

"Your friend. Her drink has melted. Did she leave, or is she coming back? I'll fix it up for her."

"Oh . . . uh, she just went to the rest room."

"She okay? She's been gone a long time."

"Has she?" Lori asked.

"About twenty minutes."

Lori jumped up, worried that Jan might have been really sick. "Hold the seats, please." She started for the rest room, but the bartender called her back, lifting the phone receiver to her. "Are you Lori Kelly?"

"Corcoran," she said. "I mean, yes, sorry. I'm Lori. My maiden name was Kelly." God, she was absolutely babbling.

"Phone call."

"Jan?"

"Your friend? Does she usually call you from the ladies' room?" he teased her, but she looked at him blankly. The young man shrugged. "Sounds like a man." You might want to move down to the corner there . . . less noise."

"Thanks."

Phone and receiver in hand, Lori moved down the length of the bar.

"Hello?"

"Lori."

The voice was a whisper with a rasping sound to it.

"Yes?"

"Take care, Lori Kelly, take care from this moment onward. I'm watching you. I can see your every move."

The voice itself was enough to send a wave of cold dread sweeping into her.

"Who are you? What do you want?" she demanded.

"First, just listen, Lori Kelly. You're wearing black slacks and a navy knit top with a scalloped neckline, smart little Timberland hiking boots. Your hair is down. Nice. I always liked it that way."

"I don't need a fashion assessment," she snapped, her wits suddenly completely restored. "Who are you, what do you want?"

"The assertive female! Don't try that bravado with me, Lori Kelly. I just want you to know that I can really see you, that I'm watching every move you make . . . ah, there you go, looking around, but you won't find me.''

''Who are you, and what do you want?''

''What I have already is very important,'' he told her. There was sibilant hissing mid-sentence, making his words rasp against her nerves as if she were listening to sharp nails snake down the length of a blackboard.

''What do you have?''

''Your son.''

She stood dead still, a feeling of dread and terror unlike anything she had known in all her life crawling over her.

''My son? Why?''

''Why? If I have your son, I have you, don't I, Lori Kelly? That is . . . unless you simply want me to kill him now?''

Her mind began to race. Was she talking to the killer, the real killer? Was this a hoax, someone out to taunt her, hurt her, tease her, someone who knew she was associated with Sean, someone mean and cruel, just playing with her?

No. She felt it in her bones.

This was the real killer, the same killer who had drowned Mandy Olin, who had robbed them all of their youth and innocence. The same killer who had so viciously attacked Ellie, Muffy, and probably Susan, and maybe many more.

And he had Brendan.

''Where's Jan?'' she asked, suddenly knowing he had her, too.

''Sick. She won't wake up for a while. It was really her turn. She'll have to wait a bit now.''

''Tina?''

''Tina. Tina is luscious, delicious. Oh, am I going to enjoy her. Anticipation is sweet. But it was always you, first, Lori Kelly. Oh, yes, Lori. Always.''

''What do you want?''

''It's time to play again. Remember how we all used to play? Well, it's time to play again.''

''Who are you? Tell me? Then, I'll know if we used to play.''

''Lori, please, don't take me for such a fool. I'm growing impatient. I don't want to have to finish this too soon. It will be fun, you thinking that you have a chance. Hope is such a charming quality. I'll get to see it die in your eyes. But you do have hope, and I do have your son. So listen. And don't forget, I'm watching you. I'm close. When we hang up, you pay your tab, walk out the door, head east, and then into the parking lot across the street. Don't pick up a phone, and don't ask the bartender or anyone else for help, and don't try to leave any cute little notes with SOS messages on them or anything. I can see you. You make the slightest mistake, and I'll start cutting your boy's fingers off, one by one, then his ears, tip of his nose . . . You get my drift?''

"Yes."

"Fine. I'm waiting for you, Lori Kelly. I've been waiting for a long time."

"If I come, will you let Brendan go?"

"Maybe. But if you don't come, I'll definitely kill him. Slowly. I've already been fairly descriptive on that point, I believe."

The phone went dead in her hand. Lori tried desperately to think of some means of finding help, but she knew that he was watching. She didn't dare try to dial the operator, hit 911, or speak with the bartender, except to pay her tab. Was the killer close enough to *hear* her as well? She didn't know. If only she could call Ricky . . .

How did she know that Ricky wasn't the killer?

Didn't matter, she had no choice, he had Brendan, oh, God no, God no . . .

"All done?" the bartender asked cheerfully. He was about thirty, bearded, pleasant.

She nodded, staring at him, trying to convey something in her eyes.

"You all right?"

She jerked her head up and down. "What do I owe you?"

"Ten even."

She groped in her bag for a twenty, hoping he would remember the exorbitant tip if anyone came looking for her.

Who would come looking? Did anyone even know where she was? Yes, of course. They'd find Jan, and Tina, hopefully. He'd said that Jan was sick, so he must have snatched her from the bathroom through a back entrance. He also said that he anticipated having Tina . . .

How had the killer gotten Brendan away from Tina, or was Tina with him had she seen anything, was she all right?

Sean, where are you? she wondered desperately.

A strange fear, unbidden, taunted her. Perhaps he was closer than she thought. Perhaps . . .

He could *not* be the killer, he couldn't possibly want to kill his own son!

Sean had left angry. He didn't trust her anymore. He felt that she had betrayed him.

But he loved her, he had said that he loved her . . .

He could not be the killer.

"No, change, thanks," she said, setting the twenty on the bill for the bartender.

He was putting a glass back on the rack; he didn't see what she had left. "Thanks. Have a good night."

Lori exited the restaurant, walked down the street, and crossed over to the parking lot.

There were dozens of cars in it. She saw that someone in the parking lot might have a clean view of the restaurant; then again, whoever had called her might have walked out, and walked back.

Her body seemed frozen. She moved with long, jerky steps along the rows of vehicles. Many of them were vans and trucks, vehicles too large to park in any of the mall garages.

Night was falling. Dusk filled the lot. She suddenly felt that there were shadows everywhere.

She heard a noise behind her. She tried to turn.

A foul-smelling blanket was thrown over her. She struggled against it, trying to scream. A powerful arm shot out, knocking her in the head and slamming her down to the pavement. Her head rang; the blanket smelled sweet.

Oh, God, Brendan, I wanted to save you! she thought.

And lost consciousness.

Sand . . . a gritty kind of sand had been found under Muffy's nails.

Sean thought that it should mean something to him, but he couldn't put his finger on the nagging thing that sat in the back of his mind, refusing to come forward.

While they were at the morgue, Bill Crowley and Alex Hanson, the two homicide cops Sean had previously met with Ricky, arrived. They were determined to study the corpse themselves in search of any small detail that might help in their investigation.

While Ricky Garcia, Crowley, and Hanson were in with Gillespie, Sean bought bad coffee from a machine. Lieutenant Joseph Trent, Dr. Gillespie's ex-husband and homicide official, came up behind him.

"My wife is right, wouldn't you say? We've a really sick killer out there."

Sean sipped from the styrofoam cup, then turned to Trent, shaking his head. "Your ex-wife thinks that I can solve this, if I can create a scenario for the last living moments of the victims."

"My ex-wife thinks that you're smart, and that you're a catalyst."

He arched a brow. "This guy was going nuts down here long before I came back."

Joseph Trent nodded. "Yes. But he chose one of your old friends when you came back, someone involved with what happened at the rock pit. And now . . . well, it appears that he's losing control. Typical of such a killer. And frightening. He'll become careless, and perhaps greedy. And want to kill more quickly. The killer has already speeded up, as if he's running too fast. I think he'll trip himself soon. But it may not be soon enough."

"Well, I think there's something you and your team should do without wasting any more time."

"What's that?"

"Start with us. Ricky—me—all of us. The group from high school."

Ricky had come up while he was speaking. His dark eyes showed a flash of anger, but it quickly faded.

He stared from Trent to Sean. "What's this about? Back to the rock pit again? Sean, we were all there, remember? It was the cops at the time, not any of us, who thought that Mandy had been murdered. Jesus, you went to jail, you went to trial, you were all but nailed on a cross—"

"And I didn't do it. But I do believe now that Mandy was murdered. And it's the same killer we're looking for now."

Ricky smiled. "So we start with you—and me?"

"Every one of us should be suspect."

"Maybe he's right," Trent said.

Ricky lifted his hands in disgust. "So grill me, Lieutenant. Make my *friend* here happy."

"I will. And there's a task force meeting later. I'll be taking over control of this investigation. We'll do some research into the whereabouts of your entire high school crew for the last fifteen years. Check out when everyone involved did so much as sneeze."

Ricky lowered his head, then slowly raised his dark eyes to Sean's. "Bye, buddy," he said heatedly.

Sean nodded. "Yeah. Bye."

"You suspect me, I'll suspect you!" Ricky said angrily.

"Ricky, you know, I *don't* think you're—" Sean began, but Lieutenant Trent interrupted. "Leave it alone. I'll handle this."

Ricky turned around and walked away.

Trent sighed softly.

"You think he's guilty?" Sean asked.

Trent stared at him grimly. "No. But I think that you're right. One of your group is. We have to find out who. Fast."

When Sean finally left the morgue, he called Arnie. They compromised on the distance between Palm Beach and Miami, meeting at a diner in Ft. Lauderdale.

"It will be on the news soon enough," Sean said. "They've found another body. I knew her, too. So did the rest of my friends, to the best of my knowledge. She was a fluffer, part-time call girl."

Arnie had mused over the information.

"How did they find this woman so quickly?" Arnie asked speculatively. "He's buried them pretty well before. Was she found in town?"

"No, she was in the swamp, same as before."

"No, not the same. She couldn't have been deep, well hidden. I think the murderer wanted her found."

"Why?"

"He's growing bolder. Cocky. Maybe he's having a little mental schism, too, getting too confident, and maybe a little more desperate. Scary, very scary. He also seems convinced of his own invincibility. He's starting to think that he's just too clever to be caught. In the end this could be good for the police. The killer might take some real chances now, and that . . ."

"What?"

"That makes him more dangerous than ever."

"Thank you, Arnie, I needed that. Trent seems to think so, too."

"Sorry, I can only tell you what I think. And you know enough about criminal psychology to know that it's true."

"Yeah, I know."

When they parted, Sean started the drive back down I-95. As he swore while stuck in a traffic jam, he started thinking about Lori, and Brendan. It made him shake to realize that he had a child, a son, a kid like Brendan.

And because of it, he'd gone off half-cocked. Angry. And sitting in the traffic, with nothing to do but think, he realized just how self-righteous he'd been. How judgmental he'd been with Lori. He hadn't been able to help himself. Maybe, if Brendan hadn't been such a great kid . . .

He hadn't used the car phone yet in his rental, and it took him a minute to find the damned thing. It was located in the glove compartment between the seats. He dialed Lori's number. He'd walked out in a rage—with one of those chips she'd told him about on his shoulder—and even though he'd gone back, she wouldn't feel that he'd been back for her—but for Brendan. He'd been angry, stunned, and he'd felt a loss he couldn't begin to explain to her or anyone else, but now time was whittling away at him, and strangely enough, what he felt was guilt. He realized that they had to talk. He'd been out of line, not giving her a chance. Yeah, he'd been hurt. But so had she. She'd been alone, with no way to reach him.

He could suddenly see it all from her side. And it was just a damned sad situation for them both, but one they could still change. Understanding didn't erase all the time that he had lost. Jail had been awful, Mandy's death so tragic, his dad's death so painful, but . . .

He loved Lori. Always had, always would. Now that he'd been with her, he couldn't imagine a life without her. He'd been hurt, and maybe he'd even been a royal ass, but hell, he'd been in shock, and surely, she would understand. He'd realized once again this morning looking into Muffy's cold dead eyes just how uncertain, unpredictable, and cruel life could be. He wasn't going to waste any more of it. He was going to talk to Lori. Make her listen even if she didn't want to.

But the phone kept ringing. Lori didn't answer.

He drummed his fingers, then tried Jan's house. There was no answer there, but finally a machine picked up. Jan's cheerful voice left a beeper number for herself, an office number, and a cell phone for Brad.

He had to call the machine twice and dig around in the compartment for a pen to write down the numbers. Thankfully, traffic continued to crawl at that point, so he had no problem taking the time. He tried Jan's beeper as he neared downtown Miami. After a few minutes he tried Brad's office number, and when another machine picked up, he tried Brad's cell phone.

Brad answered. "Hello?" He sounded curt, upset.

"Brad, it's Sean. Do you know where Lori is?"

"Yeah, in the Grove, with Jan and the kids. Sean, did you hear? Muffy is dead!"

He frowned at the familiar address. "Had you seen her recently?"

Brad groaned. "Yesterday."

"*What?*"

"I hired her, Sean."

"The threesome thing?"

"Yeah. And now . . . she's dead."

"Brad, sorry to change the subject, but do you happen to know if everything went all right with Lori getting her alarm in?"

"Yeah, yeah, it went fine."

"You're sure?"

"Yes, I talked to both Andrew and Ted earlier. Jeff's crew showed up and they did a great job, so I was told."

"Do you know exactly where Lori, Jan, and the kids are?"

"Not exactly. Why?"

"I think we should find them."

"Beep Jan. She's always got her beeper on her—"

"I did. She hasn't called back."

"Maybe she doesn't recognize your number, and can't figure out who you are. Jan is conscientious about that beeper. God, though, I just keep thinking about Muffy—"

"So do I. I really can't help it. I was at the autopsy, and it scared the hell out of me. I want to find Lori, Jan, and the kids."

"All right."

"Where are you?"

He thought that Brad hesitated. Maybe there was just a little static in the cell phone. Brad said, "I'm not far from the Grove myself. I'll meet you. Where?"

"Main Street, at the light by the mall."

Sean couldn't seem to make his way through the streets quickly enough. He tried to tell himself that Lori and Jan were shopping. Together. With the kids. Safe. Jan would be spilling out her heart, relaying her encounter with Muffy. Lori, in turn, might be explaining some of her own past while feeling sorry for the poor woman who met such a horrible end. They were probably both afraid. Once again, the killer had struck strangely near.

Maybe Lori and Jan wouldn't tarry long, they'd come home.

Maybe they hadn't heard about Muffy . . .

Brad was there, on Main in the Grove, before him. "I haven't seen them yet, but I think they probably went for a drink. I'm sure they'd want to talk today. You know how women are."

"All right, we try the bars first—wait, not like a real bar, right? A restaurant with a bar, because the kids are with them."

"Yeah, you're right. We'll try Jan's favorite Italian first, then the place on the corner . . ."

Jan and Lori hadn't been in the Italian restaurant, nor in the next two places they tried, but then they came to the restaurant on the first floor of the Mayfair. When they described Jan and Lori, the bartender nodded.

"A pretty blonde. Yeah," he said. He'd remembered Lori and Jan right away. "The dark-haired woman went to the rest room, and I didn't see her come back. Then there was a call, for Lori Kelly. I remember because she said that she was Lori and had been Kelly. She talked, and she looked real sick and upset. After the call she was white as a ghost.''

Listening, Sean gripped the bar tightly.

''The lady paid with a twenty for a ten-dollar check and left the change. Hey, buddy, watch it. Man, I'm sorry. There was some broken glass there. You just cut your hand—''

Sean looked at his hand. Yeah, he'd cut it, it was bleeding, and he hadn't felt a thing. He shook his head, absently wrapping a cocktail napkin around the injury.

''What then?''

''Hey, buddy, that looks bad, you may need stitches—''

''What happened to the blonde?''

''She hurried out.''

''Which direction?''

''Uh, toward the parking lot across the street.''

''Jesus!'' Brad breathed at his side.

''Thanks,'' Sean told the bartender.

''Sure. Anything else I can do?''

Sean shook his head. He followed Brad, who was already halfway toward the door.

''Wait!'' Sean said. ''Jan—let's check the ladies' room.''

It was empty.

Outside, they sprinted for the parking lot but stopped cold at the sound of a faint moaning, coming from behind a dumpster. They immediately went to investigate.

There lay Jan on the ground.

''Jesus!'' Brad breathed, hunkering down to her.

''She's all right, breathing, pulse steady,'' Sean said, joining him. Brad lifted Jan.

''Sweetheart?'' He patted her cheek lightly with his hand. ''Baby, what happened? Where's Tina, Lori . . . Brendan?''

Jan's eyes opened. She stared at Brad, then at Sean, blinking. ''Sweet . . . something sweet . . . Oh, God, did you hear about Muffy? What am I doing here? Where's Lori? Wait a minute. The kids, Brad, where are the kids?''

''Weren't the kids with you?'' Brad said.

''They went walking.''

''Where?''

''Around, just on the main streets, around Cocowalk and Mayfair,'' Jan said. ''What's wrong. Oh, God, we have to find the kids—''

Brad's cell phone started to ring. He answered it quickly. ''Hello?''

Sean could hear Tina's voice, she was speaking so loudly, so tearfully, and in such distress. "Daddy? I'm scared! I'm so scared."

"Jesus, Tina, where are you?"

"At the sub shop. But, Daddy, I can't find Mom or Lori, and, Daddy . . . I think he took Brendan."

"He who?" Brad demanded.

"He . . . oh, God, the guy in the van!" Tina wailed.

"Oh . . ." Jan breathed.

Sean grabbed the phone. "Tina, did you see anything?"

"No . . . but Brendan was with me, and then he wasn't. I don't want to be alone. I'm scared."

"You're okay. Your folks will be right with you." Sean handed the phone back to Brad.

"Get Jan and Tina home, Brad," he said, and left them. He started shouting Lori's name, racing up and down the rows of cars. On the ground in the third row, there was a lump. Sean bent down.

Lori's big black purse.

There were tire marks on the road beside it, as if a vehicle had quickly peeled rubber to make a speedy escape. Lori—and Brendan— had been taken away, he was convinced of it.

He closed his eyes tightly. The killer. The killer had her and their son. Desperate, and more cocky, because he thought he was invisible and invincible, he had taken mother and son.

Mandy was dead, then Ellie, Muffy, probably Sue. Only one real clue, under Muffy's fingernails, a gritty kind of sand . . .

He stood up, frowning as he realized that Brad had followed him to the parking lot.

"I told you to get your family home."

"Jan's all right; she's headed over to get Tina. I called 911; the cops will be with them soon. Jan is really all right; she told me to stay with you, to help you hunt out here for Lori . . ."

Sean looked at Brad. His old high school friend, his old buddy, chum, pal.

Brad, here with him.

Now. Here with him *now*.

Could Brad have taken Lori and Brendan away somewhere, and come back? He'd been near the Grove, on a cell phone.

Sean closed his eyes and pictured the sand, the grit, that had been in Muffy's fingernails. He'd been right; it all related back to the past. The killer murdered his victims one place, and dumped them in the swamp. Killers, Arnie had taught him, often really did return to the scene of the crime.

He knew. He wasn't just guessing. *He knew.*

"The rock pit," Sean said slowly. "The rock pit. The goddamned rock pit!"

"I'll get my car; it's fastest," Brad said.

"Catch me outside the bar; I'll call the cops."

"No need!" He reached into his jacket pocket and tossed Sean his cell phone.

Sean started to dial 911, and stopped. If he called 911, the cops would head out for the rock pit with their sirens blaring. If the killer heard sirens, he might butcher Lori and Brendan in a frenzy. He couldn't call 911.

He had a direct number for Lieutenant Trent. He dialed it, reached a machine, and left a message. He hesitated, gritting his teeth.

He dialed Ricky's direct line. A woman picked up.

"Ricky Garcia, please."

"He's out of the office right now. He calls in every fifteen minutes. Can I give him a message?"

Sean hesitated. *Jesus Christ, what if Ricky was the killer?*

"Tell him to come to the rock pit."

"What rock pit?"

Sean stared at the phone. They were all suspect, he reminded himself. "He'll know," he told the woman quietly. "He'll know."

Chapter 22

Her head hurt.

At first when Lori woke, her head hurt so badly that she could feel nothing else. But then the pain subsided to a dull throb, and she became aware of other sensations. She was seated. Streaks of pain propelled up and down her back; she could feel something scratchy against her skin.

Dirt beneath her legs.

And a tree.

Her back and her arms hurt because she was tied to a skinny tree. She was alive. For how long? Naturally, she was alive. He would want her wide awake when he tortured her to death. Panic seized her, and she tugged wildly at her arms, thinking that she was about to die, and she still didn't know who intended to kill her.

Her movement triggered a reaction. A groan, a tug in return. She froze, and realized that she was tied *with* Brendan on the other side of the tree.

She twisted around, straining to see.

Her heart catapulted in terror. Then she reminded herself that he was still alive.

Where was the killer?

Leading his normal life somewhere? Anticipating what he would do when he returned for the two of them?

"No, no, no, no, no!" Lori breathed aloud, struggling furiously against the ties that bound her. They were tight; the rope was thick. She went still. "Brendan, Brendan, baby, wake up, please, wake up, we've got to get out of this!"

Brendan didn't answer.

The ropes, she had to escape from the ropes. What did she have on her? Nothing, she had dropped her purse. Her pockets . . . empty. Empty, dammit! Oh, God . . .

Brendan's pockets. His key chain. Keys to the house, to her car . . . and the little pocketknife that Sean had given him.

She let out a strangled sob. Knife, little knife . . .

Sean had given him a little knife.

She struggled, pressing against the tree the best she possibly could, reaching, stretching. She groaned with the effort, her arms feeling as if they would pop out of the sockets. She found Brendan with her fingertips . . . his pocket. She had to get deeper, just a little deeper. She twisted. Her fingers touched . . .

A pen.

A quarter.

His pocketknife.

She managed to get the knife out . . . then dropped it. She fumbled in the dirt with her fingertips. How much time did she have? Where was the killer?

"Brendan, wake up, please, Brendan . . ."

She felt the ropes ripping her flesh, and she strained even harder to find the knife again. Finally . . . her fingers closed around it.

Her hand cramped as she tried to locate the catch and flick it open. Yet finally, she did it. She tried not to sob aloud as she twisted and turned again in an effort to saw the ropes—and not her hands or Brendan's—with the sharp side of the knife.

It had grown dark, night had come, but a three-quarter moon illuminated the pines and scruff foliage and rocky flooring of the area surrounding the dug-out pit with a strange, misted glow. Low ground fog had set in with the night. Staring straight ahead, constantly searching the swirling, silver-tinted mist in terror, Lori kept sawing. In the dead quiet of the night, she could hear the knife moving against the rope. And then, the miracle she had prayed for occurred. The rope gave.

Trying not to shout out with her sense of pure triumph, Lori wrenched at her wrists, managing to nearly dislocate her shoulder, and drawing another groan from Brendan. She tugged more carefully, allowing the severed piece of rope to disentangle the rest, then she leapt to her feet, rushing around to her son. Untied, he had slumped down to the ground. She grabbed his wrist, scared to death that he had been overdosed with whatever had knocked them out. But his pulse was strong. He simply wasn't waking up.

She looked around wildly, certain that they had to hide. She didn't know how much time had passed since she'd been brought here. She pocketed Brendan's knife, and caught him by the shoulders, dragging him from the tree and into an area of denser foliage. How did she get out of here? In the distance through the trees, she could see a glinting, and she realized with a sinking heart that the whole area of the rock pit was now surrounded by a high wire fence. The city had probably ordered the place fenced to keep from losing another child to the dangerous water. "How am I going to get you out of here, baby?" she whispered desperately.

Then she froze. She heard her name, called through the night. The sound seemed to come from everywhere.

"Lori!" From the west?

"Lori, Lori!"'From the east?

"Loriiiiiii!" From the south . . . ?

She listened to the disembodied voices.

Sean? Brad?

Her brother, Andrew? Josh . . . Someone else? She couldn't tell, the sound was so distorted by the fog and the echo off the rocks.

How many men were at the rock pit? For a moment she had a horrible vision of them all being in it together, a team of homicidal maniacs, all ready to rip out her throat.

No! It could only be one madman. And help was out there.

She opened her mouth to answer, but then caught herself. They were not all homicidal maniacs, and they weren't all part of a killer cult. Someone out there had surely come to rescue her.

But one of them *was* a killer.

She heard thrashing in the foliage, and a sense of overwhelming panic descended upon her. She quickly dragged Brendan more deeply into the bushes. Hunched down in the foliage, she saw Sean appear at the spot where she and Brendan had been tied to the tree, and she breathed a sigh if relief, about to leap back out into the clearing, calling his name.

But then she saw the . . .

Blood.

His hand was dripping with it. He was carrying a man's utility knife, a bigger version of the one he had given Brendan, and his hand, and the knife, were dripping with blood.

No!

The pain and disbelief inside her nearly crippled her. She bent over as she watched him bend low, finding the ropes she had severed. He stood, tense, jaw locked, blue eyes ebony in the darkness and shadows. His head fell back. "Lori!" he shouted, "Lori, for the love of God . . ."

Hands and knees on the ground, she tried to breathe, closing her eyes tightly. She looked up. He had moved away. Sean. She closed her eyes, shaking, her mouth dead dry.

What was she doing? She believed in him. She'd said that she believed in him. She should have run to him, despite the blood . . .

But what if he had just butchered someone . . . one of the men out to rescue her? He was carrying a knife. Blood dripped from his hand. She couldn't see him clearly, but she could see the blade glinting in the moonlight, she could see blood, dripping . . .

It was a pocketknife that he carried. A Swiss army knife, a utility piece.

But not a butcher knife, or a long knife, or the kind of weapon that could easily be used to maim and rip . . .

Still, there had been blood all over his hand. Was she in love, and therefore blind?

"Lori!"

"Lori!"

"Loriiii!"

Her name was shouted again and again, in the darkness and shadows and eerie streaks of moonlight, and it seemed again that the sound was coming from everywhere, from out of the darkness, out of the fog. A rustling from her left drove her to her feet, and she turned around quickly, trying to discover from where the danger was coming. Taking a single step backward, she crashed into a pair of arms. She spun around.

Brad. With a look of tension on his handsome face, he drew a finger quickly to his lips, warning her that they were in danger.

"Hold still! Hold still!" he whispered.

She was very still, listening. Waiting. Seconds ticked by. The place had been alive with shouting and now . . .

No shouts. No footfalls. Silence.

Just Brad behind her. Brad, holding her too tightly.

"Brad . . ."

"Shh!"

"Who—"

"I don't know!"

His arms around her hurt. She started to struggle. "Lori, don't, you're making it so hard—"

Making it so hard! For him to kill her?

She elbowed him for all she was worth, slamming into his ribs.

She turned around and kicked him with her boot. He gasped with pain, the air sucked out of him. Unable to speak, he fell to his knees. She turned and started to run.

"Sean!" she shrieked his name in the night. Oh, God, she had to find him fast, get back, before Brad could find Brendan, hurt him, oh, God, what had Brad done to his own daughter, his wife . . .

"Lori, here!"

She stopped, looking around wildly. She breathed a sigh of relief when Jeff Olin suddenly stepped from the trees. "Lori, poor Lori, come here, we'll find him . . ."

"Oh, God, Jeff! What are you doing here, how can you be here—"

"Sean called us all for help," he told her, flashing his spectacular smile. He smoothed back his rich auburn hair, and his brown eyes touched hers with a relieved look. "I was hoping so badly I'd find you first."

He stepped forward. Then she saw that he, too, carried a knife.

A real knife, with a slim, stiletto-sharp blade, at least six inches in length.

She had hidden from Sean. She had crippled Brad. And now Jeff Olin was going to kill her.

"Jeff!" she breathed, staring at him.

He shook his head. "You shouldn't have come back home, Lori. New York was a lot better for your health."

"Jeff! You . . . you did it? You killed those women—"

"Yes, of course. Sue, too. She was such a fool, such a poor desperate fool, too damned eager for any man. She just walked hand in hand with me, too stupid to realize until she was bleeding."

Lori swallowed, fighting a terrible feeling of nausea. She felt a sense of fatality, a numbness. She was praying, but praying more than anything that someone would find Brendan before Jeff did.

"Jeff, I—I can't believe this. Did you kill Mandy? How could you—she was your sister."

"Mandy was a whore. A cunt. I can't begin to tell you what it was like being her brother. She went after men, hell, she went after me. My old man didn't help—I think he was the first one to stick it to her. You never knew Mandy. I'm not even sure that I meant to kill her when I did, but there she was, underwater, and there I was, and the vine . . . first, I just thought it would be funny to pay her back for all the prick-teasing she did . . . then I saw her face, and I realized, wow, Mandy was in my power and she could die, and that sure as hell would get her, especially with me there, watching. So she died. And old Sean got the blame for it, which was good, because she was better about being such a bitch when she was with him, because she knew that he wouldn't have it, except that—he'd quit caring. It was because of you, wasn't it? The kid is Sean's, huh, not Brad's. You were a slimy little snake, not miss goody two shoes at all. Kind of makes it a nice justice that you're going to die here. I wanted you to be last, but old Sean has just about moved in these days, so I thought I should strike while I had the chance. Jan's girl was damned tempting . . . I almost snagged her tonight instead. I'll have to wait until I can have lots and lots of time with her. Too bad, I'm going to have to kill you quicker than I wanted. I really wanted to play with you, Lori. Pretty, pretty, Lori. So untouchable. Well, baby, you're going to be touched. And I'm going to have to kill your son quickly, too. He knows who I am.''

Lori desperately fought a rising sense of pure terror. He moved the knife in his hand as he spoke to her, wielding it almost absently. He could step forward and kill her in a split second, long before a scream ever left her lips. She had to stall for time, pray that someone would come.

"Jeff, don't be an ass. Everyone will know who you are, you idiot! You're going to be caught!''

He shook his head. "Me, never. I'm the caring friend. I had a very reliable company install an alarm for you today. I'm a respected lawyer, a man who suffered terrible tragedy, and made the most of his life despite that fact.''

She shook her head. "Jeff, you're here now, they'll figure it out. You will be caught, and you won't find Brendan.''

"Why?''

"He's gone.''

Jeff grinned. It was frightening to see how handsome he was when he grinned. How . . .

Drop dead gorgeous.

"The kid is around here somewhere. I'll find him.''

"Sean is here, Brad is here . . . what if they find Brendan first? And surely, they'll have called the cops by now.''

"So what? They'll just all go on suspecting one another.''

"I don't think so. They'll figure it out.''

"They haven't even figured out their way around the rock pit yet,'' Jeff said, amused. "And if they find me, well, I may have to do in a few men. It will be okay. I've picked up a guy now and then. No one ever puts two and two together when a guy is found dead.''

"Ricky will shoot you if he shows up.''

"Ricky won't shoot me, because he won't know I'm the killer.

We're all just running around in here, aren't we? All trying to rescue poor Lori and Brendan! Besides, he can't just shoot me. He's a cop. He's got to cuff me and arrest me. And then, hell, it won't get to that.''

"Jeff, no, it's not that simple."

"Trust me, it is. I've been at it a while." He was supremely confident, casual even, as they stood there.

"You killed Mandy . . . and then you started knifing people up, and nobody ever caught on?" she whispered incredulously. If she could only keep him talking . . .

"Naw . . . I started just playing. Girls. In college. You know, not one of the little sluts ever reported a rape. I mean, who would have believed them? They'd be out with me. Look at me? Why would I have to force a woman when there were plenty of women ready to go out with a guy like me?"

"Yeah. So when did you start killing people? After Mandy, that is."

"Mmm . . . eight, nine years ago? First, it was just one, a hitch-hiker, up in mid-state. They never found her, but I was scared silly for about a year. Then another . . . I made myself be careful. I rationed myself. A whore occasionally, then some nightclub sluts."

"You've been on a glut lately."

"Yeah, well, there's a guy to take the blame again."

"You really think anyone will believe Sean killed me?"

"Hell, yes! Don't you read the papers?"

She heard a rustle from behind her and opened her mouth, screaming as loud as she could, "Help! It's Jeff Olin, and he's got a knife—"

"Lori, you damned bitch, you stupid little cunt!" he thundered, spitting out the words with his rage as he grasped her, slamming a hand over her mouth and bringing the knife to her face. "Pity. You always were beautiful, you know. Almost as beautiful as me, Lori. You know, I always meant to have you myself. When you came home, I thought that I'd have you at last. Like the cream of the crop, the pick of the litter. I'd keep you a while, and I'd have you alive. But that's all right. Dead will be just fine . . . I'll try not to mutilate your face until the end."

She saw the knife glittering above her, felt his free arm constricting her against him, his fingers clamped hard over her face and mouth. She struggled, trying to kick him, yet when she was certain she would fail and couldn't possibly avoid the edge of his blade, she suddenly heard him grunt as he was ripped away from her.

"Let go of my mother, you *cockroach*!" Brendan cried.

Lori, suddenly released, staggered into a tree, righted herself, and turned back. She screamed at the top of her lungs. Brendan had fought for her, but he was still a boy, and Jeff was a powerful man. He wrenched free from Brendan, who had attacked him from behind, lifted the boy, and slammed him to the earth.

Then fell on top of him.

"No!" Lori shrieked. She pushed forward from the tree, throwing herself on Jeff Olin's back. She captured his wrist, the wrist that held the knife, with both her hands. His strength was far greater than hers. He had nearly freed himself and shaken her off when she stretched harder against him, bringing her teeth to his wrist and biting through the flesh. He let out a scream of anguish. The knife fell.

He rose with her, gripped her by the ribs, and threw her with a furious force back against the tree. Stunned, she slumped down the length of the tree, only to see that he was coming after her again.

The knife, forgotten, lay in the dirt. Brendan, too, lay in the dirt. Unconscious again.

Or dead.

"You think I need a weapon?" he demanded with contemptuous fury. "I'm going to throttle the life out of you, Lori, look right in those glittering cat eyes of yours until they pop right out of your head. And when you're unconscious, or dead, I'm going to do things to you that will make you roll in your grave for all eternity . . ."

She was nearly dead already, she thought, her head was spinning so badly she kept slipping as she tried to rise to fight him. He reached for her, and his fingers curled around her throat. He dragged her up against the tree, foam on his lips, he'd been speaking with such anger, his handsome face hideously contorted . . .

"No!" she managed to choke out. She was terrified, but she lashed back with words as long as she could. "I'll claw your face until you bleed, and this time, when they find me, they'll know, they'll *know* that you're a killer, and they'll put you in the electric chair, and they'll send a million volts through you and . . ."

She broke off as her breath left her entirely. She tried to gasp in air. She couldn't. Black beads began to form before her, then . . .

She heard a scream.

It was Jeff. *Jeff* screamed.

He released her.

She fell against the tree again, slipping to the earth, the moonlight flooded out at first by the black pinpoints before her eyes forming together. Then her vision began to clear.

Sean. Sean's knife was in Jeff's back, but it wasn't long enough to have killed.

Sean and Jeff were involved in a vicious fistfight, both swinging, both down then, in the dirt, both rolling and rolling . . .

Jeff leapt to his feet, refusing to go down, despite the blade in his back.

Lori tried to cry out; there was help out there somewhere, she had heard more voices. It was like a nightmare, in which she tried and tried, but couldn't scream. Her neck and throat were too swollen; her voice was only a croak . . .

Movement. Brendan. Brendan was crawling forward as the men battled violently just feet away. He nearly came to his knees . . . then fell again.

The knife still glittered in the dirt. The knife Jeff had used to kill so many people. The knife he would use against all of them, if he could.

Jeff staggered up. He folded his fists, ready to slam a powerful blow down upon Sean's neck.

But Sean rose, just in time, swung a fist, and grappled Jeff. The two went down again.

Lori grabbed the tree, heedless that the bark ripped her hands as she staggered to her feet. Then she saw that Brendan was moving again, inching across the dirt. He looked up. His eyes met hers.

Scream, she mouthed at him. "Scream for help."

He did. Brendan started shouting at the top of his lungs. She went to her knees, crawling to her son. She saw the knife in the dirt. Jeff's knife. She picked it up.

Lori heard a cracking sound, and she twisted around.

Both Jeff and Sean were on the ground. Still. Dead still. They didn't move.

With her heart in her throat, Lori urged Brendan behind her. She rose and staggered toward the two men, paralyzed with fear, yet determined that she would do whatever it took to keep Jeff Olin down . . .

Just as she reached the men, Sean groaned, and began to rise. She came beside him, finding new strength to help him up. He accepted her aid, but then nudged Jeff with his foot.

"I heard a cracking . . ." Lori whispered.

"I think I broke his jaw."

Sean stared at Jeff, then turned toward Lori and Brendan. He reached for Lori, bringing her into his arms. Brendan came to them, and he enveloped the boy as well.

Lori started shaking uncontrollably. She dropped the knife. Didn't matter; she wasn't going to have to use it. Jeff wasn't dead, but neither was he going to get up. Not now. Sean hadn't killed him, but he had leveled him, and in this place he had avenged Mandy's murder.

He pulled them back quickly when they heard soft laughter coming from the ground.

Lori stared down at Jeff. He had twisted over. His right eye was black, his face had swollen horribly. He wasn't drop dead gorgeous anymore. He could hardly move his mouth or tongue, but he was speaking anyway, taunting them.

"Crazy. Crazy . . . they'll arrest me, I'll be out in a year," he said. He began to cough, spitting out a tooth.

He pointed a finger at Lori, as if it were a gun. "I'll come for you. Pretty Lori, pretty, pretty, Lori . . . dead, alive, dead, alive. And Sean, big man on campus, well, it's been a hell of a life I gave you, huh? You wait and see, I'll take Lori, and no matter what, there will be those pointing fingers at you, saying you're the one who hurt her, raped her, killed her—"

A thunderous, explosive sound tore through the night.

Lori spun around.

Ricky Garcia stood in the clearing, his gun in his hand, still smoking.

He stared from Lori to Brad. "Dammit, Sean. I tried to tell you I didn't do it." He shook his head at the two of them. "You report what you feel you have to. No, I'm not God, or judge, or jury. I was just Ellie's friend, Sue's friend—and your friend."

He turned, and walked away. Lori leaned against Sean, her arm around her son, and they made their way behind Ricky.

Rescue crews arrived at the rock pit, along with numerous news teams.

Lori found herself protected from the press by Sean, her brother, and a number of Ricky's fellow cops, but she wasn't escaping a trip to the emergency room, or a night in the hospital for observation since her throat was so badly bruised. Bits and pieces of information filtered to her along with the flash of photographers' cameras, which could not be avoided.

Through sketchy conversations, she began to understand everything that had happened. Ricky had called her brother when he'd gotten the message from Sean, afraid that Lori wouldn't know whom to trust, and so Andrew had been as involved in the frantic search as the others.

Jeff was dead.

The families of his many victims might not find peace, but at the very least, they would have closure.

Sean stood clear of all suspicion.

She was somewhat alarmed that although he came to the hospital, he left her mostly to the fussing of her parents that night. Her mother wouldn't leave her side. Being a mother, Lori understood.

Gramps was there, looking really good for once, strong in his support.

"I always knew that boy was all right," he said about Sean.

"Yeah, you did."

"Did you tell him yet?"

"He knows."

Gramps seemed satisfied, and managed to get her family out of her room, knowing that Sean would be back.

It was very late when Sean returned, walking so quietly that she didn't realize he was standing there for several minutes.

"Lori?"

She opened her eyes.

"Sean." She sat up. "I almost doubted you again—"

"You heard me when I found the ropes."

"I was terrified . . . I saw the blood."

He glanced ruefully at his hand. "I cut it when I was at the bar, trying to find out what happened."

"I know . . . Ricky told me somewhere along the line. Oh, God, I'm so sorry! For so many things."

"Lori, it doesn't matter. We can't go back, and undo any of the pain of the past. I hurt you, too. But I do love you, you know," he said very softly.

"I always loved you. I just never had the courage to say so before."

Sean smiled. "Well, I guess I'm a little late doing the right thing considering the 'baby' will be fifteen next birthday, but I want to marry you, Lori. I want to stay here, build a life. I ran away before. So did you. But this is home, for both of us. And for our son. Well?" He arched a brow.

He looked great, Lori thought. He was tired. Worn. A little ragged. She could clearly see the character lines etched into his face, the pain, the humor, even a curious sheepishness. She smiled, afraid she was going to burst into hysterical tears at this late moment, when she was finally safe, and being offered a future she desperately wanted.

She nodded and said huskily, "I want to marry you, too. When do we tell Brendan?" Lori asked softly.

"That we're getting married? Well, before the wedding, I imagine."

"No, I mean that you're his father."

"I don't know yet. When we both feel the time is right. Maybe soon, before he hears too many things."

"I think he'll be glad to have you for his father."

"I hope so." He squeezed her hand. She frowned suddenly.

"Sean, after what happened, what about Ricky—"

"Ricky is in the clear. There will be questions, of course. Reports to fill out. An inquiry. But there was a scuffle; Jeff was threatening lives. As a police officer, Ricky was entirely in the right to prevent a life-threatening situation against innocent civilians."

She nodded. "Good. And Brad and Jan—"

"I think they'll be fine. And I think that Brad and I can really be friends now. And I may even get along with your brother."

Sean and Lori laughed. "He was only protecting me," she said.

"I know."

"Strange, though. Poor Michael. I should have known anyone that good to animals couldn't have been a killer. Did you know, Sean, he was the smartest among us. He told me that Jeff was a shark."

"Did he?"

"Yes—I was afraid to be in my house with Michael, while Michael was the only one with the right instincts to know the truth about Jeff."

"It's just that Jeff was Mandy's brother," Sean said softly. "Jeff was very, very sick," he added. "But it's over, and we made it, and right now, Lori, just life itself seems awfully damn good. Get some rest, huh?"

Lori nodded, and closed her eyes, exhausted, and ready to sleep. Easily. He was at her side. They had a lot of pain to face in the days to come.

A lot of healing to do.

But now they could heal without lies or fear, and for the moment, that was enough.

Epilogue

One day, about three months after the incident at the rock pit, Sean and Brendan were fishing alone just offshore from Plantation Key, where they'd rented a beach house for the weekend.

Brendan had just snagged a good-size snapper. He'd hauled it in, and while he put his fish in the ice chest, Sean rebaited his hook. Minutes later, after discussing the merits of his catch, they sat in silence again. Then Brendan startled Sean by asking, "Are you my father?"

Taken by surprise, Sean hesitated, studying the shore. He could see Lori stretched out on a towel on the beach, reading.

"Yes," he said simply. Then he looked at Brendan and asked, "Do you mind?"

Brendan shrugged, then grinned. "I never knew Ian Corcoran."

Sean nodded. "I guess there's a lot we could really explain when you're older—"

"I'm plenty old; you don't have to explain anything. I love my mother, I don't feel traumatized, nor do I have any psychological hang-ups about the situation," Brendan told him, amused. Then he said, "And I'm glad you're my father."

Sean looked toward the shoreline. Lori had risen, and she was waving, pointing to the barbecue pit. Lean and tanned, blond hair tossed in the breeze, she was indicating that it was time for lunch.

He looked at Brendan, then to Lori once again.

And he knew that it had been one hell of a long road, but he'd really, finally, come home.